The Bells and The Dark Secrets of the Bell Family

ISBN (paperback): 978-0-578-33055-6

Acknowledgments

I dedicate this to my beautiful daughter. With my journey, I would not have gotten this far without her. It shows her that anything you set your mind to, you can achieve. Shine brightly and let the stars guide you, you are the new moon. I'm grateful for my wonderful mother, who always encourages me to keep going. Thank you, James, for supporting the book and believing in the magic of friendship. Jewels, you are an amazing sister and I would be lost without you. You inspire me every single day. Let the magic of this book fill each and every one of you.

Book coverby- Primegpx @ Fiverr

Editor: Kiara

The Bells and The Dark Secrets of the Bell Family

By

W. J. SMITH

Content of Magick

Chapter 1: The end of Summer

Many of us use sleep to relax, relieve stress, and regain energy. It is said that some people remain awake even when they are sleeping. While asleep, you travel through the astral plane. August is mid-month. Plants are full of life up in the mountains of a town called Pigeon Forge, which is a tourist trap. With all the tourists coming to town in the summer, it's always very busy. There is a lot of traffic during that time of year, making it the worst time to live there. The views are gorgeous, especially during the fall, winter, and spring. Leaves change colors and snow drapes the town in graceful beauty.

Whistling can be heard as the wind blows against the windows.

Everyone in the house was asleep. During the full moon, the house was illuminated by a bright light. Shadows danced down the walls of the rooms. In one of them was an 7-year-old girl. A hint of red hue streaks can be seen in her long, slightly curly raven black hair. Bright crystal blue is her right eye, and dark emerald green is her left. She has freckles across the bridge of her button nose with a slight ski jump. Her hair hugged her small heart-shaped face and soft ivory skin.

This girl's name is Luna Star Bell. Luna was a unique person. When she falls asleep, she finds that she is out of her body in a spirit form. She discovered this ability when she was seven. For the longest time, she never told anyone. One night while her body lay asleep, her soul lifted from her and she walked through her house with a sense of curiosity.

Luna was alert when she heard her mom crying on the phone. Her mom has raven black hair, brilliant blue eyes, a heart-shaped face, and a light beige complexion. Tears ran down her face, her body hunched looking broken and disfigured. Luna was not accustomed to seeing her mother in this state. Her mother was strong, fit, and toned. She held her composure and always knew the right words to say. She had just received word that her beloved husband Adam Bell was killed in a car crash at 3 AM on his way from work.

The time was nearly 4 am and on December 25th of all days. Luna went to hug her mother, but she wasn't successful. Her arms passed straight through her mother as a ghost. "Don't cry, mommy. What is the matter?" Luna frantically asked. Unfortunately, her mother was not able to hear her. Cheyanne hung up the phone and leaped in surprise as her youngest daughter stood in the living room doorway.

Lucid Allyshie Bell stood there silent and still. Tears ran down her small oval face. Wet streaks down her porcelain skin. She was only a year younger than Luna. Luna always felt she was stuck in her childlike ways or was it that she, herself was too mature for her age. Long curly brown hair with a nose like her sisters, but smaller. Her left eye is bright crystal blue and her right eye is emerald green. She stood there wearing purple pajamas. "Why are you up?," asked her mom with her words shaky while she tried to compose the terror and pain she felt. Luna gazed at her mom then at her younger sister Lucid while tears filled her eyes.

Their mother choked back more tears, "Honey, it is almost 4 in the" Lucid cut her mom's words off, "Da...dad – daddy is gone. He went to heaven." More tears ran down those rosy cheeks while

2

sorrow engulfed her. Her mother reached for her, "How...How do you know?" she asked barely above a whisper. Seeing her mom's hurtful eyes, Lucid began to break down more. "My blocks said so." Their mother pulled her into a tight hug while they both sobbed. Luna ran back to her room and merged back into her body. Rolling over, she began to cry. Not long after, just enough time for the morning of their loss to settle.

Cheyanne watched Lucid play with her toys. When you said your blocks had told you, what did you mean?" she questioned. As she paused from playing, Lucid told her mom, "I woke up and turned on the light to get a drink of water. I blocks were lying on the floor saying DAD, CAR, and GONE. Lucid explained that when he picked them up and threw them down upset, they read "CRASH and DIE".

It has been seven years since the car crash. Luna looked at her body, she is now 5'2" tall, mostly legs, and weighs 115 with a flat stomach. She was leaving her body while it was asleep and moved around the house, a common routine for her. She opened the door to her sister's room. Her sister Lucid was a young sporty girl, who ran track, played multiple sports such as volleyball, tennis, and softball. The house lay quiet except for the family dog Rox. His brown fur was covered with black.

He lay on the stairs moping around, hoping for someone to sneak him a midnight snack or that he was bored and wanted us to play. Like their mothers, Lucid's physique was toned, fit, and strong. Her room was neat, and her wall was adorned with medals and trophies. On the nightstand by her bed were some stones that were black with red symbols ✦🜂🜔🜖🜚. Luna could not read them or anything.

      She turned her gaze to Lucid who was laying in her bed asleep. Luna reached out and touched her sister's shoulder. Suddenly she was no longer in her sister's room but somehow gone into the dream that her sister was having. The dream showed Lucid at school in the gym, the stands were filled with her adoring fans and Lucid stood on the court playing volleyball wearing black spandex shorts and a white volleyball shirt that said "Bell" on the back with the number one.

      Luna sat in the stands behind their mom, Cheyanne was coaching the team wearing a black polo shirt and black slacks with a clipboard in hand. It was for the championship. Luna, who normally doesn't attend any of the games, shouted, "GO LUCLUC!" as Lucid set up the serve for the big spike. The ball bounced off the ground after a failed serve. As the referee blew the whistle to announce the game, the announcer said, "This year's champions are-" Suddenly Luna fell to the floor and was kicked out. Lucid raised up in her bed, "Ugh…" she groaned before talking quietly to herself, "What-why was she there?" She turned on her lamp and picked up her purple velvet bag. Luna watched her sister pull out fifteen runes from the small bag and scattered them on the table 🜚🜖🜓🜔🜖🜚 🜖🜓🜚 🜖🜖 🜂🜖🜚🜖.

      Luna was not sure what to make of it and quickly stepped out and closed her bedroom door before she went back to her body. Meanwhile, Lucid looked at the runes as she began to read them Sister was here. Lucid crawled out from under the covers and slipped on some shorts and went across the hall to her sister Luna's room.

Lucid turned on the bedroom light, while Luna acted as though she had been stirred from a deep sleep. "Wha-what?" yawned out Luna fakely. Lucid was wise and not buying into it, "Why were you in my room?! She shrieked out loud. Luna rubbed her eyes. "I was asleep" she tried to persuade her sister.

Lucid placed a hand on her hip and glared at her sister, "You were in my dream, It was the championship and YOU NEVER Lucid stared at Luna waiting for an explanation. "I asked my rune stones for some things, and they told me that my sister invaded. Although Luna stared at her refusal to admit anything, Lucid ranted on, "I asked my rune stones some things, and they told me that my sister invaded. Again I asked and they said dream and the runes don't lie, but I want to know-how. So, how?"

"How what?" said Luna, hiding a grin. "Come on, don't play coy, we have the bloodline of The Bell Witch... Do you have some kind of powers too?" Lucid said while playing out the possibility in her head. Luna sighed, then let out a chuckle "Six years ago... I found out I could leave my body while I slept. I thought that I was crazy at first, but the night I found out the truth was that night mom got the phone call about dad. You came into the kitchen and explained to our mom that the blocks told you" Luna confessed. Lucid slowly sank down and sat on her sister's bed shocked.

After they sat up and talked for a good bit. Lucid looked to her sister with a curious look "Can you show me?" Even though her face showed skepticism, there was excitement in her eyes.

"Sure, but" Luna said ever so slowly while dragging out the word, "It takes about fifteen minutes to thirty minutes Luc. I have to fall asleep and once I am asleep no one can hear me or feel me while I am in that state," she explained to her sister.

Luna laid back and closed her eyes while she began to drift to sleep. Lucid sat on a blue bean bag chair while she began to look around Luna's room. The room was not like Lucid's at all. Luna's room was not tidy, books and clothes lay on the floor. She was not sure if the clothes were clean or dirty. Perhaps Luna did not know either. Lucid gazed along her walls and looked at the unicorn posters that hung up on the wall, the same ones she has had since they were little kids. A small television played on low volume and sat on a white dresser next to her closet. A blue shaggy rug lay in the middle of the wood floor, but so did many other items that covered the rug. Still plugged into the charger, Lucid glanced at her phone.

She reached up to tap the cell phone on the cluttered nightstand by the bed. She saw the time 2:45 am on the screen. She waited for a moment, before getting up. The moon poured into the room, lighting it up like a lamp. As she got up, she began to walk out when purple string lights went out above Luna's bed. "Luna? Luna?" Lucid called out. Soon the television came on, the phone started to play heavy metal music, a brown teddy bear was tossed across the room, and Lucid looked around the room. "This is creepy," she said. Things came to a halt, the music stopped on the phone, the TV turned off. There was complete silence in the room. She looked around the room "Luna?"

6

"BOO!" snapped Luna while she woke up and sprang at her sister causing Lucid to jump and scream. "Hush Luc, you'll wake up mom."

Luna and she agreed that keeping these gifts should stay secret. After a bit, Lucid got up and said goodnight to her sister before going to her room. Luna rolled over and went to sleep. - As the sun grew brighter and the sun began to shine through the windows, the only movement that indicated someone was awake was the sizzling of the sausage and bacon on the frying pan.

The house was filled with the smell of a breakfast fit for Kings. The fresh-squeezed orange juice had Luna rushing down the stairs in pajama shorts and a red tank top. When she entered the kitchen, her mom looked at her. "You are up before your sister, is she still alive?" their mother questioned, while she took a sip of her coffee.

Luna slept most of the day if she could, she should have been born a vampire. Good morning, mom. Luna said while pouring orange juice. Cheyanne laughed while she flipped the sausage. "Good morning, LuLu, go wake up your sister. We have to go school shopping" Luna was fortunate in comparison to her sister and mother. She could eat all this food for breakfast while they worked for their figures.

She had a high metabolism, Lucid had her sports, and their mom kept her figure by doing yoga, pilates, and going to the gym for cardio. After Luna ate, she went back upstairs, to Lucid's room and knocked on the door. She allowed herself into her sister's bedroom. "Lucid, breakfast!" yelled Luna. "Ugh... OK- I'll be down in a moment," replied Lucid groggily while she sat up.

A few moments later Lucid came down the stairs wearing some pajama pants and a blue t-shirt that slipped off her right shoulder. She grabbed some breakfast and sat down at the table. "Morning LucLuc," said their mom while beginning the dishes. After Lucid ate breakfast and after a moment of talking with their mom, their mother turned off the water, "you two can finish the dishes and put food away, but then please get ready." Once the two girls had finished cleaning the kitchen and swiftly moved...more like raced up the stairs nearly breaking each other's necks to get to the bathroom to shower. Cheyanne was waiting downstairs while she wore a light jacket, army green over a plum top, and dark denim jeans with tennis shoes. Luna came down the stairs wearing her black tights that had a red pinstripe skull on the thigh, a top that had a cat's head between the two stars on the shoulder between the sleeves, and a neck hole. With the skirt, black fishnet, and black combat-style boots with chains. Little bat jewelry dangling from the boots, and she wore a black leather purse at her hip.

Following her sister, Lucid stepped down wearing faded blue jeans, and a pink shirt with a large white daisy embroidered on the front. She wore her hair pulled back with sunglasses and finished the look with flats to match. The two girls walked to the large extended black cab truck. Luna climbed into the front then her sister got into the back while their mom slipped into the driver seat of the truck.

The black truck started to back up when their mom noticed the mailbox was open with a letter inside. Rhetorically asking the girls when the mail had run? "It is still too early." She stepped on the brake and asked one of the girls to get the mail. After the truck came to a complete stop, Luna hopped out and ran to the mailbox.

8

Chapter 1: The end of Summer

As she gazed at the ground, she saw a long red feather with a red sparkle, which was shaped like the tip of a flame. The feather glistens in the sunlight. After grabbing the blue envelope from the mailbox, she ran to the truck and hopped in.

Chapter 2: The blue envelope and the mysterious feather

Cheyanne drove around all day doing shopping for clothes, book bags, and other school supplies. They fought traffic and tourist all day. It was now about two in the afternoon as they began to get hungry. They saw their dad's old restaurant "Bell's Burgers" it still looked the same, a two-story building with an outside patio and a balcony with tables that overlooked the city. They parked the truck in a parking lot, and all went into the restaurant.

The place was always busy, a young teen just a year older than Luna. She had blond hair and an undercut with brilliant blue eyes, tanned skin and had sat them down. She wore dark blue jeans, a black shirt with "Bells Burgers" on the back, and white tennis shoes.

"My name is Julie; I will be taking care of you all today. What may I get you to drink?" asked the girl while she smiled at the three.

"I will have water." Said Cheyanne.

"Soda." said Luna while she smiled at the girl.

"Fruit-blast, please." said Lucid the fruit blast was a mix of tropical punch with blue mountain blast. The girl walked off to get the drinks, the restaurant had bright colors, ceiling fans hung along with the ceiling, and candles on the table. A picture of a guy behind the line cooking he had a bright blue eye and a dark emerald green eye. Short brown hair, pointed chin, long nose, and a goatee, the plaque read "Mr. Adam Bell."

After a moment the girl came back with the drinks in hand, she handed out the drinks "what may I start you all off with?" asked Julie with she smiled warmly with pad in hand. The menu had one burger from Adam's original menu, few salads, steaks, and fish.

They had placed their order in, Julie walked off to place their order in. They sat around and talked while they waited for the food to come to the table. There was light talking between them all about school starting and everything.

After a bit, a small round fellow with dark hair slipped into a ponytail with dark brown eyes and a handlebar mustache. He wore a black penguin tuxedo. He came up to the table standing only 5'5" with a broken English accent "ah, well 'ello Mrs. Bell, a pleasure to see ye, been a good bit of time." said the short round man. He slipped his monocle out of his coat pocket and slipped it in his left eye. "Pleasure to see you too Mr. Lundo.," said Cheyanne "place looks good as before."

"Yus didn't want, to change a thing. Adam was my best pal, a great owner, and a superb chef. Ye know your ticket will always be comp." said Mr. Lundo while their food arrived at the

11

table. He left the table and comp the forty-five-dollar ticket.

After they ate and leaving a nice thirty-dollar tip. Cheyanne didn't have to pay for their food, so she gave a nice tip to Julie. They said their goodbyes to Mr. Lundo. They slipped into the truck and Luna turned on some heavy rock music on the radio. The song ended and was followed by some dubstep she pulled out her phone and started to play on it and checking messages.

Lucid was on her phone making a to-do list before school started. Once they got home, they grab the bags of clothes and other school supplies. Luna scattered off to her room with some bags in hand. She took the hip purse off her hip and tossed it on the bed. The blue envelope fell out of her black hip purse. She leans down and picked it up and began to read the beautiful spiral writing.

Luna Bell
1 A Mountain Dr.
Pigeon Forge.

She began to open the letter which was written on old yellow parchment as her eyes skimmed through it quickly. Then her mouth dropped bewilderment.

Dear, Luna Bell

We have noticed over the years you have been using magick. We would like to invite you

Chapter 2: The blue envelope and the mysterious feather

to Owl Hollow School of Magick for Witchcraft and Wizards. School starts on September first. If you wish to come mark yes or no, please for your response.

YES   NO

P.S.:

Tap the letter with the feather once you answer.

Robert Rune

Headmaster

Owl Hollow school of Magick

of Witchcraft and Wizardly

Luna read the letter over and over a few times. She went down the stairs with the letter in her hand. She saw her mom reading a book sitting in the rocking chair. Her sister laid on the couch while she watched a movie. Luna looked at them and sat down on the couch by Lucid's feet. She cleared her throat.

"Rude." called out her sister looking over her shoulder at Luna.

"What is it LuLu?" asked her mom while she peered up from her book. Wearing blue reading glasses.

"I got a letter..." said Luna looking at her mom.

"Yeah?" Usually, letters come in envelopes." heckled Lucid with a grin. Luna shot a shut up look to her sister then turned her attention back to their mom "anyways mom, I got a letter from a school, I am kind of interested in it."

"Who would accept you to a private school?" chimed Lucid while she listens "your grades were really bad last year, you almost had to retake the grade." she suppresses her laughter. It was true Luna barely passed that year. Luna pulled the yellow parchment out and unrolled it. Their mom's eyes slightly widen and looked a bit baffled at this old-style paper.

"When did you apply?" asked her mom while she reached for the scroll to read.

"I didn't," said Luna handing the parchment to her mom" I am not sure how I got accepted." she sat there looking at her mom reading it over and over just as she did herself.

"It wasn't on good grades for sure." teased her sister.

"Magick? They either miss-spelled magic or can't spell. They spelled it with a "k" in it. Anyways... You know magic?" asked her mom while she stared to her daughter. Lucid spoke up before Luna could say anything "I know "magic" and I didn't get a letter!" snapped Lucid.

"I- I wouldn't call it magic. I simply can leave my body when I sleep." said Luna while her mom had a dumbfounded look on her face.

"We don't...I mean this can't be a real school. Magic isn't real." said their mom with a baffled look while she said this, she pulled her blue laptop out from under the living room table. She started to look for the website, she looked up "magic schools" found nothing more than card tricks and pulling rabbits out of hats to Wicca classes. She type "OwlHollow" no results came up, "told you, this is just a sick joke." said their mom. She was about to close the laptop, then the queerest thing happened words began to burn into the bottom of the letter saying.

W°W°W°.OwlHollow. W°WO

"Mo-mom..." cried out Lucid while she pointed at the letters burning into the parchment. Luna dropped the scroll on the table while everyone looked at it baffled.

"There is a website... I never have seen a site like that before" said their mom while she types the website. Spiral writing slowly appeared while it said. Under it had a six-box number asking for a pin number.

They looked at the scroll at the top right had six roman numerals I, V, III, VII, II, VI. They went to the computer and type in the roman numeral password. Cheyanne pressed signed in and an old man with long wavy snow white hair, long pointy chin with thick bridge nose. He wore thin half-moon glasses that showed his warm purple eyes, and a long snow white beard that was braided.

"Who is this gu-" Lucid went to speak but before she could finish off the sentence the old man in the picture began to speak and look to around to the three. "Greeting Bell family, let me introduce myself. My name is Robert Rune. I am the Headmaster of OwlHollow School of Magick for Witchcraft and Wizardly. Luna Starr Bell you had been selected for this most private school. You will hone your witchcraft skills and wizardly powers." said Mr. Rune with warmth.

"Where is this school even at?" said their mom as if she was asking the computer while scanning the computer screen. "Good afternoon Mrs. Bell, how are you?" The school is in Crystal

Owl Valley beyond the Troll Head Mountain by Coastal Town."

The webcam and microphone weren't in use. The three of them looked to the computer dumbfounded "ho-how do you know any of us or who is all here?" I never heard of Crystal Woods or Coastal Town." said their mom in slight confusion.

"Well in this world of magick pictures moves and sometimes talk. The place I would not expect anyone in the non-magick world to hear of it. It is in Crystal Region. Feel free to browse the site. If you want to attend, follow the instructions and log back into the website. Have a good day." said Rune before his picture stopped talking then vanished. They sat there with their mouth slightly gaped open and out of the blue "THAT WAS AWESOME!" shrieked Luna.

They clicked along the page exploring and finding out that she will learn all different types of potions, charms, spells, curses, herbal, fortune telling, and so much more. They clicked on a link called "clans" a small box appeared with a small discretion overlook.

~There are four Guardian Clans in Owl Hollow~

the four Guardian clans were founded by the very first four founders of Owl Hollow back in 611ad. The Guardian Clans are:

Chimerador: Founded by Warlord St. Nickulas protector of life. The color for this clan is Red and Silver. (a picture showed of a beast, a chimera an body of a beast, the head of a lion, a goat on the back of the beast, and a long tail of a serpent.) *This was the choice by*

Chapter 2: The blue envelope and the mysterious feather

Warlord St. Nickulas to represent bravely.

Crowfeather: Founded by Ember Lynn the swift, colors for Crowfeather black and purple. This was chosen by Ember Lynn to represent Wisdom.

Goldenpaw: Founded by Leo the Perfect, clan colors are Gold and Silver. (a picture showed a large black three-headed dog with golden paws.) *This was the choice by Leo to represent loyalty.*

Dracoin: Founded by Lord Kaine the Feared, clan colors are black and emerald green. (a picture showed a large black dragon with a hint of emerald green in the scales.) *This beast was chosen by Lord Kaine the Fearful to represent power.*

"This is so awesome!" said Luna full of excitement in her voice "I want to go!" she looked to the screen than to her mom with puppy dog eyes while whimpering.

"I don't know, I mean- how much is this school?" asked her mom while she looked at the computer. She began to skim through few more pages. She finished scanning the pages then she found what she was looking for. She found the price for the school, one-thousand eight-hundred pounds of gold shanties shavings. There was a list of currencies.

Silver shanties, Ruby shanties, and Gold shanties. In the Dibble-Doggle (non-magick person) world shanties meant money. Silver shanties came out as hundred dollars, Ruby shanties came

17

out to be five hundred dollars, and Gold shanties came out to be a thousand dollars. If you needed something a little less, you just took the shanties and shaved them down to the shaving amount you need.

Cheyanne's eyes widen when she saw the price "ONE-THOUSAND AND EIGHT-HUNDRED DOLLARS for one semester!," cried out their mom causing both girls to jump. "Lulu that is so much. I mean-"

"Please mom, please I'll keep my grades up. Above a D-please." pleaded Luna looking at her mom.

"I will think about it." said their mom while she got up and closed the computer. Luna sat back grumpy while the sun began to set. Their mom started to get dinner in the works, Lucid laid watching a movie while texting some friends. She slipped off the couch and went outside to go jogging. Luna laid on the bed holding the fiery red feather. Her mom knocked on the door to Luna's room. Luna looked up to the door while it open and her mom came in.

"Hey Luna," said her mom whiles he came in "so, I have been thinking IF you truly want to go to this school, I will let you go." Luna shot up to her feet, excitement wash over her face while she held the feather in and staring to her mom and ran over hugging her "thank you mom -thank you mom"

"You are welcome, just keep your nose clean and grades least up over a C plus, and for heaven's sake be careful, I don't need no letters saying you been turned into a toad or blown up the classroom." said her mom teasingly. Luna glared at her mom then a

18

split second later they both busted out in laughter and headed downstairs where dinner was ready. Lucid was back from her jog and had the plates out with cups on the counter with the sun brewed sweet tea. They all started with a salad with Italian herb dressing followed by buttery mashed potatoes, peas, baked beans, cucumbers in vinegar, blueberry muffins, and smoked ham. -

Their mom can remember the days Adam and her would cook together. When he wasn't working. They would cook, Adam and she would flirt by having flower war and throw some baking flower at each other. When Adam died, she promoted Mr. Lundo to general manager and oversee the entire operation. Mr. Lundo had owned a few businesses and when the Bells met Lundo he was over a bank, and he pushed them the money. Cheyenne still owned the Bells Burger and collected a great amount of money.

As everyone ate with light talking, Cheyanne told Lucid that Luna was going away to that school. "Does that mean I get her room?" said Lucid with a smile while pouring some tea. Her room was smaller than her sisters'.

"Of course not, it is still my room!" shouted Luna while she glared at Lucid with ham on from. "Maybe they'll turn you into a frog." laughed lucid while she looked to her sister with a grin.

"Maybe I'll turn you into a sna-."

"NO one's getting turned into anything!," snapped their mom looking to the girls, "IF so my hand will turn into a paddle."

19

Silence filled the room for a moment then the two girls looked to the mom "You know magic mom?" said Luna

"Why you never mention it to us?" Lucid added after a pause and silence fell a moment later, they all started to laugh. They finished the dinner and cleaned up. The sun settled caste a ruby color in the sky while the sun began to set.

Everyone moved into the large living room which had family pictures, a fireplace, a few knickknacks, decoration of black bears, large sixty-inch television with a black glass entertainment center. Black leather sectional sofa, beautiful hardwood floor. All sorts of books on the bookshelves, and a beautiful glass table with a statue of a black bear under it holding up the glass.

Luna picked up the pen and marked yes in the letterbox, taking the red fiery feather as instructed she tapped the letter gently. They all sat around and watched then a split second later the letter sparked a blue flame and then caught fire and burnt to ashes. Then it disappeared followed by the feather in Luna's hand. They sat in bewilderment and awe "D-did that just happened?" their mom asked as the two girls nodded their heads in surprise.

A moment later a voice came over the laptop it was Mr. Rune "Luna my dear, just got your letter so glad you are interested in going to OwlHollow school of Magick. Go to Foxin Harbor and a man, a Tigris will wait for you. His name is Maîq.,

"He is a semi-Tall furry catty with golden fur. Come Saturday, August fifteenth, go to the bus station at eleven-fifty pm and get on Gatlinburg Express, and at midnight walk through the doors to catch the bus for Foxin Harbor. Your tickets will arrive Friday in the early after." said Mr. Rune before he vanished. "Tigris... Those are my favorite race in my video game." squealed Luna.

Chapter 3: Foxin Harbor

Few days have passed, August fifteenth that Friday finally arrived. Lucid had checked the mail after she came back from a run. She seen a letter dressed to the Bell family, she opened the letter and revealed the three bus tickets "Foxin Express: Gate three "a letter was under the tickets which was the same old yellow parchment paper that was dressed to Luna. Lucid walked up the long gravel driveway which seem like that went on for miles. She read the letter while she walked up the long gravel driveway.

~ *School Requirements* ~

First years will need the following as listed, no exceptions!

Introduction to the world of magick: by Merlin the great.

History of witchcraft and wizardly: by Serge Sheray

Introduction to potions and anti-potions.

Herbology and fungi magick use: by Icy Tune.

Basic Magick spells (year I): by Nightly Jones.

Introduction to transfiguration: by Penny Moon.

Light and Dark forces (a guide to protecting yourself): By James Smutter.

Creatures and Beast of the wild by: Emily Emeralda.

~ *School Uniform* ~

Three school robes black (Summer, Spring, and Fall.)

Chapter 3: Foxin Harbor

One cloak of clan color (You will receive the first day of class)
Three winter school robes green or red (For winter use only, with silver fastens.)

Three Black plaid skirts for ladies.
Three black slacks for gentlemen.
Black Leather thigh boots (For girls)
Black leather knee-thigh boots (For guys)
Five tunics for school wear (color of your choice).
Knee high-socks (For girls)
black socks (For guys).
Cloaks must-have school badge on it.
~ Other needs ~
One medium cauldron (pewter size 2)
Healing crystal (Grade C or better)
Wand
Brass Scales
Ink oils, parchment, and quill.
Leather hip purse (Color of choice)
~ Pets ~
Each student is allowed one pet of their choice. Must be a pet off the list.
Snake, Cat, Hawk, Owl, Ferret, Fox, and Wolf.
Please make sure to have a badge made with your name on it. Parents: First years

are not allowed to have broomsticks due to their dangerousness.

Sincerely

Robert Rune

Lucid came into the house while Cheyanne was on the laptop with her credit card on the school's website buying (five Gold shanties, ten Ruby Shanties, twenty Silver shanties); She had spent twelve thousand dollars "mom, tickets are here with a long list of books and other stuff." said Lucid while she drops the bills in the bill box by the door and then handed the letter and tickets to her mom.

She went to the backyard which was large with a large red riding stable, chicken coops, and a large garden. She went into the large barn that stalled twenty horses. She grabbed her dad's horse Rogue which was a beautiful black horse with snow mane and tail. Rogue was Adam's pride and joy; he was the son that they never had. She began to wash the horse.

Luna came out after it grew a bit dark outside and Lucid was riding Rogue in the pasture "DINNER IS READY!" shouted Luna from the porch. The moon crept out behind the trees while Lucid return to the barn. Dinner was done and cleaned up, it was eight o'clock and everyone laid down to wake up at eleven to get ready. The alarms went off and everyone got about three hours of sleep.

They all showered and got dressed. Cheyanne wore dark jeans, red t-shirt with a black cardigan. She knocked on the girl's

24

doors while she slipped her hair in a ponytail and went to warm up the truck. Lucid came out with a cute pair of cut-off shorts and a white t-shirt with a silhouette of a horse and brown cow- boots. She put on her hat which was a camouflage bow-tie symbol.

Luna went downstairs wearing black Tripp pants that had red straps hanging from them, black combat boots, red fishnet arm warmers, a t-shirt with a skull with blue butterflies scattering from the mouth of a skull. Silver armband serpent, a black choker with a bat emblem. She pulled her hair back in a waterfall braid.

"Oh, it must be a full moon. The vampire came out." heckled Lucid while they walked out to the truck.

"Maybe so, this vamp will turn you into a pet bat." joshed Luna while she waved a finger like a wand to her sister. They got into the truck, and they started to drive off into the darkness of the city.-

After about a half-hour drive, they pulled up to the old bus station. They saw the "Overflow parking" and they ended up parking in the overflow parking. They climbed out of the truck and walked up to the old large bus station with two double doors.

"Looks like they are closed." Said their mom looking through the dark windows. The lights were off, no vehicles in the normal parking lot. Luna reached for the door handle and gave a tug.

"Lun-." their mom called out but the door open while Luna vanished inside, followed by Lucid tugging at the door than their mom. - What they saw next would have shocked anyone. It was broad daylight, so many people stood around wearing robes and cloaks; white robes, blue robes, red robes, so many colorful robes, pointed hats, small hats, and no hats. The bus was an old bronze Double-Decker bus. On the side said "Foxin Express" there were twenty gates with long lines.

They found their line while they stood there behind a tall man with red golden-blond hair, large ears, bushy eyebrows, high cheekbones that made his brown tiny eyes bitty button-like, short nose with a slight bridge and a large mustache, that hid his thick lips, and slender, wearing black robes with a red cloak and silver trim. He wore a black pointed hat.

"Come- come Ray and Bella." said the man with a strong English accent, his wife followed onto the bus. A short pudgy woman with short red curly hair, round face, small dazzling blue eyes. Small button nose with thin lips. She wore a brown shirt with blue jeans and a green cloak.

"Stay in line you two, Jimmy-Jim Hun you got the tickets?" the woman hollered out while the man towered over her like an oak tree.

"Yus my dear – Ray stop that!" cried out Jimmy while he gripped Ray by his shoulder and lead him onto the bus.

"Dude needs a clearance sign for himself, don't think there will be room for the top half of his body." heckled Luna in a whisper her mom popped Luna on the head.

"Hush and be nice!" snapped her mom.

A small man no bigger than a small boy wearing blue a tunic and pants with a blue pointy hat. He had a black thick beard that went down to his waist dreaded up that hid his small pointy nose and large cheeks, dark buttons for eyes with thick wavy oily hair was asking for tickets. His deep rustic voice had a growl in it "Tickets, gimme ye ticket."

"I found your garden gnome!" taunted Luna while she pointed out to the tiny man. Before her mom could say or do anything the tiny round man took the tickets and ripped off the half he needed "I'm NO GNOME! I am a dwarf ye filthy Dibble-Doggle paysanne (peasant)!" He shouted angrily at them, the crowd looked at the disturbance as the dwarf slammed the hundreds of tickets down and they scattered on the ground. Her mom grabbed Luna by the ear and dragged her onto the Double-Decker bus as they walked in there were so many seats with stairs and a door to the bathroom. They walked onto the bus till they found a seat.

It was loud and noisy, the bus was made of bronze, the inside was of dark wood, wooden benches, with maroon cushions, lanterns hung over the head from the ceiling. The benches sat four to one with an opposite bench facing towards the other. They found a compartment and slid the wood door open. In the room that had the two benches sat a family that they have seen before. The tall oak man and his pudgy wife and two kids.

"May we sit?" asked their mom looking at the four of them while they sat there. Jimmy the older man held a paper in hand. The pudgy woman smiled and offered the other bench "Of course ye may." said the woman politely.

Cheyanne smiled and sat down on the bench with Luna and Lucid while Cheyanne went and introduce her and her kids "I'm Cheyanne, this is my two daughters Luna and Lucid." The tall oak man smiled softly down on them while he sat over them.

"Nice to meet ye, I am Jimmy Ward, this is my beloved wife Katie Ward. These two are two of the four kids. This is Raymund and this is Izabella."

Raymund is fourteen years of age with golden-blonde hair, fade cut along the sides and back. He spiked it in a stylish faux hawk hairstyle. Dark brown eyes, short face but pointed chin, short nose with a slight bridge. He had small ears, a handsome boy Lucid thought.

Izabella is a fifteen-year-old girl with long fiery red hair that she did a lattice braid to her hair, that has multiple strands of hair going in both horizontal and vertical directions to create a basket-woven lattice look across her whole head. Semi oval face with pointed chin high cheekbones, bright twinkling baby blue eyes. Small nose with a slight bridge, and thick full lips. Her cloak was black with a deep purple trim.

Luna gazed disorientated at the girl as if she was in a trance almost forgetting how to blink. The first time in a bit speechless, a moment later she came too. Picking up the conversation. "This is Ray's first year at OwlHollow and this is Bella's second year. The color of the cloaks represents what clan you are in. As you see Bella's is black and purple. Her clan is

28

"Crowfeather"," explain Jimmy as you see my cloak red with silver trimming. I was clan under "Chimerador" Our older son Dane is a Pre Lord. He is in the clan of Chimerador."

"-So, boys and girls are separated like boys go to Chimerador and girls go in Crowfeather?" asked Luna "What is a Pre Lord?"

Izabella spoke up before her father did, which was a good thing. The man loved to talk and could talk for hours "no, you are assigned to a clan. To answer your question about Pre Lords, there is only one Lord headmaster or Lord headmistress. He or she is the one who does all the big picture stuff and gets things done. The Pre Lords are the ones who always have the best grades and perfect attendance.

"Pre Lords are second in charge; each clan has one. They are the ones who can help with voting, watching over the students. Voting can be used for changing, creating, or getting rid of a rule created by the students. For Example, last year they made a rule every third Saturday during spring. You can swim in the mote around the school. You have school rules and student rules.

"School rules are unable to be changed by the Pre Lords and Lord Headmaster. Student's rules are the "fun" rules or stupid rules. Then each Pre Lord picks two nobles, they help back up their Pre Lord. Sometimes though they'd vote on another clan. In the end, it is the Lord Headmaster's job to talk to the four clan teachers and Head Master to get the final approval. IF they approved then he announces it to the whole school." explained

Izabella while a cart of sweets started to make its way through the aisles. "Can Nobles, Pre Lords, and Lord Head Master be able to give some kind of punishment or detention?" asked Cheyanne.

Izabella and Raymund had grabbed a pack of "Fruit dragonflies" which looked like large bite-size of dragonflies in assorted flavors: Red (Cherry), Green (Green Apple), Purple (Grape), Orange (orange), and Pink (Watermelon). Followed by a "Chocolate Grasshopper" it was a large size of chocolate that resembled a grasshopper.

Jimmy offered to buy the Bells something off the cart. Cheyanne took a pumpkin spice coffee, Lucid and Luna took a pack of "Chocolate Witches and Wizard" came with three bars of assorted chocolate with a collectible card of a famous witch or wizard in it. He pulled out a small leather bag and reached in and pulled out a one-tenth ounce of silver shanties and paid the woman.

"Pre Lords and Lord Head Master can take points away from your Clan, take you to a clan professor for detention. Lord Head Masters can take twenty-five points and give detention," Izabella answered, "points are very important for such as getting the guardian cup at the end of the school year. She had such an angelic harmony tone in her voice.

Raymund opened the Fruit Dragonflies pack and laid the six fruit-bites in his hand as they came alive, and the wings started to flap. They began to fly around his head. He opened his mouth for a moment or two before one flew in his mouth. "D-do they not fly away or fly in your mouth when you are trying to talk?" asked

Luna amazed at the candy flying around.

"No, they will fly around. You must have your mouth open wide for a couple of seconds then one will fly in your mouth. If someone tries and keep their mouth open, they won't go to them." said Raymund while he opened his mouth and ate another Dragonfly.

Izabella opened the Chocolate Grasshopper it started to hop around till she grabbed it and took a bite of it. The outside was crunchy with hard chocolate and the inside was filled with peanut butter. Luna and Lucid watched in shock then look at their candy bars.

"Don't worry those just have three assorted candy bars and a collector card." chuckled Izabella looking at them.

Luna opened her candy bar pack. It had three bars of chocolate one was a bar of dark chocolate, the other was cookies n cream, and the last one was white chocolate. She saw the card it was a royal blue card. Holographic with name written on it in a spiral with a gold banner "Mr. Robert Rune" it showed him waving lightly with a warm smile behind his thick snow white beard. After a moment he poofs.

"He is gone?!" exclaimed Luna staring at the card.

"Oh, he has things he has to do dearie, "said Mrs. Ward smiling warmly looking at Luna who looked puzzled. "He is a very busy man. He'll be back though."

Lucid opened hers, she had pumpkin spice chocolate, mint. And chocolate peanut butter. Her card was black with purple

31

trimmed with the same spiral writing as the other card. The name was written in feather quill the name was "Ember Lynn". The card was holographic, shown a black crow with purple eyes and midnight black feathers. When the card has tilted a woman with honey cream skin tone, long wavy black hair, with deep purple eyes. Oval shape face with a slightly pointed chin. Dimples, she has thick full lips and a small nose.

    "Oh! You got the founder of Crowfeather. Ember Lynn, they said she could shapeshift into a crown." said Mrs. Ward with a soft smile looking to the card.

    After a while, they have reached Foxin Harbor bus depot. They got off the bus. It was mid-afternoon, the roads were made of dirt, the sidewalks were made of sandstone. The sea was beautiful and crystal blue. So many ships sat in the harbor at the dock from sailboats, pirate ships, to old steamboats. They walked to the entrance of the town. A large iron black word spelling "Foxin Harbor". Stores was selling potions, ingredients for potions, fortune tellers, spell books, magick equipment, and other witchery and Wizardly stores. There were so many people, all sorts of beings.

    From humans, Elves, Dwarves, to Goblins and Orcs. They saw Foxin Harbor Bank a large sandstone building with colored stained glass. At least fifty steps, being the Foxin Harbor Bank sat on a hillside that overlooks the sea and the town. They saw a cat like creature with golden fur and brown eyes. His tail had three black stripes and the end was white. His right ear had a slit from what looked like being cut from a sharp blade. He wore brown leather pants, a blue tunic with black leather curious with a red pinstripe making a dragon on the chest of the curious. The bracers and greaves were that of black with a fancy pinstripe design on them.

"He must be the one we need to talk to." said Luna pointing out to the Tigris while they walked up to the stairs.

"Um- hello, are you from OwlHollow?," said their mom looking at the cat " We are supposed to meet someone that Mr. Rune had sent."

The Tigris turned his attention to them, his tail swayed as he hopped up off the stone pillar siding. He ate the apple core that was in his paw. He stood slightly over them his royal blue cloak swayed in the wind. "Ah sim (yes), ye ust' be da Bells. I am Maîq the game huntsmen or' Owlhollow. Sim (Yes) I ust' ezcort ye around zo ye all know where wat iz wat n wat is wat."

"Dis ere' iz da Foxin Harbor Bank, or' any shanties ye own ye will find it ere'." Said Maîq with very bad English. The Bells looked at him trying to follow along with what he had said. They made their way up the stairs and went inside. It was chilly inside, candles floated over their head. Dwarves and leprechauns worked behind the large counter.

"Next! -Next! I SAID NEXT!" shouted an angry dwarf, his black beard smelled like brew mead. The bells and Maîq were standing there already as the dwarf snapped out.

"We are right here shorty. Get a box so you can see over

the counter!" retorted Luna who didn't do well with rude people.

"Luna!," snapped her mom looking down to Luna "Tell the man you are sorry, right at this instant." her mom flicked Luna's left ear.

"I am Sor-"

Luna was cut off by Maîq who stood over them peering down to the little dwarf "Luna Bell would like to withdraw three-thousand and three hundred sixty-five shanties."

The dwarf looked up to Maîq and then turned his head and yelled to a leprechaun "Ágastas, need a withdraw!" demanded the dwarf, the leprechaun floated over a tanned person same size as the dwarf, he wore green pants with black pen-stripes with a button-up shirt and green overcoat. He had a green bow tie. He had dark messy hair and small pointed facial features. He handed an empty brown leather bag but with a snap of his fingers, the bag was filled with the shanties.

"All zet." said Maîq while he gave Cheyanne the bag of Shanties and lead them out of the bank.

"So, are all Dwarves that rude?" asked Lucid while they walked along the sandstone sidewalk feeling the sun beat down on them. Maîq's ears went back, and let out a low groan "Sim (Yes)." They came up to a clothing store called *Gracie's Robes and Tunics.* They walked into the shop it was packed as everyone was gathering tunics from a variety of colors to black and green cloaks. They skim through clothes as they grabbed three black robes and three heavy green winter cloaks with silver fastening. They had bats, moons, wolves, crows, and crow silver fastens.

Luna grabbed three fastens bats. Wolves and crows. Lucid began to look around then, wham! She ran right into a boy with rich auburn blond hair it was slicked back, small slit eyes with dark purple pupils, pale skin, a long oval face, sharp chin, thin auburn blond brows, with pointed ears. He wore a black tunic with dark jeans with black boots. He snarled at Lucid after she bumped into him.

"Sor-" she went to apologize but the kid cut her off.

"Watch it! Dibble-Doggle," He looked at Lucid with a disgusted look on his face, his cold deep purple eyes. He looked her over "too many Dibble-Doggles are ruining the school and realm."

"What is your problem? I said I was sor-."

"How about you Dibble-Doggles are the problems, ruining pure bloods with your venomous lifestyle." He snarl-ed while spoke.

Cheyanne and Luna stood with six cloaks, three silver fastens, black thigh boots with buckles, three plaid black skirts, five tunics (red, black, green, white, purple, and blue). A brown leather hip purse that had a bat stitch on it, and scale armor-protected gloves.

Luna turned and seen Lucid and walked over behind the boy "you and your bloody dibble-doggle family should go back to your venomous world." said the boy with a scowl while he stared at Lucid. Lucid went to say something, Luna came up behind the boy and shoved him hard. He tripped up and fell to the ground with a loud thump." You will not speak to my sister like that!," snapped Luna staring down at the boy . While she glared down at him "you will not want me as an enemy."

Maîq heard the thump, his ears flatten against his he-ad. He let out a low groan then moved over to the by and the two girls "Nuuuu - Pare (stop)- Pare (stop)." The boy stood and glared.

"You'll be sorry." He stormed out of the store.

"Who was that?" said Lucid and Luna staring at the boy who pushed past a few of the customers while he walked off. Maîq turned to the two girls "ye new orst' enemy, Kain Bloke. He has a brother a Pre Lord at the school. They say he is the next Lord Headmaster just as bad tempered. His name is Cecil. They are rich pure-blood wizards." Said Maîq while Cheyanne came over with a few bags in hand.

They made their way to a small store on the window that had a wand with sparks decal on the stained window saying *Flick and Swish wands* they open the glass door, a bell rung overhead giving a small chime when they entered. The store was tiny with shelves lined up along the walls from floor to the ceiling with so many boxes laying on the shelves. They looked around as a tall man came around the corner from the back behind the counter. He wore a brown tunic, crazy brown hair that went everywhere as if his curly hair just sprung everywhere. Thick busy brows with tiny bitty dark brown eyes that hid behind his steampunk goggles.

"Well, guud day Maîq. What brings ye here today?" the

man asked while he smiled warmly.

"Nu, 'elping Luna with her list, first year." replied Maîq while he sat in the corner while the Bells looked at the wands on the shelves. They came up to the glass counter where the man stood.

"Well, this is always a special day indeed. There is a rule to buying a wand. The wand will pick its owner. No wands are the same," said the bushy eyebrow man "my name is TomTom Flick. - Hmm.,"

TomTom walked to a shelve grabbing a box with a label "eight in a half-inch red oak blended with a raven feather, "he opens the wand box and pulling out the blackish-red wand. "Try this, pick it up and give it a tiny wish with a flick of the wrist." explained TomTom while Luna took the wand in her hand.

Lucid watched along with their mom as Luna lifted the wand with a swish and a flick of the wand. The box flew off the counter across the store. Their eyes widen watching in awe. "Nu-nu – nu," said TomTom while he took the wand from Luna. He slipped out another wand "ten inches redwood with a peacock feather." once again Luna took the wand and with a swish and flick the candles exploded.

"Definitely not!" snapped TomTom while he snatched the wand from Luna's hand. Cheyanne and the two girls let out a screech. Maîq sat in the corner and let out a little chuckle. TomTom returns with another wand "Eight inches Griffin with willow tree leaf." said TomTom with a soft smile handing the wand to Luna.

Luna followed the same motion, Lucid stepped away from behind their mom afraid of what may happen. Because this has not turned out well last two times. Luna gave the swish her braids began to lift, and the box began to hover. They watch in awed "yes, yes that's the one." Said TomTom with such a tiny clap of his hands in excitement. He boxed up the wand and bagged it. They ended up buying the wand and began to leave the store "that was so awesome, so books now?" said Luna walking down the sandstone sidewalk as the clouds began to cover the sun casting a shadow upon them. "já – já..." answered Maîq lowly while they made their way along the sidewalk. The ocean view was beautiful as they came up to a three-story building. A large library that had a spinning sign of two *books of Spells books and Charms.* They walked into the bookstore. There were three levels of floors of books.

It was so overwhelming "we'll be here all day." cried out Luna while they walked around and she saw a large oil painting of an old woman with snow-white curly hair, thick square glasses with her brown eyes behind the glasses. She wore a large smile on her face, a small button nose, and a lot of wrinkles.

After a moment they have seen the old woman behind the counter. They walked over to her "excuse me, can you help me find these books?" asked Luna while she handed the note to the old woman. The woman took the letter and looked at it "Ah, first year at OwlHollow, of course, dear." said Ruby Golder while she came

38

around the counter. After a few moments, they walked out with a sack of eight books in a bag.

They walked to a dark alley, and they walked down it, it was almost as dark as a night sky as if the darkness had denied the sun entry. "Never come ere' alone, real dark magick. Lurks ere'." hissed Maîq while he eyed the other people going from store to store. They walked along the sandstone sidewalk and they see a large tavern called *Calix Trepidi Despumat* across from the tavern sat an old run down store. Dust covered the window seal on the inside. Luna looked to the tavern and pointed it out "What is that Maîq?"

"Dat iz da Bubbling goblet." said Maîq while he leads them to the run-down store. It had a cauldron with a few potions decal with the name *Witchery Brewed Cauldron and Potions* on the window. They went inside the dark cold store. A dark skin man stepped out with a shaved head and round face with a dark daze, his tiny brown eyes was beetle-like.

"Yes?" called out the man while he wipes down the counter looking at the lot coming through the door. Maîq glared at the man with a mischievous smirk.

"Ell' Ello Just-in Tyme." Said Maîq while he placed the cauldron, scales, healing crystal, and alchemy kit, and brass scales on the counter.

"You know my name is Justin...NOT Just-in Tyme, cat!." Justin snarled with a hatred look in his eyes while he wrote up the items and bagged them taking the shanties. He handed the bag to the Bells while he stared with daggers at Maîq.

"GOODBYE!" Snapped Justin while he glared at Maîq still.

"Sims (Yes), Just-in Tyme." Snickered Maîq while they walked out of the store. They felt Justin staring a hole into the back of them. Maîq's grin didn't break as they began to walk out of the dark alley "ell' time 'or a pet." said Maîq while he led them out of the alleyway. The town was just as busy when they got there. He walked them over to *Beast and Pets* they all walked in and seen all sorts of animals from bats to spiders to foxes to giant lizards.

Luna walked around "you are not getting a bat, spider, snake, or lizard." said her mom staring at Luna who was staring at a free-tailed bat that was red with long, narrow wings and red fur. She turned to her mom "I knoooow," she stretched the "o" out in the word rolling her eyes "it isn't on the list anyway." They looked at a few species of hawks, owls, foxes, then wolves. "Hey mom, your favorite animal is a wolf, right?" said Luna petting a gray tundra wolf pup that was in the litter of the other tundra wolves.

Lucid looked at the litter of wolves in their kennels then walked off and seen a special wolf "-yes, but I don't think you need a wolf." said her mom who was looking at a few birds.

"Já, wolves r new dis year special creatures." said Maîq looking at the pups with a repugnance in his eyes. "Come look, Luna! Only one is left." cried out Lucid while Luna ran over to her sister who stood beside a sign that said Hellhound "what is a Hellhound?" said Luna staring down at the beast.

The *Hellhound* was a small wolf cub. Bright green eyes, sharp white fangs, black fur, but something is very odd about this beast. His tail was long and fluffy like a fox. He had a fiery mohawk literally his hair was in flames for hair. Between his ears red and yellow flames. The fur that was on his chest was a smokey blue hue flame, the same goes for his paws. Blue smokey flames wrap around his paws at the end of his large fluffy tail was a large flame of red and yellow.

"Hellhounds are very special creatures; it is said they crawled out from under the underworld." said Maîq while he came over and looked at the beast. Luna reached down and pat the wolf "I don't-" their mom was interrupted by Luna "FOUND my school pet!" exclaim Luna picking up the beast and it licked at her face." I'll call you... Khan." said Luna while they paid and walked out out of the Beast and Creature store "nice meeting you." they said and departed from Maîq making their way back to the bus. Few hours have passed, and they were back at home. Placing all the bags in Luna's room and they laid down passing out. It was six in the morning when they have arrived back home. -

It was finally Saturday, August 30th, two days before the first day of school at OwlHollow. Luna had received a letter to be at school no later than Sunday. She packed her luggage and put Khan in the kennel. She had got ready and place the things in the truck. She wore shorts with a cute anime shirt and skater shoes.

Cheyanne and Lucid got in the truck while Luna sat up

front playing with the radio looking for a station while their mom drove. They did a lot of talking and Cheyanne kept telling Luna she wasn't going to turn her sister into anything while Lucid kept saying she is going to get Luna's room. They had pulled up to the bus station. It was broad daylight outside; streets were packed as they reached the bus station. They parked and made their way to the bus station.

"Well, this is it.," said Luna while she place her four luggage on the trolley along with Khan's kennel "I will say hello to our friend for you Lucid." Luna and her sister stared at one another then burst out in laughter.

"He is your friend." countered Lucid.

"Better hurry before you miss the bus. Love you." said her mom while they hugged and said their goodbyes. Someone walked by and went into the station. Luna took the cart in hand pushed it into the station while she walked behind it and then disappeared after she walked past the threshold.

Chapter 4: Trip to OwlHollow

The place was very busy, she got her new ticket out of her hip purse and found gate 7. The employees place her stuff in the cargo hold of the bus. She got on the bus with Khan, she placed his kennel on the seat next to her. His flames lit the inside of the kennel. The bus started to move while the lanterns swayed overhead. She picked up a small rabbit and placed it in his kennel. There was a grown then after a moment a whimper. A small blue light appeared in the kennel and the rabbit was no more.

A boy walks over; thin, jet-black hair that spiked up in every direction, pale as a ghost. Looks like he has never seen the sun in such a long time. Small nose, thin lips with small ears. He had two bat earrings and black snake bites. He wore jeans and a black shirt. He had small silver glasses that hid his brown eyes.

"Anyone sitting here?" asked the boy pointing to the empty seat across from Luna.

"No, go ahead." answered Luna while she offered him the seat. She moved her feet off the seat from across her so he can sit.

"I'm DJ, DJ Bréon." said DJ while he introduced himself to her, "first year."

"I'm Luna Bell. It is my first year as well. Your fourteen?"

"Yep, first in my family to attend as well."

"Maybe we'll be roomed together." said Luna while he

pulled out his white wand and began to show it off to her. "This is my wand." said DJ while he let her hold it in her hand. He smiled at her "What wand do you ha-."

DJ got cut off as a fourteen-year-old girl walked over to them. She has strawberry blonde hair that was dreadlocked up. She wore a blue headband, small round face, pointed chin, and thin eyebrows. Brilliant blue eyes, she wore the school uniform. White tunic, black robes with knee-thigh tube socks with three black us see it." demanded the girl while she sat on the other side of the kennel while DJ held his wand in hand.

"Oh, n-."

"Come on, show us." demanded the girl in a bossiness tone while she cut DJ off. He looked to Luna then to the other girl as he cleared his throat raising his wand. He gave it a swish "sunny dash Lilith, scatter stars turn this bumblebee into a butterfly." He gave his wand a swish and tapped the window. The bumblebee flew off the window seal. The two girls look at each other with a puzzlement of confusion in their eyes. A large wind burst from his wand.

"Is that supposed to do that?" said the girl holding back a snigger.

DJ's cheeks flushed while he nodded "y-yep." he stuttered out while he put his wand away. Luna and the girl looked at each other with a half of grin.

"I don't think so, "the girl chuckled and looked to Luna "Any who, I'm Jenny Striff by the way. Who are you two?"

44

"Nice to meet you, I'm Luna Bell and this "wizard" is DJ."
Said Luna with a smile while she looked at Jenny "you are very
beautiful."

"Thanks! I love your eyes."

"My sisters are the same but opposite of mine."

"Oh, that's awesome, well you two better change, we are
almost Foxin Harbor"

DJ got up and went to the bathroom and changed then
Luna went and changed. They came back and sat with Jenny while
they were all talking Luna pulled out Khan to show him off. She
introduced him to the two while they pet him. His large fiery tail
swayed while she explains how he eats the souls of other animals.-

The bus cut through the mountains and the thick woods
before it broke from the woods. The sea could be seen from the
road as the ocean was few miles from the road "next stop Foxin
Harbor" said the driver while everyone cheered while the smell of
the sea filled the air. Then Raymund came over to the group and
smiled and gave a small wave "hey Luna."

"Oh, hey Raymund, where is Izabella at?" said Luna
returning the warm smile and wave. She offered him a seat with
them. Raymund sat down by DJ while he was introduced to DJ and
Jenny. "Oh, she is on the next bus up.," said Raymund while the
bus pulled through the woods "the first years are on Double-
Decker buses six to seven. There are hundred and sixty-first
years."

"-NEEERD!" said DJ with a grin while the bus horn blew, leaving a thick black smoke in its path while it drove, and the buses came to a stop at the platform at the station. The bus horn blew its air horn while the driver announced the arrival. The buses came to a stop and all six hundred forty-five students poured out onto the platform. Then followed along the sandstone sidewalks to the docks where a large steamship sat in the harbor. The ship had two large smoke tacks, overlooked captain's nest. Two lookouts, the ship over took the view of the sea. The writing on the side of the ship was in beautiful blue spiral writing *O.W.L* (*Ocean Way Living*). The students made their way to the eight-entrance bridge to board the ship.

Luna, DJ, Jenny, and Raymund board the ship while the crew transported the students belonging from the bus to the cargo hold. This was Luna's first time on a cruise. The crowd waved and cheered for the students while they waved back to the crowd. They were assigned to their rooms, luckily Luna and Jenny got bucked together with two other girls. The moon began to rise as the foghorn was blown from the ship while it began to set sail.

They sailed for few hours then a foghorn was blown to call for dinner, the dining hall quickly filled. They moved along the line getting food of all sorts from soups, burgers, chicken, lamb, salad, fresh fish, pizza, and a variety of deserts. The four of them found a seat then Izabella joined them at the table. "We will be at Coastal Village in the morning, we will be at OwlHollow by Sunday afternoon." said Izabella while she ate her sushi, after a bit, Jenny and Luna went to lay down in their bunks.

The moon and bright stars filled the sky in the cloudless night. Luna saw Khan laying on her bunk, she pulled out a rabbit and placed it on the bed. It hopped around on the bed before Khan pounced the white rabbit. His muzzle few inches from the rabbit's face and Khan began to inhale. Blue radiance light came from the rabbit's mouth while butterflies came from Khan's mouth. It was inadvisable to the kids. Luna looked dumbfounded "so strange to watch." said Luna watching Khan suck the life out of the rabbit.

"Who knew you can eat the air from someone." replied Jenny who looked so intrigued at the sight. They laid down in bed while the ship sailed throughout the night. Morning came, they all sat down for breakfast with a lot of chattering filled the dining hall.

Kain and his brother Cecil. Cecil who is fifteen years of age. He has dark long auburn blond hair, dark auburn blond brows, deep dark purple eyes with a strong jawline. He was well built. Kain pointed to the table where Luna and they sat. "That is the girl who pushed me. I think payback is in order." hissed out Kain lowly. Cecil stared at the table with those cold purple hues with a smirk.

"What did you have in mind little brother?" whispered Cecil while they sat across from the other table. Luna looked and seen Kain and Cecil "great, my bestie is here." said Luna rolling her eyes.

"Who's tha-" Jenny went to speak then all of a sudden Luna's oatmeal bowl exploded as it covered Luna, Jenny,

47

Raymund, and Izabella. The entire school stopped and stared then a moment later burst out in laughter. Their faces quickly went pink while they got up from the table. Jenny's face was as red as her hair. They were all humiliated and they quickly rushed out to go clean up.

Before the exploding oatmeal, Kain leaned over and whispered to Cecil "be great for an oatmeal bomb."

"Indeed." chuckled Cecil while he pulled out his wand and with a whispered voice and he held the wand under the table with a slight flick of the wand, the sleeve of his robe covered his wand up from being seen "praemium". Then BOOM the oatmeal exploded and covered the group. "Oh, that is great!" laughed Kain while watching the group leave the dining all covered in oatmeal. The girls and Raymund stood in the hallway after changing while they couldn't believe what just happened.

"What happened?" said Jenny still picking oatmeal out of her dreads.

"My oatmeal exploded, but I think it was my "bestie." said Luna while she sat down on the bench "your "bestie" and his brother are the worst. They think they own Crystal Region. Cecil even though he is great-looking and carved from the Gods. He is still a cruel bully and on top of that he is a Pre Lord." said Izabella while she looked to the entrance of the dining hall.

"Do you not lose status at a new year of school?" asked Luna confused while she stared at Izabella. "Oh no you keep your status Nobles, Pre Lords, and Lord Headmaster stays." answered

Izabella while people began to come out of the dining hall.

"You should be a Pre Lord." said Luna with a flirtous smile. They talked a bit more then went out onto the deck. The ship sailed through the ocean till they made it to the Crystal Coast as a loud foghorn blew. Luna seen Kain and Cecil with two other kids.

One looked like a rat in the face with tiny bitty brown eyes and messy brown hair. The fourteen year old boy name was Zak Micheals. The other boy was little rhino boy. He was short and round with bold head, large ears, big green eyes, and a long cruckled nose which looked like it was broken twice or three times. The fifteen year old boy name is Colten Flenwick.

When the four of them got together there was always trouble. Luna walked up to them with her new friends watching. She approached them with a glass of Witch's brew tea "hey bestie, that was a cruel prank." said Luna coldly but her lips shown a mischievous smile.

"Look, its one of those Dibble-Doggles. How was your breakfast?" said kain while everyone laughed. "Oh, i came to give you a gift... Out of the botto of my heart, no hard feelings."

The boys looked to one another then she flung the Witch's brew tea right in their faces "whoops." she said slowly before running off away from them.

"GET HER!" shouted Cecil then they chased after her. Luna ran to her group and they ran through the deck then disappeared in the crowded hallCecil and his brother's pack chased

49

after them. Luna and them jumped on the old elevator and closed the iron gate as it began to start to lower. The boys seen them lowering to another floor, Luna blown a kiss "bye boys!"

They laughed while they hit a lower floor. It was chilly down in the lower halls, the walls were white and deserted "where are we?" asked Raymund while they got off the elevator.

"I'd say near the bottom of the ship."replied his sister while they walk down the long hall.

"I cannot believe you did that, you are the queen of the group." said Jenny with a laughter while they made their way through the small corridor. "I hate bullies, I'd stick up for anyone" said Luna. A door open as a crew member stepped from the room looking to them "what are you all doing here, you all should be top side getting ready to get off at Crystal Coastal Village. Now off with you four." said the man with a demanding tone. They made their way to the deck while the village came into view. The foghorn blew loudly as they came into the harbor. The village was in the sand with sandstone buildings and wood huts stood in the distance. A crowd stood cheering at the ship welcoming the students. The kids waved back as a bridge of steps connected to the eight exits. The students went off the ship and then looked around.

A large cat came over to the students "alle sammen (all) get in line, four people in a group komme – komme." yelled Maîq while he shouted orders out to the students while they all lined up. Jenny, Raymund, Izabella, and Luna parted with their trunks and luggage. In the distance, hooves could be heard and followed by hundreds of horses pulling wagons. Luna seen Maîq and gave a wave "hey Maîq!"

"Hej, Luna so glad ta see ye." said Maîq while he waved back over to her. Everyone climbed into the wagons. The sky was now a beautiful ruby red while the sun started to set. The wagons cut along the sands, they slowly hit the grassland between the mountains. The mountains wrapped around the woods and beach; the wagons took a trail through the mountains.

"Why do they call it Troll head mountain?" Asked Luna while they rode through the mountains.

"You'll see." Said Izabella while she sat in the carriage.

"So, what is the story with Maîq and Justin Tyme?" said Luna while she sat next to Jenny across from Izabella and Raymund. Izabella laughed "OH that..."

"Well back in 1995, there was this boy he was good friends with Maîq. His name was RazÉr . He was a jokester. He and Maîq had two viewing crystals. RazÉr and Justin were in the same potion class. Every day Justin was always there right on the dot, he was a short roly-poly kid.

"It was exam day if you was late; meaning if the teacher got to your desk and you weren't there she counted you as late. RazÉr sat behind Justin the exams were being handed out and the teacher was at the desk next to Justin's. Justin burst into the room with toilet paper stuck to his boot. He sat at his desk right when the teacher got there.

"Your late, you almost failed this course, Justn Tyme."

51

said the teacher while she handed him the text. "-sorry." said Justin lowly while he looked down in shame. Maîq could see and hear everything because of the viewing crystal. RazÉr made the view crystal to fit on a necklace.

"How can one be late, when your name is Just-in Tyme?,", snigger RazÉr "Hopefully, you made it Just-en Tyme for your last business!" chortled RazÉr the class burst out in laughter,

"And from that day. Justin Tyme was known as Just-in Tyme." explained Izabella while she told the story about Justin Tyme.-

The wagons moved along the sharp curved roads of the tiny trail. The higher they got up in the mountain the colder it got. Finally, they have reached the top and snow-covered the grounds. Then a very large stone shape like a troll's head could be seen in the distance. It had a large wide opening that looked like a mouth baring shape rocks like teeth. Pointy ears. Dark tunnels for eyes and nose.

The scene was frightful, then they came around the corner seeing a grand view of the mountain and noticed a waterfall spilling out of the mouth. They made it over the bridge. Then they began to descend the mountain. Inside the carriage it was chilly, the wind blew the cloth curtains back. Jenny draped her legs over Luna's lap as they curled up to keep warm.

"Can't believe how cold it has gotten." shivered Jenny while she spoke.

"-I know." replied Luna whose teeth were chattering.

"You two are adorable." said Izabella teasingly while the candle overhead swayed. Luna looked to Jenny and smiled lightly and spoke ever so gently "I'd date her." she tried to hide the flirtatious in her voice. "You're so sweet," blushed Jenny "I'm not special." -

They made it down the mountain and it was now dark out. They came from the woods and over- head sat two full moons that cast down on the stars filled the cloudless night. They came to a large iron gate that opened on its own for the carriage. They began to cut through the woods once again and there was a small stone building with a large garden and archery field. A large lake with an outflow to a river. They cut over the bridge then cut through another part of the woods before coming out of it. A stadium sat in the distance with a large pool, giant greenhouse, a few large storage sheds. On the other side of the caste were a large barn and massive pasture. Luna looked awed "my sister would love to go to the horse stables."

"All these horses belong to OwlHollow." said Bella while they look out of the window at the surroundings. Owls sat in the trees watching while everyone rode by. "So may owls, there are hundreds..." said Jenny in awe.

"Why do you think it is called "OwlHollow"." said Bella while they rode up to the castle. The castle is very large with a few large towers... Two torches sat on the wall by the draw bridge. On top of the towers flew a flag in royal blue colors with OWLHOLLOW spelled in black spiral lettering. The front right tower was flying a red flag with a crest on it of a head of a lion and the body of a beast. On the tower midsection was a large ruby carved and it spelt out "Chimerador".

The next tower was the front left tower it had a gold flag with a beast of a three-headed dog. On the midsection of the tower in gold carving spelled "Goldenpaw". A gold flag swayed in the wind above the tower. The back right tower flew a dark purple flag with a silhouette of a crow, the large tower glow in the dark like a lantern from the torches on the wall. On the wall midsection of the castle in amethyst spelled "Crowfeather".

The last tower on the back right flown a green flag with a silhouette of a dragon. The large tower had emeralds carved spelling "Dracoîn". The wagons came to a stop in front of the large castle walls. The bridge was down with the flames dancing on the tower walls. Everyone climbed out while Maîq gathered their things and laid on the ground by the students. Luna stood by the group looking awed at the view of the castle.

A woman stood outside of the castle walls on the drawbridge staring at the students while they got out of the wagon looking upon this older woman. She had a pug-like face, deep pink eyes, a small nose, her gray hair tugged in a tight bun. She wore square thin glasses that flicked in the firelight. She wore a black pointed hat, black robes, with a royal blue cloak. She wore thigh-high boots. "Welcome, students to OwlHollow!" announced the

54

Chapter 4: Trip to OwlHollow

woman.

Chapter 5: OwlHollow and the mixing cauldron!

The students stood there listening then cheered while listening to the woman, Luna looked up at the royal blue crest above the entrance of the school. A white owl, to the left of the owl at the top, was a crow, at the right top was a dragon, left bottom was a chimera, and the left bottom was the beast.

The woman looked among the students. She had a stern gaze, lips barely broke into a smile Maîq stood over by the woman now. "Welcome to OwlHollow, my name is Mistress Velvet Flowers I am the vice Head-Mistress. First years follow me, everyone else followed Maîq." said Mistress Flowers while she watched the students form two lines.

The school split up while they walked into the courtyard. There were a few buildings, a running track, a large water fountain, stone walk ways that lead from the towers to the other buildings. In the middle of the courtyard, they passed the fountain. Torches lined up along the wall, the large doors to the keep were wide open. They all walked into the keep; Mistress Flowers open two large doors as she led them into the large feast hall.

"Stand in a single file line." said Mistress Flowers in a demanding voice while she went up to the stage. The first years stood in a single fine line. Everyone else took a seat at their colored long tables. The walls were large and curved up to the large chandelier with candles. Large paintings hung on the wall of the four guardians. Luna looked around along the room, there was a long table with five thrones on a large stone stage. Doors opened up behind the stage and an old wizard walked out with his thick long beard braided, he sat down on the big throne in the middle of the five thrones.

Followed by a tall man long oval face, sharp chin, dark brown eyes with black buzzed hair. Thick black brows, his gaze was cold and hard as he sat down left to the old man he sat in the last throne. Then another man came out after the cold stone face one. This one was the opposite he was warm, cheerful. He had bright blue eyes, his blonde hair that held in a perfect style. A smile that could stop time with perfect flawless teeth. He came and sat by the cold stone face man and rune in the fourth throne.

A moment a woman came out of the room, light brown hair, pale skin, soft purple eyes. Soft facial features, she had a raven tattoo on the side of her left hand between her thumb and index finger. She took the throne by the old man in the second throne. The four sat on the thrones.

"This will be the best year yet; this school is one of the best in the regions. There are four guardians that you will be in clans with. Those guardians are "Chimerador", "Crowfeather", "Goldenpaw", and "Dracoîn.". Your clan will be your family, the dormitories will be your home. At the end of the year ALL clan points will be added up. Please give a round of applause for the headmaster Robert Rune." Said Mistress Flowers while she stood on the stage. Everyone began to thunderstruck with applause while the old man in the middle throne stood up. He was so jolly and had such a warm aura of him. The man gave a small bow and he spoke with strong confidence in his voice, he looked through his half-moon glasses to the sea of students. "As Mistress Flowers already said, welcome back to OwlHollow!," he said with thunderstruck in his voice " And for all the new students Welcome! I am Headmaster Robert Rune here at OwlHollow.,

" I Would like the Lord-Head Master, Bruno Silvertongue from the clan of Chimerador to come up and take your throne." said Mr. Rune heartily while he called out Bruno Silvertongue the students cheered and beat the tables with excitement. The Dracoîn table gave a quiet golf clap, the student stood and made his way to his throne.

He was fairly tall, lanky, and had untidy brown hair as if he hasn't brushed it in a while. He had dull hazel eyes that were hidden behind thick glasses. He wore the school uniform, with a red cloak, and it had silver trim. His school badge had his name on it with a picture of a chimera which was a lion, goat, and tail of a serpent. He waved before sitting down taking the middle throne that was in front of the stage. The seventeen-year-old boy looked among his peers. The ovation came to a stop "Now Pre Lord for Chimerador, give round applause for Dane Ward come and take your throne!." announced Mr. Rune while he stood with such warmth in his eyes.

You could hear Izabella cheer "get up there brother!" she

yelled as Raymund cheered. The heavy-set muffin top boy got up and walked over, he had curly bouncing red hair. Big ears, round face, deep sea blue eyes. He was a little dorky and heavy set. He got up from the Chimerador table and made his way across the floor while everyone cheered except for the Dracoîn clan. His red cloak bounced while he walked then he waved before the seventeen-year-old boy sat down.

"Now for the next clan, put your hands together for Bree Summers! For the clan Crowfeather."

A young girl stood, the fifteen-year-old with multiple colored hair which was black, purple, and royal blue. She was a short girl barely five feet with pale skin, freckles and her eyebrows were a dark black. Her eyes were a low dim yellow. She had a nose, ears, and lip ring. Her earrings were little gauges. She stood at the purple Crowfeather table and walked across the floor her hips swayed.

"GO BREE!" a boy yelled out from the same clan while the black cloak with purple trim bounced with each step while she made it to the third throne. She gave a small bow then sat down and fix her skirt after her legs crossed. Her badge was purple with a crow with her name on it.

"Love the hair, going with your clans color this year?" asked Mr. Rune while he smiled at her before he turned his attention back to the students. "For the Pre Lord for Goldenpaw give an around applause for Jewels Meadows!"

The room exploded with applauded while the fifteen-year-

old girl with dark purple hair, deep pink eyes, and soft honey skin came down from the Goldenpaw table while everyone cheered loudly and whistled. Her gold cloak with silver trimmed swayed with each stepped. She made her way to the third throne; she gave a graceful bow then sat down. Her long leg cross over the other than fixes her skirt.
Her badge was golden with a white three head dog with her name on it.

"Now the last Pre Lord for Dracoîn, give it up for Cecil Bloke." announced Rune. Luna's eyes rolled along with Jenny's "OF course." whispered Jenny in a groan. Cecil stood up and walked to his throne, hardy any claps but the Dracoîn clan table went crazy with cheers. Cecil walked past the two thrones, he looked to the Lord-Head Master "enjoy that throne while you can, Dibble-Doggle." hissed Cecil while he passed the third throne and took a seat at his throne right by Jewels.
Let us hear it for your Lord Headmaster and Lord Headmaster! Now, the professors for each Guardian Clan Professors. Please when you hear your name rise and give a wave. For-"

A soft tone came out around the corner of the entrance of the feast hall "Sorry I am late." said the soft voice, all the students turned and was a tall dark skin woman, she had dark brown eyes, small soft facial features; Goddess like with black dreads with a red headband with a red cloak with yellow trim. "Thank you for deciding to join us tonight, Professor Moon." said Mistress Flowers while she stared at the woman while she came up the stairs to the stage taking the first throne after she gave a slight bow before sitting down. Rune cleared his throat while he smiled down upon the students.

"Now, for the Guardian Clan for Crowfeather – please give a warm applause for Professor Raven Woods!" announced Rune while the with the raven tattoo stood and gave a light bow. The crow-feather table claps explosively with cheers. She fixed her clan color cloak and sat down.

"Next give a round of applause the Guardian Clan for Goldenpaw, please give a round of applause for Professor Sha-wn Dibbs!." announced Rune while the man with the perfect smile and perfect hair stood up and gave a wave. The Goldenpaw table blew up with cheers. The perfect model man flashes a warm smile. A girl in front of Luna and Jenny spoke up "he is sooo dreamy." her voice trailed in a long dreamy, state.

The man drapes his clan cloak over his shoulders as he sat down awes filled the feast hall "such a charmer." said Izabella to another girl at the Crowfeather table.

"Now for the Guardian Clan of Dracoîn, Professor Kanoe Thompson!" yelled out Rune while the cold stone face stood up not breaking a smile while he sat back down. "He looks so cruel." whispered DJ while he turned to Luna and Jenny. The Dracoîn table exploded with chanting "Professor Kanoe- Professor Kanoe-

61

Professor Kanoe!" as if he was a champion. He sat there staring at the students with his cold stare. Mistress Flowers took the floor now while she had a stern stare in her eyes and her voice was sharp "Now it is time to start the sorting, the new students among the four Guardi-ans. Chimerador for bravery, Crowfeather for wisdom, Golden-paw for loyalty, and lastly Dracoîn for power... It will be your task to figure out the founders and history of each clan and you must do this on your own, first yearers. Each clan is worth ten guardian clan points. "Announced Mistress Flowers while she explained. All the first yearers looked nervous.

"Test already? Luna whispered to Jenny with a lost look of hope. Luna was not the smartest, not that she was dumb. She just didn't care for school. She enjoyed being with her friends more. She spent most of her time in detention for fighting. She didn't cause it, but she stood up for the victims She enrolled in Muay Thai at the age of seven and till she was thirteen. She hung with her friends, played games, and once a week went to the *Gamer Block* where she hung out and played tabletop games such as Castle and Wizards or play card games.

Jenny shook her head "I have been studying a lot, hopefully, I will pass." whispered Jenny more to herself than to anyone around her. She mumbled different types of potions and simple spells to herself.

"Maîq, please bring in the cauldron." Mrs. Flowers called out to Maîq. He nodded his head.

"Já, Amante (Mistress) Flores (Flowers)." Said Maîq while he walked out of the dining hall. Luna's mind was racing. Were they going to have to make a potion, perform some kind of magick trick? She was trying to control her breathing as she felt an anxiety attack was going to happen. She knew she was about to make a complete fool of herself in front of the whole school.

A Moment later Maîq came back into the feast hall with a large iron cauldron and wheeled it up in front of the stage of the professors and Headmaster. Mistress Flowers pulled out her wand and tapped the cauldron *"complere "* and the cauldron slowly began to fill up with water. Everyone stood waiting to see what happens next.

"When you hear your name please come up and look into the water and gaze. The cauldron will tell you which Guardian Clan you will be placed in." explain Miss. Flowers. Names were being called out one by one they went up to the cauldron and peered into it. A large green puff of smoke puffed out of the cauldron creating a guardian. One girl peered over it and a Chimera formed then the girl lifted her head and roared out loudly like a lion. Mistress Flowers yelled out "Chimerador!"

The table of Chimerador table went crazy with cheers and banging the table while they chanted.

After a few more names were called out then finally "Zak Micheals!" Mistress Flowers shouted. Zak walked up with his rat-like smile as Kain cheered for his buddy.

"Hope his ears get stuck." whispered Luna to Jenny while chuckling.

63

"Chimerador!" Mistress Flowers yelled out while she handed Zak a clan cloak. Jenny and Luna looked at each other in disbelief.

"DJ Bréon!" shouted Mistress Flowers.

DJ walked up to the cauldron his heart was pounding and eased over to it slowly. The room seemed extra quiet as he felt his heart pounding. Then a moment later POOF! A crow appeared out of thick green smoke. His head got thrown back and he *KRAA* out like a crow, it echoed out through the whole feast hall. "Crowfeather!" cried out Mistress Flowers while she smiled. Crowfeather table cheered, and banged the table with a thunderous cheer. DJ was handed the Crowfeather cloak, he went and sat next to Izabella.

"Raymund Ward!"

Ray looked around the whole feast hall and made his way down to the cauldron. He looked up to Dane Ward his older brother who was one of the Pre Lords. He looked into the cauldron and then POOF! A large three-headed dog appeared in thick green smoke. Ray threw his head back as he started to bark loudly with a snarl.

"Goldenpaw!"

He walked over a little sadden after he got his golden cloak from Mistress flowers. The Goldenpaw table was cheering for Ray. He was bummed because he didn't get into Chimerador with his brother or Crowfeather with his sister. His new friend DJ who he met was now in Crowfeather. He saw Colt, Kain's friend at the

64

Goldenpaw table.

"Jenny Striff!"

Jenny looked to Luna and smiled before turning and walked up and peered into the cauldron. Her a loud POOF and a crow appeared in the thick green smoke. Her head flung back and she *KRAA* out loudly. She was extremely relieved as she got her cloak while the table cheered and she made her way over and sat with DJ and Izabella.

"Kain Bloke!"

Kain smiled with confidence while he walked up. Cecil nodded to his younger brother with a smudged look on his face. Kain peeked into the cauldron for not even a second. A loud POOF and a dragon formed in the thickness of the smoke. Kain's head was thrown back as he roared out loudly.

"Dracoîn!"

Kain walked over to get his cloak as he looked at Luna with a cold smirk. The Dracoîn table exploded with cheers. It was the loudest they have been. Then he sat down while the line was slowly shrinking name after name was called and finally.

"Luna Bell!"

Luna gulped as she walked to the large iron cauldron. Her heart was racing, she didn't want to be in Dracoîn at all. Kain's little click was split up among the clans. She leaned down and looked into the darkness of the water. She gazed into it as a picture of a woman appeared. An old woman with dark long stringy hair, eyes were blacked out, long crooked nose, wrinkled faced, a sharp chin, very bony facial structure.

A hand reached out of the water to grabbed Luna. The arm was wrinkled, the nails were long and pointed with black polish. The hand reached out of the water reaching for Luna.

The smell of burnt rotten flesh filled her nose. Luna threw her head back and tripped on her own feet landing on her butt. Her back arched as she stared up. A few of the students laughed as Jenny, DJ, Izabella, and a few other students stared. The professors, Mistress Flowers, and Headmaster Rune stared baffled.

Luna's head got thrown back as a loud smoke formed into the shape of the *crow*. She let out a loud *KRAA* herself. She stood up to her feet and stared at the cauldron one last time as she walked to Mistress Flowers to retrieve her cloak.

"---Crowfeather!" Mistress Flowers choked out while she stared at the scene. Then cleared her throat while she handed Luna the cloak. Luna moved over to the table as it whole room was quiet. Luna made her way down her way between the Crowfeather and Goldenpaw table to sit with DJ, Izabella, and Jenny. Jenny looked to Luna with a worried look in her eyes "are you, OK girl?" Jenny asked conerningly.

"What happened?" asked DJ and Izabella in a low whisper.

Luna looked to the cauldron as it was being wheeled off back out of the feast hall. "I---I just tripped." said Luna in a low whisper herself. She didn't want to tell them what she saw or the smell of burnt flesh. Who would have believed her?

"Now let's celebrate and have a welcoming feast!

Chapter 5: OwlHollow and the mixing cauldron!

Tomorrow classes will begin. The race of the Guardian Clan Cup is on its way and as of now it belongs to Dracoîn, snatching it from Chimerador." announced Rune while he stood at a crys-tal glass podium while he spoke to the school. Carts of food began to wheel into the feast hall on their own the platters of food floated onto the table. There was ham, pizza, multiples of pasta, a large assortment of sides, with Witch Brewed Teas, Goblin Sodas, water, and Pumpkin Spice Coffee. Followed by so much desserts, cookies, puddings, pies, and cakes. Everyone was enjoying the feast while Luna took a large sip of her Mix Berry Witch Brewed Tea. After a long feast of good food and talking. The feast came to an end.

"Everyone please follow the Pre Lords and Guardian Clan Professors to your dormitories." Said Mr. Rune while everyone began to get up from their tables while Mistress Flowers took the stage and looked at the students. "Four line-s, let's go." she barked out while the students followed their professor as each line went to their own clan castle tower. They made their way up to the spiral stairs on the walls of the tower hung photos of past students, beasts, and other professor that used to attend the school. They have reached the end with a wall and no door.

"There are passwords to make the door appear and it is "Dragon root" slow and steady." Professor Raven told the students while a beautiful circular door appeared with an engraving of flowers and crows. The door swung open, and Professor Raven lead the students into the dormitory "Come along".

The room was large and round, with a large fireplace with

four red leather seating chairs. On the other side were black sectional sofas. There is a study room with a few bookshelves and few tables. The floor was dark oak wood, over the large fireplace was an oil painting of Ember Lynn. Her deep purple gaze watched down in the room. Doors circled the walls as students poured into the common room. There were spiral stairs that led up to another floor with another living area, rooms, and study

" Your bags and belongings have been placed in your rooms already. Your class schedule is laying on your beds. For the next four years for the new students, this is your home. Keep it clean and ---don't blow the roof off." said Professor Raven as she looked at the students before turning and walked off out of the room.

"Everyone! Get around clan meeting!" announced Bree while all the students sat around the dormitory. Jenny, Luna, and DJ sat together on the black leather couch. Luna pulled a clan color blanket off the back of the couch and wrapped herself with the blanket. Bree pulled out her Ocean Blue Sparkling wand and giving it a small flick while she said "*Augue*" and a small fireball shot out of the wand and lit the fire.

Luna was still amazed at the sight of this magick. The three of them cuddled up in the blanket while Izabella and few others passed drinks out. "This is going be the best year." Said Jenny with a smile taking the Pumpkin Spice Tea.

"I would like to welcome the first yearers to our family. Last year we got our butts handed to us by Dracoîn. AS the captain of Snorkbie. There is going to be practice every Saturday morning. As we know most points are earned through Snorkbie. For my first noble it will be Bella." Said Jenny while Izabella gave a light wave while Bree went on her speech. "First yearer boys will take this floor, first yearer girls will be next floor up. Second yearer boys next floor followed by the girls. Third yearer boys on the fifth floor followed by the girls, fourth year boys on the seventh floor, followed by the fourth-yearer girls on the eight floor and finally Pre Lords and Lord-Headmistress will be on the ninth floor.,

"Third floor in the halls and the keep are restricted for they are the living quarters for the professors. The woods are forbidden to enter. If you fail any test, breath any of the rules, it will cost you to lose points.,

"This is the best year for us, lets end this meeting and put your stuff away in your rooms, and goodnight." Bree closed the meeting while everyone got up to their feet and went to their rooms. Jenny and Luna were roomed together with two other girls. The room was large each section of the room had a four-poster bed with clan color curtains, wardrobes, a nightstand, and a desk. Khan laid on his dog bed. Luna and Jenny sat together on Luna's bed to compare each other class schedules before they went to bed. Jenny looked to her schedule while Luna looked over at her shoulder and began to skim through it along with Jenny.

Khan's fiery body lit the room while they looked over the schedule "ugh, math! --- I hate math looks like we have lunch and last three together, History of Magick people, Science, and Basic

Spells for first years.." whined out Luna while she laid back on the bed staring up at the ceiling in defeat.

"Your first part sounds boring, well good night girl." Said Jenny hugging Luna before going off to her canopy bed and closing the curtains on it before snuggling under the deep purple blankets. Khan laid at Luna's feet, she turned and looked at the pictures of her mom and sister. Then she picked up one of her dad's pictures that sat on the nightstand next to the bed and kissed it "Love you."

Chapter 6: Classes Start

Luna woke up the next morning, she stood to her feet and open the large curtains to the window. The sky was still dark, she turned and saw the four girls. Jenny is in her bed asleep, Emily Hogan, Lyndsie Hearing, and her own body lying asleep.

She was now astral traveling. She moved through the bedroom to the doorway to the living quarters and opened it. Her eyes widen as she saw two spirits. One was a girl with very curly hair and a round face. Heavyset with wavy hair and brown eyes.

"I have heard she is back." said the tall ghost while he sat next to the girl ghost.

"Did you? I heard that the granddaughter is here." Said the fat ghost girl.

"That was an evil witch, and her son was just as bad."

Luna stepped back slowly and went to her room and laid in her own body. She kicked and twisted as she had dreams of the witch in the cauldron reaching for her. Hand wrapped around her throat grasping it tightly sucking the life from her. She jolted awake "NO!" Jenny had woken Luna up giving her small shakes to wake her up.

"You OK?," asked Jenny in concern "school starts in an hour,"

71

"---Ya, just a bad dream."

Jenny was already dressed in the school uniform and she hooked the fastens on her cloak while she looked to Luna with slight concern. Luna got up and went to shower and dressed. They met down at the bottom of the dormitory. They went to the courtyard, DJ and Luna walked down to the keep it was crowded with students, pictures of teachers, and several graduation classes waved. DJ and Luna made their way into the classroom. They found a table as they sat together while students spilled into the classroom.

The room was filled with multiple students from each clan before a young professor came into the room. Her hair was a light brown and pulled into a tight ponytail, brown eyes, and fair skin. The teacher began the headcount while she looked over the list and the students.

"Austin Hays?"

"Here." A young boy from Chimerador answered.

"Angela Hays?"

"Here." A girl from Dracoîn answered.

"DJ Bréon?"

DJ raised his hand as he spoke up "Here." After a few more names were called out. The teacher called out "Luna Bell?"

Luna raised her hand "Here."

"Welcome everyone, my name is Professor Hailey Brooks . I am your math teacher for the semester. Let us begin, get out yo-ur quills." Said Professor Brooks while she handed out the worksh-eets and passed them along to the students.

"I hate math." Whispered Luna lowly as she got her packet and passed it back to a student from Goldenpaw. It was one of her weakest subjects. The class dragged by each student went to the black- board and did a problem. After what seemed like such a long time. The large iron bell began to ring from the keep. The iron bell rang to release the class.

"OK class, do the two pages for homework and make sure to show your work." Instructed Professor Brooks while everyone got up from their seat and stuff their hip bags with their quills, inks, and their math packets.

Luna and DJ walked out and saw Raymund leaving Science as they waved him over "how was your first night and class?" asked Luna while they walk down the long hall.

"-O-oh...It was ok, I had science...Three pages of homework. Professor Tristan Smith isn't very pleasant." Said Raymund while he hugged his bag in his arms while he tried to fix the fasten on his hip bag. Kain, the rat boy Zak, and the fat short rhino boy Colt came by as Kain smacked Raymund's books out of his hands while they all laughed. DJ and Luna helped him with collecting his things.

"Colt Flentwick is in my clan, we are roommates," said Raymund while he stuffs them in his bag "I didn't get much sleep. He hit me with a dutch oven."

DJ looked to the two, a bit confused "He hit you with a dutch oven? Is he that strong?" Luna rolled her eyes with a chuckle "It's where the other person farts under the covers and jerks the blankets over your head and pins it over your head. Trapping you under the blankets., "explained Luna "I've done it to my sister before."

They sat down at a table with their black pointed hat. The professor came into the room and shut the door The tall woman with red hair, dark tanned, and green eyes. The room had a brown owl that perched upon a standby the desk. The ten tables that sat four students per table filled the room. Raymund, DJ, Luna, and another bot from Goldenpaw had joined their table. His name was Dagen Grimm, he was a semi-tall boy with a well-built frame. His hair was short spiky golden hair with deep green emerald eyes.

"Welcome Class I am Professor Maggie King. This class is about *Introduction to the world of Magick.* You will learn the history of White Magick the roots of all magick. Let's began the headcount."

"Josh Timble?"

"Here." called out a boy from the back he was in Chimerador.

"Luna Bell?"

Luna had her book on the table with the rest of the class. She peered up from her book "Here." After the headcount the owl watched over the class while the professor spoke and explained the difference between white and black magick.

"Magick has been around since day one of mankind. They drew power from mother earth also known as Gaia. Magick was simple back then. They focus more on Magick to help with living and helping each other. White magick was tended to help them in such ways such as turning the top of the wand in a flashlight to see in the dark or a warm ember light to close a wound, and so much more."

"Grey Magick was more elemental spells such as fire, ice, and many more. Black magick was more of your: Curses, Hexes, and Jinxes.," The professor went on as she turned to the class while they took notes. "Who here can tell me the very first wand?"

A few hands went up into the air. DJ hid behind his book, Raymund slump down into his seat, and Luna hid in her book while she looked at Raymund and DJ with her head hidden. The teacher scanned the room. Then looked to the group trying to hide.

"Mrs. Bell, can you tell us? You look as if you are looking very hard for the answer." Called out Professor King looking down at the four of them. Luna sat up and bit the corner of her lip while she thought of an answer.

"The named or made of?" asked Luna trying to stall for more time. Her eyes scanned over the two pages.

"Made of names of wands grew in time over the centuries."

Luna found the answer while the professor came to the end of her sentence. "The first wand was just the index finger." said Luna with a sigh of relief.

"That is correct, it was harder, but it was more powerful, in time the finger wand had died off when wands came around.

Five points for Crowfeather. Homework is to explain more details about white Magick."

The bell rung as the class left the room, Jenny just came out of her alchemy and potion class. She ran over to the group "hey everyone!" her face shown excitement.

"Hey." the group called out to her with a slight wave while they met up in the hall. They made their way to the second floor of the key. Kain was with his goons "make way for the Dibble-Doggles!" yelled out Kain while everyone separated in the hall making a pathway for Luna and them. They walked by as Luna glared at Kain and them while the group walked into the classroom for *History of Magick People*.

They sat in the classroom finding a table near the back of the room. The four of them pulled their book out for the class as the bell began to ring. The professor called for the headcount "my name is Professor Katt Dunn, I am the *History Of Magick People*. We will learn the best witches and wizards from good to bad." explain Professor Katt while she pastes back and forth.

The class started talking about *Merlin the Great*, discussed what made him so great "Merlin was a *Cambion*, which is a half-human and half-demon offspring of an incubus. He was born of a mortal woman, sired by an incubus. That is how he got his supernatural powers and abilities.," Said Jenny while she stood up staring at the teacher. "This is how he was commonly and notably prophecy and shape-shifting."

DJ and Luna looked to each other while Jenny explained as

DJ rolled his eyes slowly "very good... Well said, ten points to Crowfeather." said Professor Katt then she went on speaking about how he watched over King Arthur. The class took notes while the teacher spoke. The class was long and boring, Luna didn't care for history. She was more of a hands-on girl, but Jenny soaked this all in like a sponge. Finally, the bell rang, and they got up from the table and walked out of the room. -

They walked to the dining hall where they sat at their clan table. Bella came over with Bree and joined Luna, Jenny, and DJ there was so much food and desserts to choose from. "So, how was the first half of school?" asked Bella while she poured some water in her goblet. Luna explained they have been boring and dragged out. Jenny explained Alchemy and Potions were interesting.

"Oh, that is one of my favorite classes." Commented Bree while she sliced into her ham Luna washed her ham sandwich down with raspberry witch brew tea. Owls, ravens, and hawks flew into the feast hall dropping letters to the students from their family and friends Bella got a letter as did Bree.

Luna finished her lunch as the bell began to ring. The students in the dining hall begun to spill out of the dining hall. Luna and Jenny walked to the science class finding a desk together. Their mouths dropped as Kain, and Zak came in the room finding a desk behind the girls.

The professor came into the room. Dark hair slicked back,

cleaned shave, and big brown eyes. He picked up a paper off his desk as papers laid in front of everyone with today's assignment. "Afternoon class, my name is Professor Tristan Smith. You can call me Professor Tristan. I will be your Science Professor this semester." He went along with the headcount. He went along through class, and it was just like regular science in Luna's old school. It was just as boring. Kain was pushing on the chair that Luna was sitting in throughout the day. Luna Turned and hissed out "stop!" she tried to keep up with the notes.

"Luna, eyes up here." called out Professor Tristan, Kain and Zak did it to Jenny. Luna shot a glare at them she hissed out "Stop." Professor Tristan turned as he tapped Luna's desk with his wand "Ten points from Crowfeather." Luna turned next to Jenny while she sat quietly till class ended.

They had left the class, Kain and Zak had left class meeting up with Colt and Cecil. Kain told them how Crowfeather had lost ten points high fives were passed around. Luna and Jenny had picked up DJ and Ray. Luna was beside herself for losing ten points from the clan. The group told her it wasn't her fault.

Finally, it was the final class of the day. They walked into the large classroom. The desk sat two people per desk. Luna and Jenny sat together, DJ and Ray sat together. There were seven tables in this room. A raven perched upon the desk eyeing the class. Its head twitched and cocked while looking upon the room. Professor Raven came in from the hallway and closed the door and walked over to her desk. "Good afternoon class, as you all know I am Professor Raven, Head of the Crowfeather Clan. This class is basic magick spells for first yearers.," Professor Raven went through the headcount while she stood at her desk going through the list of names. Luna was more interested in this class than any of the other classes she had so far. "Today you're going to learn how to levitate.," She placed a bowl of water in front of each student on their table and her desk "so, to do a spell speak slowly and confidently. Spells come from confidence, we are going to raise this water and float it and hold it in the air for a moment and place it back into the bowl. I will show you.," Professor raven gave the wand a small swish and flicked it *"aquae supernatet"* the water began to float out of the bow.

She held the wand steady "Now I can hold it here or I can move it like so.," she moved the wand in front of her as the water moved in front of the class, the water moved like jello "Now your turn class."

Ray spoke too fast, the water splashed in the bowl and tipped the bowl over and water spilled everywhere. DJ spoke perfectly, his hand shook while the water floated and a bit splashed against the bowl. Jenny spoke perfectly, she raised the water and held it there.

"Perfect Mrs.Strif, now move it to the right." Said Professor Raven, Jenny tried to move the water. Her hand shook and the water fell on top of her and it soaked her. The class busted out in laughter. Then Luna spoke too fast and she said "aqua supernate" the water splashed all over her.

The rest of the class either got soaked or failed to do it. Zak soaked himself as Kain laugh at him. Kain spoke perfectly raised the water and moved it. "Perfect Mr.Bloak, ten points for Dracoîn." Announced Professor Raven while the bell rang and Kain dropped the water down on Luna's head. OK class, homework is to float and move a bowl of water." The class left all soaked from head to toe. "I need to go dry off and change." Said Luna.

"I will come with you girl." replied Jenny while they both head towards the dormitories. DJ and Ray made their way to the picnic tables in the courtyard while they began to talk about how they despise Kain and his gang... The two girls made it into the dorm and Luna had dried off and changed along with Jenny.

Luna and Jenny went out to meet up with DJ and Ray. Bree and Bella were at the table with DJ and Bella's brother. They did some homework together. Luna had brought Khan out down to the courtyard with her. He laid at Luna's feet in the warm grass. They did their homework and Luna looked up to the draw bridge and seen Maîq carrying a large deer over his shoulders. She hot up and walked over to Maîq while she waved to him "hey Maîq!"

He smiled while his tail gave a small wave "Olá Luna, 'ow waz ye primeiro dia(first day)?" asked Maîq

"First half was boring, second was a little better. Dealt with Kain and his goons. I learned how to float water. What are you up to?" asked Luna watching him lay the deer on the table. He pulled out his large Schrade dagger and began to cut along the deer's stomach. " 'ust sum Caçando (hunting) . Da Bloak family não é da mais amigável (it's not the friendliest)."

Luna looked towards the woods on the other side of the rolling hills past a lonely willow tree "what are the woods called?" she pointed to the woods in the far-off distance. She loved the outdoors; hiking, swimming, or just sunbathing by looking at her you wouldn't think that. She was pale as a ghost but she enjoyed the outdoors.

"Dashie, das da *Illusion Forest* very dangerous, forbidden for students."

Khan and Jenny came over to them "Jenny meet my friend Maîq, Maîq meet Jenny."

"Olá Jenny, prazer ta meet ya." He welcomed them into his sandstone hut, it had a small living room, a small cluttered up kitchen, and his bedroom. It was packed inside from animal skins to art on the wall. He came out of the kitchen with deer jerky for them that he made the other day.

"How long have you lived here?" asked Jenny taking the deer jerky from him while she took a bite of it.

"I ave been ere ten years now. I waz huntsman and merchant in da village. Done business with OwlHollow 'or long time. Dey built me dis stone house and ired me 'or da help ta supply da foods 'or da school." While they talked the large iron bell began to ring to call for dinner. They said their goodbyes while as they got up from the couch and made their way out of the house. They made their way up to the castle and join everyone at their clan table.

Every time they sat down to eat at the tables. The table was always filled with so much food and desserts. The Clan Professor sat at the teacher's table on the stage that overlooked the students. The Headmaster Mr.Rune was away, so the vice Headmistress Mrs. Flowers was on the main throne. She stood up and tapped her wand on the table a large echo ran through the dining hall as if an iron dong was rung. The kids looked up at Mrs. Flowers as she began to speak.

"As today comes to an end, I hope everyone had a good first day. Now as we know there are a few spots open on the *Snorkbie*, *The Witches Joust*, and *Broom Race* teams. Meet up with the captain of the clan if interested. Second years and higher for the *Witches Joust* and *Broom Race*." she ended the speech while dinner came to an end.

DJ, Jenny, and Luna headed up the tower stairs to the dormitories *Dragon root* Jenny called out and the door slowly appeared at the end of the hall. They walked into the room and Jenny went and changed into her pajama shorts and a crop top that showed her flat semi tan tummy.

Luna had changed into a loose tank top and pajama pants. They sat downstairs with DJ while they did their homework. "So, you guys want to try out for *Snorkbie*?" asked DJ while he looked up from his homework. He sat in shorts and a clan t-shirt that was purple with a black crow.

"Thought about it, I think all three of us should try out." Said Jenny while Luna busted out in laughter. "I am not much of a sports girl." laughed out Luna while she tried to raise the water.

"Oh, you are trying out." Said Jenny while she took her wand and raised the water and floated it around the room. Jenny placed the water back in the bowl then she and DJ picked up the couch pillows and began to beat Luna with the pillows. Luna began to laugh and covered up from the assault of pillows "fine---fine, I'll try out." the dorm began to fill up with students. Jenny got up and went over to Bree while she was working on some homework.

"Hey Bree, we'd like to try out for *Snorkbie*." said Jenny while she looked down at Bree's book.

"Oh?," Bree looked up from the book to Jenny and smiled warmly "We have two spots open. Bring your swimsuits." -

Khan laid on Luna's bed while as she finally finished her homework along with the essay about Merlin. She was able to float the water and move it around. Jenny came and sat on the bed with Luna and Khan with a bowl of ice cream in hand. She scooped a spoonful of ice cream and brought it up to Luna's mouth. She took a bite of the Rocky Troll Chocolate they laid around and talked as they fell asleep.

Luna woke up and left her body. She stood there and saw Jenny laying on the bed by her asleep. She slowly drifted into the dream that Jenny was having. Jenny had a dream of her in front of the whole school body giving a speech as she was Lord Headmistress. It showed Kain getting ready to do a prank and Luna came up and dumped a bowl of pudding onto him. Jenny saw Kain fall onto the stage causing the curtains to fall while the whole school began to laugh. Jenny got upset and stormed off the stage to the back. Luna went to chase after her but couldn't find where she went. Luna left the dream and went out into the living realm and made her way out into the tower. She made her way into the courtyard.

Three ghosts were talking one a tall man with a puffy nose with wide eyes and bald. "Ah, I have heard the rumors of the famous but evil witch has come back."

The short thin ghost with ponytails and small eyes, with a button nose, spoke up "Larry, why would she be back? She has long gone for centuries. She didn't even come around when her 9th greatest grandson came here."

The third ghost removed his small moon glasses and clean them, his hair slicked back with a cold gaze while he looked to the other two "well Linda, he was just as cruel as she was. He pushed that poor Crowfeather boy down the stairs in the keep. What clan was he in, Dracoîn or Chimerador?"

Linda shook her head "Doesn't matter Berry, he was in the best clan Chimerador. Now his daughter is with us in this school. I say anyone related to that witch is no good."

The tall one wiped his forehead "No one knows the girl's name or wants to know."

Luna decided to head back to her dorm there is an evil witch and student?! She pondered to herself while she ascended the tower back to the Crowfeather dormitory. She went back to her body and slipped back into the body where she rolled over and drifted back to sleep.

Chapter 7: Try outs

The week went on, the first half was boring as Luna didn't care for math, science, or English. She did enjoy spell class, they had worked on *aquae supernatet* for the week, making sure everyone knew how to do the spell.

At nights Luna eavesdropped on the whispers of the three ghosts as she tried to figure out the witch, the grandchild, and now daughter. She wanted to try to speak to them but couldn't. How evil were this witch, the grandson, and daughter? -

Finally, it was Friday she had survived the first week at the school. She saw Jenny in the feast hall sitting at the Clan table. She walked over and sat down to get some breakfast.

"Morning girl!," Greeted Jenny warmly while she had her books spread out on the table "how did you sleep?"

"I slept good, so can I ask you something?" Luna had nightmares of the woman in the cauldron every night since the incident.

"Of course, what's up?" asked Jenny while she with a slightly concerned look in her eyes.

"The first night here.... What, what did you see in the cauldron?"

"Sure, it was the same thing you did. Feathers that shape of a crow, why? What did you see?"

Luna took Jenny's soft hand in hers and took her outside away from the other students "what is it?" Jenny's voice trembled a bit.

"I was after Kain, not sure if he poisoned it or if something was in there."

"What did you see?," asked Jenny stopping in her steps outside, and looked to Luna " There was no way Kain could have poisoned it. There were too many people watching, sure he wouldn't want to be expelled."

Luna nodded in agreement while she replayed that night "well when I looked in the cauldron. I saw an old scary woman reaching out of the water to pull me in." Said Luna with a nervous voice.

"Why didn't you say something?"

"I didn't want to sound like a nutcase."

Jenny hugged Luna "you are safe, we will discuss this more... Classes are about to start." -

They went off going separate ways, Luna went to her math class. Same old boring stuff followed by History of Magick then History of Magick People. The class had begun, they went from talking about Merlin the great to some famous witches such as *La Voisin* who was a famous French fortune-teller back in 1640 to 1680 to *Alice Kyteler* a woman condemned for witchcraft in Ireland from 1200s to 1300s to a few more witches.

Luna raised her hand while Professor Dunn turned to Luna "yes Miss. Bell?" Professor Dunn laid the homework on the desks of the students. "Have there been famous witches that went here that went evil?" asked Luna with an earnest look on her face. Jenny and DJ looked at Luna in pure hysteria.

"Well of course... We had witches and wizards who went pure dark, why do you ask?" asked Professor Dunn while he stood in front of the class.

"Just curious. Any that we may know of?" asked Luna probing a little more at the subject.

"We'll class looks like your homework is to write about evil famous witches and wizards." said Professor Dunn while the class ugh out in disbelief and glared at Luna. The class dismissed "Miss. Bell, please have a seat." Professor Dunn's voice was stern. Luna sat back in her seat at the table she was sitting with DJ and Jenny.

"Yes Professor Dunn?"

With a swish of her wand, the blinds to the door closed "why so interested in evil witches and wizards?"

Luna cleared her throat and looked to the professor " I overheard some students talk about it. It poked at my interest."

"We don't speak of those times. It-"

Luna cut the professor off "If we try to forget about the past, the past repeats itself."

The professor took a deep breath "there are three witches that came here that went purely evil. They are in your book. To keep it safe, part of the names were dropped or changed."

"oh, what are the names?" asked Luna slyly.

"Do your research and come back with an essay of the three, your free to go."

Luna left the classroom and went to lunch. Jenny saved her a seat. Bree came over and looked down at them "don't forget there is practice is this afternoon, ten people are trying out." DJ turned to Luna while he swallowed his food.

"What was that about in class? You aren't from an evil Witch bloodline, are you?"

"Of course not, I was just curious was all." Luna grabbed a muffin from the pile of muffins and left the feist hall.

"What did I say?" asked DJ dumbfounding.

"Such a guy." said Jenny before moving away from the table to leave. Luna was sitting on the water fountain while Jenny came over "hey girl."

Luna looked up to Jenny "hey, so talk now?"

Jenny sat next to her while she nodded her head "I am all ears, what's up?"

Luna explained to Jenny what the ghosts (But she told Jenny it was a few students) had said.

"The evil witch is back and so is the granddaughter. The girl's father came to this school and he is just as evil. Now his daughter is attending."

"So, there is an evil witch haunting the school?" asked Jenny before the bell had rung making the girls jump. They rushed to science class after a long monotone Professor Tristan had taught them. Jenny and Luna met with DJ and Ray. DJ and Ray walked together down the hall together "Luna was asking Professor Dunn about evil witches that attended this school." said DJ while he looked at the map of the school.

"Don't she know you don't ask about that kind of stuff?" replied Ray a bit shocked.

"The teacher kept her after class."

"Hopefully she got set straight. Speaking of evil gives them power even if they are dead." said Ray as he pointed out to the passageway to their next class. They sat in the class while they began to use the tip of the wand like a flashlight "*mico lucis*". The class had ended dry this time. They stopped by the dormitories to grab their swimsuits and left the castle and went down the long dirt road.

A large stadium sat in the middle of the field. it had a large pool with a wooden tower for announcers with four large stands for seating and a stone building for players. DJ, Luna, and Jenny made their way to the building. The door was unlocked, and they made their way down the long stone stairs. Two tunnels one led to the left and the other leading to the opposite side of the pool. There were locker rooms and showers on each side of the stadium. They went right and a locker room door said *PLAYERS ONLY.* They walked in and Bree came over to them.

"The boy's locker room and changing rooms are there on the right and ladies come in and yours is on the left. Once you

change into your swimsuits come out to the waiting room."
explained Bree while they went in and DJ went right and
disappeared behind a door. Luna and Jenny came in and went
through the lady's locker room on the left side of the waiting room.
Jenny had changed into a multiple-colored blue striped bikini as
Luna had changed into a black bikini. They met up with DJ had
changed into red swimming trunks.

    Bree waved them over and she wore the Crowfeather
Snorkbie swimsuit. It was a purple swimsuit top with a yellow "C"
on her left breast for *captain* and on the right breast side was the
number one. The purple top faded to a black bottom, on the black
was purple words on the bottom backside spelled "*Crowfeather*",
on the right front of the hip was a picture of a crow feather.

    The students of Crowfeather that was trying out sat in the
meeting room. Bree stood with a clipboard in her hand and spoke
to the group of students " Snorkbie is played underwater with ten
players. Five players on the line are called *Blockers*. Then one
player behind the *Blockers* and that position is called the *King*. The
player behind the *King* or beside the *King*, depending on the play
is the *Queen*.,

    " There are two players on one either side of the blockers,
they are called the *Catchers* and lastly, you have the *Defender*.
The *Defender* covers five goals, two large size goals at the bottom
that are worth five points. Then two medium-size goals that are
worth ten points. Then right above them is one small goal. It is
worth fifty points.,

"The goal shape makes a star, there are twp balls the main game ball that is called *Snork Ball* which is a blue color ball. The player that wins the *Shantie* toss gets the ball. The ball is either ran or thrown down the field. The other team can tackle, or try and knock the ball loose, or catch the ball.,

"The only one that can't get tackled is the *Defender.* The second ball is also known as the Guardian Ball. It comes from the ground shooting out into the air, whoever has the *Guardian Ball* the white ball turns to that clan color. It doubles the points. Whoever gets to two hundred points wins. You're given these special beans called air beans. They let you breathe underwater for two hours." explained Bree and after the long speech, they walked into a steel room.

The door closed behind them and each student ate an air bean. The room filled with water before another door open. They swam out into the stadium. The water was a bit different you could swim, walk, and run as if it was on normal ground. Bree had the clipboard in hand while she stood underwater speaking.

"First we are going to do some stretches and warm-up. Then a mile swim and then run. That is just one lap around the stadium. Each of you will be time." Bree said as DJ couldn't help but drool over Bree was nicely toned with a small six-pack and small hourglass body.

Everybody was now swimming around the track DJ finished at ten minutes and twelve seconds. Someone else had finish twelve minutes flat but Jenny finished at eight minutes and two seconds. Everyone was impressed with Jenny's speed. Even Bree made a compliment. Another girl came up behind Jenny and finished at nine minutes and a half. Luna finally came up next while Bree blew the whistle, and Luna had begun to swim. She came around the corners as fast as Jenny. Luna came down the long stretch home even though she thought of herself, not as an athlete. She crossed over the finish line at eight minutes and fifty seconds.

DJ came up for the mile run and he had finished in twelve minutes flat. Koty Hall the boy after DJ in the swim lined up had finished in ten minutes and thirty seconds. Bree handed out another air bean while Jenny went running. She had finished in nine minutes. Sabrina the girl who swam nine minutes ran the lap in ten minutes and thirty seconds.

Luna came up and waited for the whistle finally, the whistle was blown, and she began to run hard. She kept her breathing steady and she came across the corners pretty fast while she made it over the long stretch at nine minutes and thirty seconds.

Bree looked at Matt Timble who was a year older than Bree, he was the Defender. His hair is dark brown is usually combed nicely. He had large green eyes.

"Looks like we have a fast team this year." said Bree while he nodded his head in agreement

"If they can't catch the speed is no good." he countered coldly while Luna caught his eyes. Bree grabbed the Snork Ball, and it was an oval size ball (slightly larger than a football). The ball was royal blue.

"We are going to catch this, we need two catchers for the team.," Bree looked around while she spoke "there will be ten throws we will start close till you are on the other side of the field." Bree had a strong arm. DJ had made most of the catches. Eight out of ten, he had missed the last two of the catches completely. Koty went after him and made nine out of ten catches. He made the longest catches but the short ones he had dropped.

Sabrina had caught four out of ten. Anywhere mid-field or further was guaranteed a miss. Jenny came up after her with seven out of ten catches. The long throws caught her up. Jenny wasn't too proud of how she did. She always tried to be perfect in everything that she did. Her perfection drove her. She went and stood by DJ and the others. Luna watched everyone then it was her turn finally. She had caught nine out of ten. The closer passes she had dropped.

Next, they had to catch five throws on the run and a run and stop catch. Bree was throwing lob ups or bullets. DJ on the run caught four out of five. For the missiles, Bree threw at him. He had caught two out of five. Even Matt is still surprised how hard, far, and fast Bree could throw.

Koty on the run caught three out of five. He did better on the stop catches. He had caught four out of five catches.

Sabrina couldn't keep up with running and catching. Either she overran or under ran the throw. For the stop and catches, she coward away. She complained about a nail breaking.

Jenny did the best catching five out of five on the missile catches and four out of five on the stop-and-go catch.

Luna did fairly well catching four out of five on the missile throws and four out of five on the stop-and-go catch.

"Good Job, everyone it is now time for scoring." said Bree while they all lined up and Bree handed them the Snork Ball. They had to throw ten times who scored the highest and made most goals was what they were looking at. Matt was no pushover either. He was one of the best Defenders in the school.

DJ thrown five out of ten, he had scored two hundred and fifty points and Matt had told him not bad. Koty came up and thrown three out of ten scoring a hundred and fifty points. Matt had shut him down completely, swatting them down or catching the ball.

Sabrina came up and got six out of ten scoring three hundred points. Bree had cheered her on while everyone watched from the sideline.

Jenny came up and thrown five out of ten scoring two hundred and fifty points. Jenny was a sharpshooter for the high-point goal. Luna came up last, looking at the five goals. She threw six out of ten scoring three hundred points. Everyone was close with the scoring. The practice came to an end, and everyone dried off and changed into their clothing. -

It was late when they had returned it back to the school. Dinner was about over while they joined the rest of the school.

Everyone who practiced had extra time to eat, Bree went up to the dormitory and eventually, everyone else did too. Bree and Matt talked in the study room about who should make the cut.

"I will go ahead and say no the Sabrina. She was scared of the ball." pointed out Matt while Bree nodded her head in agreement. "Koty and DJ were close overall on the catches, DJ was better at the scoring." Bree Discussed this with Matt.

"You can't lob the ball down the field every single time., " reminded Matt "DJ caught only two bullets while Koty caught four. But scoring-wise DJ made the most goals."

"Let's compare Jenny to them, speed-wise she killed it. Catching she did great at mid and short distant throws. She dropped one ball out of ten. That was the deep run and stop throws, but scoring-wise she only made half but pin-pointed the throws on the big points." Bree said while Matt nodded his head in agreement.

"Luna she was pretty fast herself. Catching wide one of the best only dropped two. Pointwise six out of ten and scored three hundred points." Matt expressed while they went over everyone else.

Koty, Sabrina, DJ, Luna, Jenny, and the rest of the ones who tried out sat around by the fireplace as everyone was saying (I bet you got it). Sabrina told everyone that she didn't get it. The door from the study room had open up and they came out.

"Everyone did good in your own ways. It was a tough decision. Our first pick is Jenny Striff.," Bree congratulated Jenny while everyone clapped "next was very tough. Had three very close people to pick from, I would take you all on my team if I could. But I can only pick one, for the final catcher is---Luna Bell." Bree said smiling while she congratulated Luna. Luna and Jenny were stoked to have made the team. After a bit, they went to do their homework to finished up the night. Luna wrote to her mom and sister on the yellow parchment telling them about school and making the team. She gave it to a crow. The Crow flew out of the window and disappeared in the blackness. Jenny came into the room with her books and laid them on her desk. She made her way to her bed and finally falling back on her bed and passing out.

Luna pulled out her *History of Magick People book* and began to scan the names. She was clueless about what she was looking for in the book. Part of her wanted to wake Jenny up for help. There have been so many Witches and Wizards in history that filled her book. She finally fell asleep and slowly awoken in her room. She was out of her body. The room was extremely quiet, and she left the dormitory and made her way to the courtyard.

The tall skinny ghost sat on the water fountain. Luna made her way over to him while he sat as if he was waiting for something. "H- Hello?" said Luna with a shaky voice from being nervous.

"Good evening Fair Maiden, 'ow ye be?"

"Good, I'm just strolling through tonight." replied Luna while she glanced at the ghost.

Larry looked at her sternly then he nodded his head while looking at her " it's not safe to be strolling alone. Especially for a student."

97

"I-I'm a ghost as well." said Luna lying to him.

"Tsk Tsk Tsk, can't lie to the dead. You may be in the spirit realm. You still have a soul. Be careful, 'ur body is an open vessel to be taken. Plus, it is against school rules to be out of the dormitories at a time like this." said Larry with a stern warning in his voice.

Luna paused while she rubbed the back of her head before speaking once again after finding what she wanted to say "The other night, there were three of you out here. Talking about an evil Witch, who is she?"

Larry took a deep breath before he spoke out " 1700's a witch came to this school, top of her class she had not many friends, but studied her heart out. She passed each alchemy, potions, spells, and shape shifting class with flying colors.,

"She could shape shift into any beast that she wanted. She was an astounding student. She was going places, she and her three cousins. Each one was great at something, but Kate has way surpassed them.," Larry pressed on with the story.

"1762 there was a massacre in Crystal Region from village to village the three cousins torment the region then left."

"Who were the other three witches, and where did they go?" asked Luna leaning forward in listening with interest.

"Dearie, it is dangerous to be out of your body. Do you want to lose it?"

Luna looked at the woman who came through the other side of the wall of the school. Luna was confused but curious about the witches "what do you mean by lose it? Who were the other three?"

"Linda, my dear, she is new to this. When you are out of your body anyone can just come in and take it over. For the other three, my old mind betrays itself." Said Larry while he was cleaning his glasses.

"You must be off to bed girl before someone takes your body. Or you are seen by a professor." said Lina staring down at Luna. Luna got up from the ground and walked back to the dormitory and seen two student ghost girls where talking, another one was talking about homework while the other one was talking about the empty body in the room. Luna ran past them and up the stairs to her room. She saw her body lying there asleep. Horror washed over her face. What happened if her body got taken? She merged into her body and slowly woke up and put her books away before falling back asleep.

Chapter 8: First Snorkbie game

Morning came way too quickly as Jenny had woken Luna up from her horrible night of sleep. They had gotten dress and headed out for the stadium locker room.

"You look beat, didn't sleep well?" asked Jenny as the sun barely broken over the mountains.

"Not really, tossed and turned."

"Oh, I am sorry. After practice, we'll eat breakfast." answered Jenny as they went into the stadium and made their way to the locker room. Their team bathing suits were hanging up in their lockers. Luna's locker was locker number ten and Jenny's was locker number fourteen. They have changed quickly, on Luna's bathing suit at the top was a number six on the right side and on the bottom of the suit was a six on the hip. Crowfeather spelled on the backside as for Jenny's was the number eleven.

They had gone to the meeting area, which had lockers, benches, and towels. Bree stood there with her team swimsuit and began one of her famous speeches "we are going to work on some old and new plays. Then we'll play them out, Blockers today you are going to play defense to stop the running and passing plays. No tackling just two-hand touch don't need no one getting hurt before the first game."

They had entered the pool and Matt had swum over to the goals, Bree took the center. Morgan Bowman was a sixteen-year-old girl with strawberry blond hair and sparkling green eyes. She played the Queen position, she either played behind the King or beside the King. Luna played right and Jenny played left. Bree had blown the whistle and each one ran a route. After a bit, they had begun catching the ball. The blockers swatted a few of the balls down or picked them from the air. -

After a couple of hours of training. They all made their way to the feast hall to get some breakfast. Luna headed back to bed after a quick bite. On her way through the long hallway to the tower, she ran into Cecil, Kain, Zak, and Colt who had blocked her way.   "Oh, hey babes." Colt the rhino boy cat called out at Luna. She rolled her eyes while she tried to pass through the group of Dracoîns.

"We just want a kiss!" cried out Zak the rat boy as Luna passed through the.

"I'd rather kiss a frog." Luna spoke in annoyance.

"Don't get a kiss from her, you'll get wor-." Kain got cut off as Zak got turned into a frog by Cecil. Zak laid on the floor and the Dracoîn cloak laid on a large wet frog with a couple of warts and bumps on his body.

"Come kiss the frog then and retrieve your prince!" commanded Cecil with the other two laughing and the frog croaked.

"No thanks, it is already an improvement." Luna had run up the stairs while Cecil turned Zak back to normal as the four laughed. -

Luna came to the hidden door and said the password where the door revealed itself. She walked into the common room where a few boys were awake, and she went up the stairs to her room. She fell face-first on her four-poster bed and fell asleep

Jenny was on the way to the dormitory herself. She ran right into Professor Kanoe. He had a cold dead stare in his eyes. His tone was bone-chilling. He was the Professor who taught *Creatures and Wild Beast still roam.* "Miss. Striff, where is Miss. Bell?" he asked with a cold tone.

"I---I think she went back to bed." said Jenny nervously as chills ran down her spine.

"Fetch her, send her to my office." said Professor Kanoe just as sharply and cold as he turned and walked to the marble staircase. He headed down them. Jenny felt her heart sink to the bottom of her stomach. She ran to the dormitory and woke Luna up.

"So, I ran into Professor Kanoe, he is scary. He wants you in his office now.," said Jenny slightly shaking and worried "what did you do?"

Luna looked just as shocked and nervous "n-nothing. I ran into the four morons. Rat boy wanted a kiss and Cecil had turned him into a frog." Luna went and put her black tights and

Crowfeather T-shirt on with her boots. -

She went down to the dungeon and seen his office. She walked into the office. It was a small office and had a small sabertooth tiger sleeping in a bed. In a large kennel was a white *hellhound.*

"Oh, I have one of those, mine is bla-" Luna was cut off by his cold voice.

"Don't care. Sit Miss. Bell.," Professor Kanoe glared while the candles flicked. Luna sat down and slowly crossed her leg over the other. She bit her lip nervously. "Do you know why you are here?!" he snapped out coldly to her.

Luna jolted a bit in her seat as her head shook "n-no sir." Kanoe looked at her hard as if burning a hole into her soul.

"Think... Think hard." he said while Luna rocked her head as she thought hard.

"Cecil had turned Zak into a frog?" His eyes were cold, and they didn't blink. His lips didn't twitch as he spoke.

"No, you are here for being out of the dormitories at night."

Luna looked at him a bit shocked "w-what?"

"Linda the poltergeist told me all about it, how you can Astral Travel. Breaking two school rules will cause you to lose fifty-five points from Crowfeather. Your Clan Guardian, Professor Raven will be getting a full report and expect detention." said Professor Kanoe with a smirk across his lips, he had seen Luna out of his office. The first week of school and already lost fifty-five points from the clan. Luna went to her room and shut the door. A note laid on Luna's bed as she opened the letter seeing the yellow parchment her heart sunk.

Dear Miss. Bell,

I have been informed by Professor Kanoe, that you have been wandering the halls at night by Astral Traveling. He also informed me that he deducted fifty-five points from you. In less than a week you lost more points than I have seen. Your detention date is October 15th - 18th. You will be helping Maîq with preparing for the Halloween Dinner.

Sincerely
Professor Raven

Luna felt even worst now four days of detention wasn't fair. She rolled over and cried herself to sleep. A few hours have passed, and the word got around about Luna losing all those points. The Crowfeather clan shunned her completely, the only one that talked to her was DJ and Jenny.-

Classes were about the same bunch of schoolwork and stacks of homework. Luna had managed to regain forty points by answering questions. It was finally October fifteenth, she walked down to Maîq's little cottage home. She knocked on the door and he opened it wearing a blue tunic with black leather pants.

"Plazer (pleasure) ta see ya, Luna." said Maîq warmly as

he stepped to the side.

"Hey Maîq, how have you been?"

"Guud, let's get dis out of da way.," Maîq has grown fawn of Luna and the gang. "First we're going to skin sum animals, pick eggs, and vegetables."

Luna went to the back of the house and seen a hut for slaughtering. They walked in and there were deer, pigs, and cows that hung there. The animals leaked blood in a floor pan.

"This is disgusting." snarled Luna looking at the animals hanging there. Maîq just chuckled at Luna. He showed her how to gut them and get the meat.

Luna couldn't wait to finish this day. Her apron was covered in blood as it grew late. She got released from her nightmare and she said bye to Maîq. Luna made her way up to the feast hall for dinner and found a seat in the back of the clan table.

Bree came over and sat with Luna, who was picking at her hamburger "not hungry?" asked Bree watching Luna pick at her food. Luna looked up to Bree and sighed.

"not when you have seen where this thing gets gutted."

"So, tomorrow is the first game of the season!"

Luna had forgotten all about that. She was so beat and now tomorrow was the first game and more time with Maîq "who are we facing?"

"Goldenpaw, their whole team is pretty much new students. Their king, Queen, and Defender are the same players. The rest of their team graduated last year.," Bree smiled at her " we have this in the bag!"

Bree went to the dormitory while Luna got up to leave the feast hall. DJ, Jenny, and Ray came over to her "hey Luna, how was your punishment?" asked Ray, but the smell of the dead came from Luna.

"It sucked. I have skinned a deer, a pig, and a cow. Then gathered all the meats and cleaned the slaughterhouse. I have to do it again tomorrow on top of that the game." she sighed in annoyance.

"Maybe... It won't be so bad." said DJ trying to cheer her up.

"Yeah..." said Luna doubtfully.-

They went to the courtyard and pulled out their books to finish some homework. Luna did an essay on the benefits of quiet casting and how it was successfully used. Then knocked out three pages of math, which took the longest. After what took a while, they made their way to the dormitory where Luna went and shower-ed then headed to bed.-

The next day, Luna and the Crowfeather Snorkbie team were changed and in the locker room. It was sunny outside and the sun cast over the land. DJ and Ray sat with his sister and brother.

"You ready everyone, this game will set the tone for us. Winning today will make us a threat. Goldenpaw is a new team. They don't have the heart or drive. Where Crowfeather is the same team and the same family from last year, we have two new members to our family. We have heart, passion, and drive. Now let's show them Crowfeather Pride!" Brec gave a speech as the players chanted Crowfeather.

The stadium seats sat every clan member, professor, and worker. Some students flew a huge purple banner that had a picture of a crow. The other side had a large golden banner with a three-headed dog. Mistress flowers sat in the announcing booth with Bruno Silvertongue the Lord Headmaster.

"MAKING THEIR WAY OUT OF THE RIHGT ENTRANCE IS YOUR CROWFEATHER!" Shouted Bruno in excitement. Purple fireworks shot off and exploding making a large crow. Everyone swam out as cheers roared from the Crowfeathers stand. Boos came from the Dracoîn as the other clans clapped.

"MAKING THEIR WAY OUT OF THE LEFT ENTRANCE IS YOUR Goldenpaw!" Announced Bruno and golden fireworks shot off and exploding making a large three-headed beast. They swam out as cheers exploded from the Goldenpaw section. Everyone clapped as the Dracoîn clan booed.

The two captains swam up to meet up with one another and Professor Ember spoke loudly "I want a good clean game, Captain Bree and Captain Jewels shake hands and call the shantie toss."

Bree and Jewels shook hands. Then Professor Ember pulled out an ancient coin "gold or emerald?" The gem is flat and on one of the sides of the gem is gold and on the other side is purple. She flicked the coin up into the air and the sunlight shimmered in the pool. The coin came down and it landed on the bottom of the pool. The gold side faced up.

"Goldenpaw!," shouted Ember "Jewels do you wish for the toss off or catch?" the stands blew up with cheers.

"We'd like the catch." said Jewels as she fist-pumped the air to get the crowd rattled up.

They moved to the positions as a loud bang shot out in the distance. The ball shot out of the wall behind Crowfeather's goal.

"The ball has landed in Charlie Blaine's hand this is going be a large leap of faith for team Goldenpaw, all but three are new players.," commented Bruno "oh, what a hard hit by Tyler Patterson. Goldenpaw is lining up. Kat Bossingham moved to the right of Jewels Meadows. Here is the snap, OH! The line of Jewel's blockers broke, and she went down. The ball is loose!,

"Morgan Bowman from Crowfeather has claimed the ball. Kevin House with the tackle. WAIT Morgan threw the ball to Bree. Bree has a cannon for an arm. Joey Hudges and Emily Simpson for the tackle. Bree got rid of the ball, Jenny Striff caught it!,

"What a catch for the first year! She is swimming, man she is fast! She is on a breakaway. Mark Tidwell on guard, Jenny throws- NO she faked it, and Mark dove for the bottom ring, Jenny scored! Fifty points!"

The game went on as Crowfeather held them at bay.

"Bree with a hard tackle!Goldenpaw is lining up and here

is the snap! Jewels lobbed it up to Pam Davis. --- Intercepted by Luna Bell! She is on the swim. Juke one, spun around the next, an---,

"OUCH! A hard hit by Kat! Crowfeather's lining up. Morgan on the move, mowed down by Timmy Moore. Luna moved down beside Jenny." Bree rotated her shoulder as a signal for Morgan to move up. She bent her right knee for Luna to move down the field by Jenny.

"The ball is snapped; Pam came around the right side. Bree fired the ball, Kevin with a hard early tackle."

The whistle was blown from Professor Ember "penalty shot, for hitting while the player doesn't have the ball."

"Crowfeather with the penalty shot. Jenny goes to throw but it was blocked by Mark. He threw it down the field... WAIT, intercepted by Keith Brooks. Big Kevin with the-,

"NO! Keith threw it to Luna... OH! Big hit by Jewels. Crowfeather with the lineup. The ball is snapped and Bree with a missile throw... Fifty points!" Bruno called out the game while everyone cheered and the Dracoîn booed.

"Crowfeather is hundred to nothing." said Mistress Flowers. Mark handed the ball off to Charles. He began to swim up the field. Luna with the tac-,. He threw her off, Jenny with a hard tack-, He swam right over her head. He threw the ball to kat! Kat threw it for the goal and Matt with the save!,

Matt kicked it down the field and Luna caught the ball and thrown it for "Twenty points! Crow-feather is on fire!" Called out

Mistress Flowers, the fans are raring, everyone is bruised up while the ball is hike. The Guardian Ball was launched, and Jewels watched everyone run to it.

"Luna, get the ball1" shouted Bree and Luna made a run for it as did Kevin. Jewels threw the ball short to Kat who was running for the Guardian Ball. Luna grabbed the Guardian Ball and it turned purple.

"Luna swam out of there just in time. Big Kevin missed with the tackle. Hunter Stokes stripped the ball from Kat! Bree retrieved the ball. They're both on the run to the goals.," announced Bruno. Bree threw the ball and Mark dove; Luna threw the other ball. "Five points! --- Hundred Points! Two hundred and ten points, Crowfeather wins! What a shut out!" Cheered out, Bruno. -

Everyone shook hands while fireworks went up making a massive crow. The Crowfeather clan roared out in cheers and ran down to the poolside chanting "CROWFEA-THER! CROWFEATHER! CROW-FEATHER" The team headed into the locker room and Bree took center stage of the team.

"Great work everyone! We crushed them, I know everyone is sore, but you all did an amazing job. MVW (Most valuable wizard) for today's game is--- Luna Bell for scoring a hundred points and winning us the game!," Bree went on congratulating her team while Luna's cheeks flushed to a strawberry pink "just don't lose these points." heckled Bree.-

The team and the school went back to the feast hall for a large celebration feast. Jenny and Luna ate so much and enjoyed the fresh pumpkin spice coffee. People came back around to Luna and began to speak to her again.

"Great job!"

"Amazing Game!"

"You did amazing"

"Can I have your autograph?"

Luna's cheeks flushed; the joyful emotions drifted away when she saw the time. She got up and grabbed her hip purse and began to walk away from the table "where are you going?" asked DJ and Jenny staring at her watching her leave the feast hall.

"Detention..." said Luna lowly while she hasted out of the feast hall. She made her way out of the castle and through the meadows. She came to Maîq's cottage and she knocked on the door

"Come ta d back!" yelled Maîq, Luna walked around and seen him gathering eggs. She walked over to him and greeted him. They both began to gather eggs.

"Sen da game, ye waz gret." Maîq told her while he filled four baskets of eggs. They began to pick so many vegetables, this chore beat slaughtering. Four baskets filled with different vegetables; the sun beat down on them. Her pale skin quickly grew red.-

The day came to an end, and she went back up towards the school for dinner. She was in the courtyard when she saw Kain,

Cecil, Zak, and Colt and they were kicking around a ball in the courtyard. Luna went to go past them to get to the keep "look boys, it's the Crowfeather's MVW." snapped out Kain with a whistle.

"To bad your team will crumble under us." commented Cecil with a smirk that showed off his pearl white teeth.

"Give HER a break!," a voice came from behind them as Jenny, DJ, and Ray came out of the keep "don't you four wissards have better things to do?" continued Ray as he looked at them.

"WHAT did you call us?!" snapped Kain in a furious rage.

"Wissards" said Ray with a shaky voice.

Cecil turned and he glared "I will show you a Wissard." He drew his wand out, Ray cowered down then Cecil kicked the ball, WHAM! The four walked away and Luna, Jenny, and DJ ran over to Ray who was holding his face, his tooth laid on the ground and blood ran from his nose.

"Let's get him to the hospital wing." Said Jenny picking up the tooth from the ground. They helped him out and Jenny handed Ray his tooth and he held it in his hand while they made their way to the hospital wing.

"I hate them." Said Luna with a furious tone.

"Why would you call them Wissards?" asked DJ with a chuckle, not at Ray getting hurt but at Ray calling them a Wissards. They got to the fifth tower and went up to the hospital floor "what is a wissard?" asked Luna out of curiosity.

"Poorly trained Wizard." answered DJ as Jenny opened the large wooden door. A short black hair woman with creamy skin

112

with big hazel eyes and a round face walked over to them. She wore a white robe with a royal blue cloak "what happened here? Come on in."

They walked him to the hospital bed, they told Madam Sunny Kimble what had happened. She made them wait at the dining hall, they began to eat and they could hear laughter from the Dracoîn's table as Cecil and Kain told the rest of the Dracoîns what have happened. An hour later Ray showed up all fixed, his tooth was back in place. Luna, Jenny, and Ray made their way over to Ray.

"What happened, are you ok?," said Luna staring at him "You was very brave"

"She fixed my broken nose and re-rooted my tooth; it was a bit painful. I am tired of them picking on you." answered Ray as Luna hugged him. Then they all headed to their table to finish dinner.

After Dinner Luna headed up to the dormitory and began to work on some homework, she knocked out her homework quickly. Jenny had sat with Jenny doing some spell homework, making the end of the wand into a heater. Luna held her wand out "Calur aer" poof a black puff of smoke filled the room quickly. Jenny stumbled to the window and open it, the thick smoke rolled out of the window. People from the courtyard looked up to the night sky and pointed at the thick smoke rolling out.

"Now they'll think I am trying to burn the dormitory down." grumbled Luna. "Nah, you are fine. Let it roll off your tongue.," said Jenny as she held out her wand "*Calor aer*" and a hot wave came from the wand and filled the room with heat. "*frigidus aer*" and the wand cooled down the room and the temperature dropped. Luna did it finally, sweat rolled down her forehead then she cooled it back down. Khan came over, his flame tail swayed, and he jumped up at Luna. She leaned down and picked up the *Hellhound* "who needs that spell when you have this beast." heckled Luna with a smile as Khan licked her face, his fiery Mohawk flicked with sparks.-

After the next couple days, she helped slaughter more animals, picked more eggs, plucked more vegetables, milked the cows, and baked so much bread. It was finally over, Luna fell onto Maîq's couch and sighed heavily out of happiness. He poured some Dragon fruit tea from his iron teapot "Bebida (Drink)---bebida (Drink), it will help restore ya energy." said Maîq while he handed her the mug. She sat up and took the mug and took a sip from it mug the drink flooded her insides with its warmth.

"Maîq, why is everyone scared to talk about evil witches and wizards?"

"Ö," his ears fell back as he spoke softly and his tail lowered "JÅ, people 're scared of dark things. Especially if the evil runs in da bloodline of another. With even pureness in dem, the evil still flows." Maîq's voice was slow and steady.

"Oh, someone was speaking of evil witches, a father came to this school and now his grandest daughter of the witch." said

Luna looking to Maîq.

"Näo (no), stay away from her if ye find out about her. All witches and Wizards know 'bout evil bloodlines. Great but evil witches and wizards have been shunned. 'Dey have cursed their families."

Luna have seen how dark it got outside and she made her way back to the dormitory, Cecil was patrolling the halls "well, what are you doing out at a time like this?" his voice was cold and steady.

"I was on my way back to my dorm."

"---Have a note?"

Out of the excitement of talking to Maîq, she had left the note on the living room table "I left it at Maîq's place."

"Hmm, breaking the rules again... Ten points from Crowfeather."

"That isn't fair, I wa "

"Keep it up and I'll take another ten points from Crowfeather.," Said Cecil with a grin "Our lovely beauty queen will lose all those points that she has earned." his lips curled into a mischievous smirk. Luna glared and balled up her fist, she was done with this.

"Lets us go to pro-"

"Professor Kanoe? --- Great idea." laughed Cecil.

"NO! I was talking about Professor Rav-" Her words got cut off as Cecil drew his wand out at her "march!" he snapped at her as her eyes rolled. She turned and began walking to the grand staircase.

"Miss Bell, Mr. Bloke... What is the meaning of this?" asked Professor Raven while she stood at the top of the grand stare case staring down at them as she saw Cecil marching Luna at wand tip.

"She was found wandering the halls, she gave me extreme attitude. I Was leading her to Professor Kanoe."

"I wasn'-"

"Silence Luna, Cecil any other punishment been taken place?"

"Yes Ma'am, as far as breaking the rules. I took away ten points."

Luna stood between her upset clan professor and a snake, she wanted to behead this snake.

"Well, she is my student. I Will puni-." Professor Raven got cut offed as Maîq ran up to them.

"Luna ye have left dis." Maîq had had a parchment in his hand, Professor Raven took the parchment and read it. It was Luna's detention pass.

"Thank you Maîq, Luna you are free to go. Don't worry about the ten points.," Professor Raven smiled "and for you Cecil." she turned to Cecil as her gaze was stone cold. Luna walked to the stairs and stopped to listen as her lips curled in a glorious smile.

"Twenty-five points from Dracoîn for drawing a wand on another student. Professor Kanoe will hear about this AND you will be questioned to step down from Pre Lord."

Luna sighed in triumph and made it back up the stairs and seen Bree, Bella, Jenny, and DJ playing Dungeons and Wizards. "How was your night?" asked Jenny and she made a spot for Luna next to her and DJ. Luna told them everything that had happened and the look on Cecil's face when Raven appeared at the top of the grand staircase. Everyone laughed as Luna left to her room to change, she returned wearing some shorts and a tank top.

"What are you playing? Asked Luna while she picked up a player's card.

"Dungeon and Wizards, want to join? You can be the elf Princess Arôstar, she can enchant stuff and her class is a ranger. OR you can be the necromancer dwarve from Shinzlark, Grimlynch." said DJ handing her the cards. Luna took the dwarf and place him on the board. When she did, she was in the game. She was a fat redhead dwarf with big round cheeks, multiple chins, the strength of an ox. When she spoke it was a deep female grumble. They played for a few hours than Luna finally popped out of the game and went to lay down for the night. She drifted off to sleep finally after a long eventful day.

117

Chapter 9: The unexpected gift.

A couple of weeks have passed, and Luna came closer with Jenny and everyone. They avoided Cecil of course, Professor Kanoe didn't do anything to Cecil and for the Pre Lord he was still there. Professor Raven summoned the clan teachers, Lord Headmaster, and the Pre Lords. They all met up in the feast hall where she began to tell them about Cecil abusing his power and drawing his wand on another student.

Professor Kanoe defended Cecil by saying "Cecil asked for a note which Luna didn't have. Told her to meet with me, she refused to. He drew his wand to have her follow his request. She was being hostile.,

"Luna has been found breaking school rules twice so far, lost numerous points for her clan. She lost ten more, but Professor Raven gave them back. Cecil was doing what was right... Or thought what was right. Professor Raven took the points away and delivered him to me, she is favoring her clan." His cold voice echoed in the large feast hall.

Professor Moon cleared her throat "look at the boy's grades, attendance, and teamwork. They are all perfect for Lord Headmaster, he is a Lord Headmaster in the making. Look at Luna, alright grades, have missed class, and lost points. Why would he ruin his chances of being Lord Headmaster?"

118

Professor Dibbs looked to the Lord Headmaster and the Pre Lords and smiled warmly "it is their call; they have heard the arguments." he got up along with the other Professor and they walked out of the feast hall. "I have seen how you treat Luna and her friends.," Bree called him out in front of everyone "I say you go."

"I had to pull my wand out once or twice on a student for breaking the rules. We are here to hold the rules and to protect the students.," countered Jewels looking to Bree "I say he stays."

"I see where everyone is at, we aren't supposed to draw wands on students as we are students ourselves. Just have more power." Dane Ward added leaning back in his throne bored.

"Dane, I helped push you to be a Pre Lord, at the time people were against you. I backed you up once or twice." said Cecil.

"I... I say he did the right thing." said Dane as his voice trembled.

"Cecil, I supposed you vote to stay... That is three against two. Cecil, you are on very thin ice." said Bruno with a glare in his eyes. Everyone left the meeting upset with each other.

Meanwhile Luna was in her *History of Magick People*, Professor Dunn told them to open to page one hundred and twenty-eight. A picture of a girl with large blue eyes, long silky black hair, short button nose, and chin. Under the photo said (Only photo known to exist).

"Mary came to this school in 1701 she astounded in

enchanting, charms, and along with (Shring) and able to move from portal to portal. I do say, we are going to talk about some evil witches, but I must warn you.," said Professor Dunn her voice was low and spoke in a warning tone "she was in Crowfeather. She had the wisdom to learn even the most advanced magick and enchantments. Her last year, she was expelled... Questions arise for the arrest of Mary for a murder.,

"They found a poor girl in the bathroom cut up only one who knew how to move from place to place was a Professor and Mary. Blood was on the floor, sink, and mirror."

Luna read the page as she thought *Bloody Mary? She's is a folk tale to scare kids. Is this the girl I have seen?* Thoughts raced through her head. Her hand shot up with a question "yes Luna?"

"Is this by chance Bloody Mary?," the students looked to Luna " Where you stand in a dark bathroom, call out Bloody Mary three times and do three circles, then turn on the light and she is supposed to appear in the mirror facing you or behind you with a knife?" asked Luna while everyone stared at her baffled.

"I will not acknowledge how to summon her, but yes that is the same Bloody Mary. IF I find out any of you try and do this old myth and summon her, you will lose ALL clan points and detention till next year!" said Professor Dunn with a threatening tone.-

The bell rang and the day went on, it was a few days from Halloween, Kain was in his room putting his books away on the book shelve "what a stupid Halloween prank.," He turned and looked into the mirror "can't believe Luna tried to get my brother kicked from the Pre Lords." The candles flicked in the room as he put each candle out and pulled his wand out, he turned around three times chanting Bloody Mary three times.

Then he placed his fingers on the candle but stepped out of the room. He had returned and lit the candle and crawled into the bed, going to sleep. He had a nightmare of Bloody Mary chasing him with a knife. He woke up very quickly, his back was burning, and he sat up very quickly.

He jumped out of the bed and seen blood on the sheets. He ran to the mirror, and he had three claw marks on his back, it was three in the morning. His face went cold, he turned to his bed and seen something out of place. Something he didn't own or even seen before. It was an old book, he walked over and sat on the bed and opened it.

It was a yearbook from 1995 "where did you come from?" he asked in a gentle whisper and open the large wood book cover. He flipped through the pages until he came across a name as if he was drowned to this name. The page number was six, the name was six down, and six across.

"*Adam Bell*"

He stared at the name, then the picture. It was a boy with blue and green eyes, scruffy brown hair, his gaze was cold "Those eyes... I know them?"

The book fell to the floor, and he picked up the book from

the floor and the memory page laid open and he read the following remarks. *Yes, Adam, I will truly... Not miss you* it was written by a boy name Nyck Bottoms. Kain looked confused *Who's this Adam Bell?*

The page flipped to another entry.

You, Adam, is just as bad as Kate B. you are evil! it was written by a girl name Molly Greene.

This book was as if answering his questions, he was thinking "*has he had family here before?*" words form on the page this time as letters form in blood.

Yes, greatest grand mom and greatest cousins. Kain's breath-ing drew heavily and fast, this was some very dark art at work in this book. He thought for a moment before asking another question *why did you show me this?* The book quickly wrote out a lengthy sentence.

Pure evil courses through family bloodline, murderess bunch. Your hatred for a girl who comes to this school. You know how Witches and Wizards are with evil bloodline! ADAM BELL IS—

The door opened and Cecil poked his head into the room, and he saw Kain awake "lights off bed!" said Cecil in a demanding voice while he looked to Kain as the other three Dracoîn slept.

"Sorry Brother." replied Kain while he climbs back into the bed, the door closed and Kain fell asleep. Morning came and

Chapter 9: The unexpected gift.

Kain woke up to the book was gone, meanwhile, Luna was at her first class, the class went by pretty quick. There were whispers amongst the Dracoîn's clan. The bell rang and Kain walked by right when he heard Professor Brooks call out to Luna. "Miss Bell, your grade isn't improving anything I can do to help?"

Kain's eyes widen, and he thought to himself *Adam Bell?... Luna Bell? OOOH, this is great!* He vanished into the sea of pointy hats of students. Finally, it was the fourth class with Professor Dunn, Luna sat with DJ and Jenny. She had turned her essay in on *Why Mary was a famous Witch.* Professor Dunn had called for row call and then picked a few students to read their essays. One student talked about how she was a great enchantress, another student talked about her charming skills, and then Professor called for Luna, Luna's stomach knotted up and she made her way up to the front of the class.

"Why was Mary a famous witch, Mary had come to this school, and exceeded in far advanced potions, enchanting, and charming. There was one thing that set her far from her schoolmates. It was how she could use (Shrining) to travel. She had sadly killed many people along with two other Witches. She is maybe one of the most famous Witches, but she is a killer." Luna went and sat down in her seat as Professor Dunn stood up

"Excellent Luna.," The bell hand rang and everyone gathered their stuff "Alright students, I do wish you a very Happy Halloween and a very blessed Samhain full of enjoyment, merriment and entertainment everyone!" said Professor Dunn

123

happily.

Luna, Jenny, DJ, and Ray walked along the decorative hallway from spider webs with real large spiders. They were the size of two grown-up hand put together, bats, and even ghost. Kain was in the bathroom washing his face and words slowly form on the mirror it looks like it was worded in blood.

Hello Friend.

Kain jumped back a bit scared "h-hello?"

Pay Back.

He read the words slowly while they formed on the mirror "Payback? Why...Who are you?" he had the biggest idea, just wanted to make sure.

Yes, payback... Salem Witch Trials... Burnt alive,

Bloody Mary! It wrote fast and sloppy this time. He had read as quick as his eyes could follow the smudges along with the mirror. Then the writing stopped and then two large words appeared

DONT SCREAM!

An old woman with long silky grayish-black hair, dark large blue eyes, long pointed chin, burnt skin on the left side of the face and the neck.

Kain stood frozen and petrified and the room grew cold. His breathing sped up and his breath could be seen from how cold the bathroom has gotten. A hand reached out of the mirror, he watched her while he stumbled back and fell on the cold damp tile floor, then...

124

Chapter 9: The unexpected gift.

BOOM! --- The bathroom door flung open, Kain screeched and covered his face. He lowered his hands and looked towards the door. Zak and Colt busted in and they have seen Kain on the floor.

"Hey man, why are you down there?" asked Zak.

Kain looked up at the mirror and it was back to normal, no words, no Witch, and no arm.

"I-I-I fell."

"You OK, looks like you have seen a ghost." said Colt, and a moment Zak and Colt burst out in laughter. There were a few ghosts everywhere. Kain stood up and walked out with them. He told them about Luna Bell and her evil bloodline. They both looked shocked and disturbed.

"That means she is evil or will turn evil." said Zak with a gulp.-

Luna sat outside with Jenny, DJ, and Ray while they talked about the Samhain Party "be my date, Jenny?" asked Luna in a friendly tone, but she couldn't hide the blush that washed over her cheeks. She had to admit Jenny was gorgeous, Jenny put orange in some of her dreadlocks with purple bands and a black bandanna with spider webs stitched in. She attached a spider charm that hung form the bandanna.

"Of course, I'll be honored to be your date." replied Jenny with a warm smile.

DJ and Ray looked at them "though we were your dates?"

said Ray while he looked to the two girls. They stood up and both kiss his cheeks, his face went as red as his hair.

"Maybe next year." they told him, and they rushed off.

DJ hit Ray on his arm "ouch" said Ray while he rubbed his left arm.

"Look at you with two girls kissing on you." said DJ while Ray went redder. Classes had ended, everyone was getting ready for the dance. Kain was in his room getting ready himself. Then on his bed was a clothing bag with a note

For tonight, found you this.
Sincerely
Your Friend.

Kain put the parchment paper away and unzipped the bag and there it was a black tuxedo with a gold flower pin and golden buttons. He lifted it and tried it on, the door open and his date Traci Brew walked in she has long dark brown bouncing curly hair, bright sky-blue eyes, fairly tanned. She walked in with red spider web stockings, black skirt that one side went down to her knees and came up at an angle. Spider web-like lace wore a red corset that hugged her perfectly. Then long black fishnet gloves and around her neck was a black choker with a green bell. She was a year older than Kain and on the Snorkbie team as the Queen. He turned and looked at her with a sparkling smile.

"My--- My, you look lovely my dear." said Kain with a

126

warm smile looking to his date, it was a rare sight to see him with such a warm look on his face.

"You, look like you're heading to a wedding. You look like you are on your way to a wedding. You do look edible.," replied Traci with a wink "Who's tux?"-

Jenny and Luna had gotten ready in separate rooms to surprise each other. They both do their makeup and Luna done her hair. Jenny pulled her dreads back in a loose ponytail with the same head bandanna and charm. Followed by a small black Masquerade mask with orange pinstripe along with sparkling perfume on her neck. Long black knee-high socks with orange candy stripes. Long puffy orange dress with black lace on the back. It had hung around her chest tightly. She painted her fingernails orange and black, and she slipped her black sparkling heels on.

Luna braided her hair up that went around her head and down the back that she let rest on her left shoulder, black Masquerade mask with purple pinstripe. She had put purple lipstick on and a purple corset, black tight slacks with purple pinstripe, and black boots. She wore purple fishnet, armband, and a black bat choker. She walked out of the room and met Jenny, she blushed while she looked at Jenny. Jenny saw Luna blushed and she walked over and gave Luna a small kiss, words didn't have to be said. Jenny pulled out an orange flower and place it on Luna's corset.

127

Bree came out with her blue, purple, and black hair now had dreadlocks like Jenny's. She wore a black short puff dress and bone tights. She was going to the dance with Dane as his date "mMm look at the two of you love birds." said Bree with a smile while she stood by the door.

"You look so beautiful Bree," said Luna while Jenny took her hand. "Annnd I did her hair." said Jenny proudly admiring her work.

They made their way down to the first floor of the dormitory and saw DJ dressed in a tux and a skeleton mask "my ladies, you two look... Lovely." said DJ while he hugged them. Then they all left down the tower stairs to the grand hall and met up with Ray. He was dressed in black skeleton tux.-

Music could be heard out in the courtyard. Five real ghouls were playing live music, guitar, bass, drummer, piano, and a singer. When the band took a break, a skeleton was at the turntables playing some electronic dance music. Lights flashed while people danced, glow wands in their hands while they were on the dance floor. Then a massive Kongo line broke out.

And Luna went onto the dance floor and danced, fog rose from the large cauldron, this had been the best school year Luna had at any school. After an hour of dancing, Luna grabbed Jenny and lead her to the DUDE! That is man-eating trap to get their picture made while they kissed. They met up with DJ and Ray and they talked about the rave. Kain was getting Traci a drink, Bree

128

came over with Dane who wore a skeleton tux. Bree hugged the group and she introduced Dane to everyone, then Bella came over with a wavy blue dress and a flower in her hair "he looks like a gentleman.," pointed out Bella at Kain, then hugged Dane "hey loser.," she smiled and then turned to her younger brother Ray "don't you look handsome." The group turned and looked at Kain.

"Where is your date?," asked Dane while he playfully flicked her nose "and what do you mean loser?"

She smiled "I didn't get one." not that she wasn't asked, she just didn't want a date to the party. She was very beautiful and well popular in the Crowfeather clan.

"I'll be your date!" said DJ puffing out his chest with a large smile.

"DUDE! That is my sister." said Ray and Dane at the same time looking at DJ, his chest let out the air making his chest shrink. Luna turned and saw Kain, and she went to speak but her words got caught in her throat, she tried to speak but spoke in a breathy sentence.

"THAT'S--- MY--- DAD'S--- WEDDING---- TUXEDO!" her face went pure white, and her blue and green eyes went watery.

"What do you mean?," asked Jenny completely confused as Luna shot across the floor towards Kain storming her way across the dance floor "LUNA!" shouted Jenny as everyone chased after her. She was on a mission, a mission to reach Kain. She finally reached him, and her voice was loud and broken.

"WHERE--- DID--- YOU--- GET--- THAT--- TUX?!"

129

snapped Luna while she smacked the drink cup out of his hand.

"LUNA!" yelled Jenny while she grabbed her arm and she looked at Luna, her eyes showed fright. Kain grabbed a towel for Traci while Professors stormed over to them quickly. The dancing stop and stared at what was going on at the commotion.

"Where did you get MY dad's tux?!" yelled Luna, her fists now balled up as tears flooded her eyes. Everyone stared at them confused. Mistress Flowers took Luna and Kain by the arm and lead them to her office. They got marched through the keep, up the eight flights of stairs. Down the large hall and finally to her door. The door opened on its own, her office overlooked the courtyard. It had a very tidy desk, two chairs that Kain and Luna had sat down in. A brown owl perched in the corner. Mistress Flowers sat on the other side of her desk and looked at them.-

"What has gotten into her?" asked Traci all snotty-like. She was a sweet girl, Jenny felt bad for what had happened to her.

"She thinks Kain had her father's tux. I am so sorry..." said Jenny with a friendly smile while she handed some towels for Traci.-

"So, Luna, what is going on here?" asked Mistress flowers with a cold dead gaze towards Luna. Luna was raging, she was furious at Kain. She felt as if the world around her was in slow motion, and she was speeding right through it.

"HE has my dad's tux... He married my mom in that tux,

130

then eight years later he... --- Died." tears filled her eyes while she spoke. A moment of silence fell on them before Mistress Flowers spoke.

"How do you know this is your fathers? I mean how could this boy get your father's tux?," Mistress Flowers looked to Luna then to Kain "where did you get that very nice tux?"

Kain looked to Luna then to the school's Mistress "it was given to me from a friend." said Kain, something he had told Traci. Luna had to wipe her eyes while she spoke with a shaky voice.

"My dad's tux had golden buttons and a flower pin, and on the tag, it had *"WHO IS "*."

Mistress Flowers gaze turned even more deadly "W-HO IS YOUR FRIEND?!" snapped Mistress flowers in a demanding sharp tone this time. Luna and Kain both jumped two feet out of their chairs.

"I'm... I'm not sure. I found it on my bed with a note." said Kain now with his voice as shaky as Luna while he stared at Mistress Flower's stone-cold face. Luna had never seen Mistress Flowers so angry. Kain only had heard stories about Flower's wrath from his brother Cecil.

"Luna, you are free to go." said Mistress flowers not breaking eye contact with Kain. Luna had gotten up and made her way out and made her way to the keep. The party was now over, and she made it to the tower, she collapsed to her knees and tears exploded out from her.

Mistress Flowers tossed the jacket on the desk, and she

looked down at the scared boy "where did it come from? It could be jinx, cursed, or anything dark. Who is your friend?" her voice had now gone from sternness to more of a concern. Kain looked at her with a look in his eyes that showed fear, he swallowed hard, and he finally found his voice again. He watched her sit at the desk and her eyes never leaving his.

"I didn't know... I had got it from someone, not sure who. They left a yearbook with... Luna's dad is in it. He is evil like his grandmother, that bloodline is in Luna. Explains why she is like she is." there was a moment of silence.

"Don't say a word, I will be speaking to Mr. Rune, go to the dormitory." She got up and walked him back to the dorm, then made him give the entire tux to her before leaving. She had put her hand out "book as well." He turned to grab it and it was gone. He stared at the spot where he had left it, then turned to Mistress Flowers and told her it was gone. Mistress Flowers had left in haste out of the dormitory..-

The next week, the whole school was weird, people spoke in a whisper when Luna came around, leaves had finally turned to fall colors. The wind blew cooler, and the halls of the school were drafty. Luna and Jenny were on their way to the class hand in hand when they stopped in their steps and their eyes widen, wrote in blood along the walls.

L. Bell has evil bloodlines in her!

The students stared and read the spiral bloody words then turned to face Luna, Luna shook her head, her knees grew weak, and felt like she would faint. Jenny took her hand and lead her to spell class, and they found their seat.

Professors scattered the students to class, Professor Raven met with Professor Kanoe about what was going on with everything and if he had heard anything about what was going on. Professor Kanoe had his cold gaze look on Professor Raven as he shrugged his shoulders bored.

"I know same as you do, Luna is evil blood." said Professor Kanoe coldly tracing his finger along with the bloody words.

"I know you have ghost and poltergeist in your ear, Kanoe.," said Professor Raven as she took a deep breath "Kanoe, a girl is in trouble... What if she is pure?"

Linda the poltergeist and Jerry the ghost float in through the wall and they looked to Kanoe and Raven. They turned and looked to the ghost and poltergeist.

"What have you heard you two?" asked Professor Kanoe sharply and just as cold. Raven's soft purple gaze shifted from Kanoe to the two ghosts.

"Not too much, everyone is speaking how good the party was. There has been word about a demon floating around." said Jerry while Linda shook her head.

"I heard Sherry Mary is back, also Bloody Mary. We know she isn't BUT whispers have been told of a boy who befriended this ghost... Demonic being."

Professor Raven's eyes widen and she spoke with a concerned voice herself "Sherry Mary? --- Bloody Mary, why would they be back here. We haven't heard from them since Mary, Sherry, and Kate had been expelled."

"As I said. Just rumors but the girl does have some very evil blood, just know." said Linda the poltergeist before they had vanished...

After school there was practice, the water was icy cold and the next game was Chimerador and Dracoîn. The practice was good as always, after practice, they had made their way to Maîq's cottage, DJ and Ray were already there. Luna sat in Jenny's lap and ask, they talked about Luna having evil blood. Then Luna had asked one question that ate away at her "did I... Did I have family that came to this school, like a dark secret?"

Maîq's ears went back, and he let out a murmur groan while his tail dropped "I not 'ne ta answer dis.," his gaze lowered. "descupla (excuse)."

They had said their goodbyes and they walked back to the castle, the sun began to lower and the sky turned to beautiful ruby color. Jenny and Luna held hands "I have an idea... Follow me, WHY didn't I think of this earlier?!" said Jenny smacking her forehead lightly while the four of them went to the library. They found a room that was a small closet-like room that was full of nothing but school yearbooks from 800 BC to the present time.

DJ's eyes widen as he stared at the pile of books "we are

supposed to find people in my family in these books?" asked Luna while she knocked some dust off a book.

"That is the plan..." Jenny spoke unconfidently. They look between 2000's nothing stood out of place. Then they looked along with the 1990s to 1999, the year 1995 was missing. It took a few hours just to find that this book was missing.

"Luna, 1995 is gone.," whispered DJ, "we better head to the dormitories before it gets too late."

They went to leave, and the librarian stop them, she wore thick large glasses and her gray hair was tidy in a large bun, deep green eyes grew large behind the glasses. Jenny looked to Mrs. Jenkins as smart and quick her brain moved she spoke just as quickly "homework, looking for someone in class of 95'" the librarian walked over to the desk and unlocked it and a file called *checkouts.* She skimmed through the file after a mom-ent she spoke up "all yearbooks are in there and counted for. Who are you looking for?"

"OK, thank yo-" Jenny was cut off by Luna who had spoken up while she walked up to the desk "someone in the Bell family." Luna had seen the look in the woman's eyes. Her head shook.

"I think it is time for students to be in their dorms."-

They had left the library and had begun to walk back to the Crowfeather dormitory "she is hiding something." whispered Luna, they went in and changed to their sleeping gown, and they met up on the first floor and worked on their homework. Bella came up behind Luna and hugged her from behind "I... We know you are not evil."

"...Thanks." said Luna lowly not knowing what to say. They had finished their homework; Luna went to her room to lay down and what she saw was a shock. She dropped her books and they landed with a loud thud, Jenny had rushed up the stairs and into the bedroom.

"What is it?"

Luna pointed to the bed and on the bed was an old piece of parchment paper. Jenny walked over and picked it up off the bed and held the page. "---Luna..."

Chapter 10: Dark Family Secret

Jenny stood by the canopy bed the purple curtains on the bed were open up. In the hand of Jenny, she held an old parchment paper from 1995, page six, six down, six across, and every other name on the page was scratched out and the other pictures sliced out. But one name, one photo stood in a place untouched *Adam Bell*. "--- Luna..." Jenny whispered as she turned to her girlfriend. Handing the paper with shaky hands while Luna took it slowly.

"...Dad?" Luna didn't know what to say about this or how to make sense of this. Adam was raised in Adams Tennessee. He wasn't a Witch or Wizard *Why was this here, what kind of sick joke was this*? Luna's mind was racing *was that Witch in the cauldron her grandmother*? Jenny had Luna sit on the bed.

"We have to get into the school records." Luna told Jenny, at this moment Luna didn't care about points, the clan cup, or Snorkbie. All she wanted was to know what her dad was doing here.

"We could just ask someone." Jenny assured Luna. Jenny wasn't about rule breaking. Luna wasn't having it either.

"We tried; Mrs. Jenkins acted if no one was here by Bell."

"Fine, I'll help you. We will do it on the game day when Chimerador face off against Dracoîn when the school is empty.,"

Jenny gave Luna a soft kiss before going to her bed "night Luna." said Jenny softly as Luna rolled over in her bed and smiled softly at Jenny. "Night JenJen." -

A couple of weeks have passed and the schoolwork grew more harder and tedious. Unanswered questions ate at Luna, she wrote a few times to her mom and sent it by a crow. She never mentions her dad to her mom or her sister. She did write about friends, how her grades were no less than a C (thanks to Jenny) and told them about Jenny and playing sports.

On the way to spell class, Luna was alone when Kain and Cecil saw her, it had been peaceful since the party. "Hey, Evil Blood." Kain shouted out, his arms had a few dark scratches on them now.

"I'm not evi-" Kain cut her off as his cold dark purple eyes locked to hers and he snapped out at her "Your dad was Evi-" Luna shot a look at him that could kill, her tone was just as sharp as a knife.

"HE wasn't evil. He WAS a good man! You don't know him!" Luna's blood was boiling, her hate for him grew fast like a wildfire, her fist had balled up tightly and her knuckles turned white.

Cecil placed his hand on his brother's shoulder "as Pre Lord, I must stop you. Get to class." Cecil ordered Kain and they walked off. Before they disappeared Kain's last words rang in her ear "Adam Bell, who got expelled."

138

Luna ran to spell class and stood with Jenny, then Professor Caitlynn was teaching a spell to reflect elemental spells. Kain spoke in a whisper while he leans forward "Your dad was an evil Wizard, 1995..." he sat back next to Zak with a chuckle. "OK class I know we haven't done much on elemental spells, but I will teach you how to reflect elemental spells. First, keep your legs shoulder length, body squared up, now loud and confidently say *Repellere*" and then a bright orb of light appeared then a blast of wind came from her wand. For ten minutes each student had done the spell till the bell had rung. They rushed out of the room.-

"Did you see Kain's arm?" Three on each arm." Ray told them while they walked down the long draft hall. "Annnnnnd?" replied Luna in an uncaring manner while she wrapped her heavy cloak around her body to block the cold draftiness halls.

"Six, the witches... Demonic number." said Jenny with a look of worried.

"Maybe it is my dad doing it, for him being mean to me." snapped out Luna.

"Have you noticed? He has been more... Active... He is being attacked, not by your dad but by being a vessel to be used. Breaking him down." Jenny's voice was shakier than ever. They had met with Bree and Bella to eat dinner before going to see Maîq as they did regularly.

They ran down the hill while Maîq was tending his garden "he Maîq." They all greeted him while they walked over to him.

"Ah, olá troublesome, how have ye all been? Come on inside." said Maîq while he led them inside his cottage. They made their way into his house. As always, his house was filled with animal hides of all sorts laying in piles on the chairs and sofas all folded nicely.

"Good." They said while Maîq has made them hot pumpkin spice cream lotta.

"Found out some reason my dad came to this school.," Luna had told him "the librarian acted as if she had never have heard of any Bells."

"Maybe, diferente Bells?" said Maîq reassuring her...-

Kain was with Cecil while they were in the locker room after practice. "What has happened to your back? You got six scratches." pointed out Cecil in concern while he looked to his brother as they all got dressed. Kain wasn't on the team, but he did help out with the practice sometimes.

"Must have done it in my sleep." he said while he made his way to the sink to wash his face. He looked into the mirror as he saw Mary behind him. Then along the mirror bloody words began to form in the mirror.

Need more followers

He nodded his head while his brother yelled for him "Coming?"-

Zak was in the bathroom. He had found a piece of parchment paper with instructions on it.

Chapter 10: Dark Family Secret

Stand in front of the mirror and turn the lights off. Turn around three times and chant Bloody Mary. Turn the lights on while facing the mirror, DONT SCREAM!

Zak laughed at the paper "What a joke." but the inquisitiveness got the better of him. HE put the candles out, turned around three times while he chanted Bloody Mary. He had lit the candles, faced the mirror, and stood behind him in the mirror was Blood Mary. He let out a screamed that screeched through the halls.

The old witch smirked and came down with her right hand. She was holding a glowing green dagger. He stepped to the side while she stabbed his shoulder blade. He stumbled a bit, and his skin grew cold, and his veins grew a blackish green color. The witch stalked her prey. Zak's breath was now visible, the door to the bathroom open, and Professor Tristan and another student came into the bathroom where the screams had come from.

Professor Tristan told the boy to go and get the other professors. The boy ran to the feast hall "MENS bathroom, HELP!" the boy shouted while the other Professors raised to their feet and rushed off to the boys' restroom. Professor Tristan had placed the boy on a stretcher. Professor Raven came up to him "What happened here?" she asked very concerningly.

Professor Tristan searched the bathroom but came up with nothing "he was stabbed, the boy has petrified to nothing more than a shell." everyone watched in horror while the stretcher began to roll on its own. Mistress Flowers showed up and gasped in fright looking at the little rat boy "is he..." she looked to Professor Tristan.

"He is alive, just poison and petrified. He got stabbed in the back." said Professor Tristan while he walked by the stretcher while it made its way to the marble staircase. It floated along the stairs.

"Pre Lords, get your clan to the dormitories now." said Mistress Flowers as the Pre Lords had made the clans marched to the dorms. Mistress Flowers turned to the other school professors "fan out the attacker should still be around."

Two teachers went along the dungeons; another group went along the inner castle walls. The school was filled with teachers, the gate had closed and Maîq watched the gates from the top of the wall with bow and arrow in hand. Professor Tristan had taken Zak to the hospital wing to Madam Sunny. Mr. Rune was in the room with them "he was stabbed by something, looks like a knife." Tristan explained while they placed the boy on a hospital bed.

"The boy is alive but frozen, his life is being drained.," Said Madam Sunny while she made a table of potions, roots, leaves, and other sorts of materials "something leached to him.," she closed the curtains to his bed "please leave so I can undo this curse."-

Kain was in his room and he spoke to the mirror, his gaze

grown more glossy "hello friend." words formed on the mirror slowly.

Hello friend, I am feeling better... Need more.

He nodded his head and wrote more instructions on parchment papers, placing them in his bag. He laid in bed and drifted to sleep. It was late, everyone in every tower laid asleep.

Luna woke up and left the bed, she was out of her body again and went through the low dim-lit hallways. An old man with gray hair and thick brows, bitty dark brown eyes with an apple size for a nose, one tooth in his dried-out mouth. He always had a long thin wooden pipe on his belt with a glass lantern attached to it. Beside him was an old grew wolf. The wolf sniffed along the halls while making his way towards Luna. Tiny was the wolf's name, but nothing was tiny about this wolf.

"Who is there?," I know you are there." The watchman is also known as Watchman Moody, just as his name. He was very moody and hated everything but Tiny. He withdrew his wand "show yourself! OR I'll reveal you."

With a deep breath, Luna broke out in a run right past the Watchman Moody and Tiny. When she passed Moddy and Tiny, she got something extra. It was a large set of a golden set ring of keys with over a hundred keys on the key ring.

Watchman Moody crusty tiny eyes widen while he seen the keys float away. "*Revelare!*" shouted Moody and a bright blue light exploded from the top of his wand. Luna went around the corner and into the bathroom. The spell hit the wall and as it

143

exploded, it went down each of the two corridors revealing Luna's footprints.

Luna stood in the bathroom where she saw a parchment paper on the floor of the womans' tiled damp floor with instructions... "Bloody... Witch?" she whispered. The door flung opened, and she jolted and hid around the circular sinks. The Watchman Moody stepped in "I know you are here." as he went in, she made her way out. She ran back to her dorm and gave the password. She rushed into the dark bedroom. The moonlit the room, the door flung open and hit the wall and cause Jenny to wake up with a jolt and looked around. What shocked Luna wasn't waking Jenny but a ghostly schoolgirl going for Luna's body "NO!"

The ghost girl turned and looked with a grin, a grin that frightened Luna. The keys and parchment paper dropped, and she ran to her body as did the ghost girl...

Jenny saw the keys and the note dropped. She got out of bed and got the keys and note. She turned and saw Luna standing behind her, Jenny jumped and held her chest tightly "you scared me. Look at what I found in the floor, the Watchman's keys, and this parchment paper."   "I think the Watchman is the one leaving these. It's not safe. For, once I think we should tell the Professor." Jenny's opened the paper, eyes-widen as she read it.

"---Bloody Mary?!" Jenny looked to Luna with a gasp, and there was a hand print, a right-hand print on Luna's side. Luna had worn a low midriff crop top and black shorts.

"We need to wake up a professor."

144

Luna's head school "tomorrow we will look for my dad. Then after dinner, we will tell a professor."

"I---don't---know." said Jenny in a murmur. Luna had convinced Jenny and they went back to bed. Luna slept with a grin that night.-

The next day, everyone got ready for the game between Chimerador versus Dracoîn. Luna, Jenny, and DJ had met up with Ray in the library. They unlocked the door and made it through the seat of books. DJ and Jenny went to the desk and seen a yearbook with the year *1995* was still on the shelf. They made their way to the books for the yearbooks and began to search...Nothing.

"Think someone stole it?" asked Ray while Luna and Jenny went to the desk and then open the desk, then open a file that was labeled *B* found a few titles as they search through it *Banishing curses*, *Banshees*, *Bats and Vampires*, *Bundle of spells*, and a file was stuffed under the rest of the files *Bell Witch*. Luna pulled it out and murmured out "*restricted area*, section six, row six, book number *666*."

They looked at Luna "*666*? That is the demonic number... This is serious stuff." said Jenny, but Luna already ran off to the *restricted area* and opened the door to the restricted area and made her way until she had a book in her hand *Tales of the Bell Witch*. She made her way back to the group "Now, to the *records*." They rushed off then stopped.

"This is crazy, we can't push our luck. Plus does anyone

know where the records are?" asked Ray catching his breath. They looked at each other. "YES!" Luna shouted then took off to the marble staircase and made her way up. They had passed the second, third, fourth, fifth, sixth, seventh, and finally, they came out on the eighth floor.

"I have seen it when Kain and I went to Mistress Flowers' office. The night of the party." They walked along the red carpet and on the walls were pictures of old teachers. Then to a door with golden letters *Records*. They had unlocked the door and stepped into the large room. The room was filled up with file cabinets from wall to wall, floor to the ceiling. They looked around the place at all the towering cabinets.

"DJ, you look for Adam Lee Bell, Ray you look for Lee Adam Bell. Jenny, you and I will look for Bell Adam Lee , Bell Lee Adam." Luna barked orders as they all began to search. Files after files they searched and finally came across *K.Bell* and a file name *A. L. Bell*. They took both files and rushed out to the dormitories to drop the file off. Then they headed to the game. They found a seat at the bench and the game was already over, Dracoîn had beaten Chimerador two-hundred and ten points to one-hundred and ninety points. They sat there watching Dracoîn celebrate. Something that wasn't right... Bree, the captain of Crowfeather and Pre Lord caught them. After the game, Luna, Jenny, DJ, and Ray tried to rush to the school.

"Where were you four? Luna and Jenny, why weren't you at the game watching the competition?"

"We... We did last-minute homework." Luna lied, trying to look all truthful as she could.

"Dining hall now, celebrate with the Dracoîn." demanded Bree while she pointed out towards the school. They groaned and moaned. They couldn't bear to be next to Cecil, Kain, or Colton.

They walked up the rolling hills, they made their way into feast hall the place was in an uproar. On the stage where the professors sat, sat Mr. Rune. Jenny nudged Luna as they sat down at their clan table. Cookies, pizza, puffins, and cake appeared on top of the table.

Luna looked at Jenny while she got up and Luna followed behind Jenny. They made their way to Mr. Rune as they both looked very nervous. "H-hello Mr. Rune." said Jenny.

He smiled at them; his blue sparkling eyes shown behind his half-moon glasses. His long-braided beard with red and green ties represented each clan. "Hello, Miss Bell and Miss. Striff, how are you two?"

They looked at him and sighed softly while the watchman stood in the dark corner with Tiny. Luna and Jenny turned to face Mr. Rune as they whispered "I.. - I'm pretty sure Blood Mary attacked Zak. I found a parchment paper in our room with instructions on how to summon her." said Jenny looking at Mr. Rune, his warm smile slowly dropped.

"Are you sure?"

They nodded as he stood fixing his blue tunic and royal blue cloak "Mrs. Flowers, I shall be back. I have plans with Miss.

Bell and Miss. Striff. Enjoy the celebration."

"Everything ok Robert?" she looked fully concerned. He stood up and left with Luna and Jenny to the Crowfeather tower. They walked up to the first-year girls' common room, then into their room.

"It's right over he---.," Jenny froze, the paper was gone off of Jenny's dresser "it was r-right here."

"Did anyone take it?" Mr. Rune turned and asked while he looked at the two girls. Jenny shook her head then she remembered the bruise hand prints on Luna's side. "Look, Luna has a bruised of a hand print on her." Luna lifted her shirt just a tad to show her lower side... NOTHING.

Mr. Rune turned and left with no word. The two girls looked at each other and sat down on the bed Mr. Rune turned and left with no word. The two girls looked at each other and sat down on the bed.-

That night, they waited till everyone fell asleep, and then Luna, Jenny, and DJ sat in the best chairs by the fireplace on the first dormitory floor. *Praemium* Jenny murmured out and a fireball shot out of her wand lighting the fire. *Mico lucis* they all whispered out and the room grew brightly.

They told DJ what had happened and Robert Rune's reaction. They opened the file containing *A.L.B* and passed the papers out to search and read through it.

"Listen to this!," Jenny whispered out shockingly "*Adam L. Bell* was in his third year before being expelled for casting a curse on three students."

"Listen to this!," DJ spoked up "*Adam L. Bell* had family attended this school a ninth-generation grandmom (*Restricted*) for the name and three cousins (*Restricted*). He started great, head of his clan, Captain of the *Snorkbie* team. In his third year, he shoved *Anderson B. Bloke* down the Dracoîn tower steps. *Adam L. Bell* denied it all happened."

Luna had taken a deep breath and paused a moment "--- Listen to this..," she took a deep slow breath "*Adam L. Bell* had his memory wiped along with his mom's as he returned to... *Adams Tennessee*, *Adam L. Bell*'s mother was a widow, her husband died in a car crash at 3 am on December twenty-fourth.," Luna stared into the fire. "My--- My dad was... Evil..." Jenny sat next to Luna and rubbed her leg and kissed her cheek " we have so much to uncover." said Jenny in a soft caring manner. DJ rubbed Luna's shoulders as he looked at the other file "We still have *K. Bell* to look through." he said reassuring her.

They had opened the file and passed out the papers. At everyone's shock the name (*Restricted*). Information on this person (*Restricted*), every part of this person was *restricted*. "We are at a dead end now." whispered Luna staring at the files in hand.

"Come on, don't you two read your spell books?," Jenny had picked up her wand *revelare*, the names and everything began to show up now. Jenny passed the papers out "listen to this," Jenny had begun to read.

" *1700, Kate Bell* had come to *OwlHollow School of Mag-*

ck for Witchcraft and Wizardly with her three cousins. *Linda DellHollow, Sherry Mary,* and *Margret Mary.* They came top of the school, *Kate Bell* mastered shapeshifting. At that time of the decade, this was frowned on. They suspended her."

DJ had picked up from where Jenny left off and began to read now.

"*Kate Bell* in her last year she was expelled and looked to be hung for twenty deaths in *Crystal Center Town* with her cousins. *Kate Bell* had escaped and the *M.B.W.W.* (*Magick Bureau Of Witches and Wizards*). They fled the *Crystal Realm.*," Luna couldn't believe this then she had begun to read.

"*1750,* the *M.B.W.W.* had found *Kate Bell* hiding in a cave in Adams Tennessee where she was killed. She had a son who lived with their father in *Adams Tennessee.*"

"Wow you have some deep roots." acknowledge DJ.

"It is getting late, let's go to bed." Jenny told them as they closed the folders and went to bed. Luna laid in bed as her mind was racing with thoughts.

150

Chapter 11: Another one is taken.

Thanksgiving was just in a few days. Zak was still in the hospital his skin had grown colder. His condition had lucky stayed the same. The school had been decorated with fall colors. The scarecrows worked out in the gardens, and turkeys had flooded the valley between Maîq's cottage and the school. Something was different, the mirrors in all of the school, the dormitories, and even Maîq's home had been blacked out with a spell. School went on as normal as any other day, classes were the same: long and boring (most of the normal classes; math and science) whispers fell about Bloody Mary and who had summoned her.

Luna, DJ, Jenny, and Ray sat in Professor Dunn's History of Magick People as they opened their book to page two hundred and thirty-five. Luna looked down at the page and it was of an older man with light brown soft hair, small glasses that hid his sparkling grey eyes. His mouth is wide and humorous with a pointed upper lip. Luna had raised her hand and Professor Dunn called on her "yes, Miss Bell?"

"Why is Benjamin Franklin in my book?" was everyone a Witch or Wizard she thought.

"Oh? Does it not say he was in the Dibble-Doggle world? Do tell us what the Dibble-Doggles taught you." replied Professor

151

Dunn looking fascinating at Luna. Everyone's eyes were on her, a-nd Professor Dunn had made Luna come up in front of the class. She looked down, wishing she kept her mouth shut now. History wasn't Luna's strongest subject. She found 1
it extremely boring.

"Class take notes." Professor Dunn had sat at her desk looking at Luna fully intrigue while Luna took a deep breath.

"Ben Franklin was a very brilliant man... He was an inventor of many things such as Bifocals, the lightning rod, the glass armonica, and few more things. He was an imprintest. He flew a key on a kite during a thunderstorm. He figured out electricity. He had signed the Declaration of Independence, the Treaty of Alliance, Amity, and Commerce with France. He helped write part of the Declaration of Independence and the Constitution."

"Very good, clearly they left out one small important detail.," Professor Dunn stood and took her place in front of the class again "he was a great Wizard, a master at alchemy and enchanter. He may not know many spells, but he could create things that no one could think of, for the lighting and the key. He did it in an alchemy circle."-

The bell rang, and they all left and headed to the feast hall. Bella came and sat with Luna, Jenny, and DJ "hey, how is all your peeps day going?" she asked with a smile.

"Good, found out Luna's related to the Bell Wit-" DJ

gasped out as Jenny elbowed him in the side and gave him a hateful look.

"What--- Really?," said Bella in shock. She looked to DJ and Luna "you cannot tell anybody at all."

"Yea, I know... It seems some of us forgot." Jenny shot DJ a pierced look. Luna stood up after eating and went outside and walked to the water fountain. A girl laid bleeding from the front of her shoulder. Luna's eyes widen and she had seen the parchment paper that Jenny and she placed on their dormitory desk. Here it is laying in the girl's hand. The girl was a first yearer name, Becca Teasley. She has long blond hair, brilliant Hazel eyes, small round head. Luna let out a gasp and ran back to the keep and made a left at the large grand staircase. She ran past the large sliding doors back into the feast hall. She ran up the professor's dining tables. Mistress Flowers and the other four clan teachers were eating and enjoying the food.

"There---has --- been--- another---attack." panted out Luna as she tried to catch her breath.

"WHAT?!" shouted Akira Miin taking a stand pushing her seat from under her.

"Where?!" asked Shawn Dibbs then he made his way down the steps and down the pathway between the clan tables towards the entrance of the feast hall.

"Everyone stay put! Lord Headmaster and Pre Lords, watch over everyone!" barked Mistress Flowers as she and the professors and Luna left the feast hall. Bruno, Dane, Bree, Jewels, and Cecil took to their thrones. A loud outburst of talk began to break out amongst the hall between the students.

"QUIET! and eat!" shouted Bruno as Bree smacked her wand in the air and a large dong echoed through the air, causing everyone to stop talking and staring up to the Lord Headmaster and Pre Lords. "Everyone calm down right now! OR we will each take twenty points, that is a hundred points gone. My clan, sit and eat, I will take our points first." Snapped Bree as the entire feast hall grew quiet.-

The professors and Luna were outside, they ran to the girl "she is a new girl, she is a Dibble-Doggle. She is in my clan." said Professor Dibbs in a shaky voice as he put the girl on a stretcher. The note was gone. Professor Kanoe turned to Luna as his cold gazed met Luna's multi-colored eyes.

"---Funny, second time you found a note then it is gone. Why is that?" Kanoe's cold gaze laid on Luna's face as the professor spoke up.

"Kanoe, Luna wouldn't make a story like that up. PLUS Mr. Rune is looking into it as we speak, seeing who is behind the attacks." Professor Moon had spoken up for Luna.

"I believe we should put her in a twenty-four-hour lockdown, showing her ways at following the school rules and things seem to happen and she is not far behind." suggested Kanoe.

Luna's eyes widen as she looked between each Professor. They all agreed to it. They walked her into the keep and up the grand marble staircase. Everyone in the hall watched, they lead her to the seventh floor and lead her to an old room that housed guests. The room was large with a massive canopy bed, large wardrobe, a blacked-out mirror. Massive candle chandelier, with large bay windows, that overlooked the hills and Maîq's house.

"This is your room for the night." said Mistress Flowers then she closed the door behind her. Luna walked around her new room trying to figure out everything...-

Jenny was in the room with Khan feeding him a rabbit, the *Hellhound* sucked the soul out of the rabbit. A few bright blue butterflies came from the rabbit's mouth into Khan's muzzle. It grew late and Jenny had read the files again over and over while she laid in her bed. Morning came, Jenny went to the seventh floor where Luna was, but Tiny laid in front of the door and Jenny knew the Watchman was close by. She went to the feast hall for breakfast, grabbed a muffin, and headed to training. She went down to the pool basement where the team had gotten dressed and ready. She changed and joined them on the field in the pool. There was talked about Professor Kanoe locking up Luna to keep her out of practice to give Dracoîn an advantage. -

The practice had ended finally, and Jenny ran up to meet up with DJ and Ray. They ran into Kain, Cecil, and Colton. They looked to Kain and them as Kain spoke up "Where is the Evil Queen Bell?"

Jenny stopped and walked up to Kain as she spoke up with a snarl and a growl in her tone "how did you know about Mr. Bell?" Her voice shook not from being scared but from being angry. Jenny looked into his cold glazed eyes; his lips curled in a snake of a smirk.

"---1995." He looked down at them, and Colton had a scratch on his neck.

"Wha-what did you say?" Jenny's eyes had widened, DJ and Ray stepped up next to Jenny.

"Her dad, 1995, came here. So did his grandmother and cousins, Bell, Dellhollow, and the two Mary sisters."

Jenny's knees grew weak as they buckled under her to keep her up on her feet. "You--- you, have summoned Mary?" Ray's voice crackled in his throat while he stared in fright. Cecil's brow raised as he turned to the Kain.

"Of course not. I don't even know how."

"People are getting hurt. Look at Colton and your arms. The two of you had been touched by a demon." Jenny pointed out as they turned and walked off. Cecil looked to Jenny before chasing after his brother and Colt.

"De'g, Ray I think we need to tell someone about Kain summoning Mary, I know he has... He has changed. I know he has been a jerk... But he is worst, his eyes are colder... He and Colton both have scratches."

"We just don't have enough evidence to show he has or anything." said Ray as they walked into the keep.

"How else did he know about Luna's family. Everything he had said was in the file; Kate Bell had cursed her family. She can shapeshift into animals. She killed her family back in 1862, I found it in an article in the Daily Crystal Readings, it was an article from December 28th, 1862. The article was in dept. They are, I believe they're seeking hosts. I think?,

"You got Bell Dellhollow, sisters Mary, two kids had been petrified. Kain and Colton both had been scratched" explained Jenny while they ran in the keep as the sky opened up and rain poured down.

"Even IF it is true, how are you going to tell anyone? --- No offense when you and Luna say anything, the things have seemed to disappear." added DJ as they went into the dining hall to do some homework. Bree came over with parchment paper in hand.

"Hey, Bree, what's up?" asked Jenny as she worked on some of her studies. Bree pushed her dreads back "Just found this in the hall." Bree opened the parchment paper. Everyones' eyes had widened.

☆*The Bell's reunion invention*☆

December 25th, 2028, 3 am. Hidden
passageway behind the golden Chimera statue outside of Chimera
Tower. Show this to anybody, and
a curse of cold dark bliss will fall upon you.

Luna A. Bell

"What is LUNA speaking of?!," shouted Bella while she looked at the group. The writing and signature were the same as Luna's handwriting. "She is gone for a night, and this appears. What kind of sick joke is this? She had attacked those students?"

Everyone sat frozen, Jenny cleared her throat while she stood "this isn't Luna, it's..." her voice trailed off as she shook her head. "It's--- Blood--- Mary."

Everyone looked at Jenny then at Bree. Bree's face went from angry to questionable.

"That's a fairy tale that was created to scare students and kids." chuckled Bree while she looked at them.

"It's not. Why do you think the professors put a protective seal on the mirrors?" replied DJ, Bree turned and walked off to the halls heading to the teachers' lounge. "We have to stop her, she thinks Luna did that note." hashed out Jenny.

They had chased after her, she was talking to Professor Kanoe and Professor Raven. "No DONT!" shouted Jenny, Bree had already delivered out the note.

"Hmm, funny when trouble strikes you, Ms. Striff and Ms. Bell are never too far." snarled Kanoe while he opened the note, but it was blank. Bella's eyes widened along with Jenny's and the rest of the group. Professor Raven looked to the kids then to Bree as her soft purple gazed fell to Kanoe's cold brown eyes.

"Disappearing ink... Foolish, students trying to play a trick on us at a time like this. Twenty points from each of -." Kanoe's cold sharp tone got cut off by Professor Raven. "Thank you, ladies and gentlemen, we will look into this. Bree has never once played a trick on a student or teacher; she is a trusted Pre Lord."

"What about the curse? That is going to fall on her for saying something?" a look of concern fell on Jenny's face. Raven looked to Kanoe then to the four of them.

"Everyone will be OK; Luna will be back in her room tonight. We will have this looked at for any curses, jinxes, and other charms." Professor Raven reassured them.-

They walked off to the outside as no one said one word about what had happened or what was said. They sat under the large oak tree as Jenny and Bree fixed their skirts while they sat there. Then Bree went and finally spoke up, breaking the cold silence. "But how, how did the words just vanished?"

"Tried to stop you, told you Blood Mary is doing this." DJ told her while the cold wind blew.

"Think the curse talk was real?" asked Bree while she sighed.

"--- No, of course not." Jenny was trying to lie to Bree and herself.

"Next week we have Thanksgiving and the big championship game." Bree stood and as she did Jenny noticed

159

something. "What happened here?" Jenny had run a finger along Bree's smooth tone thigh. There was a scratch, three scratches. Bree looked at the scratches.

"Not sure, must have scratched it somehow."

Jenny knew better, but she didn't want to say or alarm Bree. Her spirit books taught her signs of Demonic.

"--- Bree, that is not normal. You have been marked by some kind of Demon. We need to tell Professor Raven or one of the other Professors. This is serious."

Everyone stood, and as Bree went to stand up and her leg hurt as a fiery tingle shot through her. She couldn't move and fell back to the ground "OUCH!"

"RAY, run and get help!" snapped Jenny while DJ and herself had helped Bree to her feet. The sensation burnt through her leg. Few moments, Ray was returning with a Professor but the burning stopped, and the marks were now gone.

"What is wrong?" asked Professor Brooks while she reached the group.

"Bree's leg has been scratched." DJ told her while he pointed out. The teacher looked at Bree's leg, and it was just fine. She looked at all of them.

"Get to your dormitories now, your Pre Lords and Clan Professors wil-" Bree cut the Professor off while she was able to now stand on her own. "I am the Pre Lord, Pre Lord for Crow-" Professor Brooks had cut Bree of and pointed towards the castle.

"To the dormitories NOW!"-

They grumbled out, and they made their way to their towers. The common room was filled with students, Bree went up to her room on the fourth floor. "Why is this happen-ing?" asked DJ while he sat down, and Jenny sat with him.

"The Demon is trying to break us down. It feeds off of depression, anger, and sadness. Until your weak enough for it to take over."-

It had grown late, and Luna showed up. Luna and Jenny cuddled up together at the fireplace while Jenny had told Luna everything. How the Bell Witch killed and cursed her family with the help of Dellhollow and the two Mary sisters, and how Bree had three scratches. How each time things just vanished. Luna had a plan, and hopefully, it will work out. Jenny had gone to bed and Luna made it up to Bree's floor and went into the study room, where she laid on the leather couch.

She drifted to sleep, her eyes open, and she rose up to her feet just out of her body. Luna heard a door open and closed. She made her way up to Bree's room and slowly opened the door to peek in. She scanned the room, her eyes had widened, and she saw an old witch. The witch had long grayish-black hair, large black-blue eyes, a sharp-pointed chin, a large crooked pointed nose, and a half-burnt face. Luna had stepped into the room and seen the witch reaching down to Bree while Luna shouted "NO!" the witched jolted from being disturbed.

161

The witch turned, her cold-dry crackled lips curled into an ugly smile and began to drift under the floor. Luna ran over to Bree, and she have seen Bree was still unharmed, then cold to the bone screeched echoed through the tower. Luna's eyes had widened, and she turned, and she saw the witch standing at the door with the knife in her hand.

The witch spoke coldly and slowly as chills went down Luna's spine "Where is your body, Luna?!" the witch moved towards Luna as if she was stalking Luna like prey.

"Bloody- Bloody Mary?" Luna's voice trembled with fear, she took a step back and fell on her rear end looking up as she watches the witch stalk her. Dagger in her hand while Luna crawled backward.

"Hey, you stop!," a voice came out of the corner of the room, a voice Luna had heard before. The witch had turned and saw Larry standing there with his wand "step away from the girl, Margret!" shouted Larry while Mary faced him. Her cold gaze locked to his dead gaze.

"Larry, there is a free body. You can go back to the living.," snorted Mary "then I can kill you all over again." she chuckled out coldly.

"Leave and go back to the haunted grounds you crawled out from."

The witch with finesse had turned with a swift and lunged towards Luna with the dagger in hand. Luna covered her face and let out a deathly scream.

162

"*Exorcismus*!" chanted Larry loudly, and a large blinding light blasted from his wand as the room lit up blindingly, Mary let out a screech and the witch got blasted out of the room. Luna laid covered up in a shaking manner. "It's OK girl." called out Larry as he put his wand away. He looked to Luna while she came to her feet.

"Is--- She---Dead?" Luna asked shakily while she stood there while Larry floated over her head.

"Nah, she is gone for a bit. She will be back. I need to report this to Kanoe." he began to float away through the wall.

"Hey, wait... Thank you, and what was that spell?" Luna had asked as he smiled and nodded lightly.

"It's called *exorcismus*." and he slowly faded away as she picked up the dagger and went back to her body.- Time had passed, and they were now in Spell class. Professor Raven made them cast all sorts of spells that they've learned over the semester. After the long test, the bell has finally rung, and everyone stood up. Professor Raven tapped the desk with her wand. " Everyone, have a seat. We are going to learn a new spell; this spell is to blast spirits. This spell takes a lot of inner strength it's called, *exorcismus*."

After about an hour the class still couldn't get the spell to work. Wands were jumping out of the students' hands with a puff of smoke, and some of the wands were just making the users laugh out loud. "This spell is very tough, especially for first yearers with everything going on, you all need to know how to protect yourselves."-

Everyone began to leave the room, and Raven stopped Luna by calling her to the desk. "Heard of what a hero you were, please be careful. In the other world, it is very dangerous on the other side. It takes ages to free your body if a spirit takes over."

hey walked off to the feast hall as Thanksgiving dinner filled all the tables. Turkey, ham, corn, peas, baked and mashed potatoes, muffins of all sorts. Luna got a plate of food with Raspberry Witch Brewed Tea. She found a seat next to Jenny and she sat down with a smile.

"Hey, love, what was the hold-up?" asked Jenny while she cut a piece of turkey.

"Oh, Professor Raven wanted to talk about what had happened and told me to be careful. Then after dinner, I have to meet up with Professor Kanoe. I think he dislikes me... I haven't had his class yet."

Bree had overheard, and she walked over and smiled and took a seat with the two "he is scared they will lose the Snorkbie trophy to us.," Bree had poured a glass of Goblin Soda " it's going to be a rough game."

They had finished the dinner, and Luna made her way to Kanoe's classroom. On a desk were parchment paper and quill. "Sit, you are to write "I will not astral travel" you will write till that parchment paper is filled up." Said Kanoe with a grin while he sat at his desk. Luna sat and began to write This will be easy. Luna thought to herself whole she began to write.

Larry showed up, and Kanoe talked about if there had been another sighting of Mary. Larry had told him no word or sight of her. Luna had finished and made her way to turned it in " I am Finished." she handed it in.   He lifted his gaze to the paper and pushed it away, giving it right back to her " it is blank." he said coldly, she looked, and sure enough, it was blank. She took a seat and began to write again...-

Ray, Bella, Bree, and DJ laid in the courtyard under the bright stars in the cool air "can't believe she saved my life." said Bree.

" And she gets in trouble?" DJ's eyes rolled in disgust.

"I think we should beat them badly on Saturday." exclaimed Jenny as she walked over to the group, and laying down next to them, they waited for Luna to return.

"and we shall." said Bree with a smile while she stuffed her mouth with some turkey.

Chapter 12: Championship

The next day, Luna woke up in her bed. What laid next to her in the bed was the twelve-inch dagger with a slightly curved blade. The handle was wooden with rubies embedded into it. She stuffed the dagger in between the mattress of the bed. Jenny came out of the bathroom with a purple towel wrapped around her body "Happy Thanksgiving love." she walked over to Luna, and she leaned down and kissed Luna.

"So, I need to tell you something."

Jenny went behind her changing blind "what is that?" asked Jenny while Luna got up and grabbed her towel to go have a shower. She went into the steam-filled bathroom and turned on the shower.

"So, --- I can travel in my sleep, I left my body -."

Jenny stepped around the corner in her school uniform "you can do what?"

Luna slipped in the shower while she talked "I can astral travel, I left my body and went to Bree's room... I saw her..."

"Who, Bree?"

"No, Mary... She was standing over Bree, I stopped her from getting Bree's body. She tried and then tried to attack me. But a ghost saved me."

Jenny's eyes showed concern as she spoke out "astral travel is dangerous...," Jenny snapped out "hurry up, class is going to start."

Luna rolled her eyes, and she finished her shower. She got out of the bathroom, then went into the bedroom. She got dressed in her school uniform. - She finally met Jenny at the entrance of the dormitory. They walked out and down the spiral stairs in the tower till they reached the halls of the school. Professor Kanoe stepped out of his calls room and looked to Jenny then to Luna as they both felt their stomach drop.

"My classroom, Ms. Bell, Ms. Striff, get to class now." They both had looked at each other, and Luna walked into his cold classroom. His white Hellhound growled at her while it laid by his desk. Luna took a seat at a desk "Y-yes sir?" her voice broke out slowly in a tremble. And as always his voice, and gaze were so cold, he walked over to his desk.

"What happen this morning?"

She took a deep breath; she knew there was no way out of it or try to lie about it. "I saved a student's life." trying to get out of the bullet. His gaze didn't change as he nodded his head.

"Is that so, as I was told. Larry told me all about how you astral traveled." There was a coldness in his voice.

"I ca-." he had cut her off as he glared deathly towards her "SILENCE!," he roared out " Larry had told me how he saved you, I spoke to Raven about ALL this and she is going to extend her class to teach you all the protection blast. You broke school rules yet again. AFTER Thanksgiving dinner, you are to report to my classroom. NOW get to class."

He had seen her out of the classroom. He shut the door, and she made her way to math. *Was that a thank you?* She thought to herself as she made her way into her math class, finding her seat.

DJ and Ray went outside, went down to the large lake to skip some rocks. The fall winds blow chilly as it cut straight to the bone with its coldness, while they skipped some rocks. Kain and Colton came over to them. DJ's ears twitched as he heard a twig snap behind them. He and Ray turned around to face Kain and Colton.

"What do you two want?" snarled DJ as his hand moved to his back pocket to his wand.

"Came to see what the Wissard Club is up to. Haven't seen the worthless Bell in a while, still chasing after her dead daddy's footsteps?" Mockery was in Kain's voice as he chortled out. DJ's blood was now boiling, he cared for Luna a lot, his fingertips touched his wand.

"Kain, you may be pure-blood wizard, maybe rick, and may get away with a lot. BUT Luna is a half-blood, first-year witch... She is still twice, no three times the witch you are!" snapped out Ray. Colton stepped up, the large boy was twice the size of Ray and twice as many chins. He pointed to Ray.

"Come up here and say it to my face!" slowly he spoke as his gaze held Ray's.

"Colton, he is a Ward. That family is a broke joke. Four kids, the only good one is that Bella, she is the only one with brains and looks. She must have been adopted. She isn't as goofy looking

168

as your father, or as short and ugly and fat as your piggy mother. What do they do? OH yeah, your father works for the lowest side end of the job, he is at the Institution of Magickal Artifact Recovery. Your mom's what... Oh, a housewife." egging on as Kain spoke more. Ray's face grew as red as his hair, the truth was they were breaking but they made things work. His dad worked at the Institution of Magickal Artifact Recovery. as a paper pusher. His father had brilliant ideas, but he had been overlooked so many times for promotion.

DJ drew his wand quickly "shut up!" snapped DJ, his blood was boiling "*exorcismus*!" he shouted, Kain had covered his eyes and a large white light blasted out of DJ's wand, but the spell backfired. It blasted DJ back out of his boots and ten feet back into the water.

"DJ!" Ray yelled out of concern for DJ and turned to look for him. DJ had popped up out of the icy cold water. He started to swim over to the embankment.

"The idiot blew himself right out of his shoes." laughed out Kain as he spoke. They walked away and DJ pulled himself out of the water as he shivered.

"You were great, thanks for standing up for me. Not many people would of." smiled Ray as they walked back to the castle.

"Make sure you tell Luna; how great I was."

"You know she won't ever go for you."

"One can hope." They both laughed as they walked to the keep. - They had passed Professor Cook who was the Dibble-

Doggle history teacher, bald head, a large fellow with a large face, he had hazel eyes. "DJ, what happened, why are you soaking wet?," He looked out the large stained glass windows towards the sky, it was a clear sky "well it didn't rain did it. I don't see a cloud in sight."

DJ rolled his eyes as he wrapped his cloak around him to try to warm up "I decided to go swimming in the lake." he said sarcastically. He spoke as his teeth clattered. People walked by as they looked at him soaked and dripping wet.

"Why would you do something like that, you must be freezing my boy.," He looked to DJ "Go get dried off and drink some hot cocoa. IF you get sick you're still not getting out of that history homework."

"--- wouldn't ever think of it..." DJ rolled his eyes and he made his way up to the dormitory. He came into the common room of the Crowfeather Dormitory. The place was packed with Crowfeather students hanging out or working on homework.

"What had happened to you?" asked one of the older kids, he looked at DJ with a chuckle watching DJ dripping wet.

"I decided to go swi---.," He saw Luna and Jenny while they looked at him. "Ray and I were at the lake, the baby Loch Ness Monster was pulling in a wild unicorn colt. I had pulled out my wand.," Said DJ while he jumped around and jumped on the back of the couch behind people. Wand in his hand as he spoke loudly making this a big scene " went to cast a spell and the monster's tail dragged me in. I swam on top of the beast. It had let go of the baby unicorn; its large eyes locked onto me. I glared back and it let out a roar so loud,

"that I had to cover my ears, I let out a roar myself as I shouted *exorcismus*. The blast knocked it out and I had swum back to the embankment." Applause had erupted while DJ bowed his head while he looked gloriously towards the Crowfeather waving his arms over his head as if he was a champion of Crowfeather.

"What did Ray do?" asked Luna while people clapped DJ's back and gave high fives.

"Who? --- Oh, he wasn't there." DJ was lost in the moment as he replied. Luna and Jenny both look at each other doubtful at his story which he had retold a few more times. Each time he made it a bigger scene than the first time. He got up and went to shower as the room chanted "Beast Killer". Luna's eyes rolled "what do you think actually happened?" she asked Jenny.

Jenny had thought about it for a moment "probably fell in." they both laughed and got up and went to do their homework. They had fallen asleep and Luna finally woke up and moved through the tower, everything seem fine. She was out of her body as the whole dormitory was asleep.-

She went down to DJ's room and saw him asleep, her lips curled in an impish smirk, and she began to climb onto his bed. She had begun to jump up and down on it. His eyes widen and he shot awake flinging himself out of the bed, the mattress was bouncing then a pillow came floating towards him.

"G-guys!" DJ spoke scaredly as the other three students

171

woke up.

"What is it Beast Killer?" asked Worf Dunn, a black kid with dreads. The three-shot awake, and the pillow began to hit DJ

"HAUNTED PILLOW!" shouted DJ as it echoed throughout the dormitory. The pillow kept hitting him. The door opened to their room as it filled with students. They began to watch the pillow attack DJ, he shrieked out as Luna was having a blast. She went and hit Koty. The pillow fight broke out into the common room now. Then the second, third, and fourth yearers came down to see what the commotion was as they made it to the first years' common room.

"What is going o-" Morgan had stopped herself as a pillow came flying at her. The pillow smacked her as Jenny came down and her eyes widened. The room looked as if a dozen chickens had exploded as it was covered in feathers, before Jenny could pick up a pillow a voice exploded from the stairs.

"WHAT--- IS--- GOING --- ON?!"

Everyone jolted and had come to a stop. They looked towards the stairs and saw Bree standing tall at the top of the stairs. Feathers scattered across the room, pillows in everyone's hands and one floating pillow. "My pillow... It attacked me.," pointed out DJ as he pointed out to the pillow that floated by him. The pillow smacked him once again, and everyone laughed at him " I think it's haunted."

"Everyone back to your rooms.," Bree had pulled out her wand, and she pointed it to the pillow. Luna had dropped the pillow and ran to the other side of the room. "Revelare" a bright blue light that shot from the wand, and it hit the wall. The common room had got filled with blue shining light, showing bare footprints on the floor that a ghostly figure had left in her path. Luna was moving along the wall to the stairs by Bree. Everyone stared at the figured of Luna laughing. Bree ran up the stairs to the floor where Luna and Jenny were sleeping. They went into the room where she had slipped back into her body.

"OK, everyone, let's have some fun.," whispered Bree who had picked up a pillow off the floor and they all stood around Luna's sleeping body. "PST... Luna." whispered Bree ever so softly. Luna's eyes fluttered as she slowly woke up.

"Y-yes." she yawned out, stretching as she looked around. Pillows went flying around the room from the Crowfeather students. A large pillow fight had broken out. Laughter filled the room as an hour has passed...-

A couple of days have passed as the big game was going on today. Snow-covered the school grounds. Steam came from the pool. The winter wind blew across the school grounds as it howled through the hills. The school stands were completely filled with every student and professor in green winter robes. Banners had flown from the stands. The announcers were Mistress Flowers and Jewels, the Pre Lord of Golden Paw.-

Everybody was dressed warmly while they waited for

173

Bree's speech. They could hear the chanting from the stands, as they chanted for Crowfeather.

"This is it, not if but when we win, the trophy is ours. Time to take it from them, Kanoe is the referee, so make sure to play clean. He WILL do everything in his power to keep the trophy. They are up by twenty points, we will need to play hard defense. Keep the shots and hits low. When they cheat, do not play into it. He will throw you out of the game."-

"Introducing the Challenging team, making their way out of the left side of the field... Crowfeather!" the fans went crazy, fireworks had shot off exploding then a giant crow appeared in the fireworks while Jewels introduce the team.

They had swum out into the icy water. They waited for the other team as Professor Kanoe stood at the bottom of the pool "here is your Champions, Dracoîn!" cried out Jewels while everyone booed but the Dracoîn stand. Fireworks of green and black blew up creating a dragon. They came out as Kanoe pulled out the green and purple gem out and tossed it while Bree and stood staring a hole into Cecil.

"The two captains are staring each other down.," called out Jewels. The coin came down and it landed with the purple side up "Crowfeather had won the toss."

Kanoe looked at Bree as he spoke ever so coldly "Receive or Defend?"

174

"Receive."

"Shake hands and take your positions."

They shook hands, the grip was extremely firm from both sides before the grip broke. They had lined up taking their position till loud blast boomed out as the ball launched from the Dracoîn's side of the field. "The ball had shot down the field. Morgan Bowman, number 13, has the ball. Shawn Patterson Number 7 and Hunter Stokes number 8 are leading the blocks. A big hit by Eric Swift number 6, took out Shawn and Hunter. Here comes Penny Swift number 9. Both Queens are at it. Penny with the hi-.,

" NO! Morgan had thrown the ball to Bree Summers, Number 1, the Crowfeather's Captain. Bryan Whales, number 7 with an interception! Bree with the hit.," the fans went crazy while Jewels called the game. "They are lining up. Cecal calls for the ball, Dracoîn's line is holding the Crowfeathers. Here comes Morgan around the defense line, such a faster swimmer. Penny with a low hit, taking Morgan's knees right out from under her.,

"Come on Ref that is a foul! Cecil had thrown the ball to Traci Brews number 8, Luna with the - Traci had swum right over her. Here comes Bree, ouch Big Samhouse with a hard hit from behind. Traci with the throw, 20 points!," the Dracoîn clan had begun to cheer wildly as Traci showboated.

"Bree sets up the line, calls for the ball. What a missile that almost took Jenny's head off! Jenny caught the ball; she is on a break-away run. She had thrown the ball and... It had been blocked by Erica Nore Number 11, and she hands it off the Cecil. he is making a run for it, one juke, spin moved, dived over another what moves! Big shoulder hit, breaking Dan Brown's number 9 tackle. Here is the throw, --- fifty points!,

"Bree sets them up... Calls for the ball, she throws... No, it's a fake, she had broken in a run. Cecil and Penny are on their way to Bree, Bree with the throw to Morgan, Bree gets hit hard high, and low. "Come on Ref those hits are illegal they are going break Crowfeather's knees! --- Morgan with the throw, ten points!" Crowfeather had broken in a cheer while Bree rubbed her left knee. She glared as she watches Cecil get the ball, he had scanned the field as Jenny comes up with a tackle.

"Cecil steps back and gets ready to throw, OUCH what a crushing hit to Cecil's side by Jenny Striff! Trevor Nor number 5 gets the ball and makes a break-away swim for it. This is not fair one bit.," Crowfeather turned and watched in confusion as Trevor threw it and Matt was out of place.

"Matt is out of place, this shouldn't count. the ref calls for fifty points. He is saying the ball was a fumble." The crowd began to boo this time while Dracoîn's cheered.

"Bree gets the ball and she scans the field. WHAT- A- THROW! It was thrown from one end of the field to the other. Luna had caught the ball and throws the ball, fifty points! Crowfeather had cheered as banners flew.

"Cecil gets the ball and th- NO! Hunter Stokes, number 8 smacks it down and Timmy Moore number 13 falls onto it! Bree sets up and Luna moved further down to the left of the line. Jenny backs up just a bit, Bree calls for the ball.

"Morgan gets the hand off and she bulls around with th-, NO! Erica dives but it's a fake Bree launches the ball, fifty points! Crowfeather is down by ten points!"

Cecil got the ball and ran as one of the Crowfeather players dove at him. He jumped over and threw the ball as Amber caught the ball and gave a fake pass, then threw the ball to the goal.

"Matt had caught the ball, going to take more than that to get past Matt. Matt throws the ball to Luba."

Sam had tackle Luna hard before she had caught the ball, and the ball had hit the ground. Finally, the whistle was blown for hitting before the player had the ball. "Finally, he does something right. Luna gets set up at the goals. Erica is ready, Luna eyes Erica and the goals, and she makes the throw... Erica smacked it out of the way. Bree with the dive hitting it back up to goal... Ten points!,

"They are tied... What a comeback, the Crowfeather clan is going wild!" Crowfeather's banners were waving, and cheers filled the stand. Cecil glared as he got the ball and pump-faked it, then threw it to Penny.

"Cecil with the throw, Penny had caught the bal--- NO! Bree with the hit-making her drop the ball, Bree had recovered the ball. She is running it to the goal. She dodges one tackle, spins around another player, jukes another, and goes to thr--- NO! Cecil with a crushing hit!"

The whistle had blown, and Bree laid holding her left

knee, screaming in agony. Kanoe had made a stretcher appear and it floated over to Bree, she had got onto it and it floated off towards the locker room.

"Morgan, take the penalty shot for Bree." snarled out Kanoe as he looked sourer in the face now.

"What a cheap way to win if they do Morgan gets setup... She fires the ball annnnn-, it hit the rim and bounced off. Jenny dove and got the ball and throws it for... TWENTY POINTS!"

The fans go wild as Crowfeather is up by twenty points. They had lined up and Cecil gets the ball as Crowfeather is a player down. He threw the ball to Penny who is wide open. The other ball shot out, the line broke as Penny was on a breakaway swim.

"Morgan gets the Guardian ball, she goes and thro-, NO! Sam hits her hard, the ball is free. Cecil gets the ball and runs. Jenny comes up to Penny, Penny throws and scores ten points. Matt tosses the ball to Morgan, Morgan goes running, Penny hits her hard."

Penny had hit Morgan's nose with her forearm, knocking her down to the ground as blood gushed out of her nose.

"WHAT A CHEAP SHOT!" called out Jewels, Matt's eyes fell on Morgan as Cecil threw the ball for hundred points. Everyone booed as Crowfeather helped Morgan up, blood ran down from her nose.

"Your... Winner, still ch-Champions Dracoîn." exclaimed Jewels, but her voice was in disappointment while fireworks went off. Kanoe offered the trophy, to the Dracoîns. There was no celebration, no handshaking... Instead, they went straight to the locker room.

Bree had sat on the bench with ice on her knee, she had slipped back into her black shorts and a matching top. "Good job, team you tried your hardest. I-" Matt had cut her off as he hugged her.

"How is your knee?" everyone hugged her.

"Medic said I Will be on crutches till I can see the nurse." They all walked out of the locker room as the team celebrated. Professor Kanoe and Professor Raven shook hands. Bree hopped out with her team while they saw Dracoîn celebrating. The crowd came up with an uproar with chants except for the Dracoîn Clan filled the stands.

"CROWFEATHEATHER! --- CROWFEATHER!--- CROWFEATHER!"

Cecil sneered loudly "let's go." they walked off the field towards the school while the other three clans surrounded Crowfeather cheering for them.

Chapter 13: Christmas war games

The team had led Bree to the hospital wing. Madam Sunny took Bree and gave her a bed. Luna could see Zak and the other girl "how are they doing?" asked Luna while she looked at them with concern. Madam Sunny closed the Hospital curtains off to the beds.

"They should be back to normal before Christmas break. Thanks to Professor Petals in herbology and Professor Light in Alchemy and Potion. We came up with a reverse potion for the poison.," exclaimed Madam Sunny, happily smiling at the students. "Now, get to the feast hall for the celebration. You all have done great."

"- Thanks." the team said as they groaned out as they turned to walk off. Morgan had stopped in her tracks.

"Crap! I just had realized, *Christmas Wizard War Games* (*C.W.W.G.*) is just around the corner."

"What is Christmas Wizard War Games? Why do you sound worried?" Luna had spoken concerningly. She looked at Morgan then at the rest of the team. Timmy had walked up and shook his head.

"Don't sweat Mor, Madam Sunny can fix about anything. Wizard Games is in two weeks. Every day we will just have to practice, and IF Timmy has to he will ride in Bree's spot. Bella and

I are the best riders... AND to answer your question, Lu.," Matt had turned and looked down to Luna "*C.W.W.G.* is at the track in the walls, the long posts between the stadium seats. Two riders ride down on broomsticks, you blast each other with assorted spells except for *Repellere*. IF you knock the witch hat off, it is twenty-five points. IF you knock the person off the broom, it is fifty points. Four riders, if it is a tie then sudden death rule. Both captains go in the middle of the field with a wooden sword, shield, and wand. Whoever gets hit three times by lade or magick they lose." Matt had explained while they walked to the feast hall.

"That sounds so cool. Who is all on our team?" asked Jenny as they sat together at the Clan table as they began to eat dinner.

"Bree of course, myself, Bella, and Morgan." Timmy said, a short bulky kind with a flat top of brown hair and tan skin. His brilliant blue eyes met Jenny's eyes as he smiled. He took a sip of his Goblin Soda while owls, hawks, ravens, and crows had flown in and began dropping letters and some gifts to their owners. Luna had got a letter and she quickly open it.

Dear Luna,

Glad you are enjoying your new school and making all sorts of new friends, and that special someone. We have missed you so much and can't wait till you come home for Christmas break. Lucid had made captain for the Volleyball team again this year. They are in the playoffs AND no I haven't dated anyone yet. We had put the picture of you and that girl up on the fireplace mantle. You look so beautiful in your Halloween dress; I shall close up now and we will see you when you arrive at the bus station.

Love

Mom

PS: Lucid still wants your room.

Dinner had come to an end while Mr. Rune stood up and everyone grew quiet as he raise his left hand. "I want to thank you all for a good first half of the year. We have had dark times fall upon us, but we are pulling away from it. Christmas break is just coming up. IF you are going home or staying, let your Clan Professor know as soon as possible.,

"Pre Lords do not forget next weekend's first round of the Wizard Joust be ready with that. I won't see you until after Christmas break is over, I want to leave you with these words... Be Safe, Be Jolly and eat warmly."

That night, everyone was in the room studying for their exams. The door to the common room opened as Bree came into the room with crutches in hand and a blue knee sleeve while everyone made room for her to sit down. "How are you feeling?" asked Matt while Bella got Bree a plate of Thanksgiving dinner with Bree's favorite drink, Pumpkin Spicy Lotta.

"I am fine, crutches for the week and the sleeve for a month Madam Sunny had told me to take it easy, but as we.," Morgan had gone and tried to interrupt but Bree waved Morgan off " know the War Games are just right around the corner. I had already got word we are the second tier. We are the second weekend, Friday thru Sunday.,

"We are going to face Chimerador. We best be ready for them. Every day we will train, and after we win it will be Christmas break! Then once we are back from Christmas break. Then it will be for the Championship!" Everyone had cheered while a peacock feather had been passed around and everyone had signed the sleeve then went back to studying. -

The morning had come, and Luna had stuffed her bag with books, ink, jars, and quills. She headed to the dining hall for breakfast with Jenny. Snow had fallen hard throughout the night, and everything had frozen over and got covered. In the show, it was surely a beautiful winter wonderland.

Some of the students were out having snowball fights, building a snowman, and some older students had enchanted the snowman's items (hats and scarves, or wooden pipe), and the snowman would have come alive. Luna thought this was the best thing ever. She walked with the group of hers as they all hugged and wished each other the best of luck.

Luna and DJ went to their math class and took their seats. Professor Brooks had done the roll call and handed out their exams. Luna sat with quill in hand doing her classwork. She grew frustrated with it, she hated math. Half of an hour later some of the students had turned their work in. The hell had r-ung, and Luna was the last one to turn her work in.

"How do you think you did?" asked DJ while Luna had come out. She walked with him, and Ray had met up with them.

"I believe I blew it.," cried out Luna " I hate math." -

They walked into Introduction to World of Magick. The three had found their seats and sat down, Professor King had handed out their exams. Luna read through it and answered the questions.

122) What was the first wand ever used?
A) Stick of enchanted
B) Twigs gave from Goddess Gaya
C) Lonely finger
D) Whatever you could enchant.

She had answered through with confidence. She had turned in the work and the bell had finally rung. They went out talking about how long the test was. Then Jenny had popped up with a big grin "WELL, hello Cheer bear, why are you so cheerful on exam day?" asked DJ sarcastically while Jenny's smile couldn't break.

"I made 100's on my English and Alchemy and Potions." said Jenny growing more confident while she walked down the hall.

"How do you know?" asked Ray as they walked into History of Magick People. Before Jenny could answer, Luna had spoken up for her.

"OH, trust me... She's been reading her books and mine every single day and night" everyone laughed while they went into the room. They all four went to take a seat at their table. Professor Dunn had come into the classroom and given the exam papers out as she, then she had sat down after she passed out the exam paper and done a headcount. Luna didn't care much for the class. She looked around the room and saw Jenny was answering the questions very quickly as if this was a race.

3) What Wizard is the greatest of all time, he helped a young boy, took him in, and the boy became a king. He was a very powerful Wizard in spell casting, alchemy, and potions.

A) Merlan

B) Marvin

C) Moses

D) Merlin

Luna had got halfway through the text as she filled in the answers with her quill.

130) What famous Dibble-Doggle was a famous Alchemist?

A) Martha Washington

B) John Handcock

C) Benjamin Franklin

D) Merlin

Finally, the test had come to an end, Jenny had turned in her exam in just under twenty minutes. Luna had turned hers in just under the hour mark. Lunch had been canceled so the exams could finish quickly and free the students up.

Jenny and Luna were off to science as they went in, their eyes had widened as they saw Zak, the rat boy who had been found in the bathroom petrified. Everyone had welcomed him back as he couldn't remember a thing from his state.

Kain and Zak had sat with each other, while Jenny and Luna had sat in front of them. Professor Tristan came into the classroom and welcomed back Zak and then he did a headcount. He had passed the exams out to every student, Zak had taken the exams in his hands and began to scan through it.

"How is it fair for numbskull here to take the exam since he has been out for a month and a half?" asked Kain.

"Shush it, and work on your exam." said Professor Tristan as he pulled out his wand, and with a mumble, a swish, and a flick of his wrist a spark popped from his wand, and Kain's mouth glued shut.

"Now everyone, get back to work." barked Professor Tristan. -

Zak had laid in the hospital room, after school each professor had read his studies to him. Told him spells, how to make certain potions. When they were done they had tapped his forehead with the wand sealing the lesson in his head. -

They went through the science exam as Luna had struggled with this exam. Jenny yet again had finished in fifteen minutes. Again, an hour had passed and Luna had turned the exam in. The class had let out, Kain's mouth had unglued now, and everyone had laughed "I would love to learn that spell." whispered Luna, and Jenny had nodded her head in agreement.

They had made it to the last class, the last exam. Basic Spells first year, they all went in, and Luna had sat with Jenny. Professor Raven had greeted everyone while the classroom filled up.

"Hello class, and welcome back Zak." greeted Professor Raven and she began to hand out the exam. Luna had begun to work on the exam while she read the questions.

3) What spell is used to fill up a bowl, cup, or tank with water?"

A) Complere

B) Inanis

C) Caeli

D) None of above

20) What spell is used to make something float?

A) Mergi

B) Aquae Supernatet

C) Demergere

D) Aqua Amet

150) What spell is used to repel demons?

A) Daemonium

B) Exocris

C) Exspiravit

D) Exorcismus

Classes had finally ended. Winter break was now almost here, and they had such a large feast dinner, and everyone was so cheerful and excited for this. After dinner, Crowfeather had gone and trained for the war games. Luna, Jenny, DJ, and Ray had gone to see Maîq. He was now cutting some firewood behind his cottage.

"Hey Maîq." they called out to him and smiled while they greeted him. Large snowflakes had fallen now as the snow was knee-deep.

"Salve ya all?," he stopped and welcome them inside as he made some hot witch brewed tea for them "how was ye scribendae (exams)?" asked Maî, he had moved some hides out of the way so they could sit on the couch. Everyone had shrugged their shoulders.

"It was fine." everyone agreed while the fire had crackled.

"WELL I did superbly." said Jenny smiling with her eyes sparkling as she gloated.

"Ye all heading home or staying?" Maîq took a sip of his tea while he asked.

"I am staying, dad has work in the Northern Middle East in

the Dibble-Doggle Realm." exclaimed DJ as he leans backed on the couch with glass in hand as he looked miserable.

"I am heading back home to California." Jenny smiled while she placed the empty mug down.

"I am going back home myself." smiled Luna while she can't believe she had been here for three and a half months.

"We are just spending time at home." said Ray while they talked a bit more. They had finally walked out back to the keep, a snowman slid right past them on a slay. They made it to the castle, they had caught part of the last practice.-

Bree had hopped over to them, leaned down making a snowball, and thrown it at Jenny. Dane came up and picked up Bree "RAWR!" and Dane had roared out as he twirl her around in his arms. "Hey Furbreeze, how are you feeling?" Dane had asked in a concerned voice.

"God, just been practicing getting ready to kick your butt." smiled Bree as she poked Dane's nose. Once he had placed her down on the ground, Luna and Jenny both threw snowballs at Dane and Bree. A giant snowball fight had broken out, each one threw a snowball while Bree sat on the ground.-

The bell had rung finally to call for dinner. Dane had helped Bree to her feet, everyone went off to the hall and sat down to eat. Jenny stole a muffin off of Bella's plate. Everyone had been cutting up and having a fun time. After dinner, they went up to the

189

dormitory, Luna went into her room to change.

Her eyes widen as she saw that her mattress had been flipped. Everyone came into the room "what happened here?" someone cried out as a murmur broke out between students. Luna's stomach tightens the dagger was gone. Bree hopped into the room finally.

"Wha-what happened?" They had fixed the room back and Professor Raven had come into the room.

"Is anything missing?" she questioned Bree, Luna shook her head no.

"Someone had to have the password." stated Professor Raven while she glanced at each student as if studying them. She had pulled students out one by one to question them about it. She had left the room, Luna sat on the bed as it grew late. Jenny sat on Luna's bed next to her and they talked for a good bit till Jenny laid in her bed and passed out. Luna had laid in bed thinking about the last few months from the letter, the bus ride, making the dwarf upset at the bank.

Buying her first wand, how crazy that experience was from the candles blowing up to getting her ten-inch willow with griffin feather. Meeting Kain for the first time by shoving him down when he had picked on her sister. On the bus ride when she met DJ and Jenny. When DJ tried to turn the bumblebee, the spell had failed. Then the first time on a cruise, how her, Jenny, and DJ hung out. They had become really good friends with Bella. Then at breakfast, her oatmeal had blown up.

The long carriage ride, out to the castle over the mountains then--- that moment, that scary cold deathly feel savage moment of peeking into the dark cauldron... Luna's eyes had widened it wasn't Mary reaching for her. That cold dead wrinkled hand, who's was it?

Then her heart filled with joy. When she had scored points for her clan, then later on she had lost those points. She had remembered how she and Maîq had become really good friends when she was doing all those punishments for sneaking out. Her two favorite things were being taken to the Samhain party by Jenny, and the other was surprisingly she isn't a sports girl, but it was making the team and becoming MVW in the first game. As she replayed the moments in her head she had drifted to sleep. -

Friday was finally here; the whole castle was in an uproar of excitement for the first round of Christmas War Games. The school courtyard had been turned into a bunch of games, markets of many traveling shops. They had sold all sorts of stuff (crystals, incense, potions, wands, cloaks, and so much more). They had carriages of different foods and a pillory for insulting people. There were so many people from other schools and other regions.

Luna had worn her casual jeans and a sweater with the heavy winter cloak. She had made her way through the crowd looking for someone she knew. Then she heard something that caught her attention.

"Professor Tristan, I hate your boring science class. A-and

191

you smell like a troll's behind." a boy from Goldenpaw had yelled out. Professor Tristan had been locked up in the pillory. It cost one silver Shantie to insult a teacher of your choice. Then she heard a voice call out.

"Luna !--- Luna!--- Luna!"

Luna had turned and seen Jenny, DJ, and Ray coming running towards her. DJ had a large turkey leg in his hand, Ray had a funnel cake, and Jenny had two small bags.

"Hey everyone, what is this? Annnd why did no one wake me up?," exclaimed Luna. She looked at Jenny's bags " been shopping without me?" chuckled Luna.

"Yep, you looked like you needed your beauty sleep. For the shopping, I got my mom some jewelry.," exclaimed Jenny as they watch a few people play human chess. "This is the Christmas Wizard War games. It lasts all weekend, and it will be back next weekend for the next games."

They saw people sword fighting, live Dungeon and Wizards while people been zapped and they appeared on a crystal ball while they played. "They have it all, want to play some games?" asked DJ while he had finished his turkey leg.

"Sure." said everyone as they began to play human chess, Luna was the knife, DJ was a pawn, Ray was the rook, and Jenny was the Queen. The host told everyone where to move. The other host had told his pieces where to move. DJ had moved up two spots, the other pawn moved up two. Luna moved up two and one left, followed by the other team's Bishop. The game went on, DJ had taken out two pawns and a knight, Luna had taken out a pawn, another knight, and Ray held the king in place. Jenny jumped from spot to spot dancing across the board. DJ got taken out by their Queen.

Luna moved up to the King "checked" the King moved away, a pawn had moved between the King and Luna. Then Luna got taken out by the bishop. The game had gone on till Jenny got pinned and then taken out by the other Queen. Ray slides across the board taking out their Rook "check" the King moved away as a Bishop takes their pawn. The other team's Bishop had taken Ray out after a few more minutes "checkmate" their team had lost.

"Well, that was fun." said Ray happily while the horns blew in the distance. Everyone had run towards the stands at the track taking a seat. Mistress Flowers had stood from her throne and taken the stage in front of the massive crowd.

"Welcome everyone to OwlHollow, I am the Vice Mistress here at OwlHollow, my name is Mistress Velvet Flowers. I would just like to thank each and everyone for coming out to our Christmas Wizard War Games," everyone had cheered as she waved her hand and spoke again.

"This sport has been around for only three years, our dear Headmaster Robert Rune had come up with it. It is called Wizard Jousting. It is made up of four teams, each team has four jousters. They will fly down the track and shoot a spell at each other trying to score points for the team. Twenty-five points to knock the witch's hat off, and if you knock them off the broom it is fifty points. If you miss, once you pass the post. You can ride in and salute with the other and forfeit, the winner will be awarded twenty points. If neither wants to surrender, they can ride back out and try again.,

"If a tie happens then sudden death comes into play. Each Guardian Captain will meet in the middle with a sword (wood), shield, and wand. First to player gets hit three times loses it is best of two of three wins.," The crowd exploded in excitement.

"LET--- THE-- GAMES --- BEGAN!" shouted Mistress in flowers as she raised her wand up and shot off a dozen of colorful fireworks into the sky as they exploded. Bree was announcing the game with Dane, the jousting area was in the middle of a long oval track in the courtyard. Each side housed two locker rooms. Eight stands on each side of the field surrounding the track.

"Coming out on the right side of the field, riding for Goldenpaw... Number five, Kat Bossingham! --- Number three, Kevin House!--- Number ten, Charles Blaine!, and the Pre Lord, the team captain Number 1, Jewels Meadows!" Bree spoke with excitement as Goldenpaw flew in as each was called out. They flew over the crowd then had landed at the center of the field.

The fans went crazy while Goldenpaw flew overhead cheering. The riding gear was steel helmets with clan color pinstripe, making the image of the three-headed dog. Black leather robe on the shoulders that had steel pads on the shoulders with their number on it in yellow. Black leather pants with the name of the clan stitched in them, the clan cloak with the guardian on them were stitched. Then knee-high black boots and black bracers with yellow pinstripe and black gloves.

"Coming out from the left, riding for Dracoîn number eight, Big House Sam Whyte!--- Number five, Traci Brews!---Number 6 Amber Lyght, --- and the Pre Lord, the captain, he is the man-eater of the worlds, from the dark abyss, number 1 Cecil Bloke!" roared out Dane. They had flown out of the gate in the order they were announced, they flew over the fans then met the other team on the field. Each team went and sat on their bench. Dracoîn's uniform was the same but black and green. Luna and Jenny sat in the stands watching the teams fly overhead. "GO Jewels!" cried out Luna and Jenny. They sat watching as Bree began to call the game.

"The first jouster is in the lineup for Golden paw is number three, Kevin House, and from Dracoîn number five, Traci Brews!," excitedly Bree had announced out. Kevin and Traci met at each end of the hundred foo riding rail.

"There is the kick-off, some of those brooms can top out at a hundred and twenty miles per hour. Here they go! Traci with *Augu*, shooting a fireball at the head of Kevin, Kevin! He had cast *Aqua Pila*, a wave of water had put her fireball out. She got hit hard, what a crash!" Dane called the action. -

Kevin and Traci had jumped from the ground then flew at each other. Traci's Falling Star broom was slightly faster than

Kevin's Shoot for the moon broom. Dust of snow had left in the trail of their take-off. Traci had pulled her wand out with her left hand while her thighs and knees hugged the brook, right hand held the broom steady as Kevin held his wand with his right hand.

" *Augu.*" Traci shouted shooting a large fireball out of the tip of her wand, the blast went towards Kevin's face. " *Aqua Pila.*" Kevin yelled out to counter the fireball, the fireball had got put out with a large water ball engulfing the fireball, then hitting hard in the face of Traci's. The water had splashed up in her visor and eyes. It had caught her off guard, the tip of the broom handle caught the post and caused her to be thrown over the broom.

Goldenpaw had roared out as they had scored fifty points. Luna had cheered on, she had some fire-roasted peanuts, Ray bought some candy, the candy Dragonflies flew around him. The second run was Number five, Kat Bossingham against Number six, Amber Lyght. The crowd had watched as they flew at each other.

Amber rolled out of the way and blasted Kat's hat off, scoring twenty-five points. Cheers echoed through the stadium.

Third run number ten, Charles Blain came up against number one, the Pre Lord and Captain, Cecil Bloke, they kicked off the ground hard. Luna and her crowd had cheered for Charles, then a loud set of boos had echoed as a very bright, blindingly light came from Cecil's hand. Charles had been blinded and nose-dived into the ground crashing into the rail, Dracoîn was up by twenty-five points.

"Final joust of the day, Number one, Pre Lord and Captain,

Jewels Meadows riding against number eight Sam Whyte!" Bree had introduced the last riders.

"The kickoff, both are on Falling Sar brooms. They are flying across the field. Sam with *Augu*, Jewels with the barrel roll, the fireball went right over her shoulder. Jewels popped off with Augu but missed. What actions--- Can I get mustard on my wiener?," Dane called the action, he had covered the microphone but the fans still heard him as they broke out in laughter. Bree had elbowed him.

"Here they go back, Jewels- NO! Her wand had dropped out of her hand! Sam with Praemium the ground blew up under her, throwing her into the stadium wall making her fall off."

"What a fight! Dracoîn wins the first War Game, come back tomorrow for Goldenpaw versus Dracoîn for War Two." said Dane as the crowd dispersed from the stands, Luna and the gang had caught the last act of a man-eating a dozen swards.

"Gross, how does he do it?" Luna had asked in a surprised manner after the show, Luna and Jenny went window shopping at some of the traveling wagons. They looked at some dresses, jewelry, and some art. Then a sign caught their eyes. In a large glass dome jar was brown hair, blue eyes, small fairy. Wearing a small blue dress, the wings had been plucked.

~ *Has things come up missing around the house?* ~
No idea how things went from one place to another? No fear it is fairies, they are mischievous and pranksters. Pluck the wings and they have no more magick.

197

Try our Fairy be gone spray.

Luna had shaken her head "how cruel is that?" she murmured out to Jenny who had nodded in agreement. They walked around, the time had passed as they went to the dormitory, the crowd went to their camps or to the nearest town. -

Jenny had put the bags away, Luna sat on the bed "show me what you got your mom."

"Oh, it is already put away." said Jenny who had changed in her gown. She pulled out a book to read A boy and his dragon then it dawns on Luna, the billboard about the fairy...The missing dagger "we have a fairy!" she shouted out by mistake, Jenny had lowered her book and peered over it "what?"

"Oh, we have fairies in here, just dawned on me. The night when my bed was tossed. Explained Luna.

"What came up missing?" asked Jenny, she had put the book down and sat up on her elbows looking at Luna.

"--- Oh, ... Nothing too important." Luna's voice shook lightly while she told Jenny. In fact, it was Bloody Mary's Knife that came up missing.

"I am sure it will pop up somewhere." reassured Jenny as they all crawled under the blankets. They had fallen asleep that night... -

Luna was in the spirit world moving through a long hall, a

scream in the distance, she had run to the voice it was Brees... She open the doors, behind that door was a brick wall. She had turned around and seen Jenny standing in the middle of the hall.

Their eyes had met in the low-lit hall "JenJen!" Luna moved forward; Jenny's voice was cold "- what did you do?"... Why did you do this, why did yo-?" Luna's eyes had widened in shock and despair.

"W-what did I do?" asked Luna shook up, Jenny had fallen forward, the knife, that knife of Bloody Mary's was in Jenny's back. Luna reached out and grabbed Jenny, Jenny's body had vanished. It was annihilated, her body burst into smoke, then blue butterflies flew from the smoke cloud of Jenny. Tears had filled Luna's eyes.

A figure came out of a room, in a bloody gown there stood was Luna. Luna's spirit stared in those bright multi able color eyes of her own. Then the body of Luna's head cocked to the side, let out a screech of terror as the body ran to the spirit of Luna "NOOOOO!" Luna had covered her eyes and bright light, warm feeling bathe through her a sense of hope, courage, and intellect. She uncovered her eyes, the creepy grin on Luna's face the bloody dagger was a millimeter from Luna's now strong gaze, a gaze that would break even the darkest of hearts. The creepy grin on Luna's face slowly faded out to a more sorrowful quiver frown, the eyes had widened, while Luna had shoved forward " I am not afraid of... YOU!" spat out in rage and sorrow for Jenny, Lunna pulled out her wand.

199

"*Perfectus Exorcismus*!"

A strong blinding yellowish-gold light blasted out of the wand, the room grew brightly, Luna had to look away from it. A gust of wind swept through the corridor of the halls. A scream of horror echoed then died off. The gust was strong enough to blow and lift Luna's hair as if standing by a turbine, the light died down, the body had turned to black ashes, black butterflies fluttered, then slowly burst into flames. -

"... Wake up, hey wake up."

Behind darkness, eyes flickered, Luna's eyes slowly open as a bright light hit her in the face. Jenny's gorgeous face peered down with a smile. "Morning love, let's get some breakfast and see the wonders that have come." eagerly Jenny had spoken who was already dress.

"I hate you, school is out, and yet-" Luna peered up at her clock before Luna could have finished Jenny spoke up.

"It is nine, breakfast ends in an hour, by the time you get ready. You will maybe have a crumb of a muffin." thwarted Jenny, Luna had got up and fixed her gown. She walked to the bathroom " I am trying to watch my girly figure for you." sarcastically Luna cried out as she tittered.

It had fallen on deaf ears, Jenny was already in the common room with DJ, Bella, and Bree. Luna looked at the blackout mirror *It- it was only a dream.* She thought to herself with a sigh of relief, tears had filled her eyes as she got in the shower.

Twenty minutes had passed, and Jenny had yelled.

"You coming?!"

Silence had fallen, then Luna yelled back "-yeah, give me a few minutes."

Bree grabbed her crutches as everyone got their winter cloaks "we will meet you at the dining hall!" shouted Jenny.

"O... OK, see you in a bit." Luna had gotten dressed, her hair in thick pigtails, and her make-up. She dropped the blush powder brush. She had reached down under the table and froze... What she felt wasn't the powder brush, she felt a cold ivory handle, she redrew her hand slowly, and in her hand was the dagger. She had frozen looking at what seemed to take a part out of you. To hold it, it fills you with the coldness of mourning. She had put the knife in her bag and ran down to meet the others. She sat between Bella and Jenny.

"Sorry I am late."

There were about fifteen minutes left of breakfast as they talked, laughed, and ate. "Goldenpaw better win or it is over." acknowledge Bree as everyone agreed, then they headed out to the festival.

Everything was about the same, there had been new games, shows, and markets. The Dark Moon Elves had come from the far east of Crystal Region, from the Crystal Forest. They had archery games, a market wagon with Enchanted things for sale. Then later that night, the fair ladies of the Dark-Moon Elves choir were having a ceremony that evening.

201

The Dark Moon Elves were a beautiful race, tall and slender, athletic shape, hair as dark as raven feathers, to blonde as gold, their eyes were brilliant, sparkling blues, greens, and hazels. The skin was a soft honey cream tint. On each shoulder under the collar bone had a crescent moon. In the middle of the chest was a full moon. It had shown the phases of the moon.

They had walked around the festival and seen a woman. She was juggling knives, torches that were on fire, and even juggling maces. Luna and Jenny watched the act and then moved on to the archery. Kain was in line with Zak and Colton. Luna and Jenny had overheard Kain talking to Zak. "Stand there, put this apple on your head, and I will shoot it off." said Kain trying to give Zak the apple.

"I already died once... "squeaked out Zak who's face still shown terror. Luna and Jenny walked off as they both agreed *that you have to be an idiot and stand there to let Kain fire an arrow at you.*

They went and seen the Griffin ride. For one ruby Shantie, you can ride the Griffin. The Griffin was a giant bird beast, with paws large enough that could easily lift two full-grown five-ton elephants with ease in each of its paws. For one silver Shantie, you could get your picture made, for three silver shanties, you can get a moving picture. The one ruby was to ride it and get a moving picture made. The line was pretty long as Jenny was excited and looked at Luna.

"Come on, let's go for a ride!," said Jenny holding Luna's

hand. Luna's shanties were running a bit low, she had one ruby and six silver shanties. She bit her lip "I will pay." cried out Jenny whole Luna nodded her head. She now had no choice, not that she didn't want to go for the ride. She didn't like having people pay for her.

After what had seemed like an hour, they had finally reached the Griffin and Jenny paid the Griffin Keeper. "Don't pull 'is feathers, he 'ont like dat. Hold on ta da rope, he will fly round da castle, ova da mountains n back 'ere." explained the toothless bear size of a man. Jenny held the reigns and Luna held onto Jenny, the wings expanded out and a sound of thunder crackled from the large bird. They flew up and Luna let out a squawk and held on tightly to Jenny.

They overlook the whole schoolyard as they flew around, they seen the war games going on. "Look, it is tied twenty-five to twenty-five. Maybe Goldenpaw can win this." pointed out Jenny, they had flown over the Illusion Forest, then over Troll Head Mountain as the view was glorious from the sky. A bug that looks like a lightning bug but, much larger in size than a full-grown tomcat.

"Luna, come lean up here. It is a shutter fly. It's going to take our picture." explained Jenny in joy. Luna had leaned forward she thought how queer this was to get your picture made. They waved, then kissed. The shutter fly's eyes flashed it had lasted all along from the wave and through the kiss.

They began to fly back over the game, and the score was

now twenty-five to fifty "look, Goldenpaw is in the lead, one more win, and it goes to game three." pointed out Jenny. Each time the Griffin flapped its massive wings, thunder clapped loudly. They had finally landed, and the man plucked the wings of the shutter fly with a flick of his wrist. The wings had turned into a photo. The photo had shown Luna and Jenny waving then kissing in front of the sunset.-

They had run back to the stadium while Bree's voice could be heard over the speakers "a bright blast of blue light from Cecil, making Kat eat the dust." Some of the crowd had cheered, and some had booed. "Game is over and for this week Dracoîn had advanced to the finals. Come back next week and watch Chimerador beat Crowfeather!" cried out Dane as he announced the results.

"You wish, Crowfeather all the way!" said Bree in the enthusiasm in her voice. It was always a hoot to be around and listen to Bree and Dane picking at each other.

"The Moon elves' choir is about to start!" said Ray as he and DJ ran past Luna and Jenny. They had chase after the two boys and found seats up in front.

The stage was large with royal blue curtains, and the stage had curved slightly with lights shining in front. It had grown late at night by this time, The beautiful stary night, now clouds insights as the large full moon had shone down on them, casting its beautiful light down. Lights of different colors had lit the stage "this is so romantic." smiled Jenny while her voice was joyful. She held Luna's hand as soft music could be heard behind the curtain, from harps, violins, pianos. While the curtains slowly open up revealing the Dark Moon Elves. They stood in white gowns, and the elves not playing instruments were holding candles.

♪♪♪♫
LA LA LE IA IA IA
The earth- the wind- the fire- the water, let your glory rain down on us
♪♪♪♫♪♪
LA LA LE IA IA IA
Let the wind blow - Let the thunder rumble- Let the rain come down to shower our sorrows away.
♫♫♫
IA IA IA
Raise your hands up to the Gods and Goddess, deliver us to salvation from this evil we have done in us. Show us the path to this sacred land.
♪♪♪
LA LA LA LA A
On the night of a stary night, no cloud in sight, the Goddess in full white gazing down from the stary night.
♪♪♪
LA LA LA LA A
Let the wind blow- Let the fire fall- Let the wick burn down to lite

the candle on the altar of this ritual for growth and protection.
♪ ♪ ♪
LA LA LA LA A
The earth- The wind- The fire - The water, let your glory shower down on us for this sacred land. We shall dance to glorify your Godliness.
♪ ♪ ♪ ♫
LA LA LE LA A
The earth- The wind- The fire- The water, let your glory rain down on us and for our protection on this night of a stary night with no clouds in sight, the glorious Goddess in full white be our savior tonight.
♪ ♪ ♪
LA LA LE LA LA
The Earth- The wind- The fire- The water.
♪ ♪ ♪ ♫
LA LA LA LE IA IA IA

The angelic voices came to an end, the dancing from the Moon Clan Elves came to a stop of their graceful ballet. The peaceful strumming of the strings of the harp slowly died down and the beat of the powerful drums had stooped. Applause had erupted from the crowd while cheers filled the stand.

A Moon Elf had stepped upholding a goblet and she now had spoken up " May our ritual be sacred. Let our dance be seen and let the strings of our instruments be sustenance and let the might drum be entrusted. Let our song be heard and glorified."

Two elves had walked up with a cup in their hand as they walked in a big circle pouring salt on the ground on the stage. They brought an old podium with a star and crescent moon engraved on the front of it. Another elf had placed an incense stick in a holder and placed it on the altar. He walked away and another male elf walked to the girl holding the goblet and a dagger. He had placed it on the altar.

"What is this about?" whispered Luna lowly while she watched the Dark Moon elves, Jenny had shrugged her shoulders. The girl elf spoke again, her voice was soft and peaceful.

"Goddess of the moon who glows brightly, let the salt that which was poured on the ground protect us.," another elf walked up with sage burning and fanning the smoke around the circle. "Let the sacred sage of the smoke banish all evil that wishes us harm and give us temptation."

Another elf had walked up and placed a cup of water by the circle at the south side of the circle. "Let this water be blessed, to become Holy. Let the water soak in your light that no evil can ever prevail." Another male brought a red candle. He had placed it by the circle opposite side of the water, the north side of the circle.

"Goddess, your mighty, wisdom, and caring are so powerful. So righteous, let our candle burn as it is the beacon of the sanctuary. Let the watchtowers from east to west, south to the north. Let them see the mighty flame burn in your glory. Let them migrate from close to afar. Let them help bring in the new moon, the new Goddess."

A goblet of wine had begun to be passed around in the crowd and on the stage. The woman spoke before the drink had been passed around. "Goddess, let this wine be blessed and allow it to be passed around and shared. As we are children of the Goddess. Allow the wine to represent your beauty, wisdom, and care. Let us gain beauty, wisdom, and care from the sip of this wine." She signaled the goblet to be passed around.

The male and female elf in the circle had sipped the wine that was in the goblet that she brought on stage with her. The goblet had got passed around. Luna had sniffed it and her nose twisted after she had sniffed it and her lips quivered. Jenny laughed at her. Luna sipped the wine and quickly passed the goblet to Jenny. She took the goblet and had sipped it and passed it on.

Then a piece of bread was brought out on a silver platter. The woman spoke again before the bread got passed around the crowd for everyone. "Goddess of the moon, let us break bread on this night to fulfill our hunger and replenish our strength. As you are our savior and protector, let everyone fill full and mighty that eats from your flesh.,

"As you grow older and wiser. Let us rejoice and let you go on to the slumber land to rest. While we bring care and joy to the new Goddess." she had signaled for the breaking of the bread, and it was passed around. People broke bread and ate a piece of it. Luna was glad to get rid of the taste of that wine from her mouth.

After they had drunk the wine and ate the bread, the

woman began to speak once again "everyone takes a hold of each other hands and say this with us "Let our new strength be multiplied by three folds, allow the Goddess to be able to rest peacefully and our new Goddess take her place, as the dagger represents the God and the Goblet represent the Goddess.,

"Let the dagger and goblet fusion together to bring in the new Goddess into the place of the caring and righteous one. Let the new Goddess have the strength to be able to have the foresight and foretell to bring us clarity and rejoice. So mote it be."

As the crowd and the other elves say this, the female elf who Luna had now acknowledge is to represent the Goddess. The other male elf holding the dagger lit the candle. He was representing God. He now had spoken clearly.

" I light this wick to represent the brightness and warmth of the love and care that course through my body and soul for you. As I unsheathe my dagger and show you my glorious blade." he had removed the sheath of the dagger showing the beautiful ruby and gold fusion of the blade.

The crowd watched in awe while the (Goddess) spoken "let the candle represent whom I truly am bright, beautiful, and sacred. Let your wick burn to cause the wax, the tears of the candle, flowing freely as it shows how true you are of the care and joy you have and the unconditional love you show."

Jenny had squeezed Luna's hand and leaned over and whispered in her ear "you are my candle." said Jenny in a lovely tone while she stroked Luna's hand with her fingers causing Luna to blush. "Your my wick." replied Luna while their fingers laced and she kissed Jenny's hand as the Goddess spoke again. "As our love burns, it shows that love is bounded and true that together in pure harmony. Love is sacred. As my goblet lays empty, unfilled, unbarred, and unsatisfied.," the Goddess took the golden goblet and tilted it. showing it was empty and held it up in her hands and spoke more.

"I know your love is pure and true from how bright you show. I open myself up to be taken and protected eternity by you."

He places the blade into the goblet and spoke "I slide my dagger into your goblet, so you are fulfilled, bared, and satisfied. As we are fused, we are one with mother earth, Gods and Goddess, and ourselves.,

"The love and emotion are threefold stronger." she spoke after him "As you fulfill, bared, and satisfied my emptiness. I am to bear your gift and to deliver your gift. A daughter on the night of the passing of the Goddess. Let our daughter be taken to replace our Goddess, as we are children of the Gods and Goddess. So, our daughter is theirs for the righteousness taking, for our daughter is the newborn Goddess." They had placed the goblet and dagger on the altar as the candle burned, wax waterfall down the candle. God spoke yet again. "As I know you are fully satisfied. I slide the dagger out as my love burns for you even more. I sheath my blade which is bound to your goblet and only to your goblet. My blade shall not touch any other goblets. I acknowledge that if my dagger touches any other goblets that sorrow, and unfaithfulness will fill

210

those goblets. Causing my dagger to rust, breakdown, and to be broken, and I Will strip my dagger and toss it away."

The Goddess spoke after him " as my goblet lays unfilled but fully satisfied. My love is filled with you. My goblet is bound to your dagger and only to yours. My goblet shall not be touched by any other daggers. I acknowledge that if my goblet is touched by any other daggers that unfaithfulness and ungodly will be filled my goblet to bear a child will never fulfill my goblet again, the venom will curse my goblet, poisoning all other daggers."

"Let the candle of love burn all night when the flame goes out. The new Goddess is born. So mote it be." they both had said while everyone said it right afterward.

"So mote it be."-

It was late by now and they had left the dagger in the goblet with the candle burning all night. Everyone broke away to go to their tents, to the nearest towns, and the students had gone to the dormitories. Luna didn't change to her sleepwear. She had fell face first on her bed and passed out. Jenny had changed to her shorts and tank top and went to bed herself. -

A couple of days had passed, Luna and DJ sat in the feast hall, he had smiled at her, and he leaned over and took a sip of her Pumpkin Spice Latte. She had turned and faced him; her face screwed up "can I help you?" she had hissed out. He had smiled holding back a snigger as he boop her nose "you are adorable when you seem mad,- I thought it was mine."

"Is that so?," asked Luna while she sipped the Lotta "you going home for Christmas break?"

He gave his drink a tiny stir, a look of dissatisfaction in his eyes "... Staying, dad didn't make it back from the Northern Middle East." he had looked down. Luna felt bad for dampening his mood.

"I- I can ask my mom if you can spend Christmas with us." said Luna with a hearty smile.

"Oh, that would be great. Think she would?"

Luna placed a hand on his and smiled "O-of course... I mean, Christmas is to be spent with friends and loved ones."

He looked at their hands as he twisted his hand a bit to hold hers "You are the best Luna." said DJ while Professor Raven brought the exams.

"Here you two go, where is Jenny? Luna, you two are like witches brew in a cauldron. You two are always together."

"She is packing." replied Luna, Professor Raven had walked off. They had looked at the envelopes that had the school seal embedded on it sealing them. They had ripped it open, and Luna looked at her papers as she read through the exam.

Math was an eighty-three, a low C, Luna figured it would be. Introduction to World of Magick, she had scored an A in it a ninety-nine. She had missed question 122, she had picked the answer A, the correct answer was C. She was happy with it though. She got an A in History of Magick. She had scored a ninety-four which was barely an A. She had missed question number 3. She picked answer A by mistake. When the correct answer was D. Then she missed question 130, she had completely overlooked it. The correct answer was C. Then the science exam was a complete 58, a fat F. She rolled her eyes and sighed as she already knew it wasn't going to be good. She hated science. She still got two A's and once C and an F.

Then the last one was Basic Spells for First Yearers. She had scored an eighty-eight a B. She had missed question 3, she had picked answer B, the correct answer was A. Then she had missed question 20. She had picked D, the correct answer was B. Then question 150. She chosen B, the correct answer was A. She did a lot better than DJ in spell, he had got a D.

"S-so, should we go ahead and congrats her?" Sniggered DJ. They had walked up to the tower of Crowfeather and went into the common room where they had seen everyone looking at their grades. Jenny had come downstairs glowing. Before she could say anything about her grades, the excitement in her bright twinkle eyes already told the story.

"Congrats on all the A's, A+, and all the stickers that the teachers could fit on your paper." sarcasm fluently swift from DJ as he spoke. The cheeks of Jenny's flushed, her eyes showed hurt, and she looked around while everyone looked to her as she escaped back upstairs to her room. Luna had glared and snarled to DJ "what was that about?!"

DJ sighed while he shook his head "I was only teasing,

plus she was going to flaunt it just how smart she is." Luna walked upstairs; Shawn threw a pillow at DJ "good job Beast Killer."

Luna had stepped into the bedroom and seen Jenny on the bed curled up to Monkmonk, her old stuff monkey. He was missing a black button for an eye. So, Luna and Jenny had made him an eye patch. "Hey... Hey boobear," slowly Luna had approached her. Jenny had spoken with a rasp in her voice, tears stained her cheeks.

"H-hey love."

Luna had looked to her. Bags had laid all over the room from everyone that had packed up to get ready to go home for Christmas. "May I Sit?"

Jenny's legs had moved to allow Luna to sit on the bed. "So, how were your grades?" asked Luna ever so lightly as her voice was melodious.

"So you can mock me too?"

Luna's head shook and kissed Jenny's damp cheek "of course not, you are the smartest witch I know. I mean you worked hard to get your A's." replied Luna. She didn't have to look to know Jenny had all A's, she looked anyways. English A+, Introduction to Alchemy and Potions A+, Basic Spells A+, History of Magick A+, Science A+, and Basic Spells A+. "Good job Boobear.," Luna had lean over and kiss Jenny on the cheek "I got two A's, one B, a C, and an F.," She had rubbed Jenny's thigh. "DJ was only teasing you, now come on let's get some ice cream, my treat... And we can have I and you day." Luna had popped Jenny's rear playfully while she got up.

214

"--- You mean "Have you and I day, not I and you." not I and you." Jenny had corrected her, a smirk of triumph laid across her thin lips.

"Oh, you got me... Now let's go."

Jenny had rolled out of her bed and walked with Luna "-You let me have that win." smiled Jenny as they walked out of the room, out of the dormitory, and down to the great hall to get some hot cocoa. then they head outside. The land was covered in snow, the sun grew brightly, and the cold zephyr blew through the grounds. Luna and Jenny went to the lake just outside of the castle. The lake was frozen over in a thick layer of ice. "Want to try and go on the ice?" asked Luna.

They took each other hands and walked down onto the ice. Each stepped was slippery. They had slipped and slide. Giggles erupted when one of them had fallen and bringing the other one down with the other. They had done their best to ice skate, it failed! Their backside was soaked with snow and ice.

They made snow angels, a snowman. Even Khan had escaped out of the room. He let out a bark and ran towards them. His firey paws, chest, tail, and mohawk had melted the snow. Luna and Jenny broke out in a snowball fight and Khan had tried to catch and eat the snowballs.

They made their way to the stables. A young stable master was tending to the horses, he was a short man with brown hair and matching eyes. A fat face, they had petted the horses. The horses came in a variety of solid colors to patches of colors. "Ever been horseback riding before?" asked Luna while she fed the pure black horse an apple.

Jenny had pet a white horse with black patches while she shook her head "no, never, but they are such beautiful and strong animals."

"So you ride a Griffin, but never rode on a horse?" exclaimed Luna.

"No, I have flown on a Griffin." teased Jenny as she stuck her out at Luna.

"Well, this summer you will need to come over for a weekendish." Said Luna as they made their way back to the dormitory. DJ had apologized to Jenny while they drank hot cocoa by the fireplace and played Dungeons and Wizards.

Luna went up to the room and begun to write a letter to her mom on old parchment paper that she pulled out of her bag.

Dear Mother,

My grades came in and you would be so proud. I had gotten two A's, a B, C, and a Fox... How is Lucid's schooling? I will be home Monday!!! I can't wait to see you two, my room is still there, or did that snake Lucid attempt to slither in and take it? Is the guest room still open, I have a friend... Yes, I made a friend! His name is DJ, I wrote about him before. He is the one who I said failed at the spell and dumped the water on his head. He has no home to go to this Christmas. He would have to stay here all alone, anyway can he come for two weeks? Write back as fast as you can.

Love

Luna ☆

P.S: Your favorite child!

Luna had sealed the letter and waved the letter outside. A large black raven had flown by and got the letter. It had grown late, everyone had their cocoa then hit the bed.

Finally, Friday had arrived and Crowfeather's big day, Bree had been off the crutches and been walking with the sleeve on her knee now. The fair was back. Luna, Jenny, DJ, and Ray played a few games and watch a few sideshows. Luna had snuck away to go shopping. She had very little Shanties to her name. She had looked at some clothing of all sorts from shirts to dresses. She looked at bath bombs. The madam in full jewelry and wrinkles in her face and hands. The old Gypsy woman had spoken up "very best of soaps. They are enriched with the best fragrance. Those are two silver Shanties and these are called Dragon Eggs. You will hatch a dragon!" she said with real excitement.

Luna had looked at the bombs and the ones called Dragon Eggs (they were no larger than plastic Easter eggs). Luna thought to herself *these can't be real.* She had waved to the woman and made her way to another merchant wagon. She had looked at the wristbands, armband, rings, earrings, and something had caught her eyes. A glass vial on a silver and gold necklace, she had looked

217

at them as they had a small cork in the top. "What are these?" asked Luna while she looked at the vial. "Enchanted vials. Put what you wish in them. People had placed blood, tears, sand, ashes of loved ones. They are called "*Not Forget Me*", people have put a picture in them." Luna had looked at the one-eyed man.

"What are they enchanted with?" questioned Luna as her interest now peaked.

"What moment you hold dearest OR what moment the other think of, then you hold it in your hands. Close your eyes, let your mind go blank, and then the feeling drifts from that moment." Luna looked at them as she found a purple gem necklace "how much?"

"One Ruby Shantie and two silver Shanties.," the man said while Luna had opened her bag and thought hard before paying the man. "Think about what memory you want." He had handed her the necklace.

(Which memory did she want to use?) She thought hard on it *the first time, Jenny and she had met, the ride over Troll Head Mountain, Halloween dance, or the ride on the Griffan*? She had walked off and seen the group going to stands. She had run over and sat between Jenny and DJ.

"Where did you run off too?" Ray asked while he offered a pizza pretzel. Luna had taken a bite off of it.

"Ran into a friend."

Then four people had sat behind them. It was Cecil, Kain, Zak, and Colton. "Hey, Wissards Club." Kain had spoken with a

218

cold tone.

"You ready to lose this cup too?" laughed Cecil.

Then Mistress Flowers came upon the stage. Going over the rules again and welcoming everyone to and back to their (C.W.W.G.). She took the throne while Jewels had spoken from the announcing booth.

"Coming from the right side of the field is Crowfeather! Number four, Morgan Bowman! Number three, Timmy Moore, number five, Izabella Ward, and their fearless Pre Lord, captain, number one, Bree Summers!"

Everyone had cheered as they had flown out in the same leather and steel, but with clan colors and a crow on the helm. Cecil had leant over and whispered to Luna and them "should be "AND their crippled Pre Lord Captain of the crutch, Number Zero, Bree Summers!" he and his party burst out in laughter.

"How abou-" Raging DJ hashed out before Kain had cut him off. "How about you cast another spell and blast yourself out of your boots into another lake." They all cracked up in laughter while DJ flushed hard. Luna had turned to the Kain and his group now.

Jewels now could be heard calling the game. "Riding for Chimerador number Six Harley Night, number Five Blake Tolkin, the Pre Lord number three, Dane Ward, and the Lord Headmaster number 1, Bruno Silvertongue!" The crowd had cheered while Luna had glared at the lot "he is a better person than you and your pathetic brother."

"pipe down bloodline to Adam the savage satanic." snarled Kain. Luna had frozen, her stomach had tightened, and her heart dropped. She wanted to hit him with her fist or cast a curse on him. She went to speak, but her voice had failed her. Where her voice had failed her, her eyes had picked up. A tear had run down her cheek. She ran out of the stands followed by Jenny and Ray. -

Meanwhile, Jewels announced the game "fourth run Bree Summers versus Bruno Silvertongue. Here they go flying off. Chimerador is up by twenty-five points. Bree needs to knock him off for the win or tie it. Bruno fires a fireball. She had barrel roll easily out of the way, she shot a fireball. Direct hit, he had fallen off. The brook is spinning out of control and N-," Jewels had paused for a brief moment. "The broom is flying at a hundred and ten miles per hour. The broom is out of control and the handle tip had smashed right in the already injured knee of Bree. Dane ran onto the field; I know it's not how they wanted it to go. But Crowfeather wins!"

Dane had taken Bree's hand as a professor ran down and made a stretcher poof up. The crowd applaud the professor while they got Bree on the stretcher. - Luna went out of the castle to the oversize willow tree, known as Weeping Willow. The willow tree was tall for a willow tree, its branches draped down, the leaves were always green no matter what season it was. The trunk was a healthy brown. There looks to be a large (one-and-a-half foot) octagon hole... No, it wasn't a hole at all. It was a black onyx gem.

Luna pushed past the many drape branches, and she sat against the trunk. The trunk was extremely warm to the touch. As if it was a chimney with a fire blazing inside of it.

Luna's mind was racing as she thought about the memory of her dad (*at three he took her to the Christmas parade, and she saw Santa Clause. At age six he got them a dog and named him Rox, it was in a Christmas basket under the tree with a green ribbon, and how they woke up and seen the puppy. When they went to the beach every summer and her and her sister got a stuffed animal usually a fish, shark, dolphin, or an alligator. On weekends she had gone to her dad's work and watched him cook and "help" him. She loved going to the restaurant. Then at seven years old, he came home with three new horses (show horses). They did horse shows once a month. Then December 25th came... The ca-*)

"Why so gloomy child? I am supposed to be the one that is weeping." said a voice, Luna lifted her head and look around.

"H-hello?" called out Luna while she wiped her eyes.

"Up here child." the voice had called out.

Luna looked up to the tree and in the black gem was an old woman. She had long gray strands of hair, thin gray brows, large blue sparkling eyes, long crooked nose, long pointed chin, long thin lips, and a mouth with a few teeth missing. Luna's eyes widened when she saw the woman in the gem. "W- Weeping Willow?"

The woman smiled, face filled with wrinkles and her head

had cocked to the side "that is what many have called me but, I prefer Ol' Witchie Willow. So, my child, what blooms your day?"

Luna had wiped her cheek. A willow branch lowered and brushed a tear away from Luna's cheek. "No-nothing." Luna had lied. The woman in the tree just smiled.

"Now, my Deary, these aren't nothing tears."

Luna had sighed then she began to speak "there is this boy and he had said some hateful, things about my dad. Who I have found out that he came to this school a-and... He was supposed to be evil, Evil blood runs through my bloodline.," tears filled her eyes "he was so kind, caring, and full of love... Then he had passed away when I was eight."

Ol' Witchie Willow raised Luna's head with a branch "Oh Deary, sorry to hear. Death is so hard and for a person to speak so badly, amplifies that feeling so much worse. For Evil Bloodlines, we all have evil and holiness in our bloodlines. It doesn't destine who you are. Only you can decide your destiny and whom you are.,

"For death itself, it is only life. Their body is gone, but their soul is still very much alive. Some goes on to the stars, some goes to the slumber land, some stay earthbound, and then you have me who is fused with this willow. So my child, death doesn't mean always to die. Your shell is gone yes. BUT you are still living on. They say sticks and stones may break your bones, but words will never hurt you." Luna listens to Ol' Witchie Willow and nodded her head.

"RUBBISH! I say sticks and stones will break your bones

when words hurt you child. Send them to Ol' Witchie Willow."
Luna had smiled as she was feeling much better now.

"Thanks, Ol' Witchie Willow."

Jenny's voice could be heard in the distance yelling for
Luna " I must go, thank you again." Luna had gotten up to her feet
and smiled at Ol' Witchie Willow.

"You are welcome my child, come visit anytime. Do not
forget to send that boy to Ol' Witchie Willow's way."

"I won't, bye."

The branches had opened up so Luna could walk through
them. She saw Jenny and ran to her. Jumping on the back of Jenny.
"RAWR!" roared out Luna.

Jenny let out a fake shriek, but they had slipped and rolled
down the hill till they stop rolling. Jenny laid over Luna, she
looked up to Jenny. "Pinned ya." heckled Jenny.

"I let you.," laughed Luna, then she quickly stole a kiss.
"Kiss ya."

"I let you.," said Jenny then a second later they both burst
out in laughter "where did you go?" Jenny had got off of Luna.

"Oh, I went for a walk to clear my head. I am all better.,"
said Luna as they walked towards the castle to go back to the
dormitory "so, which is your best memory of us?"

They walked to the dorm as Jenny thought about it and
turned with a big smile, arms draped over Luna's shoulders "the

Halloween Party definitely." she had kissed Luna's cute small button nose before going into the common room. Luna followed Jenny and everyone crowded the chair by the fireplace.

"What is going on here?" asked Jenny with anxiety.

DJ had shaken his head while he sat in the middle of the crowd of people. "Zak and Colton happened after you all left. I punched Kain, then Zak and Colton decide to cut in.," said DJ " I did it in your honor Luna."

Luna had hugged him "my hero, I'll take care of them.," DJ's heart sunk as he held Luna a bit longer before letting go. "Thanks, Beast Killer." she had got up and headed up the stairs till she saw Bree on crutches. "What happened to you? Everyone got hurt today?" Luna walked over and helped Bree out.

"Oh, jousting accident. I'll be fine, we won." Bree had told her before Luna went to bed. -

It was mid-Saturday, Luna seen Kain, Colton, and Zak. She walked up to them and shoved Colton and Zak "HEY!" shouted Luna while she snarled. They had turned and face her then they stepped up to Luna, their fists had balled up tightly while their knuckles turned white. "Can't fight your own fight?" she cried out.

"Let's not fight here. Let's meet at Ol Wit- at the old weeping willow." said Luna staring at the three.

Kain looked to his boys Conton and Zak "fine, after the game." said Kain and he walked off with his buddies.

Luna came over with Jenny, DJ, and Ray as they found a

seat. Someone was selling popcorn, witch brewed tea, and dragon bites. Luna had bought a tea and Ray got Dragon Bites. They were little red hot candy that made you spit fire.

Cecil could be heard over the speaker "Morgan with the kick off, Harley down the straight away. Both shot a fire ball, what an explosion! They both are off the brooms."

"It is a rare sight to see them both get knocked off." said Jewels as she called heat number two.

"Here goes Bella racing off, here goes Dane... Sister versus brother which one is better?" Dane lasts a white blast at Bella!"

Bella had rolled upside down while she flew. She blows the ground up below Dane. He held on; they circled the posts for another round.

"Can't believe he held on. Here they go Bella with a blast, Dane with a counter. Such a large blast and they still held on! They are making another run; Bella shoots a blinding light. Dane with a fire blast, he had missed Bella. They're making another run! What a heat. Fourth run for them. Here they go wands in hand. Dane blew the ground up; Bella had held on. She blasts Dane in the back, throwing him forward, YES! He is off his broom. WHAT ACTION!"

The handle had caught the ground, throwing him forward. The crowd roared with claps; they began to setup for race three. Cecil took over to call the action now " Matt takes off after Blake, they sped up. Blake holding the wand out and blasts Matt. Matt had adjusted but loses his grip, he slipped off of the broom." Cecil chuckled out.

Bree had hoped over to her broom and dropped the crutches. Bella had run over to Bree. "You can't ride. You are injured." Bella reminded Bree, she had taken off on the broom leaving a trail of snow dust behind her wake.

"-What is she doing?" murmured Dane.

Bruno had taken off on his broom. Jewels called the heat this time "Bree is coming out of the gate. What she is injured, what heart she has. She drew her wand quickly. Bruno had drawn his and Bree fires... SHE- SHOT- BRUNO'S- Wand out of his hand. Here they go for another round. Bruno has to pick his wand up. Here they come, Bruno is flying upside down. Leaning forward for his wand, Bree set him up. She blasts the hat off. CROWFEATHER WINS!"

Everyone cheered as Kain, Zak, and Colton went to the willow tree " are we really going beat up a girl?" asked Zak. They stood by the tree, Luna had shown up with Jenny, DJ, and Ray.

"About time." spat Kain.

"Sorry, that's them." pointed out Luna. Everyone looked at each other.

"Of course that's them." cried out DJ waving his hands.

Colton jumped and looked to Kain "don't smack me."

"I didn't touch you." snarled Kain.

Zak had jumped this time holding his rear end. "OUCH!"

Kain turned and looked at him "What?!"

"Something hit me."

Branches lowered and grabbed the boys by the ankles and jerked them down, they turned and seen the tree was now attacking them. Lune and they bust out in laughter as cries could be heard behind the curtain of branches. The boys had run out, branches popping them as they ran.

"RUN!" Kain had yelled as they ran towards the castle. They laughed at the boys running from the tree.

"-Thank you Ol' Witchie Willow." excitedly said Luna and she waved, the Willow Tree wave its branches as they headed to the castle.

"What- was- that?" squeaked out Ray as they walked along the stone pathway to the castle keep. "Ol Witchie Willow." answered Luna while they got to the feast hall for dinner. Everyone had eaten a nice feast. Then Mistress Flowers took to her feet on stage and began to the students.

"What a very Christmas Wizard War Games we had. Tonight, will be some of your last night's here for two weeks. You will be missed. For the rest of you, we will have a great time. I just want to say to a few of you, Merry Christmas and to the rest of you Blessed Yule." Everyone had enjoyed their dinner and they went up to the room. Luna had seen a note laying on her bed, she opened it.

Dear Luna,

W. J. SMITH

Lucid tried, I stopped her. We are good glad you had passed, except for that F. Can't wait for you to come home either. Playoffs are going on, maybe you can come to a game. As for your friend, I suppose he can. For Christmas is to be spent with loved ones and friends.

Love,

Mom

P.S. You and your sister are both my favorites.

228

Chapter 14: Christmas Joy, homecoming.

Luna came out of the bedroom and ran down the stairs. Everyone was setting up the Christmas tree and decorations around the room. Jenny had a sticky bow in her dreads. The room smelt like fresh baked cookies. Stockings hung over the fireplace. DJ, Koty, and Worf were putting the train tracks together that went around the tree then around the room. Luna had walked over and poked DJ on the back of his head.

"Merry Christmas." she had handed him the note, her lips curled as she sat with Jenny and two other students to help with the tree. DJ came over and hugged her.

"Thank you, - Thank you." his voice was filled with glee. He had run off to his room. Jenny looked to her sideways.

"What is that about?"

"He is spending Christmas with me and my fam.," answered Luna "so, boobear... Do you have any brothers or sisters? What's your parents' name?" Time at the school had been so busy with schoolwork, games, and some stuff that was too easy to over-looked.

"I have two sisters. Amanda is a second year and in Chimerador and then there is Becky she will be here next year. My mom her name is Cindy, and she is an agent for Hollywood. My dad his name is John, and he is the Governor of the state of

229

California. What about you?"

"Your mom works in Hollywood! That is soo cool. - and your dad's a governor. Nice... Well, my sister is thirteen years old. Her name is Lucid, she is big in sports and is a star player in volleyball. My mom's name is Cheyanne, and she is the volleyball coach and teacher. Nothing special like your family." replied Luna as they placed the lights on the tree.

"Well, I think being a teacher is a very noble job.," countered Jenny as they had finished up with the lights. "Ray, his dad works for an office as a paper pusher. He provides for four kids, himself, and a wife. His mom is a stay-at-home wife and keeps it tidy and puts dinner on the table. Both are very noble. Just because my dad is a governor and my mom works for Hollywood doesn't make them better than your mom's job." said Jenny reassuring Luna.

"I am going to bed, night." Luna got up and headed up the stairs to the room. She had two pictures from the Halloween party. She pulled the vial out and popped the cork and placed the picture into it. The picture magically shrunk. She cut a small piece of her hair and placed it in the vial and sealed it. The vial lit to a bright golden color for a brief moment then she placed it in a small box and wrapped it in Christmas wrapping paper. Then she had laid in bed and drifted to sleep. -

The next evening, everyone was on the wagons heading to Crystal coast. "Going to miss it here." said Luna with a smile while she watched the wintry scenery go by.

"So, any plans for the break?" asked Bree with the crutches in hand as she sat in the wagon. The candle swayed overhead.

"Oh, not really." said Ray along with Dane and Bella.

"We aren't doing much, DJ is staying with us." answered Luna.

They got to the ship and Luna told Maîq bye. They boarded the ship, Luna got a bunk with Traci Brews, the Dracoîn clan girl. It was awkward at first, but they had talked about school, Christmas, and who will win the Championship for the Wizard Jousting. Crowfeather or Dracoîn. Lune had stayed steer clear from talking about Cecil and Kain, she apologize about the Halloween party. The night ended and they made it to Foxin Harbor by next evening.

Luna ran over to Jenny and told her who she had been bunked with, they made their way from the ship to the bus. Luna, Jenny, Bree, DJ, Bella, and Ray had sat together. "We'll be back in no time." said Bree as the buses began to drive off. Candy had got passed around. They had eaten some Dragon Bites and Fruit Flies. Luna's stop was coming up, it was the next stop. She turned and poked Jenny's shoulder with a smile "close your eyes." demanded Luna.

"Wh-."Luna had cut off Jenny "I said so." snapped Luna. Everyone had squeaked out "Ooh!" and Jenny had smiled and closed her eyes. "Fine."

"Put your hands out." said Luna as she placed the present with Christmas wrapping of reindeer and snowmen with beautiful red and green ribbon. "Open your eyes."

Jenny opens her eyes and saw the gift. She smiled at Luna "-Luna, what is it?"

"Open and see." called out Luna.

"Why- Why is it when someone gets a gift, they ALWAYS ask what is it? As if the person will tell them. Just open it already." blurted DJ impatiently.

"It is called being surprised and respectful Beast Killer." snickered Jenny while she unwrapped the gift and open the white box. She pulled out the purple necklace and the vial with the Halloween picture and Luna's dark hair. "Merry Christmas!" cheered out Luna.

"O-oh- I - Love- It, you- really shouldn't of. I mean-." stuttered Jenny as she looked at the vial.

"-Hope, -you like it?," said Luna as her bows lifted, biting the corner of her lip a bit. The bus had come to a stop.,"-Well, this is our stop." they had stood up to get ready to depart. DJ moved on to get off the bus. "Well... This is goodbye" she hugged everyone and then kissed Jenny "hope- you like your gift. It's called *NotForGetMe*. It takes you back to a special moment." she explained the gift.

"Come on gal! Others have places to be too!" shouted the bus driver.

232

"-I love it, Luna thank you." Jenny hugged her with one last kiss before she had left off the bus. She had walked over to DJ "...Ready?" she asked him.

"What is wrong?" asked DJ while they walked to the double doors, the bus stop was packed with people going this way, that way, and every other way.

"I- I think she didn't like it." replied Luna while she pushed her cart.

"Oh, she did... Probably upset at herself for not getting you anything."

They walked out of the stations. The trees were dressed in snow and ice, the snow was all over the ground. Cheyanne and Lucid stood outside all bundled up.

"LUNA!" yelled their mom while she ran over and hugged her daughter.

"MOM!" she had hugged her mom then turned and hugged Lucid "LUCID!".

"LUNA!," chuckled Lucid then hugged their mom "MOM!"

"LUCID!," bellowed their mom then they all broke out in laughter "how was your tr-." Cheyanne was cut off by-.

"DJ! shouted DJ while he let out a laugh that died down to no more than a chuckle.

"Trip was good. Mom, Lucid this is my friend DJ, DJ this is mo- Cheyanne and this is my sister Lucid." said Luna as she introduced them to each other.

"Nice to meet you, Mrs. Bell. and Lucid."

"Pleasure to meet you, heard a lot about you." said Cheyanne. "-Hi." said Lucid so casual and yet so bored.

"Let us get home, it is late." said Cheyanne while the moon cast over them. The night sky was beautiful as the stars had a twinkle. The next day, everyone had slept in the following day. They got home about a quarter till one in the morning. Luna had talked about her classes, the spells she had learned, the ogre that was Kain and his buddies. She didn't mention Blood Mary, Kate Bell, or about their dad.

Cheyanne had rolled out of bed at ten in the morning and got dressed. She went down the hallway and made a fresh pot of coffee and opened the newspaper. Nothing special interesting was going on in the mountains but a road closure due to heavy snowfall and snowfall for the next three days. Then the rest of the week was going to be sunny. Christmas fell on Wednesday. It was crazy how months go by so fast. Luna just got in town and two days was Christmas.

Lucid came down in her pajamas and made herself a cup of coffee "morn-" she had burnt her hand with a splash of the coffee and dropped the mug.

"Lucluc, are you OK?" her mom asked as she peered up from the paper to her daughter. Lucid looked to the mug that had shattered and began concentrated. Time had begun slowly rewind.

Chapter 14: Christmas Joy, homecoming.

The mug came back together, came up from the ground, and back into her hand. The coffee flowed from the coffee mug and back into the pot. She had put the coffee pot back. She felt lightheaded as she placed the coffee mug down on the counter. Her mom was reading the paper still. Lucid had placed the coffee mug on the counter and poured the coffee from the coffee pot. She had put the coffee pot back and took the coffee mug " morning mom." said Lucid as she sat at the table.

"Morning dear." said her mom as she got up to get ready to make breakfast. Rox and Khan came running into the kitchen. Rox barked at Cheyanne while his tail wagged.

"Lucluc, can you feed all the animals, please." asked her mom.

"Ugh, alright." Lucid had finished her coffee and got up and went to the laundry room and fed and water Rox and Khan. Rox stuffed his muzzle in the bowl and chowed down. Khan sniffed his bowl and head cocked a bit.

"You eat it." snapped Lucid, she went outside to feed the chickens and horses. DJ had rolled out of bed in the guest room. He rubbed his eyes and peered around the room at the pink sheer window drapes, soft white flower bedspread. The long dresser with a large mirror on the other side of the room. A beautiful hand-carved wardrobe. A grin crossed his lips, brows danced as his face shown mischief. He got out of the bed and opened the wardrobe door, he pushed the clothes to the side and reached into the backside and -.

"-Well, it was worth the try." said DJ before getting dress and headed out to the kitchen. "Morning Mrs. Bell, how are you?"

"I am good, call me Cheyanne. My husband's mom is Mrs. Bell. How did you sleep?" replied Cheyanne as she cooked the eggs and pancakes.

"-Strangely felt like I was at my Grangran's but I slept well. Need help with anything Mrs. Bell?" he asked while he looked around the kitchen.

"Sure, set the table, please. Cups are in that cabinet over there, the plates are next to it. The silverware is under it. OH, call me Mrs. Bell again and we will have a new stable boy." she had spoken coldly with a tease.

Lucid had come back into the house "Luc, go wake up your sister, or she'll sleep for days." said her mom. Lucid had gone up the stairs making her way into Luna's room. Luna laid sprawled out in her bed sleeping. Lucid crept over and leaned close to her sister, screeched out "LUNA! Wake up."

Cheyanne heard a cry out from upstairs from Luna yelling out at Lucid. She had let out a chuckle and shook her head while she had finished the bacon, sausage, biscuits and gravy.

"-SOoo, the stable boy was just a joke right?" asked DJ while Luna and Lucid had come down the stairs to join them at the table.

"Ask Luna, ... I never joke." she had spoken coldly while

DJ froze with eggs on his fork.

"Joke, you noooo...," said Luna while she cut her sausage "what is it about?" she had taken a bite of the sausage.

"Oh, if I called her Mrs. Bell I will be the new stable boy."

Lucid spoke up in cheer "please do, she's such a tease... Call her Mrs. Bell, yes Ma'am, no Ma'am. She is teasing --- that jokester." laughed Lucid, Luna had rolled her eyes at Lucid.

"IF he does, you will be teaching him Lucluc.," winked their mom while they ate. "Luna, take DJ and have him help you clean the stables. Lucid had fed the animals already."

"Ugh, OK." sighed Luna while they had finished their breakfast. Lucid and Luna had cleaned up after breakfast. DJ went and sat in the living room with Cheyanne. She was reading a book and DJ sat on the couch watching tv.

"So, DJ you got any brothers or sisters?" asked Cheyanne while she turned from her book. She eyed the boy.

"No, I am the only child." said DJ while she nodded.

"What about your parents, what do they do?"

"--- Well, my mom left when my dad and me. On my first birthday... -"

"Oh, I am sorry." sorrow has filled Cheyanne's voice.

"--- Oh, it's ok... Dad told me she didn't want kids when I got older. My dad is a treasure hunter. He spends half his year looking for treasures and artifacts. He found rubies, gems, and gold that belong to the Egyptian King."

"Oh, that is awesome."

Luna came into the room and sat next to DJ followed by Lucid. "Want to learn how to dress a horse and go horseback riding?" said Luna looking at DJ, he shrugged as he grew excited and nervous all at the same time. "S-sure." They had got up and began to walk of the room.

"Don't mess with Miss Sierra, she is still a bit wild. She bucked Mr. Gray off, and he had hurt his leg. He will be back after the holidays. She may bite, Lucid had been handing her a bit also."

"---OK, so the first ride should be on Miss Sierra?" asked Luna sarcastically. They walked down the stone path to the large red barn that was covered in snow. There were black letters painted on the front of the barn over the large doors (*The Bells Stables*). Lucid unlocked the door, the smell of hay and sweet pea had filled the area. Luna showed DJ where the feed and hay were, tools, saddles, the barn storage, and the office was.

The barn had twenty stables, five stables in one row opposite behind five more, then on the other side of the barn, ten more stables mirrored the first five. Luna and Lucid were in their cowgirl boots as DJ looked around at all the sights.

"So, you sure do love horses." said DJ.

"Yep, mom has one competition show horse for jump competitions, one barrel race, two show horses. I have one riding and two-barrel racing horses." said Lucid while she leaned against a stall door. Lucid gave DJ a tour through the stables and

238

introduced him to the horses. "This is white beauty is Bella and this black handsome is Onyx. They are her grand prize-winning Tennessee Walking horses. This brown one, a quarter horse mom's barrel horse. His name is Cocoa. The white hair with black spots is her riding horse, her name is Star, and she is a pinto., "This brown one is my Mustang. He is my racing horse, his name s Brownie. The two quarter horses, the black one is Rose and the white one is Moon. Then two more Mustangs Rebel and Rogue. We had Rogue for five years. He was dad's horse.

This one is another Pinto, and her name is Spots. Then the big. Meanie Sierra and is our newest Arabian. I wanted to name her night. Then we have three quarter horses for our trail walking, and their names are Hickory, Chestnut, and Cookie." explained Lucid while Luna came with three saddles then a wooden plank that shaped like a horse.

"This one here is Captain Woods, and he is your horse." teased Luna. DJ walked over to it as she showed him how to saddle a horse with the wooden horse while Lucid saddled her horse, Rose. She then had saddled Rebel for Luna. Luna took the saddle from Captain Woods "don't walk behind the horses." she snapped at DJ while she helped saddled Hickory. DJ had jumped as there was a loud bang. Sierra had kicked her stall door.

"HEY! Behave or I'll tie you up in the washing ben." Lucid snapped at the horse. They opened the stall doors and had led the horses out. They showed DJ how to get on. He jumped too hard and slipped off on the other side. Then after a few more tries, he was on the horse.

Lucid had kicked the horse sides and sped off, snow dust filled the air leaving a trail in her wake as she did quick turns "-And we will walk the horses first." said Luna while she had given a small snapped of the rein to make the horse go. They walked a bit then told him how to go faster. "I am OK with one speed." said DJ while he walked the horse. Lucid came up behind Hickory and smacked his back quarters. The horse began to gallop faster. DJ held on to his dear life while the horse ran "s-slow down horsey." DJ's voice shook with slight fear as Luna and Lucid had to case after him.

"PULL back on the reins gently!" shouted Lucid while she rode faster to catch up to him.

"Ho- horsey st-stop." DJ held on while he held the reins firmly. Luna rode to catch up with him. Lucid thrown a lasso around the horse's neck, tugging at the rope to slow down Hickory. They had come to a stop finally.

"Hey, Boy! Tug on the reins to slow down. You could have gotten hurt." snapped Lucid.

"S-sorry." said DJ in a sorrowful murmur.

Luna had ridden up and glared at her sister "It is his first time! He didn't want to go fast. It is your fault that Hickory had taken off like that. Take Hickory back and DJ can ride with me" yelled Luna as she helped DJ off Hickory and then onto the back of her horse. "Put your hands on my waist." she glared at Lucid as

240

they began to ride off.

"Gl-glady." he said as they rode around the pasture. Luna had shown him AGAIN how to use the reins. Then they had swap spots now while Luna placed her hands on his waist. They rode back to the stables, got the saddles off, and they had put Rebel back in the stall. They went ahead and cleaned the stalls and laid out new hay. They had changed the winter blankets. Lucid returned and she looked at the two. "-Hey DJ, I just wanted to apologize about the horse." she said while Luna took the blankets to the barn laundry room.

"...Oh, it is OK. No problem." he smiled at her. Luna came back over while Lucid shook her head.

"No, you could have gotten seriously hurt."

Luna walked up and smacked Lucid playfully on the back of her head "not everyone lives as fast and carefree lifestyle as you." she said. -

Khan stood over the dog dish pawing at the food, the door open as the kids came into the house. Lucid looked at the *Hellhound* and sighed out lowly "you eat it!... Luna, I think your dog... Wolf, whatever it is is mental."

Luna walked over and pat his head feeling the warm flames dance against her hand. "No, he isn't this is a new dish for him. He eats the souls of usual rabbits."

"OH, I forgot... How-- unique - he is."

241

They went into the living room and sat on the couch. Cheyanne had a game show on the television "how was the ride?" she asked them, looking from her word puzzle book.

"Err it went good. Had a lot of fun." said DJ while his gaze lowered to the floor as he placed his hands in his lap.

"Are you sure? You seem to second guess yourself.," she looked from him to the two girls "girls?"

"We-." Luna was cut off by Lucid while Luna tried to talk. "I smacked his horseback quarters..."

"Why Lucluc?" their mom had that crazy stern look in her eyes. She placed her game down on the coffee table and stared at her daughter.

".... To make him go faster." said Lucid with a lowly sigh.

"And... DJ, that was fun?" Cheyanne turned from Lucid to him while she turned the television off. DJ felt eyes on him from every single angle.

"...Well, yes. I mean after Luna, and I rode together."

Cheyanne pointed to the stairs before words shot out of her mouth. Lucid was on her feet and went up the stairs as she had now talked for her mom "LUCID! Bedroom now, think of what you did. Don't dare step out of that room. "But mom wha-" Not even if you have to use the bathroom, Girl! Have you lost your mind! IF so I'll hel[p you find it, what are you waiting for Jesus to come down and help you? Lord, help you find your darn sense child!"

DJ and Luna sat listening to her speak for their mom while they watched Cheyanne trying to hold back a snigger "Close! But I wouldn't have said darn! shouted their mom.

There was a pause then they could hear Lucid shout back "-IF I said the other word, we would be making a pit stop to the bathroom. For an all-you-can-eat bar of soap." the sound of the door closing could be heard. Cheyanna had turned the television back on to her game show. "Mom, can DJ go up and hang out in my room?" asked Luna while she sat on the couch bored. Her mom's brow raised up as if Luna had just asked for the keys to the truck. "A boy in your room, are you crazy or - Just like your sister did you lose your mind?"

"... Nevermind, we'll go walking outside." said Luna while she got to her feet and went to slip her shoes on.

"Oh, Gracy had been asking about you, may you would like to go see her?" said her mom looking at her daughter.

"OH! GOD, Gracy... I have missed her! We'll go to her house. I haven't hung out with her since July."

"Have fun, she had been asking about you. I told her you went to stay at your Aunt Margie and Uncle Gorge for the school year, you had attended a new school."

DJ and Luna had slipped their shoes and jackets on and headed outside. They walk down the long gravel driveway that went on forever. Then they started the walk down the road now towards Gracy's house. The neighborhood had such beautiful homes and plenty of wooded areas. Luna pulled out her pink phone and started to text Gracy while she walked next to DJ.

243

<Luna: Hey girl!>

DJ looked around the place while admiring these homes and saw a few deer in the distance till he heard a ding as Luna's phone got a notification.

<Grac: Hey! What's up. I have been trying to call you over the last couple mounts. ▯ ▤

<Luna: I had left my phone at Moms by mistake. It had been killing me. Are you ok?"

DJ looked at the phone and pointed as he looked baffled "what is that thing?"
Luna stopped in the middle of her tracks with a shocking expression that shown complete concern. "Oh... My- God-It is a phone, a cell phone... It is a way to communicate, play games, and Linkus. I thought I was going to die without!"

<Grac: Bet you were going crazy. No phone, and no Grac.">

DJ looked at Luna as he stopped dead in his track " Hello, I live in the world of Magick, we have birds to send our messages or view crystals, and other cool stuff."

<Luna: I need some Grac time, are you home?">
<Grac: Yea, parents are at work. Just walk on in.>
<Luna: OK, oh FYI I got you a boyfresent! ▯ ▤
<Grac: Shut up... Hurry up, I miss my ★ bear.!"-

They came up to a story log cabin home with a long curvey driveway with a large white RV parked. A pool in the backyard and a wrap-around porch. A hot tub sat on the back deck with a custom stone grill. They walked into the house; log walls ran along the walls with a lovely spiral wood staircase. A large Christmas tree sat in the living room by the stone fireplace with a loft-style upstairs.

"GRAC!" Luna had shouted while they had removed their coats and boots. A door opened from upstairs a short scrawny girl with long thick strawberry blond hair, bright green eyes, a small button nose, and a cute face with freckles across her nose and cheeks.

"STARBEAR!" Gracy had run down the stairs and jumped onto Luna hugging her "I had missed you." they both said at the same time.

"This is DJ," Luna introduced to each other "DJ, this is Gracy."

"Hi." DJ gave a small wave with a smile.

"-Oh, Hi... You weren't kidding about the boyfresent." whispered Gracy. They went upstairs to her room. Her room was covered with photos of friends, band photos, and artwork of drawings from animals to skulls. Colorful lights dangled f-rom the ceiling and a television sat on a dresser. They sat on the bed while they talked and caught up.

"So, seeing anyone Luna?" asked Gracy looking at her as they laid on the bed.

"-I'm seeing someone, yes.," said Luna softly "What about you?"

245

"No, my dad would kill me...or him.," replied Gracy "did you hear that I am on the volleyball team with your sister?"

" Oh, that is awesome! I would say I'd come and watch a game, but let's be real... I don't even watch my own sister.," giggled Luna.

"SOoo, how are you seeing? I bet he is cute." Said Gracy giving Luna a playful push.

"Oh, she is dating gi-," DJ got cut off as Luna had pinched him "ouch."

"-He is, a really cute giy. Look at the time, we must be off."

Gracy showed them out as they hugged and peck each other on the cheek with a kiss. They both said they loved each other and then waved bye as DJ and Luna walked out of the house back towards her house.

"Why did you pinch me? Why did you not tell her about Jenny?"

"One, she doesn't know I am gay. Two, Grac is my best friend... My girlfriend, she would be detestation that the girl code was broken."

"Girlfriend? I thought Jenny was your girlfriend."

Luna had rolled her eyes and shook her head while they walked up the long gravel driveway back to the house "Jenny is, a girlfriend is like... A best friend, a sisterhood."

"So, like a cult?" countered DJ while Luna shook her head

246

and ignored him as they went inside the house. Dinner was ready, a Christmas tree sat in the living room that sat naked and ready to be dress in Christmas decoration.

They had finished dinner, and everyone had migrated from the kitchen to the living room. Christmas carols were playing on the stereo while they sat up the tree. They had hung up stocking over the fireplace on the mantel. They had pulled out Santa clause and Mrs. Clause dolls and placed them by the tree.

"...This is your dad's favorite time of the year." said their mom while she hung up a Christmas bauble. The girls nodded their heads as they heard her say it every single year. They had finally decorated the tree and the living room. They sat down watching a classic Christmas cartoon and drank hot cocoa.

"Any family coming in for Christmas?" asked Luna staring at her mom skeptically. Her mom peered over the coffee mug before lowering it from her lips.

"Grandma and Pappa Green, my sister Marge and uncle George and their kids April and JR. My brother Vernon and his --- wife Vicki and their daughter Lacey. My brother Eddie (Ed), your cousins Many, and her boyfriend Brandon with their baby Shawnie. I believe that is all."

Luna had slipped off the couch and onto the floor. She dropped her head back on the couch cushion with such a heavy sigh. "... Does Ikki have to come? I mean - Vermin and Ikki can stay home, and Lacelace can stay here."

247

Cheyanne smacked her on the back of the head with a crossword puzzle "be nice they are- family." she uttered out.

"Can they sleep in the barn?" Lune asked her mom while looking at her with pleading in her eyes.

"LUNA!" cried out their mom.

"--- Your right, it is illegal in this state... I think it's called cruelty to animals. I couldn't do that to the horses" sarcastic flowed freely from Luna.

"... I think it is in all states." sniggered Lucid.

"Girls!" cried out their mom.

"-So, what is wrong with Vernon and Vikki?" asked DJ casually.

"Come on mom, tell him - about your so loving brother and Ikki." said Luna with a mischievous smile.

Cheyanne took a sip of her cocoa before she told DJ the story "they, well - just think they are better than everyone else... They have money." she said as nicely as she could. Both girls booed their mom, Luna cleared her throat.

"Lacey was five or six and got hurt playing on the porch at grandma's house. Vermin and Ikki had sued Grandma and Papa. When she hosts family gatherings, there is a bill at the end of the night. He is the board director for the railroad and she stays home and sells makeup.,

"Lacelace is now seventeen, she has always been a

cheerleader, beauty pageant queen, and president of her school."

"Maybe... Maybe they had changed." said DJ looking at Luna as he pats her head. Luna and Lucid had both shot him a cold gaze, the gaze was as cold as blades with a slight hiss.

"O- or not. Definitely not." said DJ as he backed away.

"So, where are they ALL sleeping? Seventeen people in a four bedroom --- One barn with twenty stables. "Said Lucid.

"No, fourteen of those stables have horses. We have six stables." corrected Luna.

"LUNA! LUCID! Cruelty to animals remember?" there was quietness for a moment before they all bust out in laughter. "We have four bedrooms, a study room, a den, and a large living room.,

"Mom and dad can have the guest room. Aunt Marge and Uncle George can have the den, Uncle Vernon and Aunt Vikki will take my room. Eddie will take the living room. April, Lacey, Mandy, and Shawnie, and you girls will take Lucid's room. The boys' Jr, Brandon, DJ will -."

"-N-... -N-..." Luna had stuttered out while their mom had finished what she was saying "will take your room, Lulu."

"NO!!!" dramatically overplayed on Luna's part as she fell back on the floor playing dead.

"And I will take the living room. Cause knowing Ed, he will pass out in the dining room, kitchen, or some random part of the house." she had finished off as Lucid pat Luna's stomach "better you, them me." she chortled out.

The night had ended, everyone went to sleep that night. DJ went to sleep on the couch since Cheyanne had chanted the bed sheets and bedding. The very next morning, DJ woke up and helped Cheyanne in the kitchen. She asked him to feed the dogs. He went to the laundry room to feed the dog and the *Hellhound*. An hour later, everyone was up and awake. Luna fed the horses, and Lucid attended to the chickens while DJ sat at the table. They all ate breakfast and put the dishes away. Luna had moved some clothes and blankets to Lucid's room.

Their mom sat in the living room reading a book. The kids watched a Christmas show. Sound of snow and gravel crunch in the driveway. Cheyanne placed the book down and opened the shades. A blue beat up station wagon pulled up the driveway. "Girls, Ed is here with Grandma and Papa. Go help them bring in their bags." said their mom while a knock came from the door.

Their mom opened the door. Stood a man with very thin dark hair, hardly any. Fat round face with a play dough of a nose with thick glasses. Stood in front of the thin man was a tiny woman with plenty of wrinkles, white puffy hair and small glasses hid her small sparkling green eyes.

An old man held the woman's hand. He was tall and scrawny with no hair; he was wearing a fashion brown bowler hat. He had many wrinkles and brown eyes.

"Dad, mom, Eddie come on inside." said Cheyanne as she hugged them after they came in. Luna, Lucid, and DJ had grabbed

250

the bags and brought them to the guest room. -

`   "So, how was the trip up here?" asked Cheyanne while she made them some coffee as they sat at the island in the kitchen.
          "Be better if we drove, Sunny-boy here drives like an ol' granny." said Mr. Green while the kids came into the kitchen.
          "Hey, Mama and Papa. Hey uncle ED." said Luna and Lucid while they came over to them and hugged them. But they had kissed their grandparents.
          "Hello my beautiful girls." said Mrs. Green.
          "Gosh you two grew since the last time I have seen you.," said ED "And dad, mom did teach me how to drive."
          "So, did you get a new car?" asked his sister.
          "Won her in a poker game last weekend." said ED while glowing with glee about his winning.
          "Won? The person who lost the car is the winner. That piece of crap backfires and black smoke takes me back to my war days in Vietnam back in '67.," said Mr. Green " we got stopped on I-40 east and the officer had stopped us. He asked for Ed's driver's license, insurance, registration card, and our burning permit."

          They had talked some more as a large SUV pulled into the driveway. came through the door was a tiny woman with black hair and green eyes. A slightly heavy woman followed by a tall thin man with dark brown hair and brown eyes, and a long face. A small girl a year younger (12) than Lucid came in, tiny and little to weight with dark hair and brown eyes with a heart shape face. Her little brother Junior (JR) came in. He has dark hair, green eyes, small oval face. He held his handheld game. He had oxygen tubes in his nose with a small tank on wheels. He is seven years old.

"Hey sis, George, April, and Jr. Come on in, care for a drink?" asked Cheyanne while everyone greeted each other with hugs, handshakes, and kisses. "What are you playing?" asked Luna as she walked over to Jr watching him play his game.

"Call to honor.," JR said as he showed Luna "it is a war game."

"Oh, that is cool. You like war games?'"

Jr nodded "yeah, I want to be in the marines like poppa." Luna kissed his cheek while Mr. Green looked at Jr with a smile. "That's my boy. You'll be a fine soldier. But a better general." April and Lucid went up to the room, and they talked about cheerleading and volleyball. -

George took a drink from his coffee mug then cleared his throat after Mr. Green told JR he'd be a good Marine. "The great Lord has a path for JR. Born with a hole in his heart and a lung too small, JR will be great at wherever the good Lord leads him."

"Ah- JR boy will be fine. I once met a man over in Peru who had one leg, one arm but was full of spirit. I spoke to this man, and while I was speaking to this man smoke broke out, and flames from a building. We pulled this young man out of the fiery building. Not breathing, no matter what your handicap is, put your mind to it and you can overcome any obstacle in life." Said ED while he eyed George.

Everyone talked more about how everyone has been, talked about their jobs to rumors. The sound of a vehicle pulled up into the driveway could be heard. A sparkling black sports car pulled up, and they got out of the car and came in the house was a tall slender blond hair, beautiful round face, sparkling blue eyes, nose ring, and perfect lips. She carried a tiny bald chocolate tone baby with blue eyes.

"EK! SHAWN!" squawked Luna out as she jumped up to her feet and ran over. Lucid ran down the stairs "Shawnie!?" "Hey, Mandy." said Luna hugging Mandy then Lucid greeted Mandy. "Hey Mandy how are you dear?," asked Cheyanne "where is Brandon?"

"He is getting the bags, play pen, and the diaper bag." said Mandy as she placed Shawn down as she went and hug her grandparents. "Hello Gran and Poppa. How are you two feeling?"

"Hello Dearie, I am good you look fantastic." said her grandmom as she kisses Mandy's cheek.

"I am good Manders." Said Mr. Green as he put Shawn on his lap. -

Luna went out to help Brandon bringing in the stuff. He was a handsome guy. He was well built, broad shoulders, thick chest, brown fade haircut. Hair on his chin, brown eyes, and semi

253

light brown skin complexion. Tall man, giant like compared to Luna. She made a snowball and beamed him with it "sup punk."

He turned and smiled dusting the snow off his black sweater "Psh, what is happening sport." he said sarcastically with a snigger.

"- Umm, that's Lucid." corrected Luna rolling her eyes.

"I know, how is my favorite stalker of the night, my vamp?" said Brandon as he came over and hugged her. She grabbed a bag.

"I am good, busy with school."

Lucid stepped out "hey, Mr. Heisman." Lucid ran up and hugged him.

"What is up my favorite sport, MVP... Lucuuuuuucid." said Brandon with a smile. "Come to get away from the adults?" asked Luna looking to her sister. Brandon laugh looking at Luna "Ah, so I am not an dult?," They all had bags in hand "so is Vermin and Ikki here yet?" he looked around at the vehicles.

Lucid chuckled "nah, you're a child lost in an adult body. Not yet, but... Soon they will be."

They walked into the house and took their shoes off Mr. Green looked over to see them coming to the house. "If it isn't the jolly black giant. How are you?" said Mr. Green with a sardonic grin.

Mrs. Green shook her head "-Ralph behave yourself. How are you our dear boy?"

Brandon walked over and hugged them "I am good, it is OK Nana. Ol man Jones is a hoot, how are you Nana and Mr. Green?"

"We are good." said Mrs. Green hugging him back.

"You look great son, you and Mandy need to visit more." said Mr. Green as him and Brandon shook hands. Lunch was made, Christmas dinner was in the works they had a light lunch of sandwiches and chips, and the kids ate at the kid's table while the adults at the kitchen bar. "So, Ed, is that car yours?" asked Brandon.

"- That is no car! That is a smokehouse for meats. Now I know how smoked meats feel." heckled Mr. Green as he ribbed his son. Ed smiled as he waved his dad off. "Yep, won her in a game of poke... Which reminds me of a story, a funny story When I was in Africa-."

Luna had stopped Ed from one of his famous stories. "Want to go horseback riding Brandon?"

"... I Do- I do!" shouted JR excitedly as he stood up and grabbed Lucid's arm as he jumped up and down.

"Little night stalker, I told you before... I like horses from afar or under the hood. But my people don't ride horses." Brandon looked to Luna as she placed her hands on her hips. Mandy had smiled and looked at Brandon placing her hand on his.

"Don't let him fool you, and he rode a horse at the county fair. He did it for me, I was on one horse, and he was on the back. Halfway through the ride, a group of his friends saw him and made

255

fun of him... What was it they called you?" Mandy smiled coldly. Brandon flushed up as he shook his head. Then he spoke ever so lowly. "Yippee ki yay Bucken Kept."

"Can I go horseback riding?" JR turned and asked his dad. He shook his head as he placed his hand on his son's shoulder " maybe when you're better. Good Lord has something grand for you." George aid while disappointment filled JR's eyes.

"He will be fine, he can ride with me.," said Lucid reassuring him "I am a good teacher... Now Yippee ki yay Bucken Kept. Let's go."

They all got their jackets and shoes on and stepped out Luna and Lucid both shouted before stepping outside "Yippee ki yay!"

"Don't worry George, Lucid is a great rider." Said Cheyanne while she and the other women started to wash the dishes. -

DJ, Luna, Lucid, April, JR, and Brandon were in the barm. Luna and Lucid settled up five horses. Brandon stood watching, then BOOM sierra had kicked the stall wall causing Brandon to jump. He turned and saw the black monstrous horse "That is no horse, that is a demon."

They got on the horses and Luna looked to DJ "remember how to slow down and stop?" she eyed him seriously. DJ nodded and then they rode out of the stables and into the field. Lucid put JR and his tank in between the horn of the saddle and her. -

256

Chapter 14: Christmas Joy, homecoming.

A black eighty-thousand-dollar SUV pulled up and parked in the middle of the yard. Placing windshield blinds in the window. A medium height man stepped out, round as a blimp with no hair, and a thick mustache. Large pucker fish face and itty bitty brown eyes.

His wife was shorter than him, but more rounder than him. Her black hair was pulled back in a tight bun. Large dangle earrings, fingers full of gems, and a fake tan, with blue eyes that were behind fancy glasses.

They grabbed their suitcase, a girl stepped out. She was tall, with legs that went on for miles. Slim body, thin lips, blue eyes, an adorable button nose. Long wavy brown hair. The door open and Cheyanne stepped out eyeing the three as they came across the yard "what are you doing parking in my yard? There is all that room in the driveway!"

Vernon the blimp size guy walked up the front porch "I didn't want any branches to fall on my new eighty- thousand dollar SUV. How are you, sis?"

"-Good, come on in." she said in annoyance. They came in and kicked their shoes off and greeted everyone

Everyone came inside from horseback riding "told you, you would like horseback riding." said Lucid.

"Yeah, but I still prefer my four hundred and seven hundred horsepower." replied Brandon.

"Lacelace!" said Luna while she ran over and hugged

Lacey.

They all sat around, Brandon talked to Ed about his football number jersey being scouted for the *N.F.F.* (*Nation Football Foundation*). Ed told him about a man he had drunk with, in Florida who played in the N.F.F.

Vernon spoke to Ruth and Ralph about needing to think about a nursing home. George watched the N.F.F. between Tennessee Thunder Horses versus New York Liberties. Marge and Cheyanne were getting it from Vikki about beauty tips, health tips, and colleges for the girls.

Mandy started watching the game while feeding Shawn. All the kids went to Lucid's room to get away from the adults. They put on a movie. later DJ got up to use the bathroom and walked into the hall. The attic ladder was down leading up to the attic. He climbed the ladder "hello?," he called out. He looked around the room "hello? Anyone in here?" He looked at all the old stuff from toys to boxes of old goods. He made his way to the ladder, but a cold gust of wind blew through him, bone-chilling it was. His hair stood up on the back of his neck.

A box fell with a thump, under the box on top of another box were old letters. One stuck out in a red Christmas envelope. He read part of the card.

> *Dear, my shining Cheychey.*
> *First letter ever from me.*

Chapter 14: Christmas Joy, homecoming.

DJ sealed the envelope and climbed down the latter. He retreated to Luna's bedroom. He wrote out a card and sealed it, finding an old shoe box in Luna's closet. He placed the envelope in the box and wrapped it. -

Later dinner was ready; ED have been drinking his Christmas booze and telling a story when he was in Poland about how he met a man named Khris Kringle. Vikki talked about how the turkey was too dry and how the mashed potatoes were too lumpy. Mrs. Green cooked them, same way for seventy years. Luna fed Shawn, George said a prayer for the food and blessed everyone. Mr. Green told Vikki to shut up two more three times at least, and at least there isn't a bill afterward. Mrs. Green smacked her husband and told him to be nice.

Dinner was crazy a lot of talks, but more eating. Everyone - almost everyone helped clean up. Vikki sat in the living room after dinner and played with Shawn while all the females had cleaned up after dinner. After they had cleaned up and finished. They sat in the living room, and they passed around one gift.

Brandon got a gift from ED, it was a new sports bag. Mandy got a set of candles and soap from Cheyanne. ED got a gift from Vernon and Vikki it was a book Sober life and me. Lacy got a gift from Mandy, and it was a new black handbag with her name engraved in gold stitching.

Vikki got a gift from Mrs. Green and Mr. Green it was a

new makeup bag. Vernon got a gift from George, and it was a new golf club and balls. JR had gotten a gift from his grandparents it was a few army men. April got a gift from Marge; it was a card for Emusicly. George got a gift from Brandon, and it was a signed collage card of him. Marge got a gift from Luna it was a new cookbook from the mountains. Lucid got a gift from April and it was a new gym bag with scents. Luna got a gift from Brandon a black hoodie, with a pullover hood with Dracula's face, then a set of fake vampire teeth. Cheyanne got a gift from ED. It was a horse book. Everyone had thanked everyone as DJ stood up with his gift and walked over to Cheyanne "- here is my gift ... Merry Christmas."

Everyone had paused and Cheyanne smiled at him taking the gift from him and opening it. Then the shoe box, followed by the envelope as her eyes began to water as she skimmed through it "O... Oh my."

"What is it?" asked ED.

"What is it mom?" asked her daughters.

"My first love letter from Adam."

"What does it say?" asked Vikki leaning overlooking over Cheyanne's shoulder.

"- The lover letter is private between her and her lover.," she replied while she put the letter away. "Thank you, DJ."

It grew late as people gather around the piano while Mrs. Green played some Christmas music. Everyone sung Christmas

260

carols, but Cheyanne escaped to the porch with the letter watching it snow. Moments later DJ had come out and sat on the porch chair by her.

"... Sorry, I thought it be special."

Cheyanne waved him off and she turned to him " you are fine. My husband, Adam always acted like Christmas was his least favorite time of the year. How much work it was from chopping down the tree, decorating, and the cold snow, the wintery nights. No matter how hard he tried to fake it... You always... You could always tell by the sparkle in his green eyes... It was his eyes that gave it away. How much he loved Christmas."

They went inside, everyone gone to bed leaving milk and cookies out for Santa Claus.

Chapter 15: Christmas

Everyone laid down, some had fallen asleep, some couldn't. Shawn woke up crying loudly in the middle of the night. Lucid sat up in bed, she was sharing the bed with Shawn and Mandy. She picked him up and change the diaper and fed him.

"Thanks, Luc, I was going to do it. "Yawn out Mandy.

"It is ok. We don't get much time with Shawn and you guys." smiled Lucid while Shawn fell asleep... -

In Luna's room, JR was too excited to sleep. He tossed and turned. They let him have the bed " Uncle ED, BranBran... Is Santa Claus going to make it?" asked JR.

"Of course, soldier boy." said Brandon.

"This reminds me- when I was in Spain a fantastic story. -"

DJ's eyes widen and placed a pillow over his head as he thought to himself Only if underage magick use wasn't illegal off school ground. --- May be worth it.

"The orphan boy woke up and had a very good Christmas." recited ED by the time he finished, everyone was asleep. ED nodded " well, happened again... Reminds me when of the time when I was in that pub in Ireland. ... Funny story I have to sa-.," a crow was pecking on the window, Ed watched "... How queer, you, my friend reminds me of a story in France. AH, such a lovely- but tragic story... I was in France; a beautiful maiden was in the courtyar-"

The crow flew off into the darkness as ED chucked "-and that is pretty much how it ended her leaving me at night on the streets of France with flowers in hand." He finally passed out, as he fell asleep, he saw through logs. DJ slept horribly that night. Morning finally came and DJ stepped out in the hall, Luna saw him, and her brow raised "you look, how can I say this nicely... Death came for yo-" a loud squawk erupted from down the stairs. Everyone came out from the rooms.

"Is JR, OK?!" George said as he came downstairs, heart racing. JR has been in and out of the hospital.

"LOOK- AT- ALL- THE- PRESENTS!" Jr screamed in excitement.

Everyone rushed down the stairs and Cheyanne jolted awake from a dead sleep. Presents had dressed the entire living room from tiny presents, small presents, awkward shape presents, medium presents, long presents, big presents,s seventeen stalkings filled with goodies and a present or two, and tall presents.

Everyone stared in awe, not nowhere close to the presents that they had put out last night, mouths had dropped, and eyes widened. Then ED spoke up "-Re-reminds me my time when I Was in Greenland." his father shut him up as he talked over his son "put a sock in it boy! - Which of you sixteen... Looking at you

Brandon... Which of you sixteen robbed the toy store... And how much is the reward? We are going to go for a car ride.

Brandon walked up and place his massive hand on the old man's back "pops, we all know you were the wheel man, Shawn was the lookout, and I was the heist king... Merry Christmas everyone."

The presents were organized into people's names as they were laid in piles. "So, shall we eat first? chores first? or Presents?" asked Cheyanne.

All the kids yelled "PRESENTS!!" everyone tried to find a spot to sit or stand in the mountain of presents. They did it by kids first, Shawn got two new blankets from his great grandparents. Teething bids from Marge and George. New swing from ED. A ten-dollar gift card from Vernon and Vikki, a Glow Dog that lights up and plays music, and records your voice. It was from Cheyanne and the girls.

JR got a toy tank with action sounds from ED. A new game from Mandy and Brandon, ten-dollar gift card from Vernon and Vikki, volcano kit from Cheyanne and the girls. His parents got him a new suit for church. The tag said it was from Santa Claus. His grandparents got him an army men's playset. Then Santa Claus gave him his granddad's war jacket from Vietnam.

April got a new phone case from her grandparents. New cheer bag from her parents. ten-dollar gift card from Vernon and Vikki, bath spa kit from Mandy and Brandon. Cheer class and Dance course from ED. Jewelry from Cheyanne and the girls.

Lucid got a horse lamp from her grandparents. Purse with her name stitched on from Marge and George, ten-dollars gift card from Vernon and Vikki. Volleyball class with a pro player from ED. New volleyball shoes and net from Mandy and Brandon, from their mom she got a new riding saddle.

Luna got a few dark clothes from her grandparents. A handbag with her name engraved from George and Marge, ten-dollar gift card from Vernon and Vikki. A stuff bat and spell book which was just a journal from Mandy and Brandon. Her mom told her "your gift was going to be a bit late. It had gotten lost in the mail." Luna nodded her head as her mom gave her a playful wink. "Oh, that is why you do not order by mail on holidays." said Vikki shaking her head. Some of the presents were brought there by magick. She got some candy (Dragon Bites, Atomic Bites, Sour Patch Bites, chocolate Grasshopper, and Fruit Dragons.) she got a telescope, vials, and more parchment paper.

Lacey got a new dress from her grandparents. S heels from George and Marge. Her parents got a new tier and way better dress and a car key, it was their "old" sports cart, which was only a year old, and 20. From ED he got her twenty-dollar Emusicly card. She got a book on how to make a studio in your home from Mandy and Brandon. Then she got perfume and a spa kit from Cheyanne and the girls.

Mandy and Brandon got a massage kit from Ed, some new pots and pans from Cheyanne, fifteen-dollar gift card from Vernon and Vikki, vacuum and shampooer from George and Marge. Then got a baby monitor with a camera from her grandparents. Brandon got a football case from Mr. Green with the comment "so you can sign your own football and put it up for the time when they realize you don't have no talent."

"Thanks, ole man." replied Brandon while he shook his head seeing the seer smirk on Mr. Green's face.

Vernon and Vikki got new bedding from her parents. A deep fryer from Marge and George. Three cruise tickets to Hawaii from her husband. A book called The Greed Monster from ED. New purse and wallet from Mandy and Brandon. Then a grill kit from Cheyanne and the girls.

Ed opens his gifts it was a set of plates from his parents, some small shot glasses from Marge and George, ten-dollar gift card from Vernon and Vikki. Sign football from Brandon and Mandy, a new heavy blanket from Cheyanne and the girls.

Marge and George got a family candle photo from Mrs. Green and Mr. Green. Fifteen-dollar gift card from Vernon and Vikki, a spot package from ED. Frame with the Lord's prayer engraved in it from Brandon and Mandy. Tickets to a dinner and show to a Holy Spirit Show from Cheyanne and the girls.

Cheyanne got new riding boots from her parents, some books from Marge and George. Fifteen-dollar gift card from Vernon and Vikki. New saddle for her along with a hundred- and fifty-dollar gift card from Ed. A quilt made with her daughters' picture stitched in it from Mandy and Brandon.

266

Mr. and Mrs. Green got some new smell good stuff from Marge and George, Fifteen-dollar gift card from Vernon and Vikki. A large photo of all the kids and grand kids from ED. A photo of them together from Mandy and Brandon. Lastly, they got a set of crystal set of plates and glasses from Cheyanne.

"That is everyone, Merry Christ-." George was shut off while he threw a Christmas bow at his wife.

"What about the boy?" replied Mr. Green as he pointed to DJ who sat on the couch by Luna.

"- Maybe Vern and Vikki have more gift cards." Said Ed while he smirked mischievously.

"We figured, that would be the best gifts." replied Vernon as he shot a look of disgust to ED. Cheyanne looked around the room and saw a few presents hiding off in the corner.

"There are a few more presents." she said while she picked up a present, in fact... It was for DJ from "Santa", he opens them one by one. He got vials, Dungeon and Wizards, a telescope, random candies, grow your own pet dragon, a pet crow, and a Crowfeather throw blanket.

After it was all done with opening gifts. They ate a late breakfast, and everyone had enjoyed their stuff. Luna and JR played with his army men till slept took over and they fell asleep for a nap. The boys watched the game when a knock Came from the door, followed by another knock. Cheyanne got up and open the door "Merry Christmas! How are you Gracy?, Luna is upstairs.

Come on in. How was your Christmas?" She hugged Gracy.
"It was good Momma Chey, How was yours?,," she asked as she
kicked her shoes off and went to Luna's room. DJ followed her up
the stairs. "Hey DJ, Merry Christmas." she said to him as they
peered around the corner of Luna's room.

Luna laid asleep on the bed with JR. Gracy walked in cat-
like stealth to her steps. She climbed up on the bed next to her and
slowly blew on her ear. Luna swiped at her ear lightly"-stop
Lucid." murmured out lowly. DJ and Gracy chuckled as Gracy did
it again. Luna woke up slowly with a grumble "I said stop. Luc-
GRACY!" sprung awake Luna jumped up and hugged her. JR
joked awake.

A few minutes had passed after small talk about what
everyone got for gifts, JR and DJ played with his toys. The aroma
of lunch filled the air, a knock came from the front door again.
"Who could that be, don't people know it is Christmas?" snarled
Vikki glaring at Cheyanne as she goes and open the door...

Gracy and Luna lay on the bed looking at old photos of
them from a year ago to five years ago. They laid head-to-head,
head on shoulder. JR took DJ's soldier for a prisoner. The door
open, wearing a red sweater, jeans, and cute black suede boots,
with a Christmas bandanna with a snowflake charm, dreads free-
flowing Jenny stood there.

"Hey, Luna! Merry Christmas." said Jenny with a wide
smile across her face as she stood in the doorway. Luna shot up

268

with amazement and astounding that Jenny was standing right there. In her town, not just town but home, but more important in her room. Luna ran over and gave Jenny such a big hug "I have missed you so much! How are you, how was your Christmas? How, why are you here?" Luna said in excitement as her mind raced with bliss.

Gracy looked to them then to DJ as she pointed to Jenny with a whisper "this is her giy?" DJ nodded his head while Gracy stood up and walked over to Luna and Jenny with an extended hand and sarcastic flowed frown her freely "- HI, you must be Giy... I am Gracy... Luna tooold me so much about you." Gracy stared daggers towards Luna.

"Oh- no, I'm Jenny, Luna's girlfriend. Nice to meet you. Luna told me soo much about you." fibbed Jenny, she picked up on the sarcasm very well, she lied to make things not so bad.

"Oh, really? What did she say?," replied Gracy as snugged Jenny "She hasn't mentioned you one bit."

DJ stood on the other side of the room must... Window?--- Two story dropped, may be worth it... Make a run for the door?--- To small of a gap... Angry girls.)

"-She said you were her best friend." replied Jenny while she offered a friendly smile. Gracy felt betrayed and stormed out, Luna chased after her. They stood in the entryway by the front door.

"-Gracy come on, don't leave." said Luna looking hurt as she lowered her eyes. The house grew extremely quiet, not even a

269

mouse stirred.

Then Gracy began to shout at Luna "I – SHOULD- OF-KNOWN! We are best friends, instead, you hid and lied about it... What else did you lie about... Living at your Aunts Marge and Uncles George's since school started?" Gracy stood almost in tears as she felt more hurt as she stared at her best friend.

"She didn't stay with us.," said George in a whisper. His wife hit his arm."You shall not lie, the truth will set you free." George told Marge; she rolled her eyes. Gracy overheard George's whisper. She took off her red and blue BFFE (Best friend for eternity) bracelet and laid it on the table, her face full of tears while she spoke with a hoarse voice "I can't believe you lied to me... Luna, enjoy your giy." Gracy turned to leave while Luna grabbed her arm.

"Grac, I am so sorry. I wanted to tell you, I just didn't want it to be the first thing you hear is that it was the first time I saw you in a few months."

Gracy turned and slapped Luna and left the house leaving Luna's heartbroken, stomach tighten, and tears staining her cheeks. She turned and saw everyone looking at her. Lucid sat in the living room and began to concentrate with her eyes focused and her hand out as time began to rewind. Gracy's slap didn't happen, they argued Luna backed track upstairs, followed by Gracy.

By this time, Lucid felt weak, but she pushed on for a few more minutes. Jenny walked back words down the stairs. She slipped her boots on, talked to their mom, Jenny went out, the door had shut, Cheyanne walked backward to the kitchen, a knock could be heard. "?samtsirhC s'tI wonk elpoep, eb taht dlould ohW" said Vikki, then another knock came from the door.

The room became slightly dark, and breathing was raspy. Blood dripped from her nose. She has pushed her limits; a knock came from the door yet again "I got it mom!" Said Lucid as she rushed to the door wiping the blood from her nose.

"Who could that be, don't people know it's Christmas?" said Vikki glaring at Cheyanne.

Lucid opened the door, she still felt dizzy and extremely light-headed. "Oh, hi Jenny, - Luna's not here right now."

"-Oh, well that's sadden. I wanted to surprise her." replied Jenny with disappointment in her eyes as she looked around.

"Oooh, trust me there would be a lot of surprises..." said Lucid lowly as she smiled at Jenny

"Do you know when she will be back?" asked Jenny crossing her arms to block the wind.

"No, she went to her BEST friend's house, Gracy Deerwood. They have been friends for five years."-

JR came out of the room and saw Jenny at the bottom of the stairs on the front porch. He saw her hair "A pirate girl!" he shouted out, Luna sprung up from the bed.

"A pirate girl?" --- Jenny! Gracy, come meet my friend." said Luna while she ran out of the room followed by DJ with knots

271

in his stomach. They came down the stairs and saw Luna and Jenny hug.

"JENJEN!" shrieked Luna.

"Hey, Lina! Your sister said you weren't here." replied Jenny eye Lucid who smiled ever so lightly now as she felt her cheeks grow red. Gracy walked over looking at DJ "Giy?" she whispered to him as he nodded his head. She walked up with her hand extended out.

"- Hi, you must be Giy... I -" Jeny had stopped her.

"O.M.G.! Bit is nice to finally meet you Gracy, I am Jenny. Luna's told me so much about you. Five years of friendship, that is awesome such a long time. Hope me and Luna can have a bond line that." exclaimed Jenny while Gracy stood there dumbstruck along with Luna. DJ was shocked cause Luna had never mentioned Gracy to any of them before. Gracy's cheeks and ears went strawberry red as she flushed.

"That is so sweet, nice to meet you. I need to be headed back home for dinner. BYE MOMMA CHEY! Bye Starbear.," They all hugged, and she turned to Lucid "Bye Allysaurs and DJ." They went back inside, everyone took their shoes off- and "who's her-, Lucid! Your nose is bleeding again." said Cheyanne with worry while she grabbed a wet towel.

Lucid went to clean up as Luna introduce Jenny to everyone. "Ah, your one of those traveling gyps, aren't you?" said Mr. Green while they went upstairs. Luna grabbed Jenny's hand and rushed her up the stairs to her room. They talked while Jenny told

Luna about the shadow bus that she took to get here. She pulled out a box, she wore the necklace that Luna got her for Christmas. She handed Luna the present.

Luna grew with joy and warmth. She opened the box, inside laid a silver arm bangle. The ornament was the shape of a feather when light shimmered on it, and it glowed blue. "I love it!" said Luna in excitement, Luna hugged and kissed Jenny.

"I enchanted it myself, took me a bit. It will allow you to be able to astral travel without your body being taken over." replied Jenny as she smiled feeling very good about herself being able to pull off such a highly skilled task. Luna put it on her arm, and it flashed it off to everyone. "I got it for you at the fair when you asked what was in my bags. I said stuff for my mom. I had it in there. That is why I was in shock on the bus, I wanted to give it to you then, but I wanted to wait till Christmas."-

Dinner came, everyone talked and ate. ED told a story about being in Japan last year. Cheyanne talked to Jenny, she liked Jenny very much. Vikki asked Cheyanne if Lucid's nosebleeds a lot. "Not really, few times during volleyball games." replied Cheyanne as she took a bite of the ham.

"You may need to get her checked out." said Vikki looking at Cheyanne.

They had finished dinner, everyone migrated to the living room. Luna bounced Shawnie in her lap while Jenny played peekaboo with him. "Well, we must be off." said Vernon as he grabbed the suitcases.

"Oh, - do you have to go now?," asked Cheyanne looking at him "right after dinner?"

"Yep, he has to work in the morning. Back to adulthood." said Vikki squeezing her husband's hand. They had said their goodbyes. They had left and blown the horn.

"FINALLY! Let's break out the holiday cheers." said Mr. Green, Ruth smacked his leg softly.

"Be nice hun." she kisses his cheek as she laced an arm around his. Mandy stood with Brandon with a smile "So, we have news for you all... We are -" Mady was shut off by Mr. Green.

"Having another baby?" He looked at her as he folded his arms. Ruth yet again smacked his leg again "be nice, when did you two find out sweetie?"

"Just a few weeks ago." said Mandy with a smile while she sat in Brandon's lap.

"Yep, pops we are having a baby, we need you around for another decade to babysit for us." heckled Brandon with a warm smile as he pats Ralph's arm. Everyone congratulated and hugged her.

"Kids these days are like rabbits, don't know how to just slo-w down.," said Mr. Green eye Brandon and Mandy "me being around for another decade?" You see this woman, how she beats me. I'll be lucky if I make it in the next five minutes or see the next day." he laughed as he kisses his wife. Ruth hit him again. "- See boy."

"You going name it after me if it is a girl like you said?" asked Luna as she held Shawnie.

"No, she promised me." replied Lucid taking Shawnie from Luna.

"-Girls, I am not sure what I am having, but if it is a girl, it will be one of your names and the other's middle name." said Mandy as she watched the two girls badger each other. Mr. Green let out a hard caught as he held his chest.

"Dad, are you OK?" asked George and Cheyanne while she got up to get him water and Gorge moved to him.

"He had this caught for a few months. He refuses to go to the doctors." said Mrs. Green as she held her husband's hand.

"I am fine if Vietnam and your cooking didn't kill me. Neither will this caught." said Mr. Green while he rubbed his chest smiling at her "I am fine."-

Later that night. They went to bed. Cheyanne took her room back. DJ and Brandon took the study, and ED and JR had the living room. Luna, Jenny, and Mandy had slept in her room. April and Lucid sat in her room with a movie on. April looked around the room and saw her tarot cards on a shelf by Lucid's bag of runes. She pulled the tarot cards out "what is this?," asked April looking to Lucid "playing cards?"

Lucid smiled and took the cards "no, I use these to do readings."

"Reading, like what?" replied April curious while she took the cards back and open the colorful box.

"Past, Present, or Future.," answered Lucid while they sat on the bed. April began to go through the cards "will you read mine?" she asked with puppy eyes and a soft whimper. Lucid looked at her cousin shaking her head "your dad would kill me.," answered Lucid, the look of the puppy eyes was strong with this one "FINE, I will... But this will stay between us till death does us apart. Take the cards and hold them in your hands and close your eyes. Focus... Focus your energy on them, empty your mind. Let the energy flow. "Said Lucid as she explained to April.

April took the cards and held onto them tightly. Her eyes closed after a moment she opened them as Lucid told her to shuffle the deck. She shuffled the deck in her hands. Lucid told her to draw six cards face down, however, she felt. She did that she laid six cards face down.

"Ready?, asked Lucid eyeing her cousin as she nodded her head. Lucid had turn over the first card "-tsk -tsk- tsk.," she said the first card was a picture of a tower. The card was The Watch Tower. "What is it?" asked April leaning down looking at the card. "It is the watchtower, upside down. You are supposed to be watching over someone, but you are lazy about it." said Lucid while she looked at her cousin. April's eyes had widened "m-my brother... I am supposed to help watch him a lot."

Lucid turned the next card laying upside down, it was one silver cup "-Oh, April... Your slackness will cause your brother to fall more ill." said Luna, April's eyes watered.

276

"Is... is he going to d-."

Lucid revealed the next card facing upright. Two golden cups, sitting upright. "NO, he will come out stronger than ever." April smiled big and wiped her eyes.

"Good."

Lucid revealed a card facing upside down, a demon with horns, and a flute. The death card. Lucid let out a gasp clutching her chest, then shook it off for the devil card didn't always represent death. But it was just always surprising to see it.

"What is it?" asked April in concern as she looks at the card.

"-I – it's death, a dreadful fate will fall upon you.," said Lucid with sorrow as April's eyes watered. "But don't look into it too hard. It doesn't always mean death."

Lucid turned over another card laying upside it showed a male and female hand in hand, it was the lovers. Tears filled Lucid's eyes "s-someone i-in yo-your family is going to die." April looked scared and stared at her. Lucid laid her hand on the card, eyes closed...

Time fast forward from 10 pm to 2:58 am she was in the guest bedroom. Grandparents laid asleep in the bed; Mama had stirred in her sleep. Papa took a deep breath in his sleep... 3 am struck, blue butterflies fluttered from his mouth... Lucid fell to her knees...

"-Lucluc?" said April giving Lucid a shake. Lucid gasp

for air, blood flowed from her nose, her vision was extremely hazy. Her head was spinning, tears had stained her cheeks.

"-You're bleeding." said April, Lucid wrapped her arms around her for a moment before she had cleaned up.

"We... We have one more card." said Lucid with a shaky breath while she reached out and her hand shook. The card was facing up, ten coins were the picture. "Well, good fortune will be blessed on you.," said Lucid, but the hurt was still in April's eyes "I love you." she said gently. She held her hand up with tears and touched April's cheek wiping the tear away. Then slowly rewind everything backwards, each card went back began to face down, then into the deck. April's hands embrace them, her energy flowing from the cards, back to her. Then she walked backward and put them back on the shelf...

April looked at the shelf and saw the cards then the runes. "What's this?," asked April looking to Lucid "playing cards?" Lucid's nose bled, eyes jittery, dizziness took over. "N... -" she fell unconscious. April ran over and shook her, no response "wake up Luc!" April shook more, but nothing. Then Lucid's body began to convulse vigorously having a seizure. April yelled "help! Mom, Dad... Someone?!"

Mandy ran in followed by Luna, DJ, and Jenny. "What's wro-... Lucid!" yelled Mandy, everyone had run up the stairs.

"LUC!" yelled her mom in a panic, her heart was racing. Marge and Gorge took Cheyanne downstairs. Ed called 911 "my niece is having a seizure, Lucid Bell. --- Cheychey, any history with Seizures?" he asked his sister, she shook her head as Marge held her "no Sir, no, address?.... 1A Mountain Dr, Pigeon Forge." -

Mrs. Green had rolled Lucid on her side and spoke loudly almost a yell "Lucid, come on girl... Lucid, Hey Lucid." Mr. Green made everyone go downstairs. a few minutes later an ambulance showed up and took Lucid into the back. Cheyanne stood in tears along with Luna and April "my baby... My baby." cried Cheyanne.
"Which hospital are you taking her to?" asked Ed, his breathing dance with holiday cheer.
"Pigeon Skyline. "The ambulance driver said while he closed the door.
"N-no her insurance covers Mountain Crest Horizon." yelled Cheyanne as her heart was racing.
"Madam, we have to take her to Pigeon, then transfer her." said the driver, they drove off into the darkness. Cheyanne was shaken up pretty badly. "Marge, you drive the SUV, Ma and pops you ride with her, you'll take April, JR, and DJ," George told his wife Brandon put Shawn in the sports car with the diaper bag and Mandy got in.
George locked the house up and drove Cheyanne, Ed, Luna, and Jenny. They piled into her truck. They all pulled out, Cheyanne sat in tears while giving directions. Ed rubbed her shoulders from the backseat. Luna was in tears while Jenny cuddled her.

After fifteen minutes, they pulled up it was a little after eleven pm. They rushed into the ER, and they all found a seat while Cheyanne talked to the front desk. Mr. Green, JR, April, and Ed fell asleep. They waited. finally, a doctor came out. They found a quiet corner to talk to the Doctor. "We are doing some MIR tests. No Medical history in family or anything?"

"No, she is healthy... When she gets too hot her nose will bleed." said Cheyanne, the doctor took notes and went to the back. Cheyanne and Luna had joined the family once again.

Chapter 16: Unforgettable Break

$\mathcal{It}$ was a little after two in the morning, they all sat in the cold sitting room. Magazines sat on the tables; some random artwork hung on the wall. The doctor came back and looked at them all " You can see her now, two at a time." Dr. Jones brought them into Lucid's room. They walked in Cheyanna, and Luna closed the door behind them. The room was low-lit. The tv was on some random show that Lucid was watching. She laid in a gown with wires coming from her forearm and sensors stuck on her chest, stomach, and upper arm. It was half hour till 3.

"-Hello baby, how are you feeling?" asked her mom with a slightly shaky voice as she hugged her daughter.

"Hi mom, - hey Lulu... I am a robot," Lucid raised her arm to show off the wires. The morphine made her high. The monitors had beep once in a while "-See! I beep-boop, boop- beep!."

They sat with Lucid for a bit. They held her hand "what happened?" her mom asked as the monitor beeped. Lucid's eyes grew wide "what was that?!"

"That was the machine." her sister pointed out. The machine beeped once again. Lucid ha in surprise and turned around, and she began wiggling a finger at it "hush robot, my fam is here.," lucid smiled as it beeped again "shh... That's my robot friend. Friend this is my mommy and sister."

Luna couldn't but laugh. They hugged then kissed her, they walked to the lobby, and everyone had asked how she was. Cheyanne told them that she was loopy and very high.

It was ten till three in the morning when her grandparents came in. Ralph sat down on the bed and kissed her forehead till he found the rocking chair. He fell asleep, and Ruth shook her head at her husband, then kissed Lucid's forehead while she slept. Ruth left the room leaving the two in the room.

"How is she?" asked Marge while she hugged her mom.

"She is asleep." replied her mom while she sat down placing her handbag in her lap.

"Where is dad?" asked Cheyanne. Ruth opened her bag and got some change out to get a drink.

"He is asleep as well. He found the rocking chair.," She looked to DJ and handed him the change "can you get me a drink please, hun?"

"Oh, I hope he is ok." said Marge while Ruth smiled at her.

"Sweetie, he is fine... He is seventy years old. He tires easily."-

Lucid laid in bed and began to have another seizure, alarms went off and a doctor and nurses poured into the room. A nurse turned and spoke to Mr. Green. One of the doctors rolled Lucid on her side. They counted how long the seizure lasted.

"Sir, sir... Wake up, Mr. you need to step out. SIR." the nurse shook him lightly. Then she gasped. "Get a stretcher in here!"-

Everyone sat around, a few of them took a nap. An hour later, a doctor came out with a nurse. He looked at Cheyanne and pulled her to the side "we are going to keep Lucid for two nights. She had another seizure, lasted for seventy seconds. Who is the older gentleman who was with her?" The doctor asked in a low hush tone.

Cheyanne's heart dropped "-my dad... W-what is wrong?" she felt faintness as she sat down looking at the doctor and the nurse. The doctor sat down by her "is that lovely lady over there his wife?" Cheyanne nodded her head lightly. He stepped away from them and asked Ruth to come to sit over with Cheyanne. Marge, George, and Ed all followed. Brandon had told Mandy to go with them, that he would watch all the kids. They stood in the vending area with the door close.

"Lucid had another seizure while watching over her. The older gentleman was found dead, we tried to jump his heart a few times... He was too far gone." said the Doctor with a heartfelt to him. They broke down; and Ruth fell in her son's arms as Ed hugged her. Cheyanne rubbed her mom's back while Gorge embraced his wife. Brandon told Luna to watch the kids, and he went over to hold Mandy. They came over and told April, Luna, and JR. They all broke down, Luna went out to Jenny and DJ and

283

they all hugged. ED blew up Vernon's phone, Marge blew up Vikki's phone. They went up to the room that held Mr. Green's cold body. The room was very nice, with hardwood floors and a fake fireplace. They stayed till morning came. Mrs. Green spoke with the doctors before they headed home. This joyful Christmas turned purely awful. The ride back home was in tears. -

The next afternoon, Mandy and Brandon told everyone to stay in touch. They had packed up and said their goodbyes and left. On their way back home, they stopped by Lucid and gave her a stuffed animal and a get-well balloon. -

Marge, George, Jr, and April said their goodbyes and left. They stopped by and saw Lucid and got her a get-well bear and a balloon. DJ, Jenny, and Luna were in the barn. Luna was distant. Even Jenny or Khan couldn't bring a slight of joy to Luna. "Love, it is our first Christmas together." said Jenny trying to shine some light on Luna.

"---And my sister ends up in the hospital- and my papa dies." she replied in tears and buries her face in her lap. -

Their mom sat with her brother, and their mom while they talk a bit "I- I hope Lucid doesn't blame herself for dad." she said, Ed shook his head and placed his hand on his younger sister's hand "you will just have to reassure that it wasn't her fault." Their bags were packed, everyone helped pack their dad's stuff in the bags " do you have to go back tonight?" she asked her mom and brother.

"Sadly dear. Ralph's information is somewhere at the house packed up. I am going have so much to do." said her mom while she left the house and headed towards the barn.

"Ed and I are leaving, I love you, Luna." said her grandmom while she stood in the doorway of the sliding doors. Luna got up and walked over to her as they hugged and kiss. "-And... Your grandpa loves you so much, you and your sister." This cause Luna to break down more, waterworks flooded her eyes while she hugged her grandmom even tighter.

"I... I love you... too... Why did he have to go?" she cried out in full sorrow.

"-It was his time, it's not fair. But the great Lord called for him. Now, he can watch over the whole family... I love you too.," She kissed her granddaughter then turned to DJ and Jenny " DJ, Jenny it was so nice meeting you. Take good care of Luna for us." she turned and gave Luna a kiss and hug one last time.

"We will." replied DJ and Jenny together while they waved. Her grandmom walked off to the car. Ed came down to the barn "We are off, we love you... It was nice to meet you Jenny and Doug." said ED while he hugged and kiss Luna.

"Love you too Uncle Ed.," replied Luna while she hugged him "also it's DJ... Not Doug."

"--- This reminds me of a story, funny story. When I was in Brazil-."

Lune covered his mouth "Goodbye, Uncle ED!" a faint

smile cross Luna's lips. "There is that famous smile." said Ed Giving her one last hug before he return to the car.

"-That uncle Ed of yours has some stories." said DJ. -

Ed and his mom showed up to see Lucid, they walked in the room with a stuffed animal of a dog and balloon. They popped in the room, three large balloons floated in the room, stuff animals, and flowers. "Lucid! Lucid! Are you in here, in this sea of fluffiness and clouds of balloons?" called out Ed.

"In my bed of a ship, Ahoy on over." beckon out Lucid.

"Not trying to lose mom in this sea of fluffiness. Won't ever find her." replied Ed while they walked over to Lucid.

"Oh, hush now... How are you feeling sweetie?" asked her grandmom.

"I am good, they been running tests all night, barely got any sleep. I am ready to go home!" shouted Lucid making sure the doctors and nurses heard her.

"-Did you... Hear about Poppa?" asked her Grandmom taking her hand while she spoke ever so caringly.

She nodded her head, tears filled her eyes while they hugged her "...Yes."

"I love you so much, and so did he." reassured her grandmom kissing her forehead. They all talked for a bit then the time has passed they said their goodbyes. Lucid laid there, the door opened.

"-This reminds me of a story, a funny story. When I was on

286

a ship towards England. -" Ed got cut off by his mom "she doesn't want to hear your nonsense." Ed smiled and waved to Lucid. She smiled and laughed " LOVE YOU TOO!" she yelled at ED and her grandmom. She knew the passing of her grandpa. She laid under all four stuffed animals. Dr. Aarush came into the room, a dark-haired man with sandy brown skin. He told Lucid she is going home today; everything came back good. He told her that they couldn't find anything wrong. If they made a medical guess, it was grand mal seizures.

The doctor called Cheyanne and told her Lucid can be discharged today. - Luna, DJ, and Jenny sat in the living room while her mom came in with a large smile " Luna, I'll be back. I am going pick up your sister." Luna sprung to her feet in the joy that her sister was coming home.

A few minutes later Jenny saw the time "I must go sadly too.," Luna hugged her "see you at school!" then Jenny had kissed her and gave DJ a hug. They walked Jenny to the door.

Jenny stepped out and held out her wand by the road. A black shadow mist opened up and a black double-decker bus drove up from the mist. The windows were black tinted and, on the side, it said *SHADOW BUS* in emerald green lettering. Jenny waved bye and got on the bus. The bus drove off back into the shadows.

DJ hugged Luna from behind and let go "I like your family... But that Uncle Ed is a serious loopy man." -

287

Two hours later, Lucid and their mom walked into the house " we are home!" called out their mom. DJ and Luna came from the kitchen and Luna pounced Lucid " are you OK? What did they say about you?"

Their mom shook her head handing Lucid her Keppra medicine, it was to help with her seizures "they couldn't find anything wrong with her.," said her mom "where is Jenny? I like her."

"She had to go home." replied Luna while she sat down on the couch. Lucid went up to her room. She saw the dry blood on the blanket. Shortly Luna and DJ came up to the room. The house was quiet, with no screaming kids or baby crying. No storytelling from Ed... And no grandpa and Brandon cutting up. A cold stillness fell over the Bell's house.

"Hey, how are... you?" asked Luna while she spotted the blood.

"-Are... you OK?" asked DJ while he sat on the bed with Luna and Lucid.

"I am good, thanks sissy and Deeg.," Lucid looked to them then- to her tarot cards. She looked down shaking her head. "I- I knew...," she spoke in such hush " knew... Jenny was going be at the door, Gracy and you fighting and losing a friend... Papa...I knew everything was going to happen."

Luna arched a brow " your runes or tarot cards?"

She shook her head then nodded "I can rewind time, up to twenty seconds safely... After that, I get a nosebleed, dizzy. I did

288

April's reading. I used the card as a gateway to the future and...
And I saw papa take his last breath- I came back too, in tears... I
was dizzy and had a bloody nose. April's face... I couldn't tell her
about papa. I rewind time and push myself for April... I came back
to before she could ask me about the tarot cards and that's when
my body shut down." explain Lucid while Luna leaned over and
hugged her sister."---Idiot."

    DJ watched then open his mouth "can you read me?" he
fell back off the bed from Luna kicking him off and glaring down
at him as he landed with a thud "-what's wrong with you?" she
glared down at him.

    A loud thud hit the window causing the three to jump,
they look over at the window that overlooked the barn and pasture
and they had seen a paragon falcon hit the window tapping it with
its beak. Everyone jumped then looked at the window, the grayish
falcon golden hues locked with DJ. The head of the bird cocked to
the side, the bird a roll of parchment tied to its leg. "--- Dagger?"
said DJ while he opens the window. Both girls looked at the bird
as it stepped into the room.
"...You know this bird?" asked Lucid while she eyes the bird then
DJ. His crow flew in and landed on his shoulder staring at the
other bird. "Yes, it's my dad's bird... Dagger is an old bird. He is
dad's travel companion." He took the parchment from the bird and
read it.

Boy,

Sorry for the late message, dagger went to Owl Hollow.
Then came back with information about you had left with some
friends. I do hope you had a good Yule. I will be stopping by before
you head back to school to see you and pay my thanks. I will be
leaving the Northern Middle East in a few days. I will see you
very soon.
Stryder

DJ read the letter to the girls; they didn't know how to reply to this. They had gone to bed and DJ lay in the guest room it had been a cold eerie feel to it. He had finally fallen asleep with the letter laying on the nightstand next to the bed while his Crow watched over him from the top of the wardrobe. - Five days have passed, Luna and Lucid were in the barn cleaning it up. It was New Year's Eve, Cheyanne had loaded up the horse trailer with three horses one for herself, it was one of her grand prize show horses, Bella, Then Lucid's two barrel racing horses, her black one name Rose and her white one name Moon. They had shoed the horses, put Christmas bells around their necks, and then grabbed three show saddles.

Lucid backed the truck up with the horse trailer. "-You trust her behind the wheel?" heckled Luna while her mom had finished with getting the show gear for the horses out of the storage. "Yes, I had been working with her for the last couple of months from driving to pulling." answered her mom while they loaded the horses. They had all got into the truck and drove to the New Year's Parade. They had pulled up by the river with the rest of the trailers. They unloaded the trailer and got the horses out all decked out in their Christmas gear. The mane and tail had been braided. The girls and their mom dressed up in western style clothes, hair done, and spurs on their boots with cowgirl small gallon hat. -

The parade had begun while DJ stood on the side watching the vintage show cars drive by, followed by the band from the surrounding schools, followed by some floats and balloons. Then a herd of show horses came up behind the floats, Cheyanne and the girls had tossed some candy and waved. Luna had put a chocolate grasshopper in the bunch. DJ waved to them as some kid let out a squeal when he had opened the chocolate grasshopper.

DJ stood watching then felt a large hand rest on his shoulder. DJ froze, eyes lowered, and saw a large white robe sleeve with blue trimming. The hand was nicely bronze tanned, rough, uncared sharp nails. Thick gold rings with gems dressed his fingers.

"--- Nice people, they are, aren't they?" a deep voice spoke in a whisper.

291

"They are... Very nice," replied DJ as his eyes fixed on the show. The hand was removed from DJ's shoulder. He had turned to the figure, but the man had walked off into the crowd vanishing in the sea of people. After the horses had passed and an hour later DJ came back to the trailer and met up with the Bells. People had pat and took pictures of the horses. Mr. Lundo came over "G' day, ye all look beautiful out der." he walked over to the horses and pat one of the horses "how waz ye Christmas?" he had turned and asked with a warmth of a smile. Their faces turned to a feeling of sorrow in their eyes. No words had been said about that night, and they didn't want to talk about it to anyone right now, especially Mr. Lundo.

"-Ah, sorry to hear." Mr. Lundo walked off while Lucid shivered.

"He gives me the heebie-jibbies." she said crossing her arms, then taking a brush and brushing her horse's hair that he had pat. "... He is a nice guy, just... a bit out there." said their mom. While load-ing the trailer. On the other side of the trailer came a sound, a crunching sound as if something was being chomped on.

Cheyanne and the two girls came out of the trailer to see what the sound was. A tall, hooded figure stood in white robes with blue trim. The robe went down just below the knees. He had brown leather pants and black medium boots.

"Can I help you?" asked their mom looking at the figure.

The man fed an apple to one of the horses. He lowered his hood revealing medium length wavy black hair, scruffy beard,

292

pointed chin with a strong jawline. Bright blue eyes, a scar across his right cheek from the outer corner of his right eye to the corner of his mouth. He had a very nice bronze tan completion. "Beautiful horses you have." his strong gaze had reverted from the horses to them.

"Thanks, who are you?" asked their mom while DJ came from the trailer. "Dad!"A falcon landed on the man's shoulder. DJ walked over to the man. "Dad' this is my friend from school, Luna. This is her sister Lucid, and their mom Cheyanne.," he said then turned to the Bells "This is my dad, Stryder. He just got in from The North Middle East.," Stryder extended his hand out and shook Cheyanne's hand. "How long are you in town for?"

"Long enough to give you a gift and pay them for their generosity, for bringing you in for the holidays, boy.," answered Stryder while he scanned the horizon. He pats the horse one last time then pulled out a golden necklace. "-Boy, this came from the crypts from Egypt. From the King of Kings himself, Ramses the second. They say the ruby is the heart of the desert.," said Stryder while he handed the necklace to DJ then walked over to Cheyanne with a small brown leather pouch "hope this will do."
Cheyanne had untied the bag and inside was perfect cut gems, two rubies, and four golden green coins.   "Wow, this is too much... He is a great kid, I can't accept this." said Cheyanne while trying to give the bag back to him. Stryder waved his hand denying taking it back. The two girls looked at their mom as if she had lost her mind.

"It had come from the treasure room of Neptune himself, from his kingdom."

Lucid had leaned over and whispered to her sister "it's Uncle Ed's twin..." Luna sniggered lightly and spoke in an utter whisper "this one bares gifts."

Cheyanne had smiled warmly "-Well... Thank you."

Stryder pats his son on his shoulder and he waved "I must be off. Let the Gods and Goddess guide you with fortune and health."-

They were back at home and watched the ball drop to bring in the new year. "Happy New Year's everyone." they all said. They tried to be happy about it. They retreated to bed, their heads hit the pillows, and fell asleep. A few days have passed, it was the last day being home till their bus picked them up. Luna ran to see Gracy, Cheyanne had gone to the store, and Lucid and DJ stayed at the house. They sat on the couch while DJ poked Lucid's side with his foot.

"Grooooosss... - Don't touch me with those dirty things. "Squawked Lucid with a snigger.

"-So, we are... alone." said DJ in such a soothing whisper.

"That we are, Captain obvious." replied Lucid with strong sarcasm. DJ moved over and poked Lucid's side lightly, she had turned and faced him. They looked at each other.

"-You kiss me, I'll kill you... How may I help you?" asked Lucid as their gaze didn't break.

"-Lucid...," DJ looked around and leaned in so closely and "want to read my tarot reading?" he had asked. They both broke in laughter.

"Let's go." Lucid said while she grabbed Dj's hand and lead him to her room. DJ sat on the bed while Lucid handed him the cards and explained to him how to put his energy into the cards. He had shuffled the cards. Then he had laid six cards face down.

Lucid turned the first one over and it was four golden cups upright "There is a shining of four people, a strong bond, unbreakable." said Lucid while she looked to DJ.

"Yes! Jenny, Luna, and I." replied DJ then he paused a moment "-Bree!"

She turned the second card, three of swords and it was upside down. "There will be a strong fight between three of the cups. There will grow weak and break." she said.

"Who is it, Jenny and Luna?" asked DJ staring at the cards.

"Not, sure, let us see what follows.," replied Lucid while she turned the third card. It was two silver cups upside. "-Dear – Dear – Dear... Two cups from the pack, the two golden cups are weak and lost."

"What do you mean?" asked DJ staring at her.

"Four golden cups shining bright, fight breaks out between three cups. Swords break into pieces, two silver cups still stand but weak and lost." She had explained then turned the fourth, the death card. The devil sat upright. Lucid's eyes had widened. She had paused for a moment as she felt her heart drop "-The death grows strong, a fallen out.," She turned the fifth card facing upright, it was the lover card. "Death or the fall out will cause a fallen out between two lovers, - or a new love will grow." Lucid had readout.

"Oh, - Luna and Jenny broke up?!" snapped out DJ in surprise. Lucid flipped the last card facing up and it was two golden cups upright. "The love that was shaken up came together stronger... Or the new friendship grew stronger.," she said then look to him "pick a card, for me to take a deeper look into it."

DJ looked at the cards then pointed to the number five card. The card of the lovers. Lucid closed her eyes and placed her hand on it. DJ watched in awe; moment later Lucid open her eyes as she felt dizzy. "-Well?" said DJ looking at her waiting to hear what she saw.

"-Girls have the right to keep secrets."-

Meanwhile, Luna sat in the hot tub with Gracy. Her dad had cooked dinner, he was a good cook and Luna had missed his cooking. It had reminded him of her dad. "Where is DJ?" asked Gracy while she relax in the hot water.

"Left him at home.," replied Luna. She had looked to Gracy skeptically "-why, why do you ask?" Gracy had shaken her head.

"No reason, I mean he is always by your side."

296

Luna's eyes squinted and stared a hole into Gracy. Then out of the blew she splashed her "OMG! You have a crush on him!" Luna let out girly squeal.

Gracy had splashed back while laughing "- Do not! I – I think he likes you," she battered her eyelashes "plus I have only met him a few times."

Gracy's dad Justin was semi-tall, bulky built with bright features. Blond hair and green eyes. He opened the door and called out for them that dinner was ready. The girls quickly climbed out and into the cold winter air. They ran into the house to dry off. Justin looked at Luna "how is your new school?"
Luna held the towel around her body snuggled in its warmth "it is going good. I am learning a lot, believe it or not, I am on the Sno-swim team."

Staci came in, Staci was Gracy's mom she was a short super cute woman with strawberry blond hair, sparkling green eyes with small features. They say opposite attracts, in this case, it surely did apply. Just and Staci made a super cute couple. "-You are on a sports team?m" said Mr. Deerwood "I am shocked I remember when Gracy tried to get you to join the volleyball team. You weren't having it."

"Yeah, funny how things work out." chuckled Luna. They all sat down for dinner and talked a bit. After dinner, they retreated up to Gracy's room. They lay on the large bed, Gracy turned and look at Luna "Soo, when do you and lover boy go back?" she asked facing Luna.

297

"In the words of Famous Lucid "Grrooossss". He is your loverboy." heckled Luna while she pounced on Gracy and smacked her with a pillow. "For cereal, you are going to write me and give it to my mom. She'll send it off to me." said Luna, she finally stood and Gracy grabbed Luna and kiss her cheek. She took a photo, the film popped out and slowly developed. "For you to remember your B.F.F.E... So, Jenny... A good friend or a good, go-od friend?" she looked at Luna flicking her nose.

"-She's a really good friend.," replied Luna while she wiggled her nose" we made that pact, that we would integrate them before dating." reminded Luna.

They had said their goodbyes and they dropped Luna off at her home. She walked in "mom, Luc, lover boy I am home." called out Luna, DJ's heart skipped a beat or two. He looked to Luna as his mind went to the reading.

"What was that?" asked her mom giving her daughter a questionable look.

"Oh, it's nothing just a message from Gracy." answered Luna. She sat with her family while they ate dinner. She ran up to her room while the rest had eaten. She tac the photo on her bulletin board. Then put her bags in the truck along with DJ's stuff. After a bit they sat at the bus depot, they had their bags and a few other things. They all hugged and said their goodbyes. DJ and Luna walked through the large bus depot doors.

Chapter 17: C.W.W.G. Knife in the dark

Luna and DJ both got on the bus making their way down the aisle way "Luna, DJ!" Ray and Dane had called out to them. They waved them over, Luna and DJ had joined the group of friends (Bella, Bree, Dane, Jenny, and Ray). They all sat down together before DJ and Luna had joined the group. Jenny gave them all a heads up about Luna and her family over the holiday break.

"Sorry about your loss." said Bree in sadness while she hugged her. Bree's knee was still in a sleeve.

"If you need anything, we're just a wand away." said Bella, also giving Luna a heartfelt hug.

"Thanks, everyone. You are all so great," replied Luna while she stared out the window while watching the scenery go by while the bus drove down the road.

Zak and Colton walked by and looked at them "hope, you all had a Merry ole yuletide. Dracoîn is going to take the cup back this year." said Colton while he had a devilish grin across his lips.

"Only way is if they cheat and have Professor Kanoe in their corner. We aren't losing our cup." said Bree in a harsh tone while she stared at the Rat boy and Rhino boy.

"---Whatever..." they grumbled out and walked off. The bus dropped them all off at Foxin Harbor, where they got on the ship and began the cruise across the ocean. The snow had covered the deck, and Luna had been bunked with Bree. They talked a bit and caught up. Luna went out on the deck and ran into Kain and Cecil.

"---Hi." she said so casually, trying to walk past them and not start any kind of drama.

"Hello, Bell Witch." said Kain with a grin.

"I'm not Bell Witc-... I am but, I'm not the Bell Witch." said Luna as she already felt like hitting him, and she had just seen him a moment and realized why she hated him.

"Never said you were... Just said Hello Bell Witch." replied Kain while he stared at her. Luna started to walk off to the stairs that lead to the upper deck. "Hey Bell Witch, here." She turned and caught a wrapped gift from him. She looked at the present that was wrapped in Dracoîn colors.

"Thanks?" said Luna confusingly as she stood there looking at the gift.

"Never say I haven't got you anything." said Kain. His brother Cecil looked to him with a brow arched. They walked off with whispers under their breath. She looked from the gift, then to them "why is he being so nice, what is in this box..."-

She had met up with the DJ, Ray, and Jenny who was playing croquet. She came over and leaned against the railing watching the three. They had put the mallets down and walked over to her "what is that?" asked DJ pointing to the gift.

"A gift... A noun anything presented or given; a gift.," said

Jenny maliciously "--- or if it is wrapped then one is unclear of what it is. Usually, if it is wrapped it is a gift." taking a punch remark back to the bus when DJ got "smart" with her about Luna's gift.

Luna rolled her eyes and open the wrapped gift. She tore the wrapping paper off and tossed it. It was a book *History of The Bell Witch: Cursed Family.* She looked from the book then at them "that snake... No wonder he called me Bell Witch."-

Dinner came and Luna sat at the table with the group and read a page " Summer of 1817, John Bell and his wife Lucy Bell had six kids Jessie, Elizabeth Betsy, Richard, John Jr, Drewry, and Benjamin. They live in Red River, Tennessee, which is now Adams, Tennessee.,

"John was a farmer with two hundred acres. On August 15th, 1817, Lucy and Betsy were doing laundry down at the river that evening. A loud growl started them, wolf-like grown, but it was deeper than any other dog they have heard.,

"August 17th, 1817, the Bells sat around for dinner, they heard a loud squawk coming from the yard. It was a sound of a crying woman. John and Jessie grabbed their rifles and rushed outside. What they had found was not a woman, but it was the family dog all mangled up. He had laid in pieces, a leg here, a tail there, and a few pieces of the hound dog everywhere..." Luna put the book away and went to the deck, the cold wind danced across the deck. -

"It's so damn cold and dark out here." said a watchman as he sat in the crow's nest with his buddy. One of the watchmen pulled out his wand and cast a bright light that lit the way of the ship.

"-Oh my Gods... " the watchman's eyes bulged out of his as he stared in fright. A large iceberg began to float in front of the ship.

"My- Gods, it's the hand of Neptune... RING the alarms!" said the other watchman who pulled the lever from straight forward to turn right. The ship kept pushing forward, slowly turning as it was getting too late. "Come on, ye bloody bastards turn!" shouted the watchman. -

Jenny and Bree had caught up with Luna as they watched in horror "we- we are going to hit!" cried out Luna as she watched in fear. -

A watchman pulled his wand out and cast a spell at the iceberg. The iceberg exploded as ice particles began to rain down. Bree, Jenny, and Luna took cover as the large chunks of ice began to rain down on the ship.

"Everyone OK?" Luna called out as they all stood under the small deck. Bree and Jenny both nodded, and they went back to their bunks.

Finally, after a long night, they had made it to Coastal

Village, then through the forest. Over Troll Head Mountain, and they had arrived at OwlHollow. Luna and Jenny read the book throughout the trip back to school.

"--- September 8th, 1817, A carriage wagon came to visit the Bells. It had been found tipped over. The driver, passenger, and the four horses were mangled to pieces. John Jr Bell found this on his way home, Adam's horses began to act up, and Adam rushed home.,

"October 31, 1815, John and Drewry came from a town on their way back home. A large black beast of a wolf with hellish glowing eyes, it was filled with hate, anger, and evil. The beast came chasing after them, BANG! Drewry fired a shot from the rifle. The wolf didn't flinch. "Come on boy- shoot the damn thing!" shouted John while he drove the horses hard.,

"Drewry reloaded, aimed, and fired... Bang! The wolf didn't flinch, biting at the large wagon wheels. John pulled out a revolver BANG- BANG- BANG- BANG! Adam fired four times out of six. The wolf tumbled and rolled along the ground while John and Drewry rode home."-

They pulled up to the school Mistress Flowers, and Mr. Rune stood at the large iron gate and draw bridge. "Welcome back, everyone!" they called out. - The students had made the way to the feast hall. The Professors sat in their thrones while the Lord Headmaster took his throne followed by the Pre Lords. The students had taken to their clan table. A roll of parchment laid with a feather quill next to the roll of parchment. Rune stood up while the room grew extremely quiet while he spoke. "I hope you all had a splendid Yuletide or Christmas. Some news in hand first: The corrupt has not yet been found. The good news, no sighting or word has been heard. IF anyone finds notes or any other things that appeared from nowhere turn it into a professor.,

"We had an article of clothing that had been *cursed* and a note to be a *hex*.," words broke out in the students with questions while hands raised. "Yes, Kat?" called out Mr. Rune.

"What were the *curses* and *hex*?" asked Kat while she stared at him. His lips never broke from a smile. "The *curse* on the clothing was just a *vessel curse*, to make the wearer do the things that the caster wanted.,

"For the other item, the note... The *hex* was to cause harm to occur more often. It was to break down the body and make the person weak for easy *possession*... Now first yearers, you see parchment paper in front of you with a *Nocheat* Quill and ink. You are to write what you all have learned about your Clan Guardian and the other clans.,

"Also the other scroll is your class schedule. We went from six to ten classes. Some were lucky to have eight or nine... The rest of you may return to the dormitories."

Luna's and DJ's eyes had widened "ten classes! Are they nuts." whispered Luna, Jenny was already writing down about the clans. Luna opened her parchment and began to write her clan,

~*Ember Lynn*, Born in the year of *843 BC*, a master at shapeshifting and transformation. Crow was the star form she was born under on the Harvest moon. In *893 BC*. She founded OwlHollow, it was called *cornix Pluma*. She wrote on and added on the history of Crowfeather.

~*Crowfeather Clan* was the name that *Ember Lynn* had chosen for the wisdom and intelligence of the bird. She had founded the clan under the star sign of the crow. It was the only clan for a year that attended the school.

Luna wrote about Goldenpaw next.

~*Leo the Perfect*, was born in the year of *846 BC*. Born on the waxing moon in the spring with the star sign of the three-headed dog, which was a *Hellhound*. He was good friends with *Ember Lynn*. He had become a professor and loyal to Ember.

~*Goldenpaw clan*: Was the name Leo the Perfect had chosen for the loyalty of the beast. Goldenpaw was founded in *897 BC*. At this time the school dropped *cornix Pluma* and went with the name *Guardian School*.

Jenny had turned her parchment in and went to the dormitory. DJ went through five parchments, Luna continued on with her work.

~*Kaine the Fearful*, was born in *801 BC*, under the star sign of *Draco* (*Dragon*). He was a ruthless being, ruler, and powerful warlock. He had struck fear in the lands. He found the school and came *Lord Kain the Fearful* in *902 BC*.

~*Dracoîn*: Was the new school's name and the new clan in

305

902 BC. he overtook as Headmaster and dethroned *Ember Lynn.* Dracoîn was chosen for the power and fear of the dragon.

All those late-night studies with Jenny and visiting all the clan statues had paid off. She got frustrated about it, it's a rare sight to see Jenny without a book in her hand or trying to learn something new. It drove DJ nuts how a know it all she is, but she knew a lot... She was very intelligent and loved to show it off. She never tried to come off as cocky or anything. She just took pride in herself.

~*Warlord St. Nickules*: Born in *810 BC*, under the star of Chimera in the summer of the Waxing Cresent. He came to the school in *902 BC* and fell in love with Ember. Between *903 BC - 908 BC*, there was a huge war between *Warlord St. Nickules* and *Lord Kaine.* The war ended when Merlin the great came Headmaster giving the three clans their own tower.

~*Chimerador:* became the last clan to join in *908 BC.* It was chosen from the sign in the stars of the Chimera representing it for Bravery.

~*History of OwlHollow* had many ups and downs, the long four-year war ended when Merlin showed up. Lorde Kaine got dethrone and lost his lost role as Headmaster. Merlin took over the throne as Headmaster.

~*908 BC,* is when all clans came in order. They rage rights between which one was better. Merlin came up with games held once a year to claim which clan was better.

~*925 BC* owls flocked to the hollow. Merlin the great and Mistress Ember had sat with the other head clans. They talked about the active owns that have been flocking here. They all agree to drop the name from Guardian school to OwlHollow School of Witchcraft and Wizardly.

Luna turned in her parchment and made her way to the drom. She recalled the password *Dragon root* the door didn't appear. She beat the wall; DJ came up and the door appeared. It opened and they made their way into the room "why didn't the password work?" asked Luna.

"It was changed, every semester there is a new password.," said Bree "don't you check the website? It's *Rosemary.*"

Luna sat with Jenny, and DJ came over and pulled the scrolls out "Are you excited about your classes?" asked Jenny while her legs laid across Luna's lap. Luna had pulled out her schedule.

"OF course not. OF I have ten classes."

Jenny stared at her scroll "hey grumpy bear I have ten classes too." Luna rolled her eyes.

DJ read his off schedule.

"I have eight classes!" exclaimed DJ happily while he gave a large grin.

"HOW do you have eight classes and I have ten!" replied

Jenny snapping DJ's head off.

"Because I am so smart." DJ replied glaring at Jenny.

Luna and DJ both look at each other, giving each other a questionable look. "You may want to talk to Mistress Flowers about retaking that one class you failed. Puck up that F and retake history." suggested Jenny while they poked DJ's cheek.

"You may want to take reading... Because you have nine classes... Your ninth class is *What Creature and Beast still roam* from two-ten to three. So, you'll be getting out at three." Said Luna while DJ slid down to the floor out of his seat.

"-My dream of an easy semester is over."

"We only have three classes together. This is going be a long semester." Said Luna while she rubbed Jenny's leg.

"Least we all have Kanoe's class." replied DJ as he looked up at the two. Bella and Bree came over and looked down at them.

"Why are you all so down?" asked Bree while sucking on a sucker. "We have three classes together and we have Professor Kanoe." said Luna.

"I had him last semester. He is a bit rough, good luck." said Bella while she walked off. The three had rolled their eyes. "Thanks..."-

They went to bed, lighting lit the sky, lighting the room up Bree had changed and looked out the window, large raindrops splattered on the window. "C.W.W.G. is going be fun tomorrow." she said to herself while thunder rumbled, and lightning flashed.

She saw her reflection and her eyes widened, letting a gasp she saw a woman in the mirror with stingy black hair, pale skin, and dark eyes as cold as hell itself. The woman was standing behind her. Bree turned around with a scream she was face to face with Mary.

"What is the matter?" asked Morgan standing in the doorway heading to bed. Bree looked around and her skin had flushed to pale "-nothing... My eyes must be playing tricks." said Bree while her heart race "Well, good night... We have our work cut out for us in the morning."-

Friday finally came, the school was still out for three more days. The land had tents, games, and shows. Jenny, Luna, DJ, and Ray sat in the stands with the rest of the Crowfeather Clan. Rain was coming down hard, the snow was mush and lightning lit the sky. Mr. Rune stood and waved his hand, and the crowd grew quiet.   "Welcome everyone to OwlHollow. I am Robert Rune the Headmaster of the school; I like to thank you all for making it to our Christmas Wizard War Games. The championship between the challenging team Dracoîn facing the champions Crowfeathers!,

I came up with this game to honor our past, our founders. The championship represents the four-year war. Let the games BEGAN!"

Dane and Jewels were commentating the game this weekend "Riding for Dracoîn, Sam Whyte number eight, Traci Brews number five, Amber Lyght number six, and the Captain and

Pre Lord Cecil Bloak!" said Jewels as the team flew out on their brooms and landing by their bench.

"Here are your Champions! Morgan Bowman number four, Timmy Moore number three, Bella Ward number five, and the beautiful Bree Summers the Captain and Pre Lord Number one!." Roared out, Dane.

They flew out from the right side of the tunnel. The stadium filled with cheers and glee while the Dracoîn and a few others had booed. They landed at their bench. Each team came up with a riding plan. Jewels called the first heat.

"Traci shoots out flying down the track, Morgan flies towards Traci... Traci blasts a bright blue light out of her wand. Morgan gets thrown to the side the side; the wizard hat gets knocked off. Twenty-five points for Dracoîn!"

Dracoîn stands blew up with cheers, Dane took over for Jewels for heat two. "Sam out of the gate hunched down to the broom handle. He is pushing a hundred and thirty-five miles per hour. That brook of his is a Glorious Fable, top speed is a hundred and forty miles per hour. Here is Timmy meeting Sam with wand in hand. Timmy's Pluto Duster tops off at ninety-five miles per hour. Where it lacks in speed its control and turning make up for it. Timmy with a fireball and Sam with *Praemium*, the field is filled up with dense black smoke!

Timmy came out of the smoke cloud still in tack, the bristles of his broom are smoldering. He is going to have a rough flight; they circle around for another go. Timmy shoots a ball of ice, his broom dropped making him miss. His feet are almost against the ground. Sam with a blast! Timmy rolled out of the way. Here they go for round three! And Timmy's broom is on fire now! What action!,

"Timmy, he cast *Aqua Pila* on his own broom. Sam has the advantage here... He blasted a bright blue blast, Timmy dunk under it. His broom has crashed into the ground coming to a complete stop. What an unbelievable run! Dracoîn wins this round fifty points!"-

Luna and Jenny made their way to the front row and both shouted "GO BELLA!" Jewels took over for heat three to call for the joust.

"Amber shoots across the field followed by Bella. Bella Blasts a spell at Amber, what a blinding hit! Amber's Wizard hat fell off! A quick win for Crowfeather.!"-

Bree hopped to her broom and dropped the crutches and picked up the broom "you can let us ride for you. You have to debroom him to tie up. Then beat him in sudden death." said Timmy looking worried at Bree.

"Each rider must ride or forfeit... I can't sit back and take the lost, and for Sudden Death, as Champions we can accept the tie or fight for the win."

Dane took back over for heat four. "Cecil out of the gate at full speed! Wand in hand, here comes the Beautiful Bree what heart to ride out with a bum knee. Cecil with *Praemium* right under Bree's injured leg!," the crowd booed, Mr. Rune watch the game while his lips stayed in his warmth of a smile that hardly ever broke "Bree held on, she turned her body and blast a fireball at Cecil! Wait she shot the broom's bristles. His broom is on fire, they are making another run. Cecil has lost control of his broom and crashed into the railing! Crowfeather had tied it up!"

They stood on the ground, Bree was favoring her knee while Cecil glared then smirk "this cup will be ours.," his cold gaze didn't break from her dark yellow gaze. "Are you going to let it be a tie or fight, you *Wissdoggle?*" this made Bree hot.

"Captain Pre Lord, do you wish to go on? Or do you spare Dracoîn with a tie?... OR do you accept his challenge to Sudden Death?" asked Mr. Rune while he stood from his throne. The stadium was a mix of chants.

"Take the tie!"

"Fight!"

Cecil looked at her while everyone chanted "it is OK to accept the defeat from a pure blood. You are only half the blood I am, your *Wisdoggle* family will be proud of the failure you are, bringing honor to the worthless Summer's name."

Bree barely could stand while she stared daggers at him and mumbled lowly, "we will fight." her gaze didn't break while she stared at him with a vengeance in her eyes. Her team looked at her as if she lost her mind. Whispers broke out under the Crowfeather breath.

"What is she thinking?!," said Matt while he shook his head " take the loss."

Mr. Rune pulled his wand out with a flick and a swish, two wooden swords appeared but with the illusion of steel. Shields appeared and they were the shape of teardrops, with a picture of the guardian clan emblem branded into the wood.

Bree staggered over to the sword and shield taking up to arms. Cecil took the other weapon and sword. "Rules for Sudden Death, the two Champions will bow to each other for respect. The first person to get hit three times by blade or magick loses. The winner will be awarded seventy-five points." Explained Mr. Rune while he struck the air with his wand making a loud dong sound.

Cecil ran up on Bree swinging the sword. She blocked with the sword. Her leg gave out as she fell back staring up at Cecil through the visor of the helmet. Cecil kicked the shield of Bree's smashing the edge of the shield in the bad knee. Bree had let out a cry of agonizing pain. She pulled her wand out and froze the ground, as the ground froze up to Cecil's foot trapping him.

Bree did a back roll up and pointed her wand out to Cecil and blasted a fireball to him. He hunkers down behind his shield as the blast broke him free. Bree taps her knee with the wand *Glacies sleeve* ice had formed around her knee while she winces in pain. The ice made a knee support for her. This cost Crowfeather a point.

She hobbled along while Cecil ran up, she cast a fireball and he dunk under it. She cast another one, he dodges that one. He up swung with the sword, Bree downswings with hers as their swords met. Sparks flies, Cecil gave Bree a hard shove back and swinging to her head. Bree dunked out of the way and struck Cecil in his side.

He stumbled back, and Bree stumbled forward hacking and slashing at him. He slammed the shield into her making her fall back, he pulled his wand out and she had hidden behind the shield to block the spell. He yelled out *Exarmare* the spell hit the shield and flung the shield out of her arm. She held onto the shield; pain had shot through her arm.

He brought his sword down across the bad knee breaking the ice bracer. He raised his sword and down swinging again towards her. Bree rolled on her back wand in hand *Praemium* the blast hits him square in the chest throwing him back twenty feet. He laid there in the snow. The score was two to one.

"Why didn't Cecil get the point?" asked Luna while she watched the fight.

"He hit the ice and not her." said Ray while watching the action. Bree stumbled forward, Cecil stood and pulled his wand out, and blast a fireball at her. She walked forward with her wand out and she spoke breathy *Repellere* a shimmering bright light appeared and repealed the blast back to him. He had dodged to the side while Bree came up and struck him. He blocked with his shield, then he stabbed at her chest. She sides stepped and spun around striking at him. He blocked with his sword then tried to hit her. She kicks his leg out from under him. They both hit the ground and got to their feet sword tip to her throat and wand tip at his face.

314

She blew a kiss at him then shoved away from him as he struck, he had missed, and the spell hit him turning him into a warthog. The stands were quite then--- "CROWFEATHER Wins!" said Mr. Rune while most everyone cheered.

There was a large feast after the game. Dane was waiting on Bree, hand and foot. Everyone had stopped by to say congratulations and check on her. Matt came to her and gave her a piece of his mind. Dane and Matt flew into it a bit. Mistress Flowers shut them down quickly.

Jenny was already nosed deep in her book of What Creatures and Beast still roams. "Already reading? School is in three days... Can't you be a normal girl for once?" shouted DJ. People's heads turned to them. Jenny's cheeks flushed to a shade of pink.

"What is wrong with me wanting to be smart, get good grades, and be a Pre Lord?," asked Jenny while she got up "I am proud to know the stuff I know." she got up and stormed out of the feast hall. Luna looked to DJ "seriously?!" Luna stood and chased after Jenny.

Bree watched the commotion "I think she'd be an excellent Pre Lord." said Bree getting up to her feet.

"Where are you going?," asked Dane " no one is going to take your Pre Lord spot." She turned and kisses him softly.

"To talk to Jenny, no one is taking my spot... I could be Head Mistress." she winked at him as he widened his eyes and look at Bruno. -

"Why should I be made a mockery and humiliated in front of everyone in the school, just cause I enjoy learning." said Jenny sitting on the couch with Luna while she crossed her arms in frustration.

DJ came in the room and sat down, his pet crow *Night stalker* flew to his shoulder and landed "it's not that you act like a know it all. You just flaunt it, treating people like they are stupid by telling them to retake a failed class in front of everyone."

Luna looked between the two "I don't want to see you fail." replied Jenny.

"-Luna got an F, and I don't see you jumping her. You made me feel stupid, which is worse than being called a know it all." replied DJ while his bird pecked at his hair.

The room was quiet for a moment then Bree spoke out to them "Jenny is just trying to help out. She just has... A bad way of coming off about it. DJ you have your issues of sarcastic spit off your tongue. You two are Luna's yin and yang. Jenny, you need to watch how you come off when trying to help people.,

"DJ, you need to let people do what they like doing even if it consumes them from you. Now off to bed you three."- The whole dorm was asleep, while Bree slept words had filled her ear, more of a chant "Mary, Mary contemporary, let me in and be alive." on the third chant, she woken and flung the blankets off and sat up quickly. She scanned the room, everyone was asleep... She turned and looked beside her, sat an old woman with long stringy grayish hair, long pointed chin, and nose little to no teeth. The smell of rotten burnt flesh filled the air.

The woman's robes were patched up, looked like she hadn't changed in a hundred centuries. Bree's eyes were frozen on the sunken eye sockets of the woman's pitch black sockets. Her breath had caught in her chest. She froze "Mary- Mary- Contemporary- Let me in and be alive." the old woman chanted repeatedly.

Then lunged out at Bree, hand wrapped around Bree's throat. Bree gasped for air while she tried to push the woman off as the woman kept repeating with laughter "Mary- Mary- Contemporary- Let me in and be alive." Bree pushed and struggled to get away. The woman placed her cold rotting burnt flesh of a hand on Bree's face. Bree's cries echoed; tears flowed. The woman stopped laughing and looked down at Bree. The hand around Bree's throat rested, and the other hand stroked Bree's cheek in a calming manner. Their gaze met Bree's shown fear in her yellow gaze.

"Mary- Mary..." The old witch spoke in a cold, deathly rasp.

"Contemporary." The voice grew darker.

"LET ME IN!" shouted the old witch. Bree let out a cry. The witch shoved her thumb into Bree's right eye into her eye socket. -

Bree let out a scream and flung the blankets off of her as

317

she sat up, breathing hard. She jumped out of bed, and tears rolled down her cheek as she looked at her bed. It was empty. - Morning came along, and Bree was found asleep in the common room on the couch. They woke her up, and she told them she couldn't sleep that night. She had a nightmare. -

"We got a very important day today! To beat Dracoîn fast, beat them not with the speed of the brooms but with spells. We are up by seventy-five points cause of the Sudden Death. We need to carry the same fire from yesterday." Said Bree to her team in the locker room.

The weather was still bad, the rain was down pouring, and the howling winds. The winds ripped right through you with its coldness. Jewel and Bruno spoke for the match, everyone got called out. Bruno called the first heat.

"Traci down the stretch, here comes Bella. Traci blasts Bella, Bella rolls out of the way. She is flying upside down! she blasts Traci, Traci is off her broom!" Fifty points plush the bonus of the Seventy five points. Crowfeather has the lead!"

The crowd cheered, from the wind you couldn't hear the cheers, barely the action. Jewels took over for heat two.

"Big Sam burst down the stretch away. Here comes Timmy flying down. Timmy casts a spell, Sam dodges with ease, Timmy is riding a school's training broom. Sam shoots a spell out... OUCH direct hit...Timmy is off the broom"

DJ barely could see the scoreboard "if we win one more time, it's -" Bruno announced the next heat. "Morgan Missed the

318

shot and Amber blasted Morgan's Wizard hat off! Dracoîn needs to knock off Bree for the tie, what a game!"

"Just had to say something, jinxed it." said Luna elbowing DJ in the side while she looked through the binoculars. DJ murmured out "-sooooorrrry for being excited." Jewels called out the last and important run for the night.

"Cecil and Bree down the long stretch, you know there is bad blood between these two. Their spells collided! They're making another pass and Bree with a dodge; Cecil flew up over Bree's cast. Can they afford another chance at Sudden Death?" Everyone watched as the fight went round and round.

"Snow clouds are dusting up from the speed of their brooms. Cecil barrel rolled out of the way, Bree loopy loop over Cecil's cast." They flew back to face each other. Cecil mumbled *Exarmare*, Bree held out her wand as the wand launched out of her hand.

"Bree had lost her wand! If Cecil cast *Exarmare* and cause Bree to lose her wand, he'll be disqualified! --- Bree-- she JUMPED off her broom giving the win- Wait she tackled Cecil off of his broom!. --- They awarded both teams fifty points. Mr. Rune stood and spoke with warmth "Crowfeather reclaimed the Wizard War Cup with the score one hundred and seventy-five to seventy-five. Cecil had cheated, we removed the points and awarded the fifty to Crowfeather for an outstanding two hundred and twenty-five points!"

319

Chapter 18. Letter from Gracy

The celebration of the win lasted all weekend long. Now Monday came along with new classes. Luna was late to her first class because she's not an early bird. She ran into the classroom fifteen minutes late. She walked in, fixing her hair and trying to catch her breath while she sat in her Dibble-Dog history class with Professor James Cook, an elderly man with bottle cap glasses with little to no brown hair. What hair he had made up for with the brow bushes and hair in his ears. He was a tiny man with a squeaky voice.

"Pleasure for you to join us today. Fifteen minutes late, you might as well skip and finish your hair. - Fifteen points from Crowfeather." he squeaked out.

Some of the other students from Crowfeather glared, and some students sniggered. Class ended and some girls from Crowfeather shoved past Luna "the back of your hair is still messy." said Emily and her best friend Sabrina laughed. Luna rolled her eyes and met up with DJ and Ray. They walked into the English class with Professor Emily Webb, who was semi tall for a woman. Younger than most of the Professors with bright green eyes, long blond wavy flowing hair, and little freckles. The guys were in awe over her as if she cast a love charm over them.

Zak and Kain picked on Luna bit, nothing too much or bad

for now. Ray and Luna rushed on to the other side of the school, to the third floor barely making it on time for World of Magick (advance) with Professor Nathen Sims. A simple tidy mustache and laid back black hair with lazy dull hazel eyes. Kain sat behind Luna who would push on her seat while he lean forward and whispered "Ms. Bell Witch." she did her best to ignore him.

Class ended and she walked to herbology. On her way to the large greenhouse on the other side of the courtyard, glares filled the halls. Luna walked past the glaring students to the greenhouse. Professor Caitlynn Petals looked like fall, she had autumn reddish hair, tanned skin with mild orange eyes. A short woman with leafy earrings. A student from Crowfeather pulled a parchment off of Luna's back, the parchment said I am the heirloom to the Bell Witch Luna snatched it up and the teacher cleared her throat.

"Ladies please focus. As I was saying, *Snap Dragons* have a mean bite. They are a very important part of potion making. The *Snap Dragon* root is what we need."

Professor Petals showed how to grab the *Snap Dragon* under the jaws and pull up clipping the roots. Luna got bit once or twice, she grew frustrated with it, it wouldn't stop moving and trying to bite her. She clipped the stem just under the bud of the *Snap Dragon*. The roots went from a beautiful white color to a deathly black.

"The roots are no good, that is why I demonstrated how to cut the roots and replant the flower... Instead, you beheaded it."

321

said Professor Petals.-

Class ended, and she made her way to Introduction to Alchemy and Potion she found a seat while Professor Ember Light had midnight black hair, hazel eyes, a cute tall woman. Explained the Alchemy circle and talked about how to make *holy water*. "Fill your vial with water and place it out on a full moon night, has to be in the direct moonlight."
She showed the difference between regular water and *Holy water*. The Holy water glows with a bright blue light. "A lot of potions require Holy water. Homework is to make a vial of Holy water and an alchemy circle." said Professor Light. The bell rung and Luna rushed out making a run for the dining hall to catch up with Jenny and the rest of the group. Jenny was doing homework with Bree. DJ's crow *Night stalker* flew in and dropped two envelopes, one for DJ and another one for Luna. She opened her letter it was from Gracy.

★ bear,
Hey, my ★ bear, so we made it to the Championship, Lucid had a band nosebleed. It stopped it was nothing too serious though. I miss you! So, how are DJ and your good friend Jenny? Can't wait for you to come home. It feels like you are in another world. Anyways write back, tell me more about your school.
Love
Gracy

Luna was excited to get a letter from her, sadly she felt
bad for leaving the picture at home. She really didn't know how to
tell Jenny, it should have been easy. She pulled out a quill and
parchment and wrote back.

Gracy,

Congrats on making it to the Championship!
DJ and my really really good friend Jenny are doing
Can't wait for Summer to see you. My clan, we have
clan colors, they are like hall colors. My colors are purple and green.
My clan is called Crowfeather, I'll bring you a shirt back. We won the
winter trophy. Keep writing!
Love
Your ★ Bear

Luna looked over at DJ who put his letter away. Luna
threw a roll at him. He turned and looked at her "Two things! Who
wrote you! and also, Grac said Hi." she called out to him over the
noisy feast hall. He looked at her and took the roll placing it on his
plate.

"-Dad! and tell her I said HellOoo!"

Luna cocked her head and pondered... -His dad has

Dagger...They left for class, Luna and Jenny walked into the class and she looked at Luna "you ok, you have been really quiet since mail." They sat in Introduction to Transfiguration and Shapeshift.

"Just thinking... Who wrote DJ."

"He said his dad." replied Jenny in a whisper behind the book,

"---Yea, but his dad has a fal-...I'll kill him." snarled Luna while Jenny's head cocked "wha-."

Professor Olvia Hudgins came in and closed the door behind her "You are going to shapeshift this teacup into a tea light." she passed out the teacups. She was an older woman with her dark hair pulled back in a bun, behind the glasses she had dark brown eyes. Luna and Jenny looked at the teacup in front of them then at each other.

"Open your books to pages twenty-one and twenty-two.," said Professor Hudgins "this is one of the harder classes, take your wand and tap the cup and say *Transformatio*. Image the cup changing and the tea transforming."

Her blue flower teapot turned to a white tea light with a flame wick. Everyone tried, some cups melted, cups shattered, and Jenny's cup caught on fire. Professor Hudgins put it out. The bell rang "class homework is to read pages twenty-one and twenty-two." she said while the class packed up and left. -

Jenny ran to the keep with Luna "What were you saying about DJ and his dad?" she asked while they ran through the hall

324

past the other students.

"-I think. -" Luna had been cut off as Kain and his buddies was picking on Bree and Ray "if it isn't the *Wissdoggle* and Wissard." Bree turned and glared at Kain and his buddies. "Get to class Kain, I am a Pre Lord."

Kain looked told her and snarled "---yea... And what of it, Cecil is too."

Luna and Jenny came up behind Kain and his friends "leave them alone, Kain." Bree stepped up between Luna and Kain while he turned and had that cold snake-like glare. "Kain class now, or twenty points will be taken away... I will also take you to Professor Raven."

Kain shook his head and look at the four of them "---fine." he turned and walk off with Zak and Colton while Bree turned to Luna and them. "You three, off to class as well."

Luna, Jenny, DJ, and Ray went to Basick Magick Protection. They found a seat that the four could sit together. Professor Akira Moon walked in, she was the Clan Professor for Chimerador.

They went over a simple spell to protect you from a small spell-like fire, how to cast a shield-like spell. Class ended and they ran to their other class which everyone dreaded, it was What Creature and Beast still roam. They walked in and sat, Luna, looked
at DJ.

"Who gave you that letter?" whispered Luna glaring at him.

"-No... no on-." DJ was cut off as Professor Kanoe walked in and spoke so coldly, he made the blinds close with his wand "silence, talk out alone again Mr. Bréon, you'll lose a few points." DJ turned to face the front of the room.

"-So we will be learning all sorts of creatures and beats, and how to defend against them.," said Professor Kanoe, he pointed to his white *Hellhound*. "Who here can tell me what this beast is?"

Jenny raised her hand along with Luna. Kanoe looked coldly towards the two "Ms. Bell, you have a *Hellhound* surely you can tell the class what beast this is."

"It is a *Hellhound*, sir." said Luna glowingly almost ready to pat herself on her back for answering the first question of the semester.

"How do you know it is a *Hellhound*?" replied Kanoe while he stared at her unimpressed.

"By the flame on the *Hellhound* body." DJ turned and pat Luna on the back. The Dracoîn clan glared at them, they were far unimpressed by them.

"You know what a *Hellhound* is... BUT you are wrong about what THIS beast is. Ten points from Crowfeather." Said Kanoe while he looked along with the class. Jenny was practically standing on the desk with her hand raised stretching.

"---Kain, can you tell us what this beast is?" Kanoe had snapped out. Kain cleared his throat looking to his Clan Professor.

"Everyone knows it is a White *Hellhound*." he perched up making his chest swell, he spoke very confidently.

"What does a *Hellhound* eat?" asked Kanoe while he ran his hand through the flames that sat on the *Hellhound*'s head.

"It east souls of the living."

"Very good on the diet... But just like Ms. Bell, knowledge is hard to come by. Ten points from Dracoîn... No such thing as a White *Hellhound*. Can anyone NOT Tel-" Kanoe stopped himself in the middle of his sentence as he saw Jenny waving her hand back and forth as if she was trying to hail a cab. Her knees were now in the chair to appear taller. "- I see your hand Ms. Striff, we all know you know the answer. NO ONE likes a little know it all." Kain had snapped out, her hand lowered while she retreated to her seat. The class laughed. DJ looked at Jenny seeing her face flushed a strawberry color from being embarrassed. DJ turned back to Kanoe.

"She knows the answer, let he-" DJ spoke out upsettingly. If the class could be any quieter it would have been now.

"DJ, stay after class. --- You and I will have a discussion.," said Kanoe with a smile across his lips "now, this beast is known as a *HellVixon*. For homework two essays on the difference between a *HellVixon* and a *Hellhound*. I want it on my desk tomorrow."-

Everyone left the class. DJ stayed after and Luna went straight to her Basic Charms and Enchantment with Professor

Light... Again, Luna found a table with a few other Crowfeather students. "Hello again Luna, a second time for one of my classes. How did I get so lucky?," she asked with warmth. She laid a bracelet out on everyone's desk. "We are going to take this bracelet and put a lucky charm on it. I say we can use all the luck.," she put some Holy water and a candle on the desk with a vial of green dusting.

"First clear your head and picture what does lucky looks like, how does it feel, and how do you feel?," Professor Light watches the students "when ready, open your eyes and submerge it in the Holy water.," She watches and showed them as well "--- Good, put some of the green dusting on it... All it is, is a four leaf clover, Ent root, and shavings from a horseshoe.," she hummed watching the students. "Good now. Now run it through the flame to seal it. Remember class Luck Charms are hard to give as a gift, why is that?" asked the Professor and a boy from Chimerador answered."   "It' is our luck that it was charmed with."

"Very good, Pete... Ten points for Chimerador."-

The bell rung for class to end, and everyone pack their things "tonight, read pages two thru eight. Give me an essay on Charms and Enchantments."
Luna slipped her bracelet on her wrist and walked out of the door; school was finally over. She walked by Kanoe's class and DJ was sitting at the desk writing. She remembered her time writing for her punishment from Kanoe. She walked to the keep but stopped and

saw smoke over the castle walls. She went out and went to Maîq's cottage and beat on the door.

"Come in." yelled Maîq.

Luna pushed the door open and walked in, she saw Maîq had a blanket over a large oval thing. "Hey Maîq, Merry latemas." Luna handed Maîq the bracelet. He took the charm bracelet.

" Obrigado (Thanks) Merry Christmas to ye too, ou (or) in mi tongue Feliz Natal (Merry Christmas). 'Id ye get minha (mine) presentes (presents)?" asked Maîq while making hot witch brewed herbal tea for them. He had sat down and handed her a cup.

"- I did... You left them at my house?" she asked taking a sip.

"Sim, I 'id 'idn't want ye not have a Natal (Christmas). Hope ye 'ike."

Luna hugged him "I did, thank you.," she looked at the blanket "annd what is that?" she pointed out.

Maîq looked at the blanket " nada (nothing), nada (nothing) É só um cobertor (it's just a blanket) ah." murmured Maîq in his native tongue. Luna placed her hands on her hips and glared "...Maîq." she growled out.

He sighed out "nada, nada... It iz just ah blanket." He murmured out while his ears dropped. Luna pulled the thick wool blanket off. What laid under was a large egg that shimmered brightly. A knock came from the door, Maîq quickly threw the blanket back over the egg. Luna opened the door, and on the other side of the door were Bree, Jenny, and DJ. They came in and Maîq handed them a cup of tea while they sat and talked.

"...Maîq.what is that?" asked DJ, pointing to the blanket. The egg rolled and the blanket slipped off and began to radiant multiple color lights from it.

"...What is that Maîq?" Luna stared at the egg while it shimmered lights.

"It's a am-." Jenny got cut off by Bree "Ampasaurs! An Ampasaurs, on school grounds... Seriously?!" shouted Bree, Jenny looked unpleasant to Bree for calling out the answer. DJ leaned over and murmured out to Jenny lowly.

"-Now you know how it feels to be out smartened."

Jenny's eyes rolled while she shook her head "-doesn't matter." DJ's lips curled in a large smile "Oh! Someone is bitter about being in the shadows of number one!"

Bree looked to them then focused on the concern at hand "as Pre Lord, I want to know the meaning of this! You are in a violation for housing a dangerous beast... Article ten paragraph twenty section C "No dangerous beast shall be housed on school grounds or near." Bree stared sternly at Maîq while she stated the rules.

"Bree- calm down, it's Maîq... Not like he isn't just a student, he is the-." Luna got cut off by Bree. The intensity was so thick you couldn't even cut it with a knife "I know who he is... You do not! Does she Maîq? Now, why is there an Ampassaurs here!"

"Bree! your ou-" Luna was cut off by Maîq this time as he stood by the fire staring into it intensely as if lost in thought. "She iz certo (right), I am habitação (housing) an Ampasaurs... I found dis egg all alone. I couldn't just deixar (leave) it. Der iz achados de captura de ovos (egg cachers) out der. I 'ad para salválo (to save him)."

"I must report yo-." Bree stopped talking as the egg started to roll and crack, it started to hatch. A short red scale muzzle pushed out of the egg, a crocodile-like creature climbed out. with white feathers from the neck down., long tail with feathers.

"Oh, my... I have never seen one before." said Bree staring at the creature. The beast ran towards DJ, it ran on its back legs and its mouth wide open. A loud bass sound (dubstep) came from it. Everyone covered their ears, the feathers flashed multiple colors.

DJ watched as the feathers' lights cause the body and mind to calm. Maîq tossed the blanket on the beast then pounce on it. The light show was over. DJ leaped up over the couch "keep that thing away... He was going to eat me!"

"He não é (He is not) big enough ta eat ye yet... É mais uma mordida de desmembramento (it's more of a dismemberment bite). " said Maiq staring at DJ who peered over the sofa.

"---Get rid of it!" demanded Bree before leaving his house.

"I am sorry Maiq ." said Luna in sorrow and left the house as well. -

They went to the keep to eat dinner. DJ's crow Night

Stalker flew in and dropped off a letter for him. Luna glared at him "...someone is writing him, and it is killing." she glared to him. Jenny tapped her shoulder and pointed to the Professor's table "look Luna." Luna looked to the Professors' table and saw Bree speaking to Mistress Flowers. "What does she think she is doing?" whispered Luna, her eyes filled with disbelief. DJ put his letter away and stood and made his way to the dorm.

Luna and Jenny waited for Bree to return to the Clan table "what was that about?" asked Luna while eyeing Bree.

"I had to tell Mistress Flowers. A school rule was broken, you saw how it attacked DJ... IF its parents came looking for it, then we would have a 45' foot Ampasaurs crawling around here.," Bree looked at Luna's upset face. "When you're a Pre Lord, you must hold everyone countable. No matter what." She stood and walked off. - That night, at the dormitory, no words were spoken between the four of them. They have done their homework and gone to bed. -

A knock came from Maîq's door. He opened the door and stood on the other side of the door, was Professor Kanoe, Mistress Flowers, and Mr. Rune.

"Olá a todos, que surpresa (everyone what a surprise) , Entre, entre. O que Maîq pode fazer por todos vocês (What can do Maîq for you)?," said Maîq with a broad smile and his ears perked. "quer um chá (What some tea)?"

"No, thank you Maîq. Tea isn't necessary. We are here on

OwlHollow official business.," Said Mr. Rune "may we come in?"

"Sim, sim (Yes, yes) ... Entre, O-oh, o que seria isso (What would that be)?" Said Maîq while his ears flatten but stepped to the side for the three to come in.

"Enough playing stupid Nails! Where is the Ampasaur." snapped Kanoe while he glared with pure hatred for Maîq. His ears laid back ore and groan out. "--- He iz slep."

Mr. Rune looked to Maîq and his warm smile and tone never perished "my friend Maîq, I know you mean well with full intentional. You must return him back to the Illusion forest. He must return to his home. You must know that."

Kanoe stepped in with his cold dead glare "Nailz, should be fired and return to Zert"

Mr. Rune placed a hand on Maîq's shoulder "going back to Zert would be a shame. I say you would be happy in Crystal Forest, east of here. Six moon turns, yes I'd say my friend you would find it relaxing."

Maîq's eyes widen and froze staring at Mr. Rune " iz Maîq disparamos (fired)?" Kanoe's coldness never left his face, but his lips curled in a slight smirk.

Mr. Rune smiled at Maîq and with such a casual tone "NO! not fired, no- no- no... Vacation for a month shall do, stay with the moon elves."

Kanoe let out a chortle, Maîq looked between the two " quim (Who) , 'ould Assistir (watch) va da' floresta (Forest) n Jardim (garden)? 'Or a ole' mês (month)?"

333

"I am sure we can find someone." Replied Kanoe while he stared at Maîq with a victorious in his eyes.

"That we can Kanoe, that we can." said Mr. Rune while he looked at Kanoe. -

The next day, word got around about Maîq and the Ampasaur and getting fired. Luna avoided Bree best as she could, Jenny tried to get Luna to talk to Bree. Colt, Zak, and Kain did impressions of Maîq being fired and locked up. -

Luna sat in Alchemy and Potions finishing up on a potion, which made people fall asleep. The bell rung; she went up to Professor Light "-what happens if you give a luck charm to somebody?"

Professor Light looked from her papers to Luna. Her eyes popped largely in her thick glasses "it will... very rarely bring them luck, lots of time nothing at all... And worst case it can bring bad luck... Why do you ask?"

Luna shook her head, looking down "no reason, just curious is all."

Professor Light nodded with a light smile "alright, see you in a few hours. If there is anything you need, you know my door is always open."-

Luna came into the feast hall and saw Jenny, DJ, and Bree. She turned and walked out of the feast hall, and out of the school, past the castle walls, and over the draw bridge. She walked past

Maîq's cottage, no sign of life. No smoky chimney or candles lit in the window, the cottage sat cold and alone. Even the snow had now begun to melt.

She walked down to the willow tree and sat under the droopy branches. Pulling out the book, Kain got her and opened it. "-November 14th, 1862, Elizabeth (Betsy) Bell, at age 9, was asleep one night and woke up screaming. Her mom (Lucy) and her dad (John) ran into the room, and the bed was jumping violently. Betsy jumped off and ran to her parents. The bed flung itself into the wall missing Betsy by inches."

"What is the matter my child?" asked Ol' Witchie Willow.

"---My friend Maîq got fired because my "friend" told on him. My other friend is getting letters from my--- Sister... AND not telling me, he avoids it."

"Oh, my child... Do not threaten on worry or sorrow. The wind speaks of his journey. How he is fine, he isn't fired... No, on a self-journey to find himself- reconnect with him. Yes, I can see him... He has changed, yes indeed... Not whom he once was, for your "Friend" you should not shun her, for her duties of Pre Lord. --- Bree is a righteous person. Sometimes duties of her status can put a twist on things.,

"Yes! She is the right girl for Pre Lord or even Lord Head Mistress. For your other friend,- family and friends two most important things to a child. To be felt betrayed is a burden. You are walking alone. They fear to tell you because they are afraid of hurting you. Yes, you must let them know, you are ok with this.

Then they shall tell you, my child."

Luna sighed and nodded looking up at Ol' Witchie Willow "how did you know about Bree?"

The Ol' Witchie Willow just smiled "my child, just as you, my child came and spoke to me."

"What did she say?" asked Luna.

The trunk twisted and crunch "sorry my Child, Ol' Witchie does not speak of others' burdens. I hold many tales, burdens, sorrows, and happiness. Get to class, the wind says Professor Kanoe is in a mood."

They have said their goodbyes and later Luna saw Kanoe's class outside "-what is this she whispered?" she whispered.

"Kanoe is the temporary game hunter." answered DJ in a whisper.

The class went on as usual with Kanoe's class, not well. They discussed the Ampasaurs on how they use their feathers to flash calming light and their roar is deafening. The bell rang and Jenny told Luna that Mr. Rune punished Kanoe for the Snorkbie game and he was the game hunter. -

They sat in the ding hall, Luna still couldn't pull herself to talk to Bree. Letters came in, Night Stalker brought DJ another letter and one for Luna. She sighed and looked at him "it's ok DJ... I am OK with it. - Who is righting you?"

Chapter 19: Happy Valentines Jenny and Luna

The sun broke over the mountain, a month has passed. Luna and Bree had finally made up. The snow melted away, and DJ kept getting secret letters. Luna walked over to him "who is writing to you. It has been a month now. How is it fair that I can learn to Enchant and Charm five things, learn four protection spells, make three potions, survive two tests from Kanoe, and not get one bite of IMPORTANT information from you." said Luna in disgust.

DJ looked at her and froze, then took a deep breath "do not hit me... Do not pull your wand out on me."

Luna's eyes narrowed at him " ARE- YOU- FOR- CEREAL!," she lunged at him. She pinned him with her wand in her hand to his cheek.

"What is going on in here?" Bree yelled out, arms folded at her chest.

"DJ's TALKING to my little sister!" snapped Luna while she dug the tip of the wand into his cheek.

"-Are you serious DJ?" asked Jenny staring at the two.

"-And Gracy... Ju-"

Luna sat on his chest with the wand shoved against his cheek hard "Jenny, -Bree... What is that spell to turn someone into

337

a pig?!"

Jenny pulled Luna off of him "easy girl... Explain yourself DJ."

DJ sat up and looked between each of the girls "I - I - we are all writing to each other just as friends. Nothing serious. I promise."

Luna got off of him and left the dorm. Jenny tried to grab her arm "why didn't you just say something instead of hiding it?" asked Bree sitting on the arm of the couch.

"She acts crazy. She was going to turn me into a pig!" exclaimed DJ waving his arms. Bella and Matt came into the common room from the hall.

"What's wrong with Luna? We passed her and she blew us right off." said Matt while the two sat down.

"-Love boy here is talking to Luna's little sister and her friend." Said Bree as DJ felt trapped.

"You go Lover boy- Beast Killer.," said Matt giving DJ a high five "- but on a side note... You are playing a dangerous game Friendo."

Bella smacked Matt on the back of his head "hush Mathew!- DJ, your walking on a very thin line... Breaking friend code. I do not blame her." Jenny agreed with Bella.

"She is right... I'd be upset myself. If my friend was talking to my sister and friend."

DJ slump back in his seat and sighed " We are all just friends." he got up and left the room. - Luna was in the bathroom, the mirror wasn't blacked out anymore. She looked in it and splashed water on her face.

"What a jerk." she said in a low tone. She turned to walk away and a scratch from the mirror caught her cye.

He is

She turned to the mirror and looked, her breathing came shaky, and her tone grew lower "W-who... Mary?" Luna stepped from the mirror. Words slowly began to scratch along the glass.

Betsy- Betsy Bell

Luna's eyes widen as more words scratched along the mirror.

Come home, niece.

The words burnt into Luna's mind home she thought to herself. She stood baffled, staring at the words in the mirror. DJ opened the bathroom door slowly to a crack "Luna?"

She turned and walked past him "that is the girl's room perv."

He rolled his eyes but sighed "I am sorry. I didn't mean to upset you. We are all just friends."

Luna stopped dead in her tracks and turned and looked at him with a glare, finally taking a breath "you should of told me.," she placed her hands on her hips "-sooner than you did."

DJ followed by her and bit his lip. He had an idea, a crazy idea that may be just crazy enough to make her feel better. "- This reminds me of a time, funny story -" DJ tried to sound like Ed.

339

Luna turned with a harsh tone and tears in her eyes.

"DON'T- YOU DARE pull Uncle ED on me... His last story is the last thing that reminds me of my grandpa to cheer me up.," She began to beat on his chest with her fists tears poured down her cheeks, her voice trembled. "T-that is all I have left...," she punched him more and more. "D-don't take it away.," her punches turned to slaps. "Do-don't take my poppa away from me... Yo-you have no right!," she beat on his chest with her palms now "N-no right...He's gone...," her head laid on his chest "he is...gone..."

He put his arms around her and held her close. The crowd stopped and watched. Jenny and Bree came down the spiral stairs to the main hall and saw DJ's arms wrapped around her.

"What is going on?" Bree asked Jenny lowly.

"---Not sure." replied Jenny staring at the scene from afar. Luna's tears soaked DJ's tunic as he held her "-he's gone... forever."- DJ walked her outside to her class to the greenhouse. He let her wipe her eyes on his winter cloak. "I'm sorry..." said DJ as she gave him a small faint wave and disappeared into the greenhouse. -

Tomorrow was a special day, just because it was Valentine's Day but also Luna's birthday. DJ felt bad, lunch came Luna was nowhere to be found. Jenny sat with Bree and him.

"What happened earlier with Luna?" asked Jenny while she bit into her burger. DJ couldn't even help, but his eyes watered.

340

"S-she isn't over her grandpa. I tried to help... I just made it worse." DJ got up and left the feast hall. Jenny looked to Bree with a light sigh. "Tonight we, three should do something."-

Luna was in the bathroom looking in the mirror "I miss him, I Want him back."

Words began to form on the mirror.

He misses you too.

Luna placed her hand on the mirror "-Bet- Betsy, is he there?"

Words form slowly.

My Luna...

Tears filled her eyes "I Love you...I want you back. I'd do anything to have you back in my life."

Words formed a little faster.

Miss you too, want to come back... You must sacrifice someone...

The mirror slowly cleared, in the mirror... There was an image of the dagger in her bag. She placed her hand in the bag and felt the handle, feeling the cold ivory handle. Her fingers traced along with the handle. The fingers snake around it... DING! -DONG!--- DING!-DONG! The bell rung for class, snapping her from her trance-like state. She left the bathroom. -

341

That night, everyone sat in the Common room. Bella sat with Matt, and they all talked. Bella, DJ, and Jenny sat while Luna came from the hall it was late at night. "Where have you been?" asked Jenny placing her hands out for her.

Luna took Jenny's hand and sat in her lap. She placed Jenny's arms around her and snuggled closely. People stared in awe while Jenny hugged her. No words had to be said. But they did all think the same thing Glad everything is back to normal. They all went to bed. Valentines was a big school event. Luna woke up to Jenny's bright blue eyes looking at her. She rolled away, pulling the blankets over her head. It was still dark outside. Jenny tugged the blankets off "morning sleepy head."

Luna snarled and threw her stuff pink-orange fox that had four tails at her. "Don't be like that to Starburst. She didn't do anything. Now get up Starbear." She turned the candles on as they flickered with light. Luna lazily felt around for the blanket.

"You're going to be late... Now up."

Luna snarled and mumbled at Jenny "what time is it?"

"Ten after five, now up. Today is-" Jenny got cut off "GET OUT... Waking me up two hours before class..." Luna sat up and grabbed the blankets, pulling them up over her, and curled up under them. Jenny huffed and went to the feast hall to eat breakfast and to get ready for classes.

Every morning, it was a war with Luna. An hour later Jenny came back to a sleeping Luna. She shook her "it's six."

Luna's eyes fluttered open, and she got up and began to

grumble and mumble to herself while she went to shower. They left cor class. Classes ended, and they sat in the feast hall for lunch. Bree got a singing rose from Dane that sang love songs.

DJ whispered to Luna and Jenny "-I like Dane... But how can a guy like that... Get a hottie like that?" They looked to Dane than to DJ. "He is a sweetheart," said Jenny while she worked on some classwork.-

The rung, Luna got up and went on to class. Classes went on as usual. In Kanoe's class, they talked about Griffins, the head and wings of an eagle, and the body of a lion. The bell rang, and she headed to her last class, where they made a bracelet to ward off evil.

She made her way to the keep... There they were Kain, Cecil, Colt, and Zak standing by the large school doors. "Bell Witch! Mary is looking for you!" they all laugh.

Luna stopped and glared at them "serious, that is all you have... that is sooo last semester."

They looked at her as she walked past them into the school "At least my blood is pure and not evil *Wissdoggle*, and my dad is around." said Kain with a glare. Luna froze and then ran up the long tower steps, going into the Common room. "SUPRISE!" everyone shouted and leaped out at her. Her eyes widen while looking at them, the entire Crowfeather clan.

"Thanks, everyone." said Luna while she sat down. The gifts were handed to her. From Morgan, she got a Crowfeather picture frame with the whole Snorkbie team. From Matt, she got

343

crow earrings and a choker. Bella got her a view orbs, Bree got her a *NotForgetMe* bracelet. DJ got her a picture of them horseback riding, he was on the back saddle. Jenny got her a necklace with stardust in the vial.

Luna gave Jenny her valentine gift, the bracelet (to ward off evil). Jenny gave her a *Singsong Rose*. The cake had been passed around after the birthday song. Jenny kissed Luna; Luna returned the kiss.

Jenny got up and went to the bathroom really quickly. There sat an envelope on Jenny's bed (Happy Valentine's love). Jenny smiled and opened the envelope, and her heart sank. She sat on the bed dropping the letter and the picture. She collected herself and made her way to the Common Room.

Luna saw Jenny and smiled offering a bite of her Strawberry icing and chocolate cake, Jenny refused it "I am good." She looked at Jenny sideways "you, OK?" Jenny shrugged and sat back while looking to the distance spacing out. "I am good."

Party ended and Jenny left for her room. Luna, DJ, and Bree looked at each other trying to think of what happened. Luna's feelings sunk (Happy Valentine's Day to me). "What is wrong with her, she is usually so positive." said DJ.

"Not sure, I am going to find out." Said Luna while she grabbed Bree's hand and they went up to Luna's and Jenny's room. They walked into the room and saw Jenny in her books. Each sat on Jenny's bed with Jenny between the two.

"What is the matter?" asked Luna rubbing Jenny's back. Jenny sat up and handed Luna the piece of paper.

Dear Jenny,

Wish we had more time to talk, more in private. There is so much I would love to tell you in person. Luna has yet told you, has she? She and I have been dating for two years. It's been going strong. Our last night together was a romantic, very special night. You need to know so you can back off. Sometimes if you love or care for someone you need to open your hands and let them fly away. Fair warning, she's taking you for a ride.

Gracy

Bree looked at the letter than at Luna. Luna held the paper "th- this isn't right... It's a fake, Gracy doesn't know we're d-...dating."

"Let's compare the handwriting." said Bree while Luna was getting the letters, Jenny murmured out lowly "-explains Lucid's lying... Saying you weren't at home, but at Gracy's... What do you mean you haven't told her about us?!"

Luna handed the papers to Bree while she compared. Luna replied "what? My sister lied to you! I just haven't found a good time--- yet."

"Just like you haven't found a good time to tell me about

Gracy?" replied Jenny while Bree handed the papers back to Luna.

"They... They compare exactly to each other."

Jenny handed over the picture looking at them "there is this too." Bree and Luna took the picture and both girls' hearts drop, eyes widened, and Luna's stomach knotted up "t- th- this isn't right..." she stuttered out staring at the picture than at the two. Bree shook her head.

"This isn't right, Luna."

Luna looks back at the picture, the picture showed Luna and Gracy laying on the bed. Their eyes were closed, heads tilted slightly, hands on each other cheek as it showed such a very passionate kiss. Bottom corner of the picture sealed on it in red lipstick was Gracy's lips (*XoXo Love Grac*).

"N-no... No that didn't happen at all." said Luna while she stared at it, her voice filled with confusion. Jenny looks at the photo with a weak sorrow in her voice "-did you and her kiss?"

Bree rubbed Jenny's back while staring at Luna. She sat quietly for a moment before speaking "n-no of course not! ... I mean, she did kiss my cheek. That is all, nothing more."

Jenny picked up the letter then handed it to her "this belongs to you." Luna hugged Jenny, she gazes over Luna's shoulder with a blank stare.

"I wouldn't ever hurt you, you are my Boo Bear." said Luna hold Jenny close. Jenny pulled away then look at her "I just need some space--- Happy birthday though." She got up and walked out of the room. Luna looked at Bree and shook her head

346

holding the picture and letter "this isn't real... This never happened."-

Jenny was in the Crowfeather tower with DJ, he hugged her "I am sure it was nothing." Jenny looked at him as it grew dark outside, candles lit the tower and the inner walls of the school. "You were with her for two weeks. Did she tell Gracy about me?"

DJ looked away and thought about the two weeks and thought long and hard about how to answer her as he shook his head. "No, I tried but she pinched me. Then she went to Gracy's alone on the last day. I highly doubt she'd cheat on you. You're the total Dibble-Doggle package. You got brains, know how to do second-year stuff, and your h-...good looking."

Jenny sat with her knees to her chest and nodded "thanks... Something feels wrong."-

A couple of weeks had passed, March have finally arrived the water grew warmer. The flowers bloomed and the sky was clear. Jenny and Luna were drifting slightly, even Bree and the three were cracking. They sat in the Creatures and Beast class while Professor Kanoe taught the class. He opened a cage, and a white and brown dog came out of the kennel.

The dog sniffed around the ground while the class went in awe over the beast. "Anyone tell me what this--- beast is?" hashed out Kanoe.

Hands went up, Professor Kanoe called Kain out "it's a

Doggo. They can camouflage to their surroundings. if they are scared or hunting."

"Very good... Twenty-five points for Dracoîn." Said Kanoe he walked over to the Doggo and smacked it. The Doggo whimpered while Kanoe pulled his wand out. The dog vanished and you could hear paws on the grass as he ran. -

The bell rang, and they went to lunch. Jenny sat with some new people at the Crowfeather table. Bree sat with Bella and Matt. DJ placed his plate by Jenny's, he began to eat while he talked to her "where is Luna? Are you and her still not good?"

"She is sitting with Timmy, Morgan, and Hunter. I am trying... I just keep getting a weird feeling... Something feels off, I can't put my finger on it."

They ate their dinner, Jenny stood and went to the Professor's table. DJ turned and watched her walk up on the stage to their table. "-What is she doing?" said DJ lowly to himself.

Mr. Rune stood with a smile, everyone paused and look up to the Professors' table "Can we please have all Pre Lords and Lord Headmaster come to their thrones."

Bella looked to Bree while Bree left the clan table and took her throne Between Dane, who was Chimerador's Pre Lord, and Jewels who was the Pre Lord to Goldenpaw. Cecil sat by Jewels; he was the Dracoîn's Pre Lord. Bruno Silvertongue took his Lord Headmaster's throne.

Dane looked over at Bree as everyone watched in silence.

348

Mr. rune looked at the greatest five while he spoke. "Bree Summers, summon your two Nobles."

Bree glared at Jenny while she stood up. "First Noble is Bella Ward... And second Noble is Morgan Bowman."

Bella and Morgan came down and stood on either side of Bree.

"Jenny, stand in front of all the Lords and the two Nobles. Nobles has Bree been upholding her job as Pre Lord to the most outstanding performance?" asked Mr. Rune.

Bree, Bella, and Morgan looked at Jenny as the two nobles spoke "Yes, Mr. Rune."

"-She has heart, is caring, and has pride. She holds everyone fairly, she brought our Clan to the Championship in Wizard War Games, even with a bummed knee." added Morgan.

"She will even remove points from her Clan or deliver them to detention." Said Bella.

Mr. Rune nodded while he still smiled "Jenny, do you think Bree has been upright, fair, and righteous in her duties?"

Jenny felt eyes on her from all directions. She looked at Bree and the other two, she nodded her head "yes she has Mr. Rune. She has been very fair even if we haven't seen eye to eye on things. She is a very good Pre Lord."

Mr. Rune pushed further on now "so, why the challenge for her spot as Pre Lord, is this because of the issue that contains Maîq?"

Jenny shook her head "no Sir, It is an honor to be up on

the Pre Lord's throne. I take pride in my drive to learn and my ability to push others. To get them to where they need to be."

Mr. Rune looked at Bree while she stared daggers at Jenny "Bree, why do you deserve to keep your position as Pre Lord, and not be dethrone?"

"I have been here for going on two years. I became Pre Lord last year in the fall. I hold everyone at fault students and personnel. I put my body thru so much for my clan each day. I don't push but walk beside someone who needs help Crowfeather or not.,

"This spot you must put friends and relationships to the side and be able to hold accountable without feelings interfering in the way. Jenny is the smartest and brightest first year for Crowfeather. Probably, in her school grade. I think her feelings wound interfere with her judgment."

Mr. Rune stroked his long white beard and look forward at the students while speaking " Professor Raven, your thoughts on the two... Bree and Jenny?" He turned and face Raven.

Professor Raven stood at her throne, the dining hall stayed quiet and very still. It looked like an oil painting. "Ms. Summers last year has voted number one Head Pre Lord, she kept the dive and heart. When things are unfair to her or the clan or team by luck or--- by other Professors, she kept her head up. Ms. Striff is a very brilliant young lady who is like Ms. Summers. She has the drive to learn and overcome obstacles.,

"Unlike Ms. Summers, Ms. Striff's emotions get in her way. Do I think Ms. Summers deserves to be removed as Pre

Lord?"... Yes... Certainly, we as Head Professors over the clans want to see our Pre Lords strive to do better and move on to Lord Headmaster or Headmistress...,

"She doesn't deserve to step down. Do I think Jenny deserves to be a Pre Lord?... Yes in time... Do I think today's the time? No... But it isn't my decision to decide, it is our Lord Headmaster and Pre Lords to decide that." Raven sat down and fix her cloak and long dress.

Bruno looked at Professor Raven while she had spoken out to everyone. Mr. Rune took the floor again "You heard everyone's side and thoughts. Lord and Pre Lords it is your table to decide. Students, Jenny, Professors, and I will be in the hall waiting out in the hall for you to come to a decision" -

The whole study body left leaving the Lord and Pre Lords in the feast hall. Bree snapped out "WHAT is wrong with her! Just because Luna and her having issues, she tries to take my spot. Let us get this over with."

Bruno looked to his four Pre Lord "Anyone has anything to add or disagree with?"

Cecil stood and looked at Bree with a sly smile "I and Bree had our feud, no secret at that. She tried to vote me off from Pre Lord before. I would love to see her go, but as far as a Pre Lord... This is me speaking the truth.,

"She is one of the best Pre Lords on the stand. As I said I'd love to see her go, but as a Pre Lord... She is outstanding."

They all look at him with a shocking gaze. Bree's head

cocked to the side and murmured out "thanks, Cecil?" Bruno cleared his throat "anyone else?"

Jewels added just a bit "for Cecil to say that means a lot, she has heart and love for the school. I don't think Jenny would make it, as Bree said... Jenny's emotions would get in the way."

Dane added his two scents "Bree is the best person for her throne. As Jewels, Bree, and Professor Raven said, Jenny, isn't ready. But it is your call Bruno."-

Jenny sat on the stairs while Luna sat with her "what was that about?" Jenny looked at Luna and she spoke softly.

"I think I'd be a good Pre Lord, plus it looks good on your school applications." They sat there then Jenny reached for Luna's hand. They sat out in the hall with the whole school whispering amongst the students. DJ came and sat down with them. He looked at Jenny and smiled "you've got this Pre Lord." The large dining doors slid open, and everyone had come out while everyone looked at them.

"What have you decided Lord Headmaster?" asked Mr. Rune. Bruno looked at Jenny and them. He nodded his head while he returned his focus to the Head Master. "We have..., Everyone has voted, we are glad to announce that--- Bree is still a Pre Lord."

Applause broke out while Jenny looked down in defeat. Mr. Rune smiled, and his voice was filled with warmth " Congrats Bree on staying as Pre Lord. We look forward to seeing you as you continue your Pre Lord job."-

Everyone left to their dormitories. Luna, DJ, and Jenny found a corner in the dorm to do their homework. Bree came over and looked at Jenny "hey, what was that about?"

Jenny looked up to Bree while she stood up and looked at her dim yellow hues "I would like to be a Pre Lord. I think I'd be good at it. It looks good on school applications."

Bree nodded "it is, but there are better reasons than that to be a Pre Lord.," She stared at Jenny "your emotions get you down. You have a long way to go to be a Pre Lord. I think you tried to do it, just because you were hurt by Luna. So you lost and hurt, just trying to cover it up with being a Pre Lord."

Jenny looked at Luna, then at Bree. Luna stood while looking at Bree "why are you mad at Jenny for bettering herself. You have no right to be mad at her for challenging you."

Bree looked at Luna and crossed her arms "the school body and Professors will think I can't control my clan as if I am losing control...,

"SO! Yes, I have the right to be mad. You challenge IF a Pre Lord isn't holding up to a Pre Lord's status."

Jenny looked at her and spoke a little coldly "IF that's the case, I'll never be Pre Lord because you're so good at it. Why is Cecil still a Pre Lord? He hasn't been so good."

Bree sighed and sat in a chair, crossing her leg over the other, looking at the two "Bruno, had been Lord Headmaster for two years. I am not going to go for Headmistress just to go even

353

though I'd love to be. For Cecil, we had our fair share of fights. No one challenges him... He must be doing something right."

Everyone was quiet while they sat there. Bree got up and walked off, they went back to do their homework. DJ went to his room. Luna and Jenny went to their room. They all laid down. Luna read her book under the covers.

"-December 24th, 1862, The Bell family sat around for dinner. The table got flung violently across the kitchen missing the youngest, Joel the two-year-old. Betsy got thrown into the wall, and her hair got grabbed. She began being dragged outside by her hair. Her dad leaped on his nine-year-old daughter and cut her hair to release her. A wolf, black as coal and fire red eyes glows while it ran for the door." She closed the book and fell asleep.

Chapter 20: Spring Race

A few weeks had passed. The weather grew warmer, and life fully came back to the trees and plants. Luna's been on time for her classes. They have been pretty good. She had lost a few points in Professor Kanoe's class.

It was finally spring, and on weekends, the mote around the castle was filled with students. Luna and Jenny were in their bikinis enjoying the sun. DJ and Ray jumped off the draw bridge doing a cannonball.

"Not going burst in flames are you, my vamp?" asked Jenny while they laid down in the soft grass. Luna was pale as a ghost. Jenny was opposite she was nicely tan.

"Probably will burn up." replied Luna while she lay there. Bree came over the bridge with her broom in hand. She walked off to the field and began to fly a hundred yards and back, redoing her flight back and forth. Dust trailed behind her while she flew. Bella got out of the water and shoved Dane back in. She got on her broom and flew over to Bree. Luna and Jenny watch the two race each other.

"Can't wait till we can ride brooms." said Luna. They lay there under the warm sun. - Kain, Colton, and Zak stood on the castle wall walkway between Chimerador Tower and Goldenpaw Tower looking down at them "look at those *Wissdoggle*s, laying there." said Kain.

"I- think they look hot." said Zak softly as Colton agreed.

"I agree... Let's cool them off." replied Kain while he pulled his wand out and made a water hover from the mote and he moved it over the girls and then dropped it. A loud scream came from the hill. Both girls' eyes widen while they sat up soaked.

Their towels were even soaked, they looked around the area scanning the field. - Kain, Zak, and Colt leaned against the wall "now that was great!" said Kain while they gave each other high fives. They nodded while watching the girls walk off to the castle.

DJ came up with Ray and shoved the girls into the water off the bridge. They let out a squeal as they fell into the water. The boys did a cannonball into the water.

"CANNONBALL!!" they shouted out as they landed, the water splashing over the girls. They merge up from the water with laughter.

"You guys are so dead!" exclaimed Luna and Jenny, they dunked the boys in the water. - Bella and Bree raced each other more than landed, Bree looked at Bella, Bella held the broom at her side "how do you think the race is going to go next week?"

Bree landed beside Bella and stepped off her broom "-not too good, my broom is jittery...Jewels has the new Light Speed Racer. I can beat Cecil... Maybe Bruno, but Jewels is top favor for the win."

Bree nodded in agreement about Jewels "straightaways she has it for sure. If you can beat her in the corners... Especially around the last horseshoe turn, your broom is made for fast cornering."-

Kain, Colt, and Zak walked into the bathroom the mirror had been cleared up. Zak and Kain both used the bathroom "when did Rune take the spell off?" asked Colt while he splashed his face with water. Zak came out and washed his hands. "Who knows, from what I overheard with my dad and his boss at his job. They are going to bring Rune in front of The Board of Magick Education. He will probably be can next year." said Zak while Kain came over and joined them.

"Be nice, Kanoe would be a much greater Headmaster. Why are they going to can the Ol' man?"

Colt and Kain looked at Zak while Zak stared into the mirror "from all the attacks earlier this year. The assault from the tree. Dad wasn't too happy about when I told him all of that and that the cat is here." While they all talked, words in blood began to form in the mirror.

Hello my boys, it has been a while.

They stared at the mirror before Kain spoke "hello Mary, it has been..."

It is almost time... Need one more victim...

357

Get my knife, Luna Bell has my knife in her bag.

Have her drink this. A glass vial of blue liquid rolled along the tile floor, and it hit Kain's foot. He picked it up and looked at it. It looks like Holy water.

"What is this?" Kain asked, shaking the vial.

Holy Water, it scratched along the mirror. -

They walked from the bathroom and Zak whispered "we aren't really going make her drink that are we? I mean what... What if it is poison and she--- dies. Pranks are one thing, but - I didn't sign up to kill someone."

Kain and Colt looked at the vial and then Kain spike slowly "I-I am sure it's just a sleeping potion is all... Yeah, that's it, it's just a sleeping potion."

"How are we supposed to get the knife?" asked Colt as they walked around the corner in the hall and bump into Bree, Jenny, and Luna.

"Watch it.," said Kain coldly "O-Oh, it's you Bell."

They all looked at each other "yes, it's me." replied Luna rolling her eyes.

Kain looked to the lot then to Luna's bag "Oh... You have Mary's knife." Luna looked at him dumbfounding, everyone froze and looked at her. Her face showed shock.

"W-what?"

"You have Mary's knife... Bloody Mary's knife." repeated

Kain. She shoved pass him and walked off down the hall.

"What are you talking about Kain?" asked Bree watching Luna storm down the hall.

"You'll have to ask her." he replied and they walked off down the other corridor. - Bree and Jenny huffed up the Crowfeather tower steps. They busted into the bedroom of Luna's and the other three girls. She swiftly turned from her bed, the look on her face was of fright. "SIT!" demanded Bree.

"I am no dog." replied Luna.

"Sit love, we just need to know what is going on." replied Jenny. Luna sat down on the bed in the warm room, she looked at Jenny and Bree. She undid the fastens on her bag and dumped the bag. Books, parchment, ink, and empty vials, and one vial that glow blue fell out of her bag. Luna looked at the vial "what is this?"

"-Holy water, where is the dagger?" snapped Bree sitting on Emily's bed across from Luna.

"Bree, calm down... All we know is that Kain is lying." rejected Jenny as she thought about Kain's words *Why--- how would she have Mary's knife?*

Bree took a breath and nodded in agreement "what were you doing? Luna looked between the two of them and sighed.

"I was fixing my bed..." replied Luna as her bed looks like she just crawled out from it.

"Oh! that is good." answered Bree while she pulled her wand out "*revelare*."

A blue light radiated under the blankets. Bree walked over to the bed and reached under the mattress and pulled out the dagger. Jenny's eyes widen and Bree glared at her.

"Why... Luna?" said Jenny as she stared in shock.

"I have to report this." said Bree. She turned and walked off. Luna grabbed her arm.

"Don't please, I could be expelled or lose all Clan points and then we'll lose to Dracoîn." cried out Luna.

Jenny looked at Luna with a hurtful look and rushed out of the room. Her mind was racing *is Luna really Evil Blood, is she helping Blood Mary... Luna- must be evil, WHY would she have or even get Bloody Mary's knife?* She sat in the common room while everyone came through the tower door. DJ came over and sat with her. He was still in his swimming trunks.

"You look sick, are you OK?" asked DJ while he sat facing her.

She just sat there lost in thought, the world around her just stopped and left her behind. He gave her a small shake. She turned and laid her head on his chest. He rubbed her back. - Emily and Lyndsie came into their room to change. Bree looked at them then kicked them back out of the room. Bree stared coldly at Luna. Luna's eyes averted downward "I- didn't know what to do... When I do right, things vanished or something. It's like Professor Kanoe already said when things happen, I am not far behind. If I showed up with the dagger, it really would make me look bad. I thought... If I kept it out of the spirit, world I could keep it safe. My intentions were for the good. You have to believe me." pleaded Luna with tears in her eyes.

Bree looked at Luna and shook her head "-I -I'm sorry... But as Pre Lord... I must, you could have put all of us in danger with this act. I am sorry Luna." Bree turned and walked out as Luna spoke up for one last defense.

"-Just remember... I saved your life... I had to break school rules for the good of saving your life."

Bree opened the door and sighed "I am truly sorry Luna." she walked out and shut the door behind her. She came downstairs to the common room and told the two girls they may return. Then told Bella she'll return, that she was on her way to see Mistress Flowers and Mr. Rune. She walked out of the Common room and into the tower. A moment later Jenny came after her. "-Wait... Don't do this, she deserves it... But she is about to lose someone who means a lot."

"Jen, this is why you are not ready to be a Pre Lord. Your emotions get in the way. It has to be done." answered Bree.

"-Please... Think about it, she saved your life." her tone showed desperation.

"What am I supposed to do with this? I am in a bind... I am sorry Jenny" said Bree as she began to descend to the stairs. Jenny followed her and took Bree's arm. "Isn't a Pre Lord supposed to uphold rules, show care and compassion,... Passionate to the students?" It's her first year at school and in this world... This year has been hard on her. She found out she is related to the four evil witches, found out that her dad came here, and he was evil... Her granddad died, she had missed his funeral. She's- about to lose me."

There was silence between them, nothing was said for a moment "get to the dorm..." said Bree softly while she turned and walk off. Jenny sighed and went to the dorm then up to her room. She saw Luna packing up her bags. Jenny sat on the bed, then Luna turned and hand starburst the stuffed animal, the orange-pink six-tail fox. "I want you to keep her."

Jenny smiled but turned to a frown "I can't... She is yours... I am sorry Luna, but- I think we should break up. You and Gracy, the hidden secrets... I think it's for the best. You couldn't tell Gracy about us. Are you abashed by me? Of me being with you or being your girlfriend?"

Luna froze, eyes watered, felt her throat grow sore, and tears dance down her cheek. "N-no, of course not... I just didn't know how to tell Gracy, that I- I'm gay. You are my JenJen, I-I -."

Jenny put Starburst in Luna's bag before grabbing her blanket, pillow, and her Monkmonk. She left to the Common room to sleep. She cried herself to sleep while sinking a song that her dad had sung to her when she was very young.

♫ Close your eyes baby girl, fall asleep tonight. Let your sleep drift you to the dreamland. ♩ Relax baby girl, close your eyes. and fall asleep tonight. Let the stars shine down on you and the moon wash upon you tonight, keeping you safe. Baby girl, sleep tight, let your mind drift you to sleep. Close your eyes baby girl. Fall asl... -♫

Jenny fell asleep near the end of the song. - Luna laid in the bed with Khan and cuddled to him as she cried into his warm side till she fell asleep. -

The next day, Luna woke up at nine. Sleeping in three hours, she got out of bed. Her Bell book fell off the bed and opened to page two-thirty one *December 25th, 1862, Lucy and John Jr found John on the floor dead, then heard a cold voice the Bell Witch saying, "big dose of that will fix it." Tears filled their eyes. They had buried their dad, the very next day John Jr found a small bottle on the counter. He poured some of the liquid in the cat's bowl and a moment later the cat died... THE BELL WITCH had poison John!*

Luna quickly picked up the book and got dress in her school uniform and grabbed the vial and ran to her herbology class. She got to class late, she snuck in slowly while the class was in middle of feeding the Snap Dragons.

"Ms. Bell, nice to have you join us. You are late... Twenty points from Crowfeather." said Professor Light.

Luna went and fed her Snap Dragon, which took a few bites at her "I hate Snap Dragons." she murmured out. A Snap Dragon spat at her, and she growled at it, the bell rang and she rushed out to her potion class. She sat in potions as they made blue flames. Professor Light explained how to do it "now you'll need an empty jar, crystal water, blue rose petals, and flame coal. Put it in your cauldron and grind it all up into powder. Pour it in your vial, tighten the lid and give it three shakes and -.," The jar glowed with a bright blue flame "there you go class.," the bell rung for lunch "class, read pages three hundred to three hundred and four to learn how to make a mute potion."

The class left and Luna came over with her vial she found in her bag "-can you tell me what this is. I found it on my way to class." she said holding the vial in her hand. Professor Light looked at the vial while pulling her wand out "looks like Holy water." she tapped the vial with her wand. The blue light water slowly turned to a green liquid. "It's an ancient poison... Advance alchemy, I must take this. Where did you say you found it?"

Luna looked at it dumbfound while she shook her head "o-outside by the hill... Yesterday."

"Get to lunch Luna." replied Professor Light with a soft tone. -

Luna saw Bree with Matt and Bella, Jenny sat with DJ. She went and sat with Timmy and Morgan. They got up and moved away. Luna sat all alone and looked down at her plate. Mail came in by birds. Luna saw DJ get two letters and Luna got only one. She lifted the goblet to her lips to take a drink, but she stopped. She tapped the cup with her wand "*revelare*." The brown-red tea slowly turned to green. Her eyes widen and looked around the room *Someone tried to poi- Bell Witch... John. she* thought to herself. The bell rung whole she poured it in her vial.

364

She looked for Professor Light, everyone went to the stadium for the broom race. She sat once again alone. The Pre Lords sat at the starting gate.

Bruno's voice came over the speakers " Riding for Dracoîn, number four Cecil Bloke!, riding for Goldenpaw number Three, Jewels Meadows!, Riding for Crowfeather number Two, Bree Summers!, and for Chimerador, number One, Dane Ward! Twenty laps for the win and the Broom racing trophy."

All the clans went crazy with cheers when they heard their Pre Lords name. A loud bang shot from Mr. Rune's wand. "They are out of the gate! Jewels is leading the pack followed by Dane. Cecil and Bree fighting for third. They are coming around the first turn. Dane over taking Jewels, Bree pushing pass Jewels. Cecil and Jewels fighting for third. Dane on the straight away, Jewels blocks Cecil. Bree blocked by Dane."

They all watch and cheered on while watching them speed by, dust clouds filled the tracks. Each lap got more intense. "They are coming up to the last lap. Bree is leading, Jewels is gaining on her. Cecil is speeding up to catch Jewels. Jewel passes Bree, the last straight away. Their pushing all they've got!--- OH!! Bree wiped out, her broom crashed her into the wall. Dane pulls into second place, Bree's back on, Cecil passed her. Jewels hunched down and--- she passed the checkered line! Goldenpaw WINS- Goldenpaw WINS! Goldenpaw WINS! Four hundred points to Goldenpaw!"

Chapter 21: Fools!

A couple of weeks have passed, people in year two and up were complaining about the April Fools Goblin who prank the school. He comes out only on April Fools, a mischievous menace, no more than a pest.

Luna woke up to a girl's hair that went from black to hot pink. Jenny came into the room soaked from head to toe. She change clothes. Everyone was late for class. Luna went to the shower and got in, and began to wash. -

Jenny beat on the door "Luna! I need my towel." a shriek came from the bathroom "I'm not going to class!" Jenny, Emily, and Lyndsie stared while the door opened and they all gasp.

"Ooh- my- gods. -" said Lyndsie slowly. Then a small snigger came from the closet. "-Fool!"

Luna came out dyed blue from head to toe "I am going to kill it." Emily opened the closet door... POOF! Black smoke came from the closet, and she coughed and came out covered in soot. A voice from the Common Room, a small deep voice with a snigger "-Fool!" Emily turned and looked at the other three girls, and she had a very large handlebar mustache. "He isn't in here." said Emily looking at the girls which had a dumbfounded look on their faces.

Lyndsie spoked up "-Emily... You have a mustache."
Emily felt her face and let out a scream. - Luna went to her potio-

ns class. Kain, Colt, and Zak saw Luna and began to laugh at her "it's the blue Lagoon Monster." said Zak.

"It's the Water Imp." added Colt.

"It's the Ice Queen, Frosteon!" exclaimed Kain. Luna turned to walk out the hall, laughter broke out in the room. "-Fools!"

Kain, Colt, and Zak stood covering themselves up as they stood in their boxers (Kain's was a tie-dye, Zak was bright blue and Colt was an emerald green polka dot). Luna burst out in laughter as Professor Raven came by "-what is the meaning of this boys? Get dressed now! fifteen points from Dracoîn, Goldenpaw, and Chimerador."

Luna ran off the class with a smile on her face. She got to class, Professor Light came in and saw a blue Luna. "Oh dear, Goblin of Menace got you... Poor child." said Professor Light pulling out her wand and giving it a small wave "*Normalis "*."

Luna went from blue back to pale again, she found her seat and the class went over a potion to cause someone to go mute for a short period of time. Professor Light took her small mixing cauldron and added blue rose petals (4), frog breath, Stevia root (4), and mushroom caps (1) and she blended it all together. Poof! Professor light lost her voice.

"-Fool!" the same small deep voice from earlier spoke up, the bell rang to release class. - Lunch came around and Luna passed a boy from Goldenpaw with a long rat tail in tears. She sat down with some of the other kids from Crowfeather. DJ and Jenny sat near the top of the table. DJ looked at Jenny and ate his roll "-this chicken is good... Take it you and Luna haven't made up?"

Jenny poked at her food, then looked over at Bree, then over at Luna "-nope, not ready to talk to her.," replied Jenny gloomily. DJ put the piece of chicken in his mouth and froze "what is it DJ? She has just done a lot, and I just need time... Don't give me that look."

DJ spat his chicken out and a small yellow chick came out of his mouth and onto his plate. Everyone stared at Dracoîn's table bust out in laughter. "-I am done eating." said DJ feeling sick staring down at this chicken.

"I think I am going to be sick." replied Jenny pushing her plate away.

"-Fools!"

The table let out a scream as the Professors' table shook their heads. "Robert, anything we can do about this Goblin the Menace?" asked Mistress Flowers.

Mr. Rune sighs out while he strokes his beard "I have tried to get rid of him. When I first came to this school. His magick is far superior then any Wizards that I have met. No, in time he will be gone."

Laughter broke out "look Candice can only walk backwards." Said a boy from Chimerador.

"-Fool!" said the Goblin. -

Lunch had ended, DJ came up to Bree as he look over at

Jenny and gulped "-hey Bree... Can I speak with you for a moment?"

Bree looked at a Chimerador student that she was walking with. "I'll catch up with you shortly Amber.," said Bree while she turned and looked at DJ "what's up?"

He looked at her and pondered how to ask, "are you cool with Jenny and Luna?"

"I don't have time for this.," she said while turning to walk off "Luna hid something and lied. Jenny wants me to jeopardize my position as Pre Lord. I took care of the issue."

He walked with her while he replied "how much trouble is she in?" concern filled his voice.

"-Get to class or Ten points from Crowfeather." replied Bree while she walked in her direction. -

They sat in Professor Kanoe's class while he taught about the Ferrethin a little ferret that its tears can heal. Professor Kanoe's back was to the class, student's eyes widen... None spoke or laughed. The back of Kanoe's cloak had turned into a hot pink dress with flowers.

"-Fool!"

Professor Kanoe turned, and his cold gaze scanned the classroom "-why the concern stares?"... Ms. Striff, you are always ready to speak first. Why do your eyes show fear?"

Jenny dare not to say a word as she sat in discomfort. Professor's cold voice spilled out slowly "the first time you didn't dare to answer... Fifteen points from Crowfeather." The bell rang while the class ran out of the room. -

The school was finally over. Luna ran into DJ and Jenny. They looked away from each other DJ sighed "come on you guys, you two were best of friends. Can you two forgive each other? You two were, stuck to each other like glue... Now it's like you two are trying to think the other doesn't exist now. Jenny, Gracy, and Luna are just stupidly close friends. Luna, Lucid and I are just friends. Gracy and I are talking, the reason I didn't tell you is so you could see how it would feel. Can we glue you two back to normal?"

Jenny and Luna didn't say a word, but Jenny's head shook slightly. A voice of the Goblin spoke up "stuck like glue, I indulge in that... That be amusing."

Jenny and Luna got flung together side to side. They tried to pull apart with all their might but couldn't "-Fools!"

"That's not what I meant..." shouted DJ looking around the corridor. Luna and Jenny stumbled off, shoulder to shoulder. They walked up the tower of Crowfeather. - DJ sat on the bottom of the steps.

"What having a gloomy day?" said a voice.

"More like a down pour." answered DJ gloomily. DJ's eyes widen as a black cloud appeared over his head. Lighting lit up the cloud, thunder echoed through the halls. The cloud poured down on him.

"-Fool!"

"I'm no fool... Wait, fool... I have sunshine down on me."

said DJ looking up at the cloud "-Good Fool!" The rain cloud began to turn to a beautiful blue puffy cloud as a rainbow came from it, casting a bright light down on him. "My eyes wish to see the Prankster of Mischief."

The goblin slowly manifest itself into view, he was no taller than three feet tall with large over wide jaws, long red thin lips, bushy snow-white chin hair that was braided. Large multiple shimmering eyes. He wore a white penguin suit with a white bow tie and a very large top that was three times larger than the goblin. He had no hair on his head. He had a black wood-knotted cane. He poked DJ's nose with his cane. "-Fool!"

DJ looked at the white albino goblin and pushed the cane from his face "-you sure love white."

"-Fool, you can't see me. I am the greatest mischief of all time."

DJ sighed and poked the goblin's arm "you are right here." The goblin turned and jab DJ in the stomach with his cane "You must be the chosen one, the last person was... let me think... Merlin, Benjamin, Nailz, Adam, Str-."

DJ spoke up cutting the goblin off "Did you say Adam?!" he blurted out. The Goblin hit DJ in the shin with the cane "don't interrupt me, I am your Mentor, and you Fool is the pupil... AS I said Merlin, Benjamin, Nailz, Adam, Str-."

DJ clapped his hands "what is Adam's last name?"

The goblin struck DJ in the knee "I will require fresh-brewed Witch Raspberry tea."

"...Fine, come with me." said DJ while he got up from the stairs and head up them. "I required to be carried." said the goblin looking up at him. "-Your kidding... Right?"

The goblin hit DJ in the shin with a nasty glare "I shall never kid about being carried. Now offer me your back, my pupil." DJ knelt for the goblin to climb onto it. *It was better when I couldn't see this annoying pest* DJ thought to himself then BAM! "OUCH." said DJ groaning out while he rubbed the top of his head from the hit. The goblin had bonked him on his head with the cane.

"Better not to see your mentor?" snarled the goblin.

DJ kept his mouth shut and carried him up the stairs. All ten stories... He recalled the password and walked in. The goblin snapped his fingers and a pale of water appeared over the door while Bree and Morgan came from the room. CRASH!

A scream could be heard from up the stairs. Luna and Jenny were still stuck together. One of the kids said, "this homework is going to eat me alive."

"-Fool!"

DJ's eyes widen but the goblin snapped his fingers and the books and parchment started to bite at the boy. Matt had seen DJ and waved "hey Beast Killer, how is your day?" DJ nodded and ran to the small kitchen and began to brew the tea.

"S-so do you have a name?" asked DJ.

"Ah! Fool, everyone has a name... I am Shmôg. The April Fools Goblin." said Shmôg as he had introduced himself.

DJ poured the fresh tea and handed it to him "so, we were

discussing Adam-"-

Luna and Jenny were upstairs tugging at each other trying to break free. They had stared daggers at each other "I want to go and see Maîq before it gets too late!" Luna hashed out tugging hard.

"We have finals coming up at the end of this month, twenty-seven more days! Six weeks till school is out. We need to crunch down on the homework for the next twenty-six days. I don't plan on making anything lower than an A." replied Jenny trying to tug away from Luna.

Luna rolled her eyes "DJ is right, you are more concern about yourself than your friends!" she screeched at Jenny.

Jenny looked at Luna with a glare "only IF you knew what I have done for you. To keep you in this school. I spoke long and hard with Bree."-

DJ sat on his bed looking at the large bat-like ear goblin watching him drink his tenth cup of tea. "-Sooo, Adam bell?" DJ slowly asked.

The goblin made a table appear while placing his tea down and sat "I come from a far off realm, Amethyst Realm, now I came across the sea long, long, long, long, long, long, long, long, long, long, long, lon-"

DJ cut him off and looked at him waving his hands at the goblin "I don't care about that, that's not important. I just want to know about Adam Bell."

"-Fool! My stories are legendary, Golds and Goddess, Kings and Queens shared the finest of tea to hear my adventures, my stories ... Now, it was 830BC when I came from Amethysts Realm, now I came over the sea."

DJ zoned out keeping his mind clear as possible till Shmôg's story had ended. Finally, it came to an end, and DJ looked at him "-Fantastic story... Now Adam?"

Shmôg smiled flashing his sharp fangs "which was your favorite part? What was so fantastic about life and death? Say... Do you have - Evil Blood, reminds me of a story..."

DJ fell forward on his bed and screamed into the pillow. WHAM! Shmôg hit DJ on his head again. "-Fool! Pay attention, listen to your Evil Bloodline. 1700's a Witch named Kate Bell came to this school with her beautiful cousins. *Linda DellHollow, Sherry Mary*, and *Margret Mary*- I'll require another pot of tea.," DJ made him a pot and poured a cup "The Witches were fantastic at things. Kate Bell was able to shapeshift and transform. Her favorite thing was to turn into a wolf. Linda DellHollow could use the worst curses you could imagine.,

"Sherry could enchant things, most advanced enchantments that this school had seen. Margret could open portals. Kate had taught them how to transform. Well, Margret fell in love with a guy. The guy cast down on her for he loved another girl. Margret fell apart and told her sister Sherry about this, she enchanted a dagger...,

374

"The girl stood in front of the mirror in the Crowfeather's dorm Second floor, room three... second Sunday in May, three in the morning, the witches hour. The girl went to the bathroom. Following the next day, she was found dead... Bloody prints on the sink and mirror. The four witches got expelled."

DJ got up and knelt down "hop on!" he said in a rush.

Shmôg hit DJ with the cane " do not tell Shmôg what to do!" He climbed onto DJ and DJ left the room in haste "Jenny! Luna!" he cried out. -

Luna and Jenny came down the stairs looking miserable as they were still stuck together. They looked at DJ from the stairs "What, DJ!" yelled Luna upsettingly.

"We are trying to do homework." said Jenny staring down at him. He looked at them and smiled, He walked up the stairs to them. He scratched the back of his head looking from at the two "you know what is funnier than being stuck together?," he said so casually" being thrown apart!" He made himself burst out in laughter.

Jenny and Luna looked at him brow raised, looking confused "thrown- apart, that is funny" said Shmôg with a snap of his fingers. Luna got thrown violently into the wall and Jenny got thrown violently into the other wall. "-Fools!" sniggered Shmôg.

Luna and Jenny groan in agonizing pain while they stood up "Oww... My back.," Luna sprung to her feet in glee "-I'm FREE!"

"Oww... I'm not stuck to you." said Jenny in glee as she

hugged DJ. He looked at Jenny and grabbed her hand. "Get the picture and note of Gracy. I have an idea."

Jenny looked at him and shook her head "- I don't want to see it." she replied with hurt in her eyes.

"Trust me... Please, trust the Beast Killer." said DJ softly while he looked at her. Luna walked over while Jenny ran up the stairs.

"What are you doing DJ?" said Luna confusingly, she eyed him skeptically.

"Hopefully my idea works and not oof." said DJ lowly.

"-It's going to be a BIG OOF, your ideas seem to just crash." replied Luna while he ignored her. He looked over his shoulder at Shmôg.

"Can you reveal fake notes and photos." asked DJ.

"Shmôg can, yes but I will require a -" DJ cut Shmôg off, he turned and looked at Luna as she stared at him as if he lost his mind . "Luna make me a fresh pot of tea. ---Ow" demanded DJ while Shmôg hit him on top of the head for cutting him off yet again.

"Who are you talking to?" asked Luna, DJ waved her off while Jenny returned covered in feathers. "-Fool!". Jenny placed the photo on the table, Bella and Bree came and sat with their homework. Shmôg tapped his cane against the photo and the note. The words began to smoke and vanished. The picture began to smoke, and the picture bubbled up before the colors caught flame.

"-What does this mean?" asked Jenny.

DJ looked at Shmôg while he waited for an answer "-Fools! And naive you all are for you all can't tell right from wrong, fix to broke. You all overlooked it. - Fools!,

"The truth and lies that lay before your eyes. Your tiny eyes show what you wish to see, but not what you see is what you must see. For these, you see which you think it is true is how closed-minded you truly are, indeed.,

"-Fools! A child shall see pass these lies as they're not narrowed-minded... and stupidly minded... - stupid- Fools!"

They sat looking in silence before Luna looked at Jenny and said very slowly but a bit sharp "told you I didn't kiss her." She got up and went off to her room leaving Jenny and DJ. -

Jenny came up the stairs and into their room, room three. Jenny sat on her bed as it grew late. She looked at Luna then away "-pretty crazy day today... Kanoe sure looked funny in a pink dress... Funny we were "glued" to each other last semester and this semester we were actually glued... -" said Jenny before going quiet.

"Must be our destiny." murmured Luna.

"-Yeah... Destiny for a good friendship, but... I just want to say, sorry...I can honestly say I am sorry about not believing you about the photo and the note. I can't get over the lies...Yet, goodnight." replied Jenny as she crawled under her blankets.

Luna lay there in bed thinking to herself, looking over at Jenny in the dark "I am sorry Jenny. I just tried to spare feelings and protect everyone."-

The tower lights went out while everyone fell asleep. The moonlit the castle up. A bright white horse with a glow and large wings landed pulling a golden carriage. Mysterious figures a set of four stepped out and went inside the school.

Watchman Moody and his wolf Tiny met the four figures in the grand hall with a low growl in Moody's voice "-didn't think you would have come... Keep it down and come along."

"Things have been a bit - murky." said a woman with an angelic in her voice. The four figures wore white hooded cloaks with blue trim that hid their faces.

"-Indeed, dealing with a traitor and now this." added another man with a deep voice. -

In the dorms, everyone lay asleep, not even a stir from any students. Not even a mouse dared to stir at night. SPLASH! Everyone woke up soaked as if they had jumped into a pool. Groans filled the dormitories. The moon slowly turned till it was a few seconds from midnight.

"-Fools!"

"SHMôG!" DJ yelled out.

"-Goodbye chosen one. - Fools!"

Chapter 22: Mysterious Figures and can it be fix?

Chapter 22: Mysterious Figures and can it be fix?

The following day, word broke out about what was going on. They sat in the feast hall for breakfast. Kain could be overheard from the Dracoîn's table "they are taking the old man away. For how he ran the school into the ground this year."

"I heard he is going to *Tenebrae Prison*." whispered a third-year girl from Dracoîn's table. Cecil looked at them.

"Whatever the *Wizards of The Round TableTable* are doing here, it is never good. Mr. Rune won't be here too much longer."

Luna showed Jenny her homework for her to look it over. "Number six is wrong. Look on page four-thirty-nine in your Potions book. You have the wrong base. - You are actually up early."

Luna pulled her book out and scratched out the answer she had and changed it. "Figure I have somethings to fix. I miss having breakfast, lunch, and dinner with you." said Jenny while she worked on her homework. -

Bell rang, and everyone went to class. - Mistress flowers sat in Mr. Rune's circular office. A large stone fireplace just left of his mahogany desk. His ferrethin lay in a bed in the large cage that looked like a replica of the school. He had oil paintings of the founders on the wall. A large royal blue round rug with the Guardians-s' beast lay in the middle of the room. "Robert Hun, why are the *Wizards of The Round TableTable* here? You've done no wrong! You are the son of Merlin, the best Prof- Headmaster we have seen in centuries. I mean IF Mrs. Fallingstarr stayed Headmistress and that child died, then you should stay Headmaster.!" hashed out Mistress Flowers.

Mr. Rune just smiled while he sat in his large royal blue leather chair. He looked at h Flowers through his half-moon glasses "Indeed, but it isn't my call. Times have changed in three hundred and twenty-four years. They are not going to remove me, my dear.,

"If they do, you'll make an excellent Head Mistress. - Now let's bring in our lovely guest."

Mistress Flowers turned with a sigh and opened the doors. "- Welcome, *Wizards of The Round Table*. - Glad to have you at OUR school, this is OUR great Head Master Robert M. Rune." said Mistress Flowers as she introduced Rune to the four figures.

The four mysterious figures came in, Mr. Rune made five seats appear and offer them a seat. "So glad you all made it. How was the travel?" his warmth and friendliness never broke.

The white hoods with blue trim were lowered. There was a Fox , anthro, large ears, large sparkling green eyes, dark flowing hair, and a large busy red tail with a white tip. Under her muzzle was white fur that ran down from her muzzle down her neck and disappeared behind her white cloak. Her paws are dark orange with

380

white pads.

The fox looked to Mistress Flowers, one of her large ears twitched while she spoke with a soft Irish accent "Tú (you), ar not hapi with R m nil (no)?"

Mistress Flowers looked at the fox not saying a word. A man on the other side of the group leaned over, he was dark skin, long black hair with high cheekbones. On his neck was a tattoo of an eagle claw. "-Now Vixen, be nice. We are guest here, indeed though she is upset.," said the man while he looked at Rune "I am sure you know why we are here?"

Mr. Rune nodded "indeed, why did you wait so long?"

A man with red scales, thick crocodile skin with dark slit orange eyes with no hair. His fork tongue flicked "-we had other...issues.," the reptile man looked at Rune while his large tail swayed "-concerning a traitor. We know he came to this school nineteen years ago. Believe he has a son here."

The last figure spoke it was a tall Moon elf, dark flowing hair, bright emerald eyes, and light honey tone skin. On the side of her face was a crescent moon tattoo that went from her forehead to the corner of her lip. "Have the attacks been handled? Do you know who the attacker is and their whereabouts?"

Mr. Rune looked at the four of them, leaning forward on his elbows and his fingertips laid against the other. "We only had two attacks... We believe it to be Margret Mary, we are still figuring out who summoned her. Someone is being used as her puppet. We found a few things appear and disappear, Mrs. Firefly."

381

"-Bloody Mary is back?" the reptile man said with a slight shakiness in his voice. "Indeed, we sealed all the mirrors in and around the castle Mr. Mystic." Said Mr. Rune.

Mrs. Vixen's face never changed its expression along with the other Wizards while she spoke. "- And the third attack?"

Mr. Rune looked at Mistress Flowers as they turned back towards the four "three? There has been two." said Mistress Flowers confusingly.

Eagleclaw spoke up as his dark gaze met Rune's "The Ol' Witchie Willow attacked three students. Bloody Mary can wait, what can we do about this tree?... For the safety of the students?"

Mr. Rune nodded "we will handle her. She just doesn't attack to just attack. I mean we can remove the jewel of the tree."

They nodded and looked at Rune. Mystic spoke with a snarl " the more important business... Where are Stryder and Nailz?"

Flowers looked at Rune while he pondered then a twinkle in his eye as he smiled "not sure, haven't seen him since Adam has been expelled. For Nailz, never met him. When, IF you find Stryder can you please for the sake of the school... Please tell him to return his library book it is nineteen years past due."

They stood with a glare while his door opened on its own. Eagleclaw turned to Rune with a glare "we'll like to talk to the kid, now!... No more attacks, we'll be watching the school. Now get the kid." They walked out of the office while leaving Rune and Flowers alone. A concerned look fell on her face.

"-Robert, what has Stryder done? What has he gotten himself into?"

"I do not know... I dare say he is in danger." said Rune softly. -

The students sat in the feast hall for lunch. Luna sat with Jenny and DJ again while they spoke about class and the exams coming up. "Will you tutor me Jenny?" asked Luna while they ate their food.

"I must have died, Luna asked to be tutored?" replied Jenny with her mouth dropped open. They heard a cluck and down at DJ's feet sat a yellow chicken.

"This thing won't leave me alone!" exclaimed DJ.

"Looks like we have a new pet." Said Jenny. The bell rang while they walked out to their classes. Kain, Zak, and Colt ran by and snatched the baby chicken.

"Can't you guys just grow up? He's just a little chick." snapped out Luna. They tossed the chick while DJ tried to get it between tosses.

"I think my hawk, Mars would like to meet your little chick." said Colton while he whistled A red hawk came and landed on his shoulder/ The hawk's eyes followed the tossed chicken.

"Don't you dare Colton!" shouted Jenny. Professor Kanoe showed up and saw the commotion between the six. He looked to them with his cold eyes.

"-Class now... DJ follow me." said Kanoe as Kain tossed

the chicken to DJ while they ran off laughing. DJ looked at Luna and Jenny. Fear swept over his face while he got marched to the keep. He spoke with a squeak in his voice "-where are we going?" Kanoe walked him up the stairs, floor by floor they walked. They stopped on the seventh floor. Kanoe turned and looked at him "you have been summoned by the Wizards of The Round Table. Do fear these--- creatures."

DJ froze, his mind racing what did I do? Can I make a run for it? Kanoe opened the two large doors and lead him into the room. The floor was dark wood, a large fireplace, pictures of old professors and a few beasts sat on the wall. A long table that sat ten people, large windows that overlooked the valley and the woods. "-Sit." demanded Kanoe as he turned and left.

DJ sat at the end of the table, nerves, shot as he fiddled with his wand. He sat in the large dining hall quietly. -

Luna and Jenny had caught up between classes while they walked together "wonder where DJ went to?" murmured Luna.

"If Kanoe took him, can't be good." replied Jenny. They separated into their classes. Classes grew more challenging, work stacked upon them to get them ready for the exams. Luna took down notes, DJ's seat was empty. The class ended, she told Jenny she'll catch up in a minute. She walked over to Professor Kanoe.

"-Professor Kanoe... Sir, I was umm... Wondering if well-" Luna tried to figure out how to ask him about DJ.

"He is probably in tears of pain. Yes, indeed they're

torturing him now Ms. Bell... Get to class." said Kanoe with a small smile. Luna left and head to class mumbling under her breath-

DJ sat in the dining hall, the large wooden door creaked open, he slowly peered around the high back wooden chairs. The four wizards came in along with Mr. Rune and Mistress Flowers. Mrs. Vixen looked at Mr. Rune and Mistress Flowers "you two are dismissed, we will take it from here." her large tail swayed. DJ looked at them desperately for help. Mistress Flowers went to speak but Mystic already answered for her.

"He is your student, yes but this is our grounds. We are over Headmasters, we are the top tier of the Magickal World. Now you are dismissed."

They stood for a moment than Mr. Rune just smiled with a bow of his head " indeed, you are correct. Come Mistress Flowers. " they turned and left. DJ sat watching them sit at the other end of the table. His stomach sunk. Mrs. Fireflyz spoke up across the table "I am Chloe Fireflyz, this is James Mystic, here is Rocky Eagle-claw, and this is Hailey Vixen. We are with the Wizard of The Round Table. You boy is someone who can help us find someone."

DJ stared at them trying to figure this all out, why was he here? Mr. Mystic hissed out at him; his fork tongue flicked out. His large arms laid on the table while his claws tapped the table "she already told you why you are here. Now, where is your father!"

DJ's eyes widen as he looked at them dumbfounded "I don't know, I haven't seen him since last year. - Why?"

A Quill, Ink, and parchment appeared in front of him. He looked at it then at them. "What do you want from me?" said DJ while he grew a little angrier slowly.

Mrs. Vixen leaned forward looking at DJ "write to your father, his whereabouts." -

Ray rushed over to Luna and Jenny out of breath. He looked at them and sat on the stairs in the grand hall trying to catch his breath "why did they take DJ to the third floor or whatever?," Luna looked at Ray sideways, while he talked "I came out of my class and saw them stopped on the stairs. Words were said between the two and they went on up the stairs."

"Poor DJ." replied Jenny softly.

Luna looked at Jenny and saw Bree walking towards the Crowfeather Tower double doors. She told Jenny and Ray she'll be right back. She ran over to Bree and opened the door "-Hey Bree."

"Hi Luna, what can I do for you?" said Bree, her hair had bright streaks of blue and purple in her jet black hair.

"-Love your hair... I am just wondering about the knife... Why am I still here? Figured I'd be expelled." Said Luna in a low murmur so no one would hear them. Bree pulled Luna into the tower. Her hand wrapped around Luna's throat and pinned her against the wall. Luna's eyes widen in shock.

"-You would have been. I did it FOR Jenny as she pleaded on your behalf. I snuck out and threw it into the lake. I save you this once, don't take my niceness for granted. I take honor and pride as a Pre Lord. I expect you to back me up every time." hashed out Bree, she let go of Luna and made her way up the stairs then stopped "and thanks, going for spring colors." Luna rubbed her throat then went up the stairs to the dormitory. -

"DJ, just write your dad a normal letter and send it." said Mr. Eagleclaw so calm while he watches DJ pick up the raven quill and dip it into ink.

"What did he do?" asked DJ staring at them while he wiped the excess ink off. Mystic drags his claws along the table.

"We will tell you. WHEN you write out the letter!" he hashed out, DJ's eyes lowered to the parchment as he slowly pushed on "-is -he -in -trouble?"

Mrs. Fireflyz shook her head with a warm smile. Vixen stood up and walked over to DJ while Mrs. Fireflyz went to speak "-no, no... of course not, we need him back at the table."

Mrs. Vixen placed her paw on his shoulder, eyes closed "the boy lies. He saw his father over Yule Holiday. - Briefly though."

DJ's eyes widen then felt his head get shoved to the table. His cheek pressed into the table as he peered up at the others. Her paw rested on his head holding him down.

"-Now Vix, no need to get rough.," said Mr. Ealgeclaw so

casually. He waved her off "sorry boy, she tends to lose it when she is lied to. Now, write the letter and send it out." DJ rubbed his head when he felt the paw removed from it. He picked up the quill and began to write.

Dear Dad,

Hope you are good. I haven't heard from you in a bit, guess that is usually for you anyways. I made all A's last semester. School is going great, so where are you at now? I do hope you are good, and I can't wait to hear your stories!

Love you

Boy

He made his way to the window and opened it, holding the envelope out. Nightstalker flew by and grabbed it. Then POOF! Mr. Eagleclaw turned into a black eagle and flew off after the crow. DJ's eyes widen out while he watched. He turned back to the table and looked at the three as he was about to speak.

"-No you can't leave kid, not until Eagleclaw returns." said Mr. Mystic. He sat down at the table and looked at them and spoke with such a harsh tone filled with hatred "WHAT did my father do!" -

In the dining hall, everyone sat eating dinner. No word of DJ has been heard of. What did Kanoe do with him, Kain's the one who started it by throwing around ChickiDee. Should I tell Professor Raven? She poured Jenny some pumpkin spice latte, made her a plate of food. They even discussed DJ, she told Jenny what she had been thinking. Jenny crossed her legs and fixes her skirt while laying a napkin in her lap.

"- I think we should ask, but then again. Mr. Rune and Mistress Flowers are gone too. Not sure Professor Raven would even have an answer.," replied Jenny "besides, I am totally confident that Professor Kanoe wouldn't hurt -anyone... studnt."

"Yeah, but Beast Killer has been gone ALL day." added Matt as he sat next to them taking a bite of a roll. Luna rolled her eyes and got up and walked out of the hall, she went down to Maîq's and she knocked on the door. There was no answer, she knocked again. "-Strange, he is always home."

She turned to walk off, the door open and a hand reached out and snatched her in. She let out a scream "-Shhh, wat ye 'oin 'ere? At a Tempo (time) ike dis?" said Maîq in a murmur. His blinds were closed, one candlelit his dark house up. He sat down " bad Temp (time) ta come."

Luna looked at him "who are these people?"

Maîq covered her mouth and held his claw up to his mouth "shh... Gat ta be queito (quiet). Dey will her us.," he removed his paw from her mouth "Feiticeiros da Mesa Redonda (Wizards of The Round TableTable, from da escuro, reino ônix (Dark, Onyx Realm). Dey holds ties to TODA magia (ALL magick). Ye must go now!"

Luna left the house; she had a very bad feeling about these people now. She had never seen Maîq look so scared before, she made her way back to the castle. The sun began to go down casting a beautiful ruby color in the sky. -

DJ looked at them with a glare as he hashed out once again, "WHAT did he do, and why do you want him, and this Nailz?" he hit the table. He was steaming a tear ran down his cheek. But it was not a sad, sorrowful tear. No, this tear was full of anger and hatred "he is my dad, I have the right to know!"

Fireflyz nodded her head "indeed boy you'd. Yes." she stood from her seat and went to the window and stared out of it. "The Wizards of The Round Table was founded. After the fall of King Arthur and the Knights of the round table.,

"Merlin teleported the table from the Dibble-Doggle world to a restricted place. In early of 2000, we had an open seat which, Stryder whom we been eyeing on over last few years and his-ways of traveling would be a big help.,

"Yes, he was a grand wizard and knew his way around a sword. Your father was the table's enforcer who we used to claim evil out of realms. He grew up as a bandit and thief along with Nailz, then he went back to his bandit roots and stole something of ours."

DJ listened to this woman speak about his dad "what did he steal?"

The woman turned and shook her head lightly "that is

Classified."-

    Luna walked into the keep where she saw a girl, a little taller than Jenny with the same sparkling blue eyes, long thick blond hair "hi, you must be Jenny's sister. I am Luna."
    The girl smiled and looked at Luna, her voice was soft "nice to meet you, heard so much about you. The good and yes, the bad. I'm Amanda. She talked so much about you. I was wanting to meet my sister's girlfriend, school is so big and keeps you so busy."
    Luna nodded her head in agreement "sure does, I miss her." They walked through the long corridor.
    "You need to show good faith... FYI, she misses you too." replied Amanda as they stopped at a crossing corridor "it was nice meeting you Luna, you seem kind... Keep your head up and show that faith, that you have for her."
    They went their separate ways. Luna went to her tower and into the common room. She walked straight up the stairs not saying a word to anyone and went into her room. She sat on the bed and began to write with a smile across her lips.

Gracy,

Hey my Grac, how are you? So, I need to tell you something. Something very important, something I wish I could have told you around Christmas. I didn't want to hurt you, I tried to keep it a secret to keep from hurting anyone's feelings. I'm gay, yep, I dropped the "G" bomb... LOL.

Been gay for a year. I hurt someone well two, three people... I hurt you for hiding this from you. I am dating Jennym you're my BFFE. You should have known. I hurt Jenny badly who I **was** dating... I broke her heart and she left me. I hurt myself for the lies I made to try and spare everyone's feelings. I love Jenny soso much, I wanted you to be the first one to know.

Love you, My Grac
★ Bear

Jenny came into the room and looked at Luna and sat on her bed looking perplexed. Luna walked over and unveiled what she wrote. Jenny's face was mystified.

She enclosed the envelope and placed her hand out of the window. A moment later, a crow came by and snatched the letter from her hand. Her heartfelt light she now was filled with blissful joy. She turned and walked out of the room. Jenny looked up with a low whisper "-you, you love me?" Luna turned and looked at Jenny over her shoulder with tears staining her cheeks. She stepped out and closed the door. Jenny sat on the bed feeling foolish *come on girl, chase after her... no, I- I just can't* Jenny, thought to herself.

She grasped her *NotForgetMe* necklace in her hand. Her

eyes closed and drew in a long slow deep breath. Her mind grew blank, the hand began to glow incandescent with orange and black lights. -

Jenny began to relieve the Halloween dance. There on the dance floor is Bree and Dane, they do make a lovely couple. There goes Ray and DJ trying to find a poor girl to dance with. Shame, Ray is an oddball, but he is sweet. Then DJ, well he's DJ...

Jenny and Luna began to dance, Jenny's arms drape over Luna's shoulder and Luna's hands rested on Jenny's hips as they gazed into each other's eyes. Jenny fixed Luna's little black and purple sparking mask.

They held hands and walked over to the red carpet with the Venus man-eating flytrap. A beautiful blue flower with large shimmering leaves with such a luscious scent of an aroma. One picture was arm in arm and the second was the kiss. The flash of the Shutterfly and Jenny was awoken. - She came too, a tear slipped from her dim blue eyes and down her cheek. -

DJ came into the dormitory and it was very late. Luna was asleep on the couch. He gave her a light shake, her eyes fluttered open "hey, why are you down here?" he asked in a low whisper.

Luna sat up and looked at the sun-and-moon dial to see the time, it was midnight. "- I was waiting on you to come in. Where have you been, are you OK?" said Luna apprehension in a low whisper.

393

He sat with her and told her everything about his dad being in the Round Table, stole something important, and the man with the bird tattoo how he turned into an eagle. "Then he returned along with the Nightstalker. Dad is in a place called " Land Down Under" in the Dibble- Doggle Realm and then they all left."

She hugged him "oh, I am so sorry.," with a dolor in her low tone "get to bed I will see you in the morning." They parted ways he went to bed and Luna went to her room and saw Jenny holding Monkmonk in her arms. Luna crawled under the blankets and sailed away to sleep. -

Three weeks have passed, Luna went to visit the Ol' Witchie Willow. She was flabbergasted, she found the Ol' Witchie Willow was no more than a stupid willow tree. She found some flowers of red, yellow, and blue roses and laid them out at the trunk of the tree. The large Onyx gem was gone. Kain, Zak, and Colt walked by and let out a burst of roaring laughter. She turned and felt hurt as if she lost a member of her family.

She ran back to the castle to return to classes to finish the exams. She was glad exams were almost over. Jenny's been a nightmare. - She went to her Creatures and Beast class. She got the test and sat down, beginning to answer.

60) What is an Ampasaurs?

A) Large Bird

B) Lizard

C) Dinosaur

394

Chapter 22: Mysterious Figures and can it be fix?

D) Feather crocodile

70) What ability do the Ampasaurs have?
A) Flys
B) Deafing stereo base roar and calming light feathers
C) Camouflage
D) Breaths fire

     Luna knew the answers for this due to the fact Maîq hatched one, the roar was ear piercing. It felt as if your ear laid flat on a speaker at a concert that was playing electronic dance music. The lights of the feathers flashed like a light show. The long snout of the crocodile. How this little creature, causes so much trouble and ruined friendship.

145) What is a Doggo?
A) Common Dog
B) #GayDoggo
C) Furry
D) Cat

150) What is the ability of the Doggo?
A) Nothing
B) Being adorable/ Rainbow powers of happiness.
C) Being Trash

D) Camouflage

Luna chuckled and marked B for *#GayDoggo* Reminds me of my BFF; she thought and knew it was the wrong answer. It was too good not to skip up. Then she chose C for Camouflage. She wanted to pick B but didn't want to miss too many questions and fail. She worked hard on studying and didn't want to flunk it.

The bell rang to release class, and she walked with Jenny, DJ, and Ray. ray looked at them "so, how do you think you all did?"

Luna spoke up with excitement in joy " I did great, I believe, I did miss one... Hashtag Gay Doggo!" she shouted, then burst out in laughter. "You are an idiot." DJ and Ray said together.

"You're full of an imbecile." banter Jenny.

"No, I am Hashtag GayDoggo." replied Luna while they all walked along the stone path, she went to her last class of Charms and Enchantment. An hour later she turned in her work and sat down. The sun shines down into the classroom with its warm rays. The bell rang, cries of cheers broke out in the classroom. The students fled into the hall, a boy could be heard "I don't have to deal with Professor Kanoe anymore!"-

Luna walked to Maîq's and saw him with the brown doggo. She walked over and the doggo camouflaged into the grass. "Olá (Hello), Luna 'ow waz exames (exams)?" asked Maîq as he catered to his garden.

396

Chapter 22: Mysterious Figures and can it be fix?

"It went... Surprisingly good, who knew those long painful long homework nights with Jenny would have paid off." she sniggered.

"I amar (love) ta stay n talk 'ut I 'ave work ta do." replied Maîq as he picked a few tomatoes.

She said her byes and left for the castle. - She came into the dormitory and Jenny gave Luna an envelope. Luna looked at Jenny then at the envelope and opened it.

Hey  Bear,

You are right, you did hurt me. I wish you had told me. We are supposed to be BFFEs. I am sorry for your loss with Jenny. I liked her, hopefully, things work out. GUESS WHAT!... Did you guess, No? Too bad... I could tell you or make you wait. I'll make you wait <wink face>. To tell you something you'll be shocked. I have been talking to a guy and I'm not dead, MY dad knows too. Tell Jenny to give you another chance your just... fatuous. "

Love you  Bear
Grac

Luna read the letter and showed it to Jenny. Jenny read the letter and smiled softly. Looking from the letter then at Luna "well, she is right about one thing. You are fatuous." she said with an antic tone. Luna looked at her and placed her hands on her stomach.

"I'm not fat." replied Luna running her hands over her stomach.

Before Jenny could reply DJ opened his mouth beating Jenny with his reply "it means fat butt. I think uous is Latin for butt." Luna threw a pillow at him.

"Don't look at my f- thick butt..." she snarled at him. Her cheeks flushed to a rosy red. Jenny shook her head "you two are both blockheads. Uous isn't Latin for butt. Fatuous means marked by lack of intelligence and rational consideration."

Bella burst out in laughter with Matt about uous means butt in Latin. "Luna, you have a nice fatuous." said Matt. Bella hit his arm.

"Watch it." snapped Bella while she glared at him.

"-Your uous is just fat and nice." replied Matt as he kiss Bella. Everyone burst out in laughter

"-I knew uous didn't mean butt... I- I was making a joke." said DJ in a low murmur. Keith smacked DJ on the back while laughing. "Good one, Beast Killer- Jester.," Bree walked into the dormitory, they watched her come in while the laughter lowered. "Ooh, Furbreeze your so fine with that uous." Keith tittered out slowly.

Bree looked at him in sideways bafflement. She went up

to her room. The room broke out into laughter, Luna leaned
forward and hugged Jenny and whispered in her ear. -

DJ looked over and saw them. His crow Nightstalker
came and dropped a letter in his lap. He opened it and read it. Then
a large falcon came and dropped a letter in his lap, he opens that
one.

Boy

*I am nowhere near the Land down under now. Seen a large eagle follow
the crow you sent. It is not safe to send messages. The Round Table is a
very dark group. The darkness of good and evil I can only help for now
by staying away. They have many spies. Their tongue spits many lies.
When you send a crow do not hope for a return message. Dagger will
bring messages to you. I have found a Goddess in a damsel.*

*-Boy! When the Summer sun shows seek south for a town
named Zert. Seek out a cat folk name Nxily, Naily Malra. Tell him
Stryder had sent you. Pray to the Gods. that the Wizards of The Round
Table Table hasn't found him. So many secrets we hold.*

*-Next year stay away from the school. Evil seeks out forth
towards Crystal realm UNDERSTAND BOY!*

Stryder

DJ's face went white not come back? he though. I am pure blood
he handed the note to Luna and Jenny. They went dumbfounded

over this "what a uouz!." Luna spat out infuriatingly. DJ looked at her with dismay never seen her hash out such words as uous even though they made up uous to mean butt. He could only imagine what uouz meant. Jenny poked Luna in her side. Luna turned and looked at Jenny. Jenny whispered in Luna's ear. Luna smiled with a nod then spoke with such tender in her tone "-Yes... Yes, I will."

Chapter 23: The Three Broken Swords

The following week came last week before the weekend to go home. What a journey we all had from the terror of the cauldron, two attacks, to making the snorkbie team. Being MVW, to having two best friends anyone could have, to a perfect... Almost perfect Halloween date. Then going to the fair, riding a griffin, having the best girlfriend.

Then the second semester happened... Lost a good friend, lost a better girlfriend, but a better girlfriend. - Then Shmôg happened., April Fool's day! It was a prank war from the goblin. -

Luna laid in bed with Khan against his warm fur. The heat from his fire was bright but not hot, she pats him on his head. The flames engulfed her hand but didn't burn her. Today was the last school game of the year. Everyone grew with eagerness for which Clan was going to win the trophy for Wand War.

"Luna! Hurry up!" DJ yelled in alacrity.

Luna came down the stairs in normal clothes, she was done with knee high tube socks, plaid skirts, tunics, but still had to wear your clan's badge and cloak. She came downstairs in white skinny jeans with a twelve-inch black crow stitch on the right thigh. With smaller crow feathers cascading down and around the left thigh then spilling into words *CROWFEATHER 2028.*

She had a black band shirt on *Distinction Jaded*. The words were written in bones, on the shirt shown a skull tilted back with red roses sticking out of its mouth and some rose petals were blue butterflies fluttering from the mouth, and black right arm sleeves and purple left arm sleeve. Her hair had been dyed. Half of it was black and the other side purple. She came down in her black half calf combat boots. She smiled when she came downstairs "O-Oh my... Your mom is going to kill you.," exclaimed DJ as he looked at her with a coveting filled heart "you look stunning." They walked with Morgan who looked at Luna's pants.

"Love the pants, their super cute."

"Thanks, made them last night. The crow and feather, all the patchwork is leather." replied Luna. They all climbed the castle stairs to the upper wall level. DJ opened the wall door for them. The walls were crowded with students.

"So, you have a date for May Madness Dance?" DJ asked while the professors sat things up.

"Actually, I do. A girl from Goldenpaw." replied Luna. Stones raised up from the ground creating caves and barriers. Thick bushes to help with the barriers. Pools of lakes filled as the land shifted. It was a large maze.

"Welcome everyone, to Wand War. The last Clan war between the Pre Lords and their two nobles. Rules are simple. The first team to lose all teammates is eliminated. This game is worth four hundred clan points! Now coming out at the Goldenpaw tower the two nobles- Kat Bossingham and Emily Simpson! and their Pre Lord Jewels Meadows!" announced Mr. Rune.

Goldenpaw broke out with applause and cheers "GO Kat!" a Goldenpaw boy yelled out. Jewels stood on a rock and fist-pumped the air to push Goldenpaw to get louder. The three held their wands up and shot gold and white stars shot into the air.

"Coming out in green and black from Dracoîn tower, The two Nobles- Traci Brews and Sam Whyte! And the Pre Lord himself, Cecil Bloke!"

They came out into the jungle side. It had the illusion of nighttime. They had raised their wands and fired green fireballs into the air. Dracoîn clan went crazy with cheers. "YOU GOT THIS TRACI!" Yelled Kain.

"Coming in with black and purple from Crowfeather the two nobles Bella Ward and Matt Timbles! Their Pre Lord with heart and spirit Bree Summers!"

Crowfeather roared in ovation cheering and chanting " CROWFEATHER- CROWFEATHER- CROWFEATHER!" They were on the beachside, water knee-deep. The three fired their wands and black and purple fireworks blew up.

"Now from Chimerador in red and silver the two Nobles Amanda Striff and Blake Tolin!" The Pre Lord Dane Ward! annd Lord Headmaster Bruno Silvertongue!" They came out into the hot desert, wands raised and fired off red and silver stars.

"Let the last of the War games begin!" cried out Mr. Rune.

Team Crowfeather began to walk along with the beach wands in their hands. They kept their eyes peeled "stay in a triangle formation. If you get pin down fire a purple fireball. If you spot a team shoot that clan's color fireball." said Bree as they plan their attack. -

Jewels and her team began to fan out quietly into the bushes. Kat peered into a dark cave, so dark you can't see your nose "*mico lucis*" her wand lit the long tunnel up. - Dracoîn took to the trees and sat on the branches and waited. "We will sit and let them knock each other out.," said Cecil with a smile "I have this for us." he passed around a silver bangle with doggos' fur on it. They slipped it on and camouflage to the trees. -

Chimerdor went along the desert and saw a rock tunnel that had a light illuminating from the cave. They stood on either side of the cave entrance. "Shh." whispered Bruno.
"*mico lucis*" said Kat as she stepped from the cave. BOOM! Amanda and Blake both cast a spell at Kat and she vanished to the dormitory. They made their way through the cave. -

Crowfeather came to the desert and walked through the hot blazing sun. Matt noticed prints "hold on.," he said while he knelt down and investigated the signs "their footprints. Let's go.," They came to the cave, and he ran his hand lightly along the ground. "Someone got blasted." they went through the cave. -

Traci sat bored on the limb "-real fun this is." she said with a cold sarcastic tone. "Hush!" snapped Cecil. Traci snarled at Cecil. - Emily and Jewels walked into the dark forest wands out. They walked slowly through the dark forest "where did Kat go?" asked Emily while they walked along the trail.

"Not sure. Hopefully, she is OK.," replied Jewels in a low whisper. BOOM -ZAP -KaBOOM! Bright lights of gold, blue, and green came from the treetops. "WATCH OU-" howled out Jewels. The explosion threw Jewels back. She shot a spell off into the treetops. "CAMOUFLAGE is against the rules!" she yelled out. -

Chimerdor came to some stones and looked around the place. Bright light hit the rock right beside Amanda. "CROWFEATHER's here." she shouted as she hunkers down behind a rock. Fireworks of spells shot back and forth between the two teams. -

Jewels hid under a small tree trunk that lay between two hills. She peered over the trunk – BOOM! She dunks just in time. She took a pop shot hoping to hit someone. A crunching noise of a snapping of a limb than a loud thump. Jewels made a run for it, to retreat. Sam saw Jewels' head pop out of behind the tree trunk and cast a spell. A bright ball of light shot from the turned-over tree, hitting the branch then it splintered up and then snapped. Cecil fell and hit the ground hard. He lay groaning out in agony of pain.

"Cecil are you OK?!," cried out Sam as they climbed

down the tree. Cecil pulled the bangle off "my back." he groan out in pain. - "Push around!" demanded Bree while she and Bella held off Chimerador. Matt flanked to the right stealthily. He sly through under the now night sky of the forest. -

Chimerador was pinned down in a small cave. Each of the four had returned spells at Crowfeather. "Where did they come from?," asked Bruno. He looked at his team "stop casting." -

Jewels ran into Matt, he drew his wand and she stood frozen in her steps "wait!" she panted out between breaths.

"Why should I, where is your team?" Matt held his wand pointed at her. Her hands raised slowly "wiped out, least Emily is, not sure about Kat. Dracoîn is cheating... They are invisible. They blasted Emily away." she spoke with as much truth in her voice as she possibly could. She stared at him her arms still raised.

"What the he-" BOOM! A large explosion threw Matt and Jewels back. Sam and Cecil cast *exarmare* and pulled Matt's and Jewels' wands from their hands.

"Where are your teams?" demanded Cecil as he snarled. Sam looked around the forest.

"-You cheated; you cowardly killed my team!" snapped Jewels.

"You can never play any games without cheating." growled Matt. Cecil blasted Jewels and she had vanished. - She appeared in the dormitory "--- how did you do?" Emily and Katt asked as Jewels just shook her head and explained Cecil and they are cheating. -

Bree went to move up and came up behind the rock. Bella flanked out and hid in some bushes.- Matt looked at Cecil, fist balled up "let's go you and me!" Cecil walked over and glared "you are just upset we outsmarted you. We are going to win this trophy." Matt pulled his arm back to get ready to slug Cecil in the face. "*Mico lucis*" Sam blinded Matt while Matt took a swing at Cecil. He dunked the punch and blasted Matt in the chest with a spell, Matt vanished from the field. Traci came up from the woods "They are east at the rocks."-

"Want to go in and I'll cover you?" asked Bree watching the entrance of the cave.

"Sure... If something happens get out of here." replied Bella. Bree nodded while Bella made her way up slowly. She kept her wand out in front of her as she stepped into the dark cave. A bright light came from the cave then died down.

"B-Bella!" cried out Bree. -

"Guess, someone is in the cave." murmured Sam. Tracy pointed her wand out at Bree and shot a spell and - Poof. They waited while Blake ran out and spun around in the opening with his wand out in front of him. "CLEAR!"

They came out by force "where she run off too?" asked Dane, he saw a shimmering of silver "- Drac-." Dracoîn spread out while they popped up blasting spells. Dane vanished; Traci rolled out of the way of a spell. Bruno vanished, Blake and Amanda made a run for it. Blake shot over his shoulder at Dracoîn. Sam got hit and he had vanished. Cecil gave chase and blasted at them but missed. Amanda turned and fired off a spell and then ran again. "Keep running!" she yelled out. Traci came from Blake's left and blasted him. Amanda had lost Cecil. "Oh... Ow, my Knee... Get help I think it's out of socket or... Worst." cried out Cecil as he laid on the ground.

Amanda looked from behind the tree and raised her wand to the sky. "-Thank you, I wo-." Amanda lowered the wand at him.

"Like you showed Bree mercy?" exclaimed Amanda as she came from behind the tree as he looked at her worried. Cecil pulled his wand and blasted; he had missed Amanda. She cast a spell at him, and he had vanished.

Traci came up behind Amanda. She presses the wand against Amanda's back "I would have done the same thing if I was you." said Traci softly.

"You should challenge him.," said Amanda "I mean you'd make a great Pre Lord." she fumbled with the wand slowly. Her hand still held out, while she held the wand reversed in her hand.

"I'll give you the honor of forfeiting. To walk off the field." said Traci. Amanda shot a spell but missed Traci by a hair. Then Traci gave Amanda a little tap on her back instead of casting a spell and Amanda had vanished back to the dormitory. -
The Dracoîn clan roared with joy as they won the last cup. Luna saw Jenny and waved. Mistress Flowers called the game "Your

wand war winner this year is Dracoîn!"

The land shifted back to the old school grounds. Mr. Rune took the stage and raised his hand while he looked towards the students as his voice grew with an amplified tone. " Children, I'll like this time of great warmth of pleasure and thank you all for another wonderful year.,

"Most likely our best year. This year we have been awarded best school of the year! And the Dibble-Doggle award for the most increase to half-blood and Dibble-Doggles to attend our school.,

"Even though half bloods are magickal beings. The board looks at them just as Dibble-Doggles. I am going to award each clan two hundred points! Now in two days is the May Madness Dance. The polls are open to vote for this year's Guardian Clan God and Goddess. We encourage you all to go and vote. The polls are in the grand entry hall,

"I know we are all excited about that. Then Friday our large feast, then the large Guardian cup ceremony. Then you all get to pack up and Sunday you all go home. I just want to thank you all."

Cheers roared from the stands, everyone pulled their wands out and blast their clan colors into the sky as firework size explosions took place. They all retreated to the dining hall. The smell of hot food filled the air, Luna walked over to Bree with a low murmur "you guys did good."

Bree smiled and nodded "thanks."

409

DJ came and sat with Jenny and Little ChickieDee followed him "so, you have a date?" asked DJ while he looked at her with a loss of hope in his eyes.

She shook her head "Nope, not going. I know a cute chick that will love to go with you."

DJ;'s ears perked as he looked at her "who!?"

Jenny smiled and leaned in with such a soft whisper as it tickled his ear and neck "--- ChickieDee." He look down at the yellow chick who was helping herself to his plate.

"... Stupid Shmôg." snarled DJ.

"Just be glad you weren't eating a beef burger or steak. Then you'd be spitting out a cow." heckled Jenny. Luna came over and sat with them "I got my dress for the dance."

"-You in a dress? Hallow dance you wore a... Pretty much a tux, who is taking you?" marveled DJ.

"Charles, Charles Blaine from Goldenpaw, the blocker on their Snorkbie team, and number ten in the joust. He asked figured why not." said Luna with a smile.

"I- I thought you were gay." said DJ in bewilderment.

"She's a girl, she can change her mind." Jenny chimed in. -They made their way to the dormitory. Bree came over and sat with them "you want to play Dungeon and Wizards?" she asked softly. They pulled the game out and began to play. Their characters transform into them. They played till almost the sun came up. Everyone had fallen asleep, almost felt like old times. -

Two days had passed; everyone had got their exams back Luna rushed to the feast hall in her tank top and pajama shorts. She saw DJ and Jenny as she sat down on the bench next to them.

"Nice legs!" yelled out Kain, Luna's legs like the rest of her were pale.

"...Forget to change?" DJ question Luna while he looked down at her legs.

"I- I got excited about my exams.," retorted Luna. She picked up a Strawberry Danish Pastry and put some eggs with bacon on her plate. "Alright on three, we'll open the envelopes together." she said counting to three. They tore into the envelopes as if Christmas came early.

"I got-"

"All A's again... Good job." acknowledge DJ as he pats Jenny's head. Luna's smile had faded to a frown as she looked at her score "- I- can't- believe it."

Jenny and DJ looked at her "I'm sure it's not that bad. I mean, I am proud of you. You stayed up late to study with me." said Jenny's tone while she rubbed Luna's leg.

"I've got two A's, four B's, two C's, and one F. Not too bad." solaced DJ while he pats their heads.

"...Why are you petting us?!" question Jenny as she pulled away from him.

"Figure since ChickieDee is following me around as a new pet. And that we are always together. That I claim you two as my kitties." teased DJ.

411

"...Anyways, what did you get?" asked Jenny while anxiously waiting to hear what Luna got for her grades.

"--- I got... A's... In all my classes!" said Luna in astonishment. "That is great!" they said while they hugged her.

"Now you have no reason you can't keep all your grades at an A's." said Jenny with a grin.

Luna's eyes widen in shock "N- N- NOO! I wanted to beat you on those long dreadful nights! Luna shouted to herself. They went outside into the halls.

"You, quit being lazy and get dressed. Meet us at the willow tree." said Jenny as they went their separate ways. Luna went up to the dormitory to shower and dress in her punk rock clothes. She saw her music player and she slipped her hoodie on that Brandon got her for Christmas and slipped her earbuds in and turned on the player. She began to listen to Distinction Jaded, a letter sat on her bed.

Dear Luna,

Can't wait for you to come home. I miss you so much, so does your sister. That man has been stopping by for visits, DJ's dad Stryder. He is a very good man. He had told me he would help with Sierra. She is still so wild. Mr. Jackson still can't tame her. She must have had very bad previous owners, poor girl. Mr. Jackson said the best thing for her is a fifty-five-cent shotgun shell and put her down. He said she has too many demons and she is going to end up hurting someone or herself. He said he would take care of it for us. He tamed all of our horses, even your dad's horse Rogue. Not sure what to do... Anyways, I will be picking you up Monday! I am so excited that you are coming home.

Love
Mom

Luna sat on her bed I hate for Sierra to be put down. It seems death follows me like a shadow she thought. She turned on the music player all the way up. While her favorite song came on by Distinction Jaded (*Falling into Detriment*) She walked out of the dormitory listening to the epic drum solo and the squeal of the electric guitar. The strong bass.

♫ *<Chris singer> When I close my eyes to fade away from this pain. Into the blackness to escape my detriment.* ♩ *<Ember growls> My detriment.* ♭ *<Chris singer> I am falling, falling into the darkness of this curse. I can't break out of this curse.* ♫ *<Ember growl vocal> Break out of this Curse. -*

Luna got to the willow tree and sat with DJ and Jenny "can't believe Ol' Wheepin willow is gone, now it's just a stupid willow." said DJ while he lean against the tree.

"It's... My fault, Ol' Witchie Willow is gone. If I never sent

413

Kain and his goons down here to her. She would still be here.,"
replied Luna heartbreakingly. She laid her head back on the tree
"seems, whatever or whoever is by me either dies or is on the way
to be taken by death. I can't escape my detriment curse." she said
lowly in a melancholy. "That's not true. I mean things happen." said
DJ trying to to be emboldened her.

"...My dad. my hamster Wiggles, and Brownie, my
multiple fishes, that cat Oreo, my pet rock Pebbles, my chickens
that mom had -... It's still so hard to talk about. My-... Grandpa, Ol'
Witchie Willow, soon to be Sierra. Almost Bree, my relationships
with you, Jenny. My friendship with Bree. Kain is right it's a
because I am evil blood." Luna spoke with a heartache of sadness.

"Oh... How do you kill a pet rock?," asked DJ, then Jenny
had punched his arm. -

Lucid was laying on the floor in the middle of the living
room on the warm day in her pajama shorts and top. She had her
phone in her hand. Cheyanne came into the living room and saw
Lucid "going be lazy all day and stay in your pajamas?"

Lucid looked to her mom and smiled "-yep, how was the
teachers conference?"

Cheyanne sat down after removing her heels "long, they
want to defund the art class, music class, and they brought up to
vote to get rid of the volleyball team. So, they can upgrade the
football stadium, and get new uniforms."

Lucid sat up in a fit of rage "THEY can't do that! We on

the Championship, two years in a row. Next year it will be three... How many did the stupid football team win?--- Oh yeah, it's been what four years? What did you say?"

Cheyanne looked at her daughter who was fuming "I told them that we have won the last two years. We are on a hot streak. That our football team isn't the money issue. It was the coach, they wouldn't hear it.,

"I asked about them about my job as the volleyball coach and you girls. They said the girls can try out for the cheerleading team or softball.... Your already on the softball team and cheer. For me they said thanks for your coaching service." her said as she sat back upset.

"They can't do this mo-." There was a loud knock on the door.

"Who could that be?" question her mom. Lucid got up to her feet while another knock came from the door "coming! "Lucid yelled out while she walked to the door. She opened the door and stood there was the little dwarf man in his fancy tux. "-Hi, Mr. Lundo." said Lucid with a clamorous tone. He looked at her with a smile behind this thick beard.

"Good day, is ye mum home?"

Lucid stepped to the side to allow him in "living room..." she said coldly.

"Thank ye, ye played a good Championship game. Ye looked lovely out der. Yez indeed, a real showstopper." his whiskers curled in a smile.

415

"... --- Grooosssss... Mom, I'll be in the barn." said Lucid while she walked Mr. Lundo into the room and then rushed to the back door.

"Hey, Mr. Lundo didn't expect you to show up. After I replied to your email about selling Bells Burgers." He sat down on the couch and place his black briefcase on the table. He looked at her "such lovely daughter ye 'ave. She waz dashing out on da court. Such a big win for her... And her team. I brought over the papers to show you the numbers and figures they are offering us." He opened the briefcase.

"I have seen the numbers and I appreciate all the money Adam and you had put into Bells Burgers. You are taking care of the banks and financial help to keep the business alive. I am trying to come up with the money to buy the company back. I know, they are offering a lot, but Adam is in that building... I can't put money over Bells Burgers. Sorry that you have wasted a trip out here. I, we are not selling. Have a good day, Mr. Lundo."

Mr. Lundo stood and smiled with a slight bow "we will speak more later... By chance Mrs. Bell, would you let me take you out for some splendid wine and dinner?"

She walked him to the door and looked down at him, she smiled warmly "-no, I am good. We are done discussing the sale of Bells Burgers. I may come in for work a few times a week."

He nodded his head and left as his driver opened the back door. Cheyanne waved bye.

416

"--- Grrroossss." she said as she sat down getting comfortable, another knock came from the door. She sighed and got up and open the door "-Yes Mr, Lun... Stryder, come on in." she stepped to the side. He came in while Dagger rested on his shoulder. He lowered his hood. "Evening, I was passing by and figured I'd stop by."

"May I get you a drink?" she offered him a seat.

He waved his large rough hand" no thanks, I came by to warn you. Do not send, Luna? Back to the school next year. I found word of something happening. I am being hunted. I wish not to see her get picked up by these... Wizards, I have told the Boy to stay away too."

Cheyanne's eyes widen as she looked at him "oh dear... Where are you going?" her words were filled with concern as she stood staring at him.

"I am going west, is all I can say." he kept his answers little to none. They walked to the barn. Lucid was washing Rogue. Cheyanne and Stryder walked into the barn. "Lucid, - Stryder, DJ's dad is here." her mom called out. Lucid turned with the hose in her hand and still in her pajamas.

"Hello sir, how are you?" she greeted him while she turned the hose off.

"I am good, beautiful horse."

"Oh, he is my husband. We had two girls and... Tried for a son but I sadly had a miscarriage. So, Adam came home with this horse, but at the time he was a little colt. Adam told me he adopted us a son.," Cheyanne laid her hand on Rogue's snout and petted him "he is very protective over the girls."

Stryder walked up and looked into the horse's dark eyes "he is stout hearty... Great horse.," he reached up "shh, friend." he spoke in such a soft whisper. He began to pet the horse. Cheyanne and Lucid looked stunned watching Rogue let a stranger pet him. A loud bang came from Sierra's stall.

"CALM DOWN! in there." Lucid yelled at the horse in her stall.

"What is that?" inquired Stryder while he walked over to the stall.

"Our angry girl. Who is... On her last string of hope." answered Cheyanne with heartache.

The horse kicked the wall of the stall again while it moved around in her large stall. Their eyes had met, Stryder took a large breath "indeed you have... Shh girl.," He spoke softly. Cheyanne and Lucid watched, "you are alright... Yes, you have been a real scared girl... They can't hurt you anymore." Cheyanne looked at lucid, while they watched in pure quietness.

"She has been beat and abused nearly to death. She has zero trust. She has the stride and heart of a strong horse." said Stryder while he turned and faced Cheyanne and Lucid.

"Anything you can do for her?" asked Lucid.

"Indeed... I can't change her, we must build her trust

back.," She kicked the door again "you want to be out?--- I'll let you go in the pasture. Do you need to be lead?" The large horse's head shook and snorted. He opened the gate to the stall, and she ran out of the stall and through the barn.

"You must build her trust back and lead her with an invisible rope.," he nodded "in time, she will trust you."

"Thank you, Styrder." said Cheyanne with a light smile. -

He stayed for dinner and slept in the barn. The next day Lucid came out before the sun came up to check on him. He was gone, Sierra was in her stall with a note on a barrel.

Dear Bells,

Thank you yet again for the hot dinner last night. I enjoyed the convivial we all shared. You all are so gracious. Sierra came back in on her own last night. She is a grand horse, for my thanks I have left a small ruby in her stall.

Let the Gods guide you

Styrder

Lucid went to Sierra's stall and saw the flawless Ruby laying in the stall of the mean Sierra. Are you kidding me? she thought. She walked over to the stall door "-hi girl.," The horse snorted and kicked the door. "Are--- you for cereal!" -

419

Jenny looked at Luna while DJ rubbed his arm "one- A rock is an inanimate object... and second -You're not cursed by detriment. And thirdly, - I am surprised you know a big word or even know what it is." said Jenny staring at her .

"She is evil blood." Kain's voice came out of the blue behind them while he stepped around the tree.

DJ stood up with his fists up "leave her alone."

Kain smiled as his purple eyes twinkled "may want to steer clear of her or - we'll be having a funeral for the two of you. Just like for this stupid tree. He sniggered as a strong guest of wind blew across the grounds. The branches swayed in the wind. A spider the size of a palm of a hand to fall onto his shoulder. His eyes widen while smacking at it with tears in his eyes.

"G- get it off." he jerked his shirt off over his head and threw it on the ground as he ran. They all burst out in laughter. - Then headed to the keep to eat dinner. They saw Kain at his table "SPIDER KAIN!" they yelled at him. He grumbled. Night finally fell on the school, the sky lit up with twinkle stars as the two moons sat overhead. - Kain stopped at the bathroom in the grand hall. He pulled out the dagger "just as where you said it was, in the lake. " He said as he was soaked. He dripped water as he held the dagger in his hand.

The old burn scar Witch reached out of the mirror and took the knife. "Good, good puppet boy." She vanished from the mirror. The bathroom door flung open, and Mr. Moody the Watchman

420

came in and saw Kain.

"- Dormitory, now Mr. Bloke."

Kain turned and something of importance fell from his bag while being escorted away. He walked Kain back to the Dracoîn Tower. "No more roaming, why are you wet?"

Kain smiled and walked into the dormitory. - Mr. Moody traveled along the halls, and his wolf Tiny came to him with a piece of parchment "Wat we got der boy?.. Ohh my..." -

Finally, it was the day of the May Madness Dance, everyone was running around getting ready trying to find last minute dates. DJ saw Ray outside, he came over and shook his head "- looks like it is you and I for the dance, together again. I think we should coordinate colors." heckled DJ.

Ray looked at him with a look of grief "I - I have a date." DJ looked at him in disbelief.

"O-oh... Who?," he swallowed hard "I mean we went to the Halloween dance together... I figure we'd go again."

Ray saw the disappointment in his eyes "Amber Lyght. You know the joust rider and Snorkbie catcher for Dracoîn?"

"Dracoîn?! Seriously... Well, guess I'll spend my time packing with Jenny, I'll have a packing date with her." said DJ while he stretched.

Ray looked at him sideways in full concern of addled "- she is going to the dance." DJ was all confused and alone for the dance. "She said she wasn't going...," ChickieDee clucked in his shirt pocket "Looks like it's just you and me ChickieDee."

Ray looked to him "I love you, my man."

DJ turned and walked off waving him off "-Get the girl man."

"- Cluck!" Chirped ChickieDee. -

Luna was in the room that night doing her hair in a Milkmaid Braid. She took two pigtail braids and then wrapped them up and around, crossing them over the top of the head. Her makeup was done with glitter perfume. She placed glitter in her hair. Her black and red lolita dress hugged around her chest with a corset top and the dress flowed down to an angle. The cut at mid-thigh and flowed down at an angle to her knee. The corset had black ribbons on the front. The dress is paired with black fishnet. The dress itself was dark wine red. She painted her nails red.

"Oh... My god... Who is this girl?" Luna asked herself as she stared into the mirror. She was all dolled up; her black and red tint with half scalp purple flowed so well in the braids. Her eyes shadow looked so good, breaking up the paleness. Then the eyeliner made her crystal blue and emerald green eyes pop. The light red lipstick bought her lips out.

She walked out of the room, everyone gasps looking at this vampire girl who wore skinny jeans and combat boots as if that were the only clothes she owned. DJ looked at her "oh, -my you sexy... Charles is a lucky guy."

Bella came in her hair wavy, make-up done, and long blue dress. "Look at you Luna. Is this a new Luna?" asked Bella.

Luna shook her head "no, heck no... Who are you going with DJ?"

DJ sighed in gloominess "nope... No one, I'm sitting here all alone." Bella came over and sat with him "DJ- DJ... Beast Killer Jester, will you take me to the dance?"

DJ sprung up to his feet "let me get ready." he rushed off to his room.

"That is sweet, Bella." said Luna.

"He was sulking like a sad puppy." replied Bella. They all got up and went to the door "COME on Bree and Jenny!" they yelled out for the two as they waited.

Bree came down her dreads flowed freely, make-up is done, and wore a white wavy dress with a blue ribbon around the waist. The dress sparkled.

Jenny came in with her dreads pulled back with a Crowfeather bandanna. With a feathered emblem, make-up is done, a red corset with a chain that crisscrosses on the chest, a black pinned stripe, and black slacks with red heels. -

They came down while DJ met them in the hall "wow Jenny, you make a hot dude." said Bella while they made their way downstairs to the first floor common room.

"How do people, Luna wear this. It is sucking the life out of me" said Jenny as she place, her hands on the front of the corset resting on her stomach.

"Jenny going as a wo-man tonight, looking good." said

423

Timmy as he came into the room looking at all the girls. They all made their way to the dance. DJ held Bella's hand. Dane showed up and stole Bree away. They walked into the courtyard; the large moon cast over them. DJ saw Ray come up with Amber, she wore a black and green dress.

"YOU took my sister!" shouted Ray as he stared in shock.

"Hush Ray, he wasn't going to come. So, I ASKED him." said Bella glaring at her younger brother. Charles showed up in a black tux and looked around the courtyard.

"Luna, your date is here.," said DJ. He turned around to Luna and, but she was gone. "Where did Luna and Jenny go?" he looked around. Everyone looked around dumbfounded that Jenny and Luna had disappeared.

"Maybe they went to wash up." Said Bree as her arms hug around Dane's arm. They walked into the grand hall. Bella and DJ took to the dance floor, Ray and Amber stood and talked. There on the dance floor, arm in arm was Jenny and Luna. Music played loudly, and lights flashed. "What the heck?" said DJ baffled.

"Hmm, what is it?" asked Bree as she danced with DJ.

"Luna and Jenny dancing." replied DJ as he nodded towards their direction.

"-Oh, they wanted it to be a secret. No one knew, they have talked to me and Amanda about it. They didn't want to flaunt it. Have to say, they are made for each other. They sure are Yin and yang. Jenny is the Yin earth, femaleness, passivity, and absorption. Luna is the polar opposite she is the yang, heaven, light, and activity." Said Bree while her head lay on his shoulder.

Jenny and Luna danced as the song came to an end. Luna smiled at Jenny as she stared at Jenny, and they swayed. "I missed you." Said Luna smiling at Jenny.

"I have missed you too my Boobear." replied Jenny while they held hands while they dance. "A perfect night." said Luna with a twinkle.

"No, it isn't!" snapped Jenny.

"What do you mean?" asked Luna in confusion while she stared sideways at Jenny.

"-Shut up!," snapped Jenny "and kiss me."

Luna leaned up a tad and slowly press her soft lips into Jenny's soft cherry blossom-flavored lips. They had kissed, the kiss lasted a little longer for a moment. "- Now it is perfect." said Jenny in pure bliss. They walked off to get their dance pictures made. They walked over to the group by the refreshment stand. "Hey guys." they greeted everyone.

"--- Don't hey guys us, we had the right to know. When I say we... I mainly mean me!" snapped DJ in a harsh tone.

"We wanted to surprise everyone." said Luna as she kissed his cheek along with Jenny. DJ's cheeks flushed to a strawberry red. Then Bella kissed his cheek.

"Thanks for the dance." she walked off to Matt. A few hours had passed. Mistress Flowers stopped the music and stood up "We are glad you all made it to the May Madness Dance! Are we having fun?," everyone had cheered "This is the last dance of the year. I'd like to announce the Guardian Clan God and the votes are in and came very close. This Year's Guardian Clan God is --- Bruno Silvertongue by one vote!"

Bruno walked up to the stage and sat on the throne by the Professors. Mistress Flowers placed a crown on his head. "This year Guardian Clan Goddess is not even a surprise to us. --- Bree Summers! By hundred and fifty votes, come and take your crown!"

Everyone cheered while she came up and sat down on the other throne. Mistress Flowers placed the crown on Bree's head. Bree smiled over at Bruno " scared yet?," she whispered, "to lose Lord Headmaster next year?"

Bruno looked away with a sour face "give it up for this year's God and Goddess. Let them take the floor for the Guardian God and Goddess dance." Bree and Bruno took the floor, and they dance to the their own song. Mistress flowers took the stage after Bree and Bruno had their Guardian God and Goddess dance. "I like to remind you all Friday is the Awards and the last large Feast, and who is this year's Guardian Clan winner.," each student started to yell out their clan's name "Now we have two more songs for the evening."

Luna took Jenny to the floor and danced, Bella and Batt came onto the floor. Bree and Dane, Bruno and Jewels, and Ray and Amber were on the dance floor. The energy was so alive that night, everyone was having a good time. "Well almost everyone." said DJ sigh as he sat on the sideline by the refreshment table feeling bummed out.

426

Cecil was with Erica, Kain was with Traci... Even the rat boy Zak had a date, so did Colt. DJ slid back in his chair with a sigh *be funny if a chick ran up to me and asked me for a dance... Shmôg* he thought to himself while he watched everyone dance... Then he felt a tap on his shoe, he looked down and saw, yes... ChickieDee somehow this little chick had a small white bow around her neck. DJ gave a small chuckle and thought *-Fool!... Shmôg, you are the Goblin of Menance.* He picked up ChickieDee and held the chicken in his palms close to him and went to the dance floor with everyone. Luna and Jenny both smiled at him and pat the chicken "beautiful chick you have there." joshed Luna.

"I wasn't being serious about bringing ChickieDee." said Jenny with a whimsical smile as she rolled her eyes.

"- I didn't plan on it, Shmôg decided to pull one last prank. "Answered DJ. They all danced through the last songs. They made their way back to the Dormitory and fell asleep.

Chapter 24: The meeting

The next morning, Luna felt a dabbing to her nose. She wrinkled her nose. Then felt another dabbing. She brushed her face with her left hand with a slight grumbled, another assault of dabbing, this time hidden behind muffled giggles. Luna's eyelids slowly fluttered before she opened her eyes. She saw the bright, positive person yet at this time the most irksome person ever.

"Good morning love, "Jenny laid across Luna's stomach "open up." she broke a piece of her banana muffin off, and Luna opened her mouth while Jenny fed her.

"What time is it?" asked Luna while she ate the muffin.

"Seven, hate for you to sleep in ALL day." Jenny fed her another piece.

"-You woke me up at seven, are you for cereal?! What time did you wake up?" asked Luna between bites.

"I could have woken you up when I got up. I got up at five. Did a little light reading till six-thirty when breakfast was ready." Luna looked over Jenny's shoulder at her bed where a book laid at. With at least two thousand pages. Luna laid back down and snuggled into her pillow. "That's not light reading." she snuggled under the blankets and closed her eyes "how many pages consist of light reading?"

"I just started it. I'm only on page three hundred and forty-

428

two. I was trying to get to four hundred."

"... Three hundred and forty-two, really light reading. DJ's right... You're not a human." Jenny leans down and kissed her cheek "goodnight." she went back to her book while everyone slept. after a bit, she got up and went out of the dormitory for the day.

There was so much commotion downstairs in the Crowfeather dormitory. Luna woke up and looked at her sun-and-moon dial, and it was a little past two *what does a girl have to do to be able to sleep in* she thought to herself while she got up and headed to shower. - DJ, Bella, Matt, and a few others were playing human chest; Timmy got the human chessboard for Christmas. The four-foot pawn pieces moved across the floor on their own. Then Bella moved and overtook the pawn. DJ saw Luna at the top of the stairs. "Hey, sleepyhead."

She found a seat and curled up with a pillow, her feet tucked under her "you know it's rude to wake someone up?" she eyed the room as they continued to play.

"-Sorry., Princess." chuckled DJ.

Finally, the game had ended, and DJ, Matt, and Morgan's team won as they were the black pieces. Luna told DJ to come with her to hang out. DJ grabbed his note from his dad and followed her. Nightstalker flew behind as Khan followed.

"Why do you have that note?" questioned Luna with a puzzled look. "Figure you wanted to see Maîq, figured he might know about this Nails or this Zert town."

Luna shrugged "maybe." they walked out of the tower, the hot sun beating down on them. Kids swam in the moat around the castle. The Loch Ness Monster had its long neck and massive head out of the water taking in the sun. Deer were out in the valley along with some flowerindeer (grassy green fur with flowers blooming running along their spine).

Luna and DJ came along through the valley to Maîq's cottage. They knocked on the door of the large oval wooden door. The door opened. Jenny smiled from the other side of the door "Yeesssss?." she giggled "-sorry we don't want anything that you are trying to sell."

Luna rolled her eyes and walked in "Oh, you are stupid. Hey Maîq." she said as they sat down while Maîq poured them Witch Brew Passionflowre tea.

"Olá Luna n DJ, Wat brings ye 'ere?" asked Maîq while they sat down.

"We missed our feline friend.," answered DJ. He cleared his throat and looked at Maîq's large cat eyes "so, you're from here aren't you?"

Maîq took a sip of the tea "sim, in da Sul (south) of da deserto (desert). Wen I waz medium Tigris. I left casa (home) to Cidade Costeira de Cristal (Crystal Coastal Town). I supplied peixe (fish), clams, n other foods 'or da escola (school). Den Directora (Headmistress) Ruby gave Maîq trabalho de caçador (huntsman job) on da order of Mr. Rune. Whom at da Tempo (time) waz vice diretor (vice Headmaster). Why ya ask?"

Luna, Jenny, and DJ looked at each other before DJ looked at Maîq "what year did you come to the school/. What town did you grow up in?" asked DJ.

Maîq's tail raised and swayed with a questionable look "--- porque (Why) ye ask?" his ears twitched. He let out a small fierce hiss. Luna pulled out DJ's note from his pocket "DJ got this from his dad." Maîq took the letter and scanned through the letter. "-1995, Sim (yes).," he handed him the letter "Sim, Maîq came ta da escola (school) in 1995. Maîq waz caçador de caça (game hunter),

". Maîq 'ave 'ever attended the escola. I 'ad da 'est dois (two) amigos (friends). Adam n a guy in ma village Zert, RazÉr. He Found ma town at age seis (six) yer older den Maîq., "He lives two huts down wid dis felina (feline female) and felino (feline male)." Maîq looked at DJ as if he was playing word chess to figure out his next words.

"Few anos (years) 'ad passed. Maîq found work at Cidade Costeira de Cristal (Crystal Coastal Town). RazÉrgot a free ride ta OwlHollow. 1993 is da Temp (time) we separado(separated). We explored Montanha Troll Head (Troll Head Mountain), ilusão de floresta (Illusion Forest), N da dois (two) templos (temples), between 1993 to 1995. We found waz ta 'ake shanties."

They listened to Maîq's story "who's RazÉr, did you know Stryder, Stryder Brêon and do you know this Nailz?"

Maîq grumbled while his ears flatten. "RazÉr waz good amigo (friend). Stryder... Stryder RazÉr do 'ot recall dat name. 'Ot safe ta spit dat name. Feiticeiros da Mesa Redonda (Wizards of The Round TableTable) 'as many espiões (spies). Dis Nailz ye speak of iz a mito (myth)... contos (tales), criatura fictícia (fictional creature), Maîq people made up. Der just Contos de Nailz (Tales of Nailz). Wen Summer comes do not seek Sul (south), Go Wid Luna, go home wid her."

DJ sighed and looked at them then back to Maîq with a nod. "What is Zert like?" asked Luna.

Maîq took a sip of his tea. He looked at them "Calor brutal (brutal heat),areias quentes de fogo (hot sands of fire). Da folks r rough, assassino (assassin) type of folds. caçadores (hunters) 'or shanties n other artefatos (artifacts)."

They stood up and waved bye to Maîq "we must get going now, bye Maîq." -

They said their goodbyes and they left. They walked off to the willow tree. "-Do you feel like Maîq was hiding something?" question DJ with a puzzled voice.

"Why would he lie or hide something?" replied Luna a bit frustrated.

"-I don't know. I am with DJ on this... His tone and aura changed. - As if he is hiding something." replied Jenny looking at Luna while they sat under the tree.

"He has nothing to hide. Rune trusts him and IF Rune has so much trust in Maîq, so can we. I believe he is telling the truth." Luna snapped out.

432

"... I mean, even the Wizards of The Round Table was asking about Nailz. They are like old...Like ancient old. I don't think they would fall for a myth." said DJ to make his argument point.

"--- I agree with DJ." added Jenny.

"...Whatever, believe what you want." said Luna while she got up.

"Where are you going?" asked Jenny looking up at Luna.

"A walk away from the two of you before we fight." replied Luna while she walked off.

Jenny sighed watching Luna walk off into the distance "--- she is definitely your yang." said DJ. Jenny looked at him sideways with a puzzled look of shock. -

Luna walked to the courtyard; Kain yelled and ran past her "stay away from Bell, death follows her!" she sat on the ground while Professor Raven came out of the castle with something big under a thick wool blanket.

"Ms. Bell, what brings you out here alone weeping?"

Luna looked at Professor Raven with a deep breath while she crossed her arms. She was still upset "stupid fight over something."

Professor Raven looked at her with a nod "walk with me, tell me what it is about."

Luna waved her off and shook her head "no thanks, I am fine."

Professor raven spoke with her soft tone staring down at Luna with an austere stare"- I wasn't asking, now come."

Luna sighed heavily while she got up and walked with Raven as they head towards the valley. She told Professor Raven everything, from all the deaths around her. Losing her friend Ol' Witchie Willow when she had no one. Then DJ and Jenny, basically calling Maîq a liar.

"Oh child, stories mean different things for everyone. Stories are just - stories... The meaning could be different fro you then for me. Depends on how you read into it." explain Raven while they walked over the rolling hills of the valley. This didn't make Luna feel any better about things. They had reached the willow tree. There was no DJ or Jenny could be found.

"Why are we here?" asked Luna looking at Raven. Professor Raven pulled the blanket off and revealed the large black octagon gem. Luna smiles largely, heartful of joy "Ol' Witchie Willow!"

Raven placed the gem onto the trunk of the tree and tapped it with her wand. Fog slowly stirred in the gem, then the Ol' Witchie Willow came into view as the smokey gem cleared up. She woke up with a yawn.

"Such a long sleep. Oh, Child Raven, what is the meaning of waking me?" asked Ol' Witchie Willow with a toothless smile.

"Dear Willow Mother, Mr. Rune believes it is safe to return you back to the Willow." explained Raven with a tender smile.

"Ah, yes... He is an old and wise, almost as old as Ol'

Witchie Willow. His father was a great and powerful wizard. I fear the shadows will not break, this curse of darkness will linger on till five spirits can rise."

Raven's eyes widen with full anxious in her tone when she spoke "what do you mean Willow Mother? What curses do you speak of?"

Luna stood in shock listening in. "The wind speaks to me, a traitor amongst the wizardly world, and a boy in the web of a puppeteer. at works.," Ol' Witchie Willow turned her gaze and smiled that toothless smile at Luna, the branches closed around Luna hugging her in the branches. "Ah, my dear child. have missed you my little one."

Luna hugged the trunk of the tree "I have missed you too."

"What traitor and what kid?" question Raven looking perplexed.

"Ah, Child Raven. I do not know; I am weak and I need my rest." replied Ol' Witchie Willow with a yawn.

"Of course Mother Willow." Said Raven while they said their goodbyes and walked back to the castle. They made it back to the keep of the Castle. They walked into the school. Raven turned and looked at Luna " do not speak of what you heard. We do not need this getting out. Thank you for the walk. " said Professor Raven with a smile.

Luna walked into the large feast hall and saw Jenny and DJ. She came up behind them and hugged them "sorry for how I acted. Let's just drop it and enjoy this fine pasta."

They looked at her as if she was out of her mind. They ate so much till tiredness fell over them; ChickieDee helped herself to DJ's pasta. - They went up to the dormitory and sat in the Common room.

"Who do you think will win the Clan trophy tomorrow?" asked DJ as he laid upside on the couch looking up at the girls.

"So far, Dracoîn is up by two trophies. It depends on the points." said Jenny while she draped her legs over Luna's lap.

"Chimerador didn't win one, so they are at least last." added Luna while she rubbed Jenny's leg. Night fell on the school, and they all laid down till slept took them. -

Kain looked out of the window while words spelled out slowly Get Luna to leave her body, Saturday night. I am ready to bring home a body to sacrifice to bring back one of the relatives. Kain nodded his head and spoke in a murmur.

"Yes Mistress."

Good puppet. -

The next day, excitement fell over the whole school. It was the awards. Everyone in the school dressed up in formal wear. The school was all decorated out in clan colors, candlelit in clan colors down the halls. Clan banners hung along the wall, and Clan colors rolled of colors down the corridors.

They all walked from their towers following the colored clan carpets as they look around in awe as photos of the school year hung along the walls. They walked into the feast hall. Professors, Mistress, and Headmaster sat in their thrones. Lord Headmaster and Pre lords sat in theirs. The students took to their seats at their clan tables. Luna, DJ, and Jenny sat with Bella, Matt, Worf, and Koty. The large black cauldron sat in on the stage. Luna saw it and remembered looking into it. The old witch appearing, the old, wrinkled hand reaching out for her brought back the cold nightmare of terror.

Mr. Rune stood, everyone called and cheered. He gave a slight bow with his head and clapped his hands as did every professor joined in. He spoke with such warmth and a twinkle in his eyes. His tone was just pure of glee.

"Welcome everyone to the most important day of the school year! We have awards to give out for recognition. and some information. When you see your name, come up here and claim your reward."

Everyone cheered, they watched the smoky cauldron "Frist award, is for Best Attendance... She is a first yearer, a bright young girl. She is from the Crowfeather clan... Give around applause to --- Jenny Striff!

The cauldron spat her name out in purple spoke. Jenny blushed while she got up and walked to the stage. She shook hands with all the professors, Mistress Flowers, and then Mr. Rune. He handed her a black plaque with a picture of a purple crow at the bottom, and in beautiful spiral writing were the details of the plaque.

~ *Best Attendance of 2024* ~
Owl Hollow would like to
honor this award to the
first yearer, who missed
zero classes
and
not late once!

Jenny Striff

Velvet Flowers	*Owl Hollow*	*Robert Rune*
Vice Mistress	*School of Magick*	*Headmaster*
	OF	
	Witchcraft and Wizardly	

Jenny took her seat looking at the award with a heart filled smile.

"This award is for the highest grades of the year. She is -" Dj whispered lowly "come on up, Jenny." Jenny glared at him as she began to get up.

"a second-year from Chimerador... give round applause for. --- Amanda Striff!" everyone clapped while Amanda got up and went to the stage. Jenny sat down as her cheeks flushed.

"WOW! Got beat by your own sister." said DJ with a grin.

Chapter 24: The meeting

Jenny looked at him with a grimacing smile trying to hide the fact she was upset "...She deserves it." The cauldron spat out Amanda's name while she claimed her award. The plaque was red with silver spiral righting with a picture of Chimera printed on the bottom. She made her way and shook hands with the professors, Mistress flowers, and then Mr. Rune

~ Highest Grades of the Year 2024 ~
Owl Hollow would like
to honor this award to the
second yearer who held all 100's
throughout all school year!

Amanda Striff

Velvet Flowers	Owl Hollow	Robert Rune
Vice Mistress	School of Magick	Headmaster
	OF	
	Witchcraft and Wizardly	

She made her way back to her clan table. Mistress Flowers took the stand "guess I'll take over, so this ol' man can rest his voice. This award can go out to a lot of you students. It is the most

Improvement, this girl went from all over the grade scale last semester. to ALL A's. She is a first yearer from Crowfeather. --- Luna Bell!."

The cauldron spat her name out while she ran up shaking hands. She took the plaque, the plaque looked just like Jenny's.

~ *Most Improvement for 2024* ~

Owl Hollow would like

to honor this award to the

first yearer who improved overall

throughout all school year!

Luna Bell

Velvet Flowers	*Owl Hollow*	*Robert Rune*
Vice Mistress	*School of Magick*	*Headmaster*
	OF	

Witchcraft and Wizardly

Luna came down and showed her award off to DJ and Jenny "good job, love!" said Jenny giving Luna a kiss as they held hands.

"Now our most prized individual award, Best Pre Lord of

440

the year, this was a tough one to give out. We had so many great Pre Lords this year. This individual, she shows pride, care for others, and school spirit. She is someone you can go to for anything and she will help anyone out, she will go out of her way. Please give around applause for --- Jewels Meadows!"

      The cauldron spat her name out in gold smoke. Jewels ran up and shook hands with everyone as she took the award. The plaque was golden glass see through with silver writing and a picture of the three headed dog on the bottom.

~best Pre Lord of the Year 2024~

Owl Hollow would like to

honor this year for Pre Lord

for the

Care ~ Respect ~ Pride

Jewels Meadows

Velvet Flowers	*Owl Hollow*	*Robert Rune*
Vice Mistress	*School of Magick*	*Headmaster*
	OF	

Witchcraft and Wizardly

Everyone cheered as Goldenpaw table blew up with a roaring of applause while Jewels returned to her throne. She slipped the crown back over her head. "Now comes the Professor of the year award. Don't worry we didn't forget you. The Professor of the year award, this professor came to our school two years ago. From Crystal Magck University, she is a tough professor, but she shows care and love for all the students. She is a Clan professor for... Crowfeather, come on over Professor Raven Woods!."

Crowfeather clan blew up with cheers and applause as Proffe-or Raven shook hands with the professors, then received a hug from Flowers and Rune. She got her award and held it up while the cheering continued.

~Professor of the year 2024~
Owlhollow would like to
honor this award to
for outstanding teaching and care!

Professor Raven Woods

Velvet Flowers   *OwlHollow*   *Robert Rune*
Vice Mistress   *School of Magick*   *Headmaster*
OF
Witchcraft and Wizardly

Mr. Rune stood back up and took the stand "thank you for the rest. Now you may rest, you old bat. I would like to honor the game trophies. The first trophy is the Snorkbie trophy. The games were splendid each clan did a spectacular job. This year's winner goes to... Crowfeather, for that Dracoîn, had cheated in the Championship game." his voice went from its usual warmth to a more sterner while he eyed Cecil.

A gold three-foot trophy appeared with someone diving to catch a ball. On the base of the trophy said "*Crowfeather 2024*", the plaque was black with purple writing. Bree came up and received the trophy, then sat down placing the crown back over her head. She looked at Jenny with a snub look.

"The next trophy is the Wizard Jousting, a very outstanding event. This year's winner is Crowfeather!" Bree got back up and went to receive the trophy. It was a foot-tall and a foot-wide trophy with a silver star with a wand at an angle resting on the tip of the star. The end of the wand sat on the tip of the star. Same plaque as the other trophy.

"Now the broom racing this year's winner is Goldenpaw, for such a great race!" Jewels got up and walked up to retrieve the trophy. The trophy was gold in the shape of a sphere with a broom resting on it. The plaque was gold and silver "*Goldenpaw 2024*". She sat down while Goldenpaw clan cheered like crazy.

"Our last game trophy is Wand tag. Very intense game. This winning Clan is Chimerador! for the Dracoîn had cheated to their way into victory. By using the fur of the Doggo." the room was quiet then Chimerador blew up with cheers and whistles. Bruno and Dane got up and received the trophy. The trophy was a golden star with three wands on the tips of the star. The plaque was red with silver writing "*Chimardor 2024*".

"This will look good in the Chimerador's trophy case, thanks Cecil." said Dane in mockery. Cecil gave a nasty snarl at them.

"Now the Guardian Clan cup, we will look at each total points of the year for each Clan...Chimerador with combined points of *four thousand five hundred and eighty.* " Said Rune, the cauldron spat out the score in red spoke as it floated over the Chimerador's table. The clan beat on the table cheering.

"Now, Crowfeather had combine points of *four thousand five hundred and thirty-five points*, but Matt tried to hit another student. So we took fifty points away. They have a total of *four thousand four hundred and ninety-five points.*" The cauldron spat the score out in purple smoke as it floated over the clan table. The Crowfeather clan cheered loudly.

"Now, Goldenpaw with the combine points of *four thous- and, three hundred and seventy-five points!*" gold smoke came from the cauldron and floated over the Goldenpaws table while they cheered.

"--- We lost." said Luna gloomily while defeat showed on her face.

"Don't worry we got next year." replied Jenny trying to make Luna think positively.

"Now lastly, Dracoîn with the combined points of *five thousand one hundred and fifteen points!*" The cauldron spat out green smoke as it hovered over the table. Dracoîn had the loudest cheers while every other student just looked in disappointment.

Rune took his wand and tapped the air and the clan colors shifted from all the clan colors to green and black. Dracoîn's banners flew, and photos hung on the wall from the school year. "Mr. Rune, I found dis in a student's room. I busted Kain one night after school hours. Tiny brought me this parchment.," said Moody the Watchman while he dragged his foot on the stage while he made his way to Rune. Tiny stared at the students growling and snarling while drool foam from his mouth. He handed the leather bag to Rune. It had Kain's name stitched on it.

Rune took the bag and opened it. There were so many parchments on how to summon Bloody Mary. The students sat in awe as the room grew quiet. "--- Oh Robert..." Flowers gasped in fright while she looked in the bag.

Professor Raven made her way to the two and looked into the bag and gasp "Oh, Mr. Rune I told them if anyone had tried to summon Mary, their clan will lose all points and detention till next summer."

Whispers broke out in the sea of students. Mr. Rune nodded as he took such a deep breath. "--- This has been brought to my attention, things of discovery. Dracoîn will lose ALL Clan points. This year's Guardian cup goes to... Chimerador!." He took his wand and gave it a wave as the colors changed from green and

black to red and silver decorations. "Now for Dracoîn, Pre Lord...
As Headmaster of OwlHollow, I see you have lost control of your
Clan and the pride you once used to carry. You may step down
from the throne and back to the table."

Dracoîn gasped and stared while Cecil removed his crown
and laid it in his seat. He walked back to the table while a low
whisper of cheers came from the other students of the clans.

"Dracoîn has no Pre Lord." Whispered Jenny while she
watched in shock.

"... Maybe you can get his Pre Lord spot." sniggered DJ
behind his hand. Luna elbowed him while Jenny glared at him.

"That isn't funny." Jenny replied. Bruno smiled while he
watched Cecil walk in shame.

"Bruno and Dane, come get the Guardian clan cup." said
Rune. The large trophy had a lot of loopy loops that broke off in
different ways like a branch. Each branch held a Clan color Gem.
The trophy was clear crystal. Bruno and Dane went up and lifted
the Trophy while their clan gave thunderous applause.

"When school comes to an end, keep an eye out for the
envelope for next year. We will gain new students and lose some.
For the ones who are leaving, we will miss you and may bright
roads guide you.," everyone cheered out "for the Pre Lord spot in
Dracoîn, we will announce the Pre Lord at the beginning of next
school year. Now let's eat and enjoy our time together." Food appeared on the table and everyone dug in even little ChickieDee
began to eat.

Bree came over and sat down by Jenny; she looked at Jenny with her arms crossed "because of your challenge, it made me lose the Pre Lord of the year award." Bree stood up and tapped her goblet with her spoon while everyone stopped talking and stared at her.

She raised her goblet into the air " Chimerador, you all had an splendid year and keeping their heads up when things went south. You guys have a great Pre Lord and Lord Headmaster. --- To Chimerador!."

"To Chimerardor!" everyone said with hearts filled with joy. Except for Dracoîn, who sat with a sour look on their face. -

The next day, everyone was up. Luna had slept in till three, DJ and Jenny sat in the Common room. He looked at Jenny as she polished her award "can't believe your sister got the smart person award.," he chuckled out "I thought you were smart."

Jenny rolled her eyes "I am my sister is just as smart." she looked to the stairs. "Think we should wake the beast up?"

"Nope, she was upset yesterday when we woke up." replied DJ while he watched her polish her trophy. -A half an hour later, Luna came downstairs. She rubbed her eyes while she laid on the couch with her head in Jenny's lap "morning love." said Jenny while she ran fingers through Luna's hair.

"- You mean Good afternoon... Explains why your sister got the smart person trophy." heckled DJ with a gadfly tone.

Luna kicked him in his side "don't ruin my pampering."

Jenny gave Luna's hair a tug with a smile "you should let me dread up your hair like I did Bree's and mine."

Luna lay there thinking about it. She looked to DJ while he shook his head "your mom would kill you... Then I'll get your room, yeah go ahead! Dread up your hair." said DJ with a smile.

Luna's eyebrow arched looking puzzled "why would you get my room?"

"Cause your mom likes me." replied DJ.

"- She likes you for the stable boy aspect." joshed Luna.

Bree came in and Jenny looked at her "Hey Bree, I want to say I am sorry... My heart aches because I ruined a great friendship, a sisterhood. Each time I see you I am tearful, I only challenge you because I wanted to be Pre Lord,

"I am sorry you didn't get Pre Lord of the year. You deserve it, it was pitiful for me to do it. I think next year you should go for Lord Headmistress; you deserve it. Your exceptional, I mean it. Luna and I both are." said Jenny with heartache and tears in her eyes "- I am so sorry."

Luna sat up and nodded "we miss you Furbreeze. I am sorry... Sorry for everything. We want you back in the sisterhood."

DJ sat quietly Awkward. Maybe I should say something stupid... Or get up and leave. "Zeta!"

"-What?" they all said looking at DJ sideways.

"It's the sixth letter in the Greek alphabet."

"How do you know that?" said Jenny.

"Fine, I'll forgive you.," Said Bree with a smile "truth be

told, I miss you two as well *Awkward. Maybe I should say something stupid... Or get up and leave.* "Zeta!"

"-What?" they all said looking at DJ sideways.

"It's the sixth letter in the Greek alphabet."

"How do you know that?" said Jenny.

"Fine, I'll forgive you.," Said Bree with a smile "truth be told, I miss you two as well. the three girls hugged. Jenny looked at DJ, still puzzled "how do you know what zeta meant?"

DJ looked at her with a smile that danced across his lips while he hassled Jenny "- maybe next year I'll get the smart person award."

She hit him playfully in the arm "shut up."

"Tonight, bring your plates up here. We are having a congratulations party for all the awards, trophies, and all the effort you all gave." said Bree while she stood in front of the clan. -

Luna, DJ, and Jenny ran down to Maîq's Luna's award in her hand. She beat on the door as he opened it. "Sim (Yes), Olá everyone, come in... 'Ow waz da prêmios (awards)?" asked Maîq while they came in and sat.

"It was good, me and Jenny both got an award. We won two trophies." repled Luna beaming with delight.

"Bom (Good), Bom (God), Parabéns (congrats) ye dois (two). DJ no prêmio (award)?"

DJ shook his head "I went mostly for the food." heckled DJ.

"DJ, ye got grandes amigas (great friends)."

DJ nodded with a smile " I do, even though they abuse me." he said with laughter. They all sat around and talked for a bit then left the cottage. It was a gloomy cloudy day.

"I'll catch up with you all shortly." Said Luna as she turned and waved before running off.

"Where are you going?" hollered Jenny.

"Don't worry about me!" she hollered back as she ran.

"Where is she going?" question DJ. -

Luna ran through the valley; it had begun to rain. She ran over to the willow tree. The branches had opened up slowly. She felt the branches wrap around her, the feeling of the willow embracing her.

"- Child, why are you out here in this downpour?" asked Ol' Witchie Willow with her toothless smile.

"I wanted to see you one last time, and show you this award that I got." said Luna proudly while she held up the award.

"Oh dear child of mine, congratulations. Little one, I will mis-s you. I will see you next year. Thank you for the flowers, they are b-eautiful."

"Your welcome. I will miss you too, you've been a really good friend." said Luna as she hugged Ol' Witchie Willow. She waved and ran back to the castle. Her foot slipped on a rock, and she fell. Crunch! She sat up holding her arm, the bangle that Jenny got her for Christmas had broken. Blood ran down her arm.

"Ouch... O-oh no, shoot my Christmas gift." sorrow filled her heart while she leaned down and picked up the broken pieces. She rushed off into the feast hall and sat down with Jenny and DJ.

"You are bleeding, what happened?" asked DJ.

"-What happened?" asked Jenny with concern.

"--- Cluck!" said ChickieDee. -

They took their plates back to the dormitory "I don't care about that, my Christmas gift broke" said Luna tearfully.

"I... Can fix it?" replied Jenny in a questionable tone as she was not so sure about it.

"I'm sorry, boobear." said Luna with tears in her eyes.

"It's ok, I'll put it in my bag." replied Jenny as she put her plate down and ran up to her room putting the broken bangle in her trunk. Luna sat with everyone while the whole clan ate.

Jenny came back and sat with Luna and DJ. She picked up her plate as everyone had a slice of pizza with garlic knots, bread sticks, and some had wings. Luna's cup was filled with Goblin Soda, DJ was drinking Mountain blast Goblinraid, and Jenny had her Pumpkin Spice Latte.

Bree stood up and cleared her throat while everyone gave their attention to her. She had a warm glow to her; her voice was soft... Pure not like it has been the last couple of months. "I know this year was a rough and bumpy road. Not just for me. - But for Crowfeather. We came home with two of four trophies; we should have won first place. I am proud of all of you. We may haven't won the Guardian Clan Cup this year.,

"But next year we will. We were down by ninety-five points. Next year I challenge each and every one of you to push yourselves. I'll also like to take this time to say Congratulations to Jenny whom I believe; deserves the two trophies. For best attendance and Luna for most improvement. I'll admit... I didn't think you would have lasted all year. You had a very rough start. I didn't think you finished strong; I am proud of you. On three, Crowfeather! --- One... two... three."

"CROWFEATHER!" everyone vociferated in glee. The party lasted most of the entire night. There was talk about everything from school year to summer break. Khan laid on the floor eating the soul of a rabbit. ChickieDee rested on Khan's back, and Nightstalker flew in and landed on DJ's shoulder. "So, why did you name your crow Nightstalker?" asked Luna.

"- Reminds me of you, when Brandon called you Nightwalker or something." answered DJ as he fed his bird.

"He calls me stalker of the night, and that is weird." said Luna looking at DJ. Matt heard them and shouted out to DJ.

"Quit chasing Luna's ouos, you have another ouos to chase." DJ's cheeks turned bright red. Luna popped out her Emusicly player and put an earbud in and the other end into Jenny's ear. She skimmed the playlist and picked the band Sacrosanct Sacrifice. Then picked one of their songs (*I'm Falling*). The song played the guitar chords strum along, the mighty drum beat, and the bass guitar plucked along.

<Brandon sings> I lost my strength, I'm near the edge of it all looking down. *<Ava sings>* Over the edge. I'm falling. *<Ava growls and the Brandon sings>* You're falling. *<Ava grow>* You are falling away from the edge. *<Brandon sings>* I'm holding onto the edge with the last of my hope. Hoping you can reach me before I fall again. *<chorus>* I fall again. *<Ava growl>* Reach out and take my hand for I have the strength for you>

Jenny removed the earbud and kissed her cheek "too much growling for my taste. I mean the story of the song is good of the hero is falling and the weakest one came in to save him"

Luna was flabbergasted at Jenny's remark. She sat there with a dumbfounded expression on her face "-what?" asked Jenny.

"-You... Do you always have to look into the meaning of everything? You ruin a great song. It's called heavy metal." replied Luna while she put the other bud in.

"That's how you learn." answered Jenny.

"You know what this means?" Luna asked Jenny before getting up and stomping off to the room.

"- Means you are upset!" answered Jenny.

Luna lay in bed while listening to her music. Night overtook the students with sleep. Luna woke up and got to her feet; she could hear the music of Distinction Jaded. It was the song (*Falling into Detriment*), she turned and saw her body asleep. She could hear the music. She wandered out into the tower and sat out in the rain, and lightning lit the sky while; she sat listening to another song by Distinction Jaded it was the song called (*Torment*).

<Andrew sings> I stare into the mirror as I see this face staring back at me. The mask I wear to escape the memories of the past and the pain I try to hide from behind this clown's mask. <Chorus> Escape the memories of the past, the pain I try to hide from behind this <Ember growls, Chorus > clown mask. <Andrew sings> I am ready for the hangman to come and claim me. I feel the tightening of his nose around my neck. Why can I still breathe? Why am I still fighting for? Why am I strong and not weak! <Chorus> why can I still breathe? why am I still fighting for? <Ember Growls> Why am I strong and not weak! wish the pain would fade awaaaaay. I wish I found the strength to take the razor and shed this pain awaay from me. Opening up the Red Nile River. up as I carve my flesh awaay to escape the pain.

<Chorus> Opening up the Red Nile River as I carve my flesh away to escape the pain. <Andrew sings> I feel the warmth of the Red Nile River overtake my arm as I feel the pain ease away. <Chorus> feel the pain ease away.

Luna sat there in tears washing away from the rain while the song ends. The woman in the song who growled spoke up after the song "Suicide isn't the answer. We sing about our fight with suicidal thoughts to cope and help others so you're not alone. IF you feel suicidal. Please talk to someone, parents, friends, teacher, hotlines (1-800-273-TALK (8255)), or Distinctionjadedforthefight.com Your life means more than you think. This is Ember Gunn from Distinction Jaded, and I want you to know we love you. Your life matters. -

In the dormitory, second floor, room three. Jenny woke up and went to use the bathroom. She washed her face and turned around. - Luna heard footsteps, it wasn't by her on the school grounds. She could hear running water. -

Jenny turned around and saw Luna with a sideways grin and a crazy look in her eyes. A creepy stare, the green eye dropped to a low gaze and the blue eye kept forward. "- That's creepy." said Jenny. - Luna gasped and ran towards the tower. Then - a heart stopping shrill filled Luna's ears, heart pounded, tears filled her eyes. She ran into the dormitory to her room. Jenny walked forward gasping, hand on her chest blood coated her hand and her purple gown.

"Jenny!" yelled out Luna tearful of pain washed over her.

"- L- Luna..." Jenny gasped out while she fell forward. Luna caught Jenny feeling her body grow cold. Puddles of blood covered the floor. "N- no.." Luna buried Jenny's face in her neck and shoulder. "- God, no, please... I love you, Jenny!" a bright blue light began illuminating from Jenny's chest. Luna wiped her eyes "- what?" then blue butterflies began to flutter out from her chest. Not one but many blue butterflies, "w-what this? - NO! It's her soul!" screamed Luna in despondent.

Then she heard a stabbing than a gasp of breath... Then a

voice "- Flee, I have one more job." they ran down the stairs as the butterflies scattered towards the window. Luna looked to the door.

Chapter 25: Home sweet home

The butterflies flew to the window; Luna heard the footsteps then looked at the door and saw... Bree and Luna, Luna's body turned and smiled in the same creepy smile with those creepy eyes before running off. Luna got to her feet for a chase. She stopped and ran to the last butterfly; she jumped with both hands reached out, and grasp the butterfly, just one. Luna's eyes widen as she hung on the edge of the window seal with one hand.

"Would I die if I fell?" asked quietly as she felt her grip loosen. She felt her hand slip. Then a hand gripped her hand.

"-No, you don't child." said a voice. He said while he brought her back up into the room it was Larry the ghost with Linda and Berry the three ghosts from when she first got here.

"Child, you could have died... What on heavens are you doing?" said Linda concerningly.

"My fri- girlfriend... Jenny is dead..." said Luna in tears. A bright blue light was illuminating from her hand.

"- Child, she will be OK if you don't lose that last soul of hers." Larry told her; Luna placed the butterfly in a jar. They rushed off to the hall. Luna could hear snoring, then a gasp.

"They are in a dormitory!" cried out Luna in a panic.

They ran into the main hall, Mr. Rune came down the stairs and saw Larry and them. Luna stepped behind Larry. "What is the meaning of this, did you find them?," asked Mr. Rune with more of a sharper tone than usual. "- I can see you, Luna."

Larry shook his head with a downfall gaze "I, we only found da girl... She said there is snoring."

"It's all my fault, Mr. Rune... I am so sorry." said Luna sadly. "Dear, dear it's not your fault. We use our powers and forget the consequence of the action. - As if you didn't leave your body, you wouldn't be able to save Jenny. Only in the spirit world or a strong third eye allows you to see the blue butterflies. The soul of life." said Mr. Rune while he sounded m-ore like the cheerful man he is.

He took the jar and gave it to Linda "place this on my desk, Berry, take Jenny's body to my office. Luna, you and I along with Larry will look for your body and who else is on foot."

They went along the hall of the large castle "- Sir, Mr. Rune they could be anywhere." said Larry while he floated along.

"Indeed, yes, but we have their ears... Luna can hear them." said Rune while they walked along the long hall.

"-There!" Luna shouted while she pointed to the end of the long hall. Luna's body swayed wearing the nightgown. Her bare feet tapped along the floor. They chased after her. Larry pointed out of the window "There!" lighting struck, the flash lit up the sky while the rain pelted off the stained window.

"-BREE!" exclaimed Luna loudly, Bree ran off into the illusion forest. Larry sent chase while he floated through the wall and towards the illusion forest. "Luna what do you hear?," asked

Mr. Rune "*revelare*" while he pointed his crystal wand and the halls lit up and it showed hand prints and footprints that were all over the floors, walls, and the ceiling. "-My they been planning this attack for a while."

Luna listens closely, her eyes closed. "-Running water... Bathroom!" they rushed to a bathroom, nothing... They went up another floor, nothing... Then they went to the fifth floor to the bathroom, they rushed into it and Luna's eyes widen, her body hung halfway out of the mirror crawling into it. Rune took his wand and with a swift of the wand. Luna's body jerked from the mirror "no you don't Margret." Luna's body lay lifeless; she looked at Mr. Rune with an anxiety perplexed look. "It's ok, she got away. Tomorrow we will do a headcount for everyone." said Mr. Rune with a depressed tone while Luna submerges back into her body. Her eyes fluttered open slowly as she took such a deep breath, her chest raised and fell. Rune turned and spoke to the thin air next to him.

"- I figure you would have lost her in the forest.," there was a moment of quietness "indeed, I do believe so.," Luna sat listening to Rune speak "I shall think they will be p to removing me as Headmaster after this event tonight, no there was no avoiding this."

Her eyes widen with disbelief "... Yes, I may be in prison in *Tenebrae Prison.* Do not threaten, Mistress Flowers will make a fine Headmistress. I've made plans with her just in case if I am removed." there was a moment of quietness while Luna's heart race and thoughts rush through her head   "Kate Bell said she'll get her revenge on me, for her death that I had ordered." He turned to Luna who sat in tears. He smiled with such sympathy and delight in his voice "now, let's go save your girlfriend. Tonight, not all was lost." -

They went up to the eighth floor and into his large circular office. On the desk laid the jar, to the common eye it looked empty. In a chair sat Jenny's body. He laid her body down on the floor and the *ferrethin* climbed up on Jenny and a tear fell on her deep gash cut on her chest.

The wound slowly closed up. He took the butterfly and place it into her mouth while chanting some ancient words. Her mouth lit up and butterflies flew by in hundreds. They flew into the blue light that acted as a beacon as they flew back into her mouth.

"She'll keep the scar. But in the morning, she'll be back to normal." Said Rune as he made a cot bed appear with a flick of his wand as he laid her on it. "Now, go back to the room and get some sleep." -

Luna was escorted back to her dormitory. It had a chilly eerie feel in the common room. Luna went up to the room, the blood was cleaned up. She grabbed Captain Monkmonk and curled up with him on her bed. She felt a stinging sensation on her left thigh. she reached down and felt it, she winced in pain. She had been bitten.

"...Khan?!" she yelled out. Lyndsie laid in bed just on the other side of Luna's lit her candle. "...God shut up Luna, trying to sleep." Lyndsie said before pulling the blankets over her head.

The common room lit up in red, yellow, and blue light. A deep growl rumbled from the common room. Khan came in, Khan's deep emerald eyes shimmered in the dark. His body was engulfed in flames. He let out a deep growl, sparks of flame spat out from his muzzle. Luna had never seen Khan like this before. Words were stuck in her throat. His paws dug in the hardwood floor; small flame paw prints left in his trail. His tail fire grew largely.

"K- K- Kh." Luna stuttered out as fear took over her. His fangs coated in red, in Luna's blood. The hellhound jumped on the bed, Luna got up and ran out trying to find her voice which was lost in fear. Khan stalked her like pray. She ran into the common room, then...

Thump, she felt him pounce her. His large paws were on her shoulders. Large fangs dropping with steaming hot drool, his throat sparked up with the bright shimmering light of flames. He lowered his head, his muzzled opened to her mouth.

Footsteps ran up the stairs to the Common room of the second floor "-LUNA!" shouted DJ in fear while this wolf engulfed in flames had her pinned. A bright blue light cast from Luna's mouth a butterfly began to flutter out from it.

"-K-Kh- Khan-" Luna said slowly as she passed out. DJ stood frozen but something happens, the light fad-ed. Luna took a

461

deep gasp of breath as her chest raised and fell. Khan pawed at Luna's face with a light whimpering coming from him. Luna came too and gasped. She shoved Khan back off of her; DJ ran over to her and hugged her. Khan's fire died down. He laid on his stomach with a whimper.

"What happen?" asked DJ in anxiety. Luna told him everything from the attacks to; Khan biting her, and then Khan almost ate her soul. She eyed Khan. She put out a shaky hand; he crawled over and licked at her hand. She got to her feet and laid in bed and passed out.-

Morning came very quick. Luna was woken up by Bella "time to bring our stuff downstairs." Luna tossed and turned most of the time she tried to sleep. She sat up and saw Jenny's stuff had been removed. She stood up and got dressed.

She carried her bags down to the Common room downstairs. "- Jenny!," she dropped her stuff and ran over to her "oh, my god!" tears streak Luna's cheek.

"Luna!" Jenny opened her arms for her. Luna leaped into her arms. Arms wrapped around each other. Luna wrapped her legs around Jenny's body.

"DJ!" yelled out DJ, then wince from Matt and Bella, smacking the back of his head "hush." they snapped out at him. Luna hung from Jenny; Jenny held her close in her arms.

"I'm so sorry." said Luna crying.

"Shhh." said Jenny in a soft whisper while she held her.

Jenny looked at Luna and kissed each tear away slowly. She hugged Luna. Everyone watched in quietness. "I love you too." said Jenny heartful of pure joyous bliss. They kissed in such a loving manner. Luna didn't w-ant this to end. This moment was special. This is the first time they said the "L" word. The feeling was unreal as if no one else was around, they were lost in paradise just the two of them.

"OK! Kids bring your things down!" yelled Professor Raven. - Yep, paradise had ended. Jenny put Luna down on the ground and they went to the carriages. Professor Raven went to Mr. Rune along with the rest of the Clan Professors.

"Everyone's counted for besides - Bree." said Professor Raven distressed.

"Everyone's counted for in my Clan." said Professor Moon.

"Goldenpaw is counted for." confirmed Professor Dibbs.

"Dracoîn is in order. "Professor Kanoe said coldly.

Mr. Rune watched as everyone got in the wagons while he stroked his long white bread. "- Indeed, Luna said she heard a gasp... I say, there was just one more attack we are unaware of. I feel it in my old bones. I believe someone is possessed."

The teachers looked at him with anxiety while the wagons trailed off "do you know who?," asked Mistress Flowers "or suspect anyone?"

"I dare say, I do not know... Only time shall tell us sadly."

"-Oh... Robert." replied Flowers while she watches the

wagons disappear into the woods. -

Luna and Jenny sat with DJ. They leaned out of the window and waved bye to everyone while they rode off. "You will have to visit Jenny." said Luna while they cuddled up. DJ looked at Bella and Ray. "- Can't believe you took my sister to the dance." snapped Ray. - A burning sensation came from a girl's arm, she rubbed her arm as words form slowly *Feels good to be alive* the girl looked down at her arm where it burned but the words were gone. They crossed the mountains, through the valley, and onto the beach. They got out of the wagon at Crystal Coastal Village. Luna, DJ, and Jenny waved bye to Maîq. They boarded the steamship, the people in Coastal village waved bye to the students. Luna got bunked with Kat this time. They talked for a bit before Luna left the room and ran into Traci Brews.

"Hey, Traci." Said Luna while she felt uneasy.

"... Hi Luna." she replied while she still remembered the

.

"I want to say I am sorry. For the way I acted at the Halloween party." replied Luna.

Traci nodded "well, thanks... Well, I must be get going." Luna walked off and saw Cecil and Kain, she turned and walked off figured they were in a mood. She saw Jenny on the deck. She came up and wrapped her arms around her waist.

"Hello beautiful." said Luna with a smile.

Jenny leaned back and smiled "Hello my knight in shining armor."

"-How bad is the scar?" asked Luna while she look at Jenny.

Jenny turned and tugged the front of a shirt down a bit, close to her heart was a three-inch wide scar "Mr. Rune told me I was lucky. IF you didn't save the last... Butterfly? I wouldn't be here. You are my savior." Jenny said softly but heart strong.

"I love you." said Luna kissing her softly.

"I love you too," replied Jenny while she leaned against Luna with her eyes close as the cool breeze blew against the, -

The day turned tonight, night turn to day. They have reached Foxin Harbor. They got off the ship and onto the bus, they watched the scene go by.

"Four months till school, any plans?" Asked Bella.

"Horse shows, camping, and maybe the beach." answered Luna.

"None unless you count going with my dad to all the fundraisers and speeches. Maybe a vacation." replied Jenny.

"I'll be alone, dad is always away on adventures." said DJ while he stared out the window.

"We'll be in France." said ray happily.

Luna nudged DJ while she scrunched her face up and spoke deeply to do her best Uncle ED's impression "Ah, reminds me of a funny story actually." DJ died in laughter, a real shriek. Everyone looked at him as if he was going bust a gut.

The food cart came around, they stocked up on candy and glass bottles of Goblin Soda, Mountain Blast Goblinraid, and a few other flavors of Witches brew teas. Stop after stop the bus was emptying. The moon cast down when Luna's stop was coming up.

"So, Ray – Bella, how are you going to France if your parents are broke?" asked DJ with a composure.

"Dad saved up, we are going stay in small rooms. We all are going share." answered Bella.

"- Must be hard and annoying to sleep in a room with six of you." questioned DJ while Luna stood up grabbing her things.

"You have no idea." chimed in Dane. -

The bus stopped, and they said their byes while ever-one hugged. Luna looked at Jenny "You have to come to visit this summer! Stay a week, I'll cook."

"... You cook?" - I'm scared... I had seen how you make your cereal in the mornings." joshed Jenny.

"I can... I love you." said Luna with a smile.

"I love you to." replied Jenny. -

They got off the bus and out of the bus depot waiting there was Mom and Lucid "MOM!," Luna called out and ran up and bugged her.

"LUNA!" shrieked their mom and hugged her.

"LUCID!" yelled Luna and hugged her.

"LUNA!," Screamed Lucid "MOM!"

"LUCID!" yelled their mom.

DJ put the stuff down in the bed of the truck.

"-DJ!"

"-DJ!" a soft voice yelled.

DJ peered around the truck, and there stood "GRACY!" DJ cried out. Luna saw Gracy come around the truck. Gracy ran over to Luna and them "GRACY!" shrieked out Luna.

"LUNA!" they hugged.

"GRACY!" cried out Cheyanne.

"MOM!" screeched Gracy while they hugged.

"LUCID!" yelled Gracy.

"Oh, no, we're not doing this again." said Lucid bluntly.

"If you want to go home you -"

"- GRACY!" heckled Lucid.

DJ came around the truck and blurted out, "DJ!" a wide grin crossed his lips, and he got a hug from everyone. "M-Cheyanne! - Luna! - LUCID! - GRACY!" DJ yelled out, then he went over and kissed Gracy. His cheeks flushed.

"-Grroooossss!" snapped Lucid.

Luna glared at them and got into the truck. Khan's fire lit up the back of it. He stood leaning over the side. They got home, and Gracy stayed the night. They lay in her room listening to Sacrosanct Sacrifice (*California Girl*).

<Brandon sings> The warm breeze blowing in my hair, driving around with the top down. I wish I had a California girl <chores> Wish I had a California girl. <Brandon> The calmness of the blue sky and the bright sun. You would look so good in this sun my California Girl. <Chore> California girl>

"I should have known." said Luna eyeing Gracy. *<Brand-
on> My California girl is out there>*

"We are dating. As you told me about Jenny." replied
Gracy staring back at Luna with an arch brow *<Chores> My
California girl is out there.*

They laid there in the bed Luna sighed "- we are even. I
love you."

"Love you too Starbear." replied Gracy. -

Morning came, Lucid made DJ help with the horses
"remember how to feed them and saddle them? We are opening up
the barn today." she told DJ while she got all the saddles down
from the loft.

"What does opening the barn up mean?" asked DJ while
Luna showed up in the barn.

"Means we are giving trail rides." answered Luna while
she looked to Sierra's stall, "...Where is Sierra?" her voice was low,
she knew what happened.

"Oh, Stryder... DJ's dad tamed her. She comes on whistle
now." answered Lucid. She whistled a few moments later Sierra
came running in. Luna sighed in relief "I'm glad." - A couple of
hours later people showed up for horseback riding. Cheyanne
collected the money, DJ was watching. Luna and Lucid were doing
small group rides, five horses at a time. Pretty much a family ride.
Thirty dollars for a half-hour, fifty for an hour. They went into the

valley, through the woods, and into the creek and back. After a long day of seven hours with five rides, they bathe the horses. Cheyanne cooked dinner and they sat down for dinner.

"How is Jenny?" asked their mom.

"She is great!" answered Luna as she cut her steak.

"They sat and talked for a bit, a knock came from the door. DJ yelled as he got up "Want me to get it?" he asked while he walked towards the door.

"Yes, please and thank you." answered Cheyanne from the other room. Another knock came from the door. DJ opened the door "- Oh my... N-no..."

"Ah, Danial, is it? Good ta see you again, my boy. How have ya been? I have a story you'll surely love; I was in Switzerland in my earlier years. -" -

Lucid and Luna heard Uncle ED's voice in the foyer. They walked to the door towards the den. "Girls, don't you dare leave this room." snapped their mom. -

"I was selling Swiss cheese door to door. A young boy opened the door. Funny you're a young boy... Anyways, I looked at the boy. I said, you know why Swiss cheese has holes in them?" The boy's face looked almost just like yours baffled.,

"Anyways, I told him I was a soldier for the Swiss army, we used the cheese for target practice. Because if you notice, no other cheese has holes but the Swiss.," He walked in and smacked

DJ's back. "The boy was laugh struck, couldn't laugh or move. Maybe kin of yours." said ED with a smile while he came into the living room "Hey, little sis, and my girls!" he said with jolliness.

DJ looked out the door Run for it... Run Danial - Darn it DJ! Run it is Christmas all over... Story after story.... Must hide...

"-How was school, congrats on the Championship, Luc." Said Ed while he sat down on the couch with the girls.

"Oh than-." Lucid tried to thank him but he heckled her off "Reminds me of a story when I was your age, Funny stor-"

"Love to hear it, got to get to bed. Got to get up early for work." said the girls while they got up and rushed upstairs. -

"Oh my... That was close." said Luna while they sat down on Luna's bed.

"Too soon." replied Lucid.

Gracy texted Luna <Grac: Hey, figure you forgot ▢ ▢Did you guess?>

Luna totally forgot and texted back.

<Luna: No of course not... Your dating DJ.>

<Grac: Yep, but that's not the wink face guess >

<Luna: What is it then?>

<Grac: You are my BFFE, I knew your gay.>

<Luna: I love you>

<Grac> Love you too ★bear>

They fell asleep, a couple of days had passed they were out

getting ready for horseback riding for the day. A black Sub pulled up and a tall man, 6'3", brown clean cut hair. Well-groomed with blue eyes. A fit man, button-up shirt tucked into his jeans.

A semi-tall woman climbed out with long blond hair that pulled into a ponytail, hazel eyes, fit frame body. She wore a summer dress; she was very attractive. -

Uncle Ed poked his head out of the back door "CheyChey!," He barked out, "the president is here!"

Cheyanne lead two people to Luna and Lucid for trail riding. -

A girl climbed out of the SUV she had blond hair in a ponytail with hazel eyes. she wore shorts and a shirt. Two other girls climbed out of the SUB they walked around to the back. Cheyanne smiled "Oh? Hello, Jenny nice to see you again."

"Pleasure to see you, Mrs. Bell, this is my Dad John and my mother Cindy. and my two sisters Amanda and Becky."

"Pleasure to meet you." Said Cheyanne as she extended her hand out to the two. Mr. Striff looked at her, and they shook hands "nice to meet you. Jenny wanted to come and visit figure we'd take a family vacation up into the mountains."

Mrs. Striff looked around the ranch "you have such a cute little house. It must be easy to keep up. It reminds me of that show... John, what is that show, has that actress Lunetta Whann?"

"-Little House in the Mountains. So, you offer horseback

rides?" asked John while he looked at the barn.

"Oh, I love Lunetta Whann. I run the stables with my daughters; they should be back soon."

"Lunetta Whann is a piece of work, she won't be seeing her name in lights." replied Mrs. Striff in a bored manner. -

They rode back and then a shriek echoed from the barn "Jenny!" Luna ran up and hugged Jenny. She tried to kiss her, Jenny turned her head so Luna's lips met her cheek.

"- Tell you later, keep it friendly." whispered Jenny

"... Nice to see you too." whispered Luna bit aggravated.

"Nice to meet you, Luna.," said Mr. Striff " I heard a lot about you."

"Are you going for a ride?" asked Cheyanne.

"We will, let the girls go for an hour." said Mr. Striff. Jenny, Becky, Amanda followed Luna and Lucid into the barn. They asked if anyone rode before. None of them did. So Lucid explains how to work the reigns and such. They started to walk the horses to the woods. -

Mr. Striff got a phone call and walked off to the distance " ev-en on vacation he is working." said Mrs. Striff.

"What does he do for a living?" asked Cheyanne while she got them a cold glass of iced tea.

"He is the Governor of California. What do you do for a living, besides this barnyard work?" asked Mrs. Striff while she sat down at the picnic table.

"I am a teacher for the middle school and the volleyball coach, and I run the stables." answered Cheyanne with a slight annoyance.

"That is good, must be nice to have this beautiful simple living. I am an agent for Hollywood. I help movie stars find their parts in movies and shows." replied Mrs. Striff while she flashed her brilliant smile.

"-Oh, it's not that simple living.," answered Cheyanne remarked with a slight sharpness to her tone "upkeep on the house, barn, truck, keeping the horses and chickens maintained, and two and a half kids... Real simple." -

They made their way through the creek; it was quiet and peaceful while they rode. "They say there is an Indian burial ground around here somewhere." said Lucid. Jenny rode along by her sisters Becky and Amanda. Luna was in the back while Lucid led. Luna rode galloped up beside Jenny.

"So, what was that about back there?" asked Luna.

"Oh, my dad is not for Gay Rights. He is closed minded on a few things. He is stressed over the elections; they are coming up soon and there is a woman for Gay Rights. He and his team are threatened by this." answered Jenny.

"-Oh! Luna look what I found a couple of weeks ago!" Shouted Lucid. - Mr. Striff came back and sat down with the two women "sorry about that. It was my team, always wanting to keep me so busy. So, Mrs. Bell, we rented a cabin and went sightseeing.

This little mountain town is a busy place. We ate at Bell's Burgers; it is a great restaurant by chance is it yours?"

"Oh John, what did they have to say, anything with Carol Hue?" asked his wife.

"Bell's Burgers is my late husband's place. He partnered with a friend. We didn't have the money. So, his friend helped.," answered Cheyanne "I am glad you liked it."

"- Just getting dirt on Ms. Hue... How she is for Gay Rights and things. I have a counter for it thought. Mrs. Bell, what is your thoughts on it? Gays, Gay marriages, and a month to celebrate Gays. I actually like to invite you all to Bells Burgers tonight for dinner." Mr. Striff said with a pleasantness to him. -

They rode up the steep mountain. The horses had trouble finding traction. They slipped a bit "- you think this is safe, Lucid?" asked Luna with anxiety while they climbed the mountain.

"- I made it... I mean I hiked up it." replied Lucid with worrisome. After a moment Lucid made it, then Jenny followed by Amanda then Luna. Becky's horse spot the pinto lost her footing. A rock rolled under her and the horse fell rolling down the steep hill with Becky. The sound of limbs cracking and crunching then quietness fell.

"BECKY!" everyone yelled out in full concern. It was quiet not even a critter stirred. Luna jumped on Rogue and made haste. "Stay here." said Lucid while she rode Rose down the mountain. They saw a path of destruction. They reached the bottom of the hill. There Spot had laid motionless, head twisted back completely, under the horse. - "Oh, God..." gasp tearfully Luna and Lucid. Under the horse laid Becky, left foot tangled in the stirrup. Her head busted open against a large rock.

"-She's - is she?" asked Luna in a sorrowful whisper as she can't bring herself to fully asked the question. Lucid stood by Becky and nodded.

""-Oh... God..."tears filled their eyes, "-can... Can you? Can you do something!" Luna looked at Lucid with a hopeful look in her eyes.

"- I never... messed with death... I ... I can try."

Lucid placed her right hand out, the horse rolled up, blood poured back into Becky's cracked head. The horse rolled up the hill, the horse's head flopped around. Becky's body was flung around like ar rag doll.

"Luna, ride up there and lead her behind the others." ordered Lucid. "- What about you?," asked Luna in concern.

"- GO! I'll be fine!" shouted Lucid. She pushed time back while Luna rode up the hill. Luna saw Becky get smashed by a tree between the horse. The crunch of the horse's neck echoed. After a moment the three girls was climbing down the hill. Luna climbed up behind them.

"Though we lost you." said Becky.

"Oh... No, I thought I saw something. Becky get behind Amanda.: they all made it up the hill. Luna's heart was racing as she had avoided this terrible tragedy.

"Where is Lucid?," asked Jenny while she looked around "she was just right in front of us."

"I - she'll be up here." said Luna in anxiety. -

Cheyanne looked at them while she took a sip. Uncle ED and DJ came out of the house "Oh, this is my brother, Ed-die or Ed. He is a real character, and this is DJ their other friend." Cheyanne introduced them then a faint whisper "perfect timing."

"ED and DJ, this is Jenny's parents. Mr. John Striff and his wife, Mrs. Cindy Striff, they came all the way from California."

"Pleasure to meet you. Eddie and DJ." said the Striffs.

"Nice to meet you, California ya say? I had been the-re once, reminds me of a funny story... I was out there three years ago, and I was on the Hollywood Boulevard. -" -

Lucid sat on her knees head throbbing. She felt blood pour out from both nostrils. She stood up; knees shook. Rose came over and nudge Lucid slightly. "- I'm OK girl..." she said weakly. Rose knelt lowering herself to the ground. Lucid barely could climb onto her. Rose climbed up the mountain.

"There she is!" yelled out Becky while Rose carried Lucid.

"- You, OK?" Luna asked her sister while she took the lead.

"...Yeah." Lucid answered weakly. They came to a small clearing in the woods, there was a small stone building building. The door hung off the frame, the other door was stuck. The stain windows were coated in dirt and grime.

"What is this building?" Asked Luna while she hopped off Rogue. They all got off the horses and tied them up. They went into the small stone building. Amanda hung around outside "you coming Amanda?" asked Becky.

"Nah, you have fun with the spider webs and critters." replied Amanda. They went in and there were six pews all covered in dirt and leaves. A small stage with a old organ, cobwebs had coated everything, leaves and dirt dressed the floor. "This is a church.," said Luna.

"My own little sanctuary." replied Lucid while she held her head. Becky tried to open a door to what looked like lead to a closet or office.

"GUYS!" Amanda yelled for outside in a panic. Everyone ran out and they gasped fright "LUCID!"

Lucid laid on the ground while she shook violently, Amanda rolled her on her side. Lucid's head thrashed around. "She is having a seizure! You have a blanket or anything?" asked Amanda while she cradle Lucid's head.

"No." replied Luna while Amanda tugged off her over shirt. She put her shirt under Lucid's head for a softer support held Lucid on her side while the event continued. Everyone stood and watched. They watch Lucid's body twist and shake. After a minute or so she slowly came to a stop. She slowly opened her eyes, she laid there; eyes wandering around while she looked disorientated and absent minded. "Lucid... Hello... There you are!" said

Amanda looking down at Lucid.

"Are you OK?" asked Becky while she knelt.

"- Lucid, how are you feeling?" Asked Jenny while holding Luna's hand.

"LUC!" cried out her sister squeezing Jenny's hand.

Lucid laid there for a moment, voices was strain, her body extremely sore as she slowly sat up. They helped her up to her feet. A few minutes later they rode back to the stables. -

"I had seen Jimothy Deeno, I yelled out Jimothy Deeno and to the man. Well, turned out it was just another man visiting for Pride Month. Very interesting holiday, I met some lovely people and a woman named Carol Hue, she is a very lovely woman.," said Ed while he sat with a cold drink in his hand.

"She is trying to gun for my job." said Mr. Striff bit sharply, "she is trying to get the Gays and hipsters votes. My thing is WHY does a lifestyle you choose need a month of it's own. Its a choice they had chose and want to get upset when they are "attacked" for it. You know, you may be shun for your lifestyle if you flaunt it. They bring it on their selves, God is already casting down on them."

The girls came back and walked the horses to their stalls "It is their choice, IT is their life... How is it fair for you or "us" to be the judge of someone's life on how they wish to live... What they find to make them happy. They been attack-ed by strangers, friends, and even loved ones. They have a right to stand together hand in hand, same as you and your wife. For God he has so much love and passion, depends on how you live your life makes God's choice for you.

"Live good, straight or gay, show your righteous then the gates of heavens open up. If you live evil, sinful life. Straight or gay then the gates of hell opens up for you. For you to judge them you are no better than the Anti-Christ... Love is blind; love sees no color or lifestyle... Love has and will always be heartfelt... Full of pride, loyalty, and love...,

"How can you sit and judge someone for their love. I have a story, funny story... I was in Tibet; I met a blind man and we talked about love. He said "you know what the blind man and love has in common? Blindness and Wisdom.,"

"The difference between the blind and love? The blind man will still judge and be a man. Love is non-judgmental, full of love.,

"Then the man said, you know the difference between the blind man and a man who can see. I said "What" he told me... Nothing at all, he may be blind, the man may see but he is still blind for he tries to judge for what he doesn't understand. He said a man who is fully aware able to truly see will lose his judgment on love, race, and everything that blinds the seeing man." said ED in a long breath of ranting, speaking harshly.

"D-did we come back at a bad time?" whispered Jenny lowly.

"No, no we were just chatting with a blind man. I must be

off. It was nice meeting you Striffs, love you girls and sis. - Darwin." said ED while he walked off.

"-Darwin?" whispered DJ rolling his eyes. He went off to feed the chickens. "We must be off too. - Eight o'clock if you wish to eat dinner with us." said Mrs. Stiff. They got up and walked off their vehicle. Jenny said bye to Luna. Then they had drove off.

They closed up for the day "what was that about, never heard Uncle Ed speak... So smartly." said Luna while DJ came and sat with them.

"I don't think he cares for Jenny's dad... He called me Darwin."

"Get dress or in Mrs. Striff's wording pick something chic. Because tonight we dine on the Governor." said their mom. -

Two hours had passed it was little after seven. They got dress, hair did up and dolled up. Lucid wore a blue plaid western button up shirt, front tucked in to show off her cow-girl Bucking Bronco Championship buckler. Followed by her favorite black show boots with rose embedded into the leather. Luna came down in her Distinction Jaded shirt that had a grave with a headstone with a guitar leaning against it with a crow on the neck. Black leggings with a plaid skirt with her black combat boots.

DJ stepped out in jeans and a white s-shirt and his black school boots.

Cheyanne came out in her black slacks, blue dress up button top and black heels. "- seriously Luna, would it kill you to dress up for a change?" asked her mom staring at her out.

"Mom, you know she is the Queen of the Darkness." joshed Lucid.

"You do want to impress your father law." said DJ in a taunting manner.

"-DJ!" everyone shouted at him.

"No need to fuss about it. The blind man is waiting." said their mom while they all laugh and got into the truck. They drove down the curvy road.

"How was the horseback riding?" asked their mom.

"- It was good.," said Luna "it went like the last... five." added Lucid.

They pulled up to Bell's Burgers. The patio was lit up by string lights, the upper deck was full and lit by some string lights. They walked in, and the main floor was packed with customers. The bar was full not even a single seat. Julie smiled and waved "Mrs. Bell, they are upstairs. The Striff's are waiting for you."

Julie led them up the stone stairs, something caught Cheyanne's eye. It was Mr. Lundo sitting at a table with a couple. Then Cheyanne and everyone was led out onto the patio. The view overlooked downtown Pigeon forge and a view of the mountains.

"Glad you could make it. I ordered drinks for everyone, Luna, is it? Jenny said you like sweet tea, Lucid I ordered you a glass of water and I ordered the bottle of the house's best wine, *Sapphire Mountain River.*" Cheyanne choked on her water, it was the top shelf wine of wine. Mr. Lundo kept it locked up. It was four to five hundred dollars a bottle. Mr. Striff wore a tuxedo with a black tie. His wife wore a white dress, dressed in jewelry. The three girls wore white dresses and dress in jewelry.

"- Sorry, we feel under dressed." joshed Cheyanne.

"You are fine, I am teaching my kids ALWAYS dress to impress." said Mr. Striff.

Julie returned with a smile "What can I get you all to eat?" Ashe asked. Everyone had placed their orders in. Jenny played footies with Luna while they ate. The large moon sat over them "boy, we didn't get your order." Mr. Striff waved Julie down and DJ ordered a soda, a burger, and fries.

"So, sorry about that." said Julie sincerely.

"No, it is fine. We took up two tables." said Mrs. Striff while DJ took a bite of a mozzarella stick. A few minutes later the food DJ ordered came. they sat around and ate. Cheyanne was fuming about the menu change. The ticket came, he placed his bank card in the black binder. Then he laid two hundred dollars on the table. Cheyanne put ten-dollars under her plate.

Lundo came by their table and smiled warmly with his deep raspy voice " 'Ow waz everything? I meant to come by da table earlier, buzy night."

"It was all good. Very beautiful place you work at." Said Mrs. Striff while she slipped her fur coat on.

"I am Co-Owner, actually. Mr. Bell waz my friend n he needed money and da help. I helped wid da money and contracts. That our lawyer wrote up. Ye all have a good night." Cheyanne wanted to know who he was talking to earlier, that was more than how was your food the couple was older, not his friends. He had no family. They all left to their vehicles.

"We are going sightseeing tomorrow, love for you all to join us." said Mr. Striff while he invited them, they all left. Everyone climbed into the truck. DJ was in the back with Lucid.

"Can't believe there is only one item left on the menu from Adam's menu." said their mom sternly.

"Told you I don't trust him." Lucid spoke up.

"Can you fire him?" asked Luna.

"I can't, he owns the other half. I'll have to dig out the contract that his lawyer and him and Adam had signed. He was twenty-four when he found Lundo, when the place was for sale. Lundo at the time worked as the Bank's manager. He gave A-dam the loan and we stayed at my parents' house for two years.,

"Then Adam got the bank to loan us the money for the house, Lundo told Adam he will help out in any way he can. He quite the bank after the contract signing."

DJ poked at Lucid's side over and over while she was on the phone "STAWP!," snapped Lucid "GOD you're so annoying."

"- DJ, leave your sister alone." said Cheyanne while she drove.

Everyone looked at Cheyanne, "DJ, leave Lucid alone... He is over every day, might as well be treated like family."

"-He has no home to go to..." DJ said in a hurt felt whisper. Dads too busy to see me, the home has always been a tent in the woods. Since I was five. He thought while he stared out the window at the night sky. -

They got home from dinner. They kicked their shoes off and went to the living room to relax. "They were nice people." Said Luna.

"Kind of flashie." answered their mom. -

Lucid went up to her room, DJ went and sat on his bed sadden how rough he has had it. Luna went to her own room and text Gracy and told her everything that has happened. -

"- LUNA! - DJ!" Lucid yelled out in a deathly holler. Everyone ran into the room of Lucid's "WHAT!" they yelled out. Lucid pointed to her bed where twenty black stones laid all facing down but twelve.

ᚺᛖᛚᛈ ᛗᛖ ᛁᛗ ᛒᚱᛖᛖ

Lucid read with worrisome "Help me I'm Bree."

Bonus Magic

Chapter

Bonus Magick: 1992-1993

September first, 1992, was the date, the date a young
boy fourteen years of age. He stood at 5'5"; scruffy brown hair
pointed chin, slightly long nose; with a brilliant crystal blue right
eye, and an emerald green left eye, and slightly pale. He rode in the
carriage with three other students.

A girl at age fourteen, her hair was dark brown, and wave.
Soft pale skin with such brilliant beautiful purple eyes; her features
were soft. Small chin, high cheeks, large eyes, and a button nose.
On her left hand, she had a raven tattoo between her thumb and her
index finger. She is a cute girl at five feet.

Another boy sat, he had sharp features, medium-length
black hair, sharp chin, strong jawline, bright blue eyes. Across his
right cheek from the corner of his eye; to the corner of his mouth
was a scar. He had a nice bronze tan. He stood at 5'6"

The last boy was pale, silver slick back hair, with dark
purple eyes, soft jawline with a sharp chin. He stood at 5'4". They
sat in the blue carriage wagon, the candlelit the inside of it up. The
wind blew the red curtains out of the way. They sat in the wagon
wearing blue tunics and black slacks with leather boots that
buckled up. The girl had her leg crossed over the other. She
flattened out her black skirt. They wore black robes.

The girl looked from her book while everyone sat around

491

looking in a daze. "- Is anyone going to talk? I'm Raven, Raven Woods. What is your name?," she asked while looking at the brown-haired boy, "-your eyes... They are remarkably interesting." The boy with the two eye colors spoke softly while he looked at her "I'm Adam."

Raven smiled warmly at him "does Adam have a last name?"

He nodded slightly "... Of course, it's Bell."

The boy with the scar stared out of the window. His eyes shifted to Adam while he spoke softly "-don't spit that name out. As it is venomous in this land."

Raven and Adam both looked at the boy with the scar. Adam cleared his throat with anxiety "- what do you mean? Who are you, and what happened to your cheek?"

The boy with the scar stared out of the window "... I do not know... Just a feeling, a bad feeling. I'm RazÉr, I do not recall where I had gotten this scar from..."

The wagon came to a stop by a large white stone castle with four towers and a large keep that went up like a tower. Everyone climbed out of the carriage. They looked at the boy with silver hair. Adam put his hand out "what is your name?"

The silver hair boy cast his dark purple gaze down at Adam's hand then looked back at him "... Interesting." the boy spoke drably. He walked off but stopped "I'll say, you will not make it... Through your last."

Raven sighed and looked at them, then spoke with heartfelt joy "don't let him bother you. He is a Bloke, they are all purebloods, as I am." A man came out to greet them. He had long wavy brown hair, a long thick brown beard, bright blue eyes, a long pointy chin, with a thick bridge nose. He was a tall man, not a giant, but a tall slim man. He smiled warmly and when he spoke, he spoke with such warmth and jolly in his voice. "Welcome to OwllHollow School of Magick of Witchcraft and Wizardly!" The horses and carriages rolled away while everyone stood looking at the man in black robes and cloak.

"Welcome back and all the new students, Welcome to OwlHollow. My name is Robert Rune, I am the Vice Headmaster. All the first yearers please follow me, and the rest follow the grounds man Timonthi Took."

Mr. Took was a short man, a child to the eye of the beholder. He had red curly hair, dark tan with large bright blue eyes. With large adult size feet.

They walked in the courtyard as the clouds covered the two moons and the stars. There was a large fountain with three fairies: three-winged girl figures all in bronze. A little goat boy playing a six-hole ocarina. Each note that played cause the water to shoot out of the ocarina. They walked into the keep, the glass was stained glass, three halls lead from the entrance way along with a beautiful marble staircase and to the left was two large sliding doors. Everyone walked pass the large sliding doors into the large feast hall. The large walls went up and slowly curved up into the ceiling. Pictures of beasts hung up on the wall. An older woman stood with a cauldron on the stage. She had long white hair, round face, and hazel eyes with half-moon glasses. Mr. Rune took a chair by the four professors. The woman spoke with such harsh tone.

"Welcome everyone to OwlHollow School of Magick for Witchcraft and Wizardly. I am Mistress Jupiter, for the years you are here, you'll learn all different kind of spells and potion making. You will learn the past wizards.,

"There are four clans: Dracoîn, Chimerador, Goldenpaw, and Crowfeather. It will be your own job to learn the founders and history of each clan. When you hear your name, come and look into the cauldron and you will be placed into a clan."

All the new students lined up in a single fine line while everyone took to one of the four color clan tables. Black for Dracoîn with green words wrote across the table. Red table for Chimerador with silver writing, black table with purple writing for Crowfeather, and lastly Goldenpaw had a golden table with silver writing.

"Marv Stargaze."

A boy little, smaller than Adam with blonde hair, dark skin, and brown eyes came up and bent over a bit. POOF! A black smoke puffed out creating a crow. The boy pulled out and KRAA out.

"CROWFEATHER!," Mistress Jupiter snapped out while he sat down. "- Raven Woods!"
Raven stepped up and looked in the smoky cauldron then a crow formed in the smoke. "CROWFEATER!" Mistress Jupiter announced while Raven sat with the clan, "RazÉr Bréon!"

RazÉr went up before he could look in the large cauldron. Puff of smoke came up creating a beast with a lion body, head of a lion, with a goat on the back of the beast, and a serpent for a tail. Everyone stared stunned, the room grew quiet.

"-Chimerador!" called out Mistress Jupiter. He sat down at the table as the students just stared at him not saying a word as they were in awe. Rune sat back in his throne; his eyes twinkled while his beard hid his smile.

"Adam Bell!"

Adam walked up and looked in the dark cauldron which was filled with water. --- POOF! Same beast, the Chimera smoked up while Adam roared out.

"Chimerador!" Mistress Jupiter snapped out while Adam walked over and sat down.

"Anderson Bloke!"

The silver hair boy walked up and peered into the cauldron then a large dragon appeared while he roared out.

"Dracoîn!" called out Mistress Jupiter, after a few more students had been sorted. Food appeared on the tables. Everyone began to eat while Timonthi removed the cauldron out of the feast hall. Mistress Jupiter sat with Mr. Rune and the four Clan

Professors.

"-That boy, RazÉr who is he Robert. He must be special."
Said Jupiter eyeing him with interest.

"I do not know Marie… Indeed, he is astonishing. I say he
will do wonders here." Said Rune softly. – Later dinner was over,
and each clan was led to their towers. RazÉr and Adam sat in the
Common room. They laid around.

"RazÉr, is it? Are you from her o e…earth?" question
Adam.

"- Boy… You have a lot to learn, this is called Crystal
Realm or Crystal Region. Another part of the earth that is hidden
behind the third eye. I am from Zert a small village in the south in
the desert. Boy, do not steer from here." Answered RazÉr while he
stared at Adam as if he was studying him.

"Why do you call me boy, we are the same age." Question
Adam slightly puzzled.

"- I do not know… I feel older… Way older… Ancient." -

The next day Adam went to his spell class with RazÉr, and
Raven. They sat in class together doing spell work. The bell rung
and released the class. – Few days later Adam tried out for the
Snorkbie team he was astounding. He shined in the sport, him and
RazÉr became really good friends, they would sneak two horses
and rode them out to Coastal Village where a friend of RazÉr's
lived. His name is Nailz a cat creature who stood a 5'6", long torso.

Blonde fur, blue eyes. With his right ear had a slit in it. His long cat tail swayed, the tip had three black stripes and a white tip.

"- Nailz." RazÉr called out while he walked over to the cat creature. He placed his right hand out and Nailz placed his arm out while they grip each other's forearm. "Olá (Hello), RazÉr, 'ow r ye?" asked Nailz.

"Came to see ye, amigo (friend). Diz is Adam." Said RazÉr while he introduced Adam. Adam waved to Nailz, Nailz nodded slightly After a bit of talking Nailz grabbed his bow and arrows. He slid his daggers in the belt as he tossed RazÉr a sword with a grin. Adam looked uneasy at the two.

"What is going on?" asked Adam.

"Vamos caçar (Lets go hunting)." Said Nailz with a sly grin.

"Sim (yes), lets go." –

They all left and went and hunt Flowerindeer (deer with a grass for fur and flowers on their spine and antlers). Nailz fired two arrows at once. The arrow hit the back of the Flowerindeer, the creature began to run. Then Nailz fired a third arrow while RazÉr followed its tracks. Then the ground shook. Nailz looked to the Woods. RazÉr gripped the hilt of the sword, his eyes slanted. His gaze grew hard "ADAM, get to the village!" shouted RazÉr.

"W-what – why? What is going on?" question Adam kind of nervous.

"GET BACK TO THE VILLA-" RazÉr got cut off by a

loud thunderous roar. A tree fallen. A large brown snout beast with large tusk stepped out holding a club with massive spikes.
Everyone stood and stared at the troll "- that's why! A Mountain War Troll!" growled RazÉr while he held the sword tightly.

"IR (GO)!" snapped Nailz while he nocked an arrow. Adam ran off to the village. Nailz fired an arrow, it struck the troll's arm. The troll charged as his large spike club crashed down into the ground missing Nails barely. RazÉr ran up and slice the troll at the knee. The troll tried to stomp on RazÉr. He rolled out of the way. –

Adam could feel the ground shake then slowly came to an end. They came out of the woods and to the sandy village. RazÉr handed the sword over to Nailz. They said their goodbyes. "What happened to the troll?" asked Adam.

"We killed it. It was a child war troll, Nailz he is going to skin his hide and remove the tusk and sell them." Answered RazÉr while they rode back to the school. They got back to the school and saw Raven.

"And where have you two been? We were supposed to study together, remember?" Raven sat at the fountain giving them a stern look.

"Sorry, we got caught up in other stuff." Answered RazÉr.

"- Is that blood?," asked Raven her eyes showing worry, "what happened?"

"Nothing at all." Replied RazÉr

"Tell me now... Or I'll report the two of you." She stood

and placed her hands on her hips. They looked at her while RazÉr turned and walked off towards the keep.

"I killed a Mountain War Troll." His tone was so casual. Raven stared with a dumbfound look, just in pure shock. She was just mum. A moment later she chased after him. "--- Are you serious, are you so fatuous? You could have been killed."- Months passed Adam and the Chimerador's Snorkbie team was undefeated. His grades for the year were all A's. At the end of his first year, they won the Clan cup. He went back to his home in Adams, Tennessee where he lived with his dad and mom in a white two-bedroom farmhouse. He went to the woods and saw a cave. He went in and the cool air flowed through it. He felt the cold damp walls of the cave. He saw something alarming. Two dark red orbs of pure hell... Adam could fill hatred, anger, and death. The beast snarled; Adam ran from it. –

That night he could hear scratching at the walls of the house. Same breathing, snorting could be heard. Adam couldn't sleep that night. – Year two came, he returned to the school. He sat with Raven, RazÉr, and a new friend Marv. They came close friends. Adam snuck off with RazÉr and Nailz, he picked up on Nailz's language and learned how to ride horseback. He has extravagantly prevailed over all his classes. He became the Snorkbie team captain.

He was such a brilliant kid; he was fifteen years old now. – The Halloween dance came. He dressed in a black tux with a red tie. He took Raven to the dance; she wore a dark purple lacy dress and her hair braided. They were on the dance floor. "Figure you would have brought RazÉr to the danced." She teased with a wink.

"He was my first choice, but I saw you… So, I changed my mind, you're better looking." He joshed with her while she laid her head on his chest. "Well, I am glad you saw me. You are very charming.," she said with a smile while they dance. After a bit, she smiled and peered up at him, "- thanks for the dance."
They hugged, he went and found Marv with a piece of parchment in his hand standing at the mirror.

"Hey Marv, what is that?" asked Adam looking to him.

"- Leave me be… You are far from a friend." Marv said with a shaky voice full of abhorrence.

"What are you talking about? Of course, we're friends." Adam said with care in his voice. He saw Marv's dark blue eyes swell up, "- you're going be the death of this place" Marv stomped out leaving Adam fully flabbergasted. He turned and went to his dorm. – Few weeks passed, whispers filled the school about a witch, an evil witch… Bloody Mary and her sister Sherry Mary, and … Kate Bell. –

"No way you are related to Kate, Bloody, and Sherry, and Linda. I can't believe it, I won't." Cried out Raven while she sat on a desk in an empty classroom. "- This is why I said don't spit your name around, - boy." RazÉr made a sharp remark about it while he stared at Adam.

"YOU KNEW- YOU KNEW WHO THEY ARE?!" Adam

snapped out in furry. RazÉr sat so casually with a yawn, "boy! Of course not. I do not know why I told you that, I do not know that name isn't safe. OR why I was right." RazÉr spoke so calmly, so cool, and collected. The classroom was on the third floor. The moons cast down on the school lighting it up with her gaze.

"LIES!" Adam yelled out in frustration.

"- Boy! I need to spit no lies."

"STOP IT!" Raven cried out in worrisome as tension was getting tighter. It was growing late, Adam threw a punch at RazÉr, but RazÉr swiftly stood up catching Adam's right arm under his elbow causing his arm to lock up. Adam couldn't break free. Adam punched with his left fist. RazÉr caught that arm the same way.

"Stop it guys… STOP IT!" Raven cried out upsettingly.

Adam tried to jerk away. He went to bring up a knee to RazÉr's stomach. RazÉr slung himself back, his foot shoved into Adam's torso, and flung him across the room into the tables. RazÉr rolled up to his feet.

"- Boy! As I said, I do not spit lies." RazÉr said just as cool, calm, and collective as he walked out of the room. Raven ran over to Adam.

"Are you OK?" fright and sorrow washed over her face and eyes. He climbed out from the pile of tables. He winces in excruciating pain. "-Ow… Y-yeah…" Adam winces hard.

"- You're bleeding.," Raven frown, she took her wand out and tapped his arm "Sana." His cut slowly closed as they fixed the tables. They went back to their dormitories. – Christmas came, he went back home where it was covered in snow and cold. He stood in his bedroom looking into the mirror, parchment in hand.

He spun around three times "--- Bloody Mary – Bloody Mary- Bloody Mary." He turned on the lights and sat in front of his mirror. Long crooked nose, long pointed chin, long black hair. Appeared in the mirror. He let out a scream, an arm reached out and grabbed him. His dad opened the door, he was a tall man with brown hair and a thick mustache with blue and green eyes.

"What is the meaning of this Adam! Get to bed." His dad shouted at him. Adam's face was pale and sweat broke out. He looked at the mirror there was no old woman. He stared at himself, he turned his gaze to his dad and nodded.

"-Yes Sir." He went to bed that night, morning came. He helped with chopping wood and collecting the firewood. That night he went to the cave and Saw those eyes. He stared back at them coldly. A large black wolf stepped out. Snarling, drooling, and fangs baring. It circled Adam as he stood there, "- hello cousin." Said Adam softly. A voice from the house yelled "Adam!," his mom yelled for him "dinner's ready!"

Adam smiled and left the cave to the house. They sat around and ate dinner. – Next day was Christmas. He had a good Christmas he got a new bike, some games, and a broom a Starz model. It had a beautiful red oak finish. He returned back to the school a week later. He caught up with RazÉr and Raven.

"How was your Christmas?" asked Adam while he leaned against the wall of the school.

"I don't celebrate Christmas, but we had a good Yule Tiding.," Said Raven with a flashy smile, "we went to Spain and visit family."

"I spent it with Nailz." Said RazÉr while he looked around the hall. They hand the Championship game for Snorkibie, it was against Chimerador. The game went on for a whole twenty-four hours. It was the most intense game they had seen in a decade. It came to an end, Chimerador had won by five points.

Adam scored the last shot. That night they celebrated and ate like kings, or at least ate like someone who hasn't eaten in twenty-four hours. Raven came over and smiled with a yawn "good game." She turned to a Raven and flew up to the Crowfeather tower. Everyone went to bed early that night. Adam lay in his bed while he smiled coldly. –

A few days have passed, Nailz, RazÉr, and Adam snuck into the forest and found a house. A small cottage, they peeked peered in through the window, and it seemed to be empty. They told Adam to keep an eye out. Nailz picked the lock. They peered around the corners then they searched and found some silver shanties. A man yelled from the woods.

"HEY! What are you doing at my house?" question the man with a harsh tone. RazÉr peeked out of the window. "- Come on, boy." Whispered RazÉr while he eyed the man. The man picked up his shovel and marched towards Adam "are you stupid boy? Why are you at my house?!" He snapped at Adam angrily while he

503

raised the shovel.

"- Nailz, Ire tempus puto (I think it is time to go.)" said RazÉr in a silent whisper. Adam pulled his wand out; the man shook his head. "Stupid boy." He raised the shovel higher, then the man froze. A wolf with red glowing eyes… Same red eyes from the cave stood behind Adam. "- I'll kill you!" the man yelled out finally as he swung with the shovel. The wolf moved with haste and swiftness. It pounced the man, RazÉr opened the door and ran with Nailz. "- Come on Boy!" They ran out and parted ways. –

Finally, the year was over, Adam's grades were nothing but A's once again. Mistress Jupiter took the floor in the feast hall "I would like to thank everyone for a grand year this year. Mr. Rune and I created a special position for a student this year. It is called Lord Headmaster. We would like to announce Adam Bell to the throne. All A's two years in a row, two Snorkbie Championship, and Clan cup again. Will Chimerador hold the cup for a third?" Mistress Jupiter gave a bow along with the rest of the Professors. Raven looked at Adam while he sat in the throne. She gave a warm smile and waved lightly to him while she flashed a smile at him.

"-Of course… We can hold the cup." Murmured Adam Coldly while he sat on the throne staring at the other students.

RUNES!

A-   H-   O-   V-

B-   I-   P-   W-

C-   J-   Q-   X-

D-   K-   R-   Y-

E-   L-   S-   Z-

F-   M-   T-

G-   N-   U-

Thank you for everyone for getting this book. I hope you all enjoyed the little adventure and hope to see you on the next journey for the Bells, please leave a review on Amazon and or any other place you had received your book.

)✪(

If you ever feel lost, look to the star to the Goddess of the moon dress in white guide you on your past. Allow the stars to be the road to your Gloriousness.

W.J. Smith is a loving father, cosplayer, and gamer. He enjoys the simple things in life. He can be outside or downtown working on his next book.

Made in the USA
Middletown, DE
17 March 2022

62811312R10285